Hun
Hunter Jack D.
The cure

JUL 1 6 2003

$25.95
1st ed.   ocm51478045

THE CURE

THE CURE

JACK D. HUNTER

A TOM DOHERTY ASSOCIATES BOOK

NEW YORK

THE CURE

Book design by Michael Collica

A Forge Book
Published by Tom Doherty Associates, LLC
175 Fifth Avenue
New York, NY 10010

www.tor.com

Forge® is a registered trademark of Tom Doherty Associates, LLC.

Library of Congress Cataloging-in-Publication Data

Hunter, Jack D.
    The cure / Jack D. Hunter.—1st ed.
        p.   cm.
    "A Tom Doherty Associates book."
    ISBN 0-765-30648-4 (acid-free paper)
    1. Cancer—Treatment—Fiction.   2. Oncologists—Fiction.   I. Title.

PS3558.U48C87 2003
813'.54—dc21

                                                            2003040021

First Edition: July 2003

Printed in the United States of America

0   9   8   7   6   5   4   3   2   1

Again – as always – to Tommy

ACKNOWLEDGMENTS

This work of fiction intends in no way to disparage those legions of physicians, nurses, medical scientists, pharmaceutical manufacturers, and public servants who work honestly and resolutely to heal and to save lives. It is, in truth, an implied bow to them.

It's also a soldier-type salute to the bravery of that small lonely troop of medical scientists who persist—in the face of unrelenting professional harassment, personal vilification, and economic loss—in their quest for alternative weapons in the war against cancer.

My gratitude, too, for the invaluable technical advice of Dr. Philip Binzel and the lucid expositions of G. Edward Griffin.

And, of course, very special thanks to my good and savvy friends, Phil May, Sandra Birnhak, and Stan Budner, for shoving me into gear.

Our mission is about monopoly. Absolute pharmaceutical monopoly. The efficacy of any drug in the universe is entirely secondary to our purpose. Our purpose is to own, control, or constrain all chemical compounds that in any way have a role in the maintenance of health among the world's population. And if we don't own, control, or constrain a drug, our mission is to destroy it before it can become a competitor.

—Gerda von Reichmann

PART ONE

1.

Morton tried to feel bad about the death of Anson Lunt, his old friend and benefactor, but it didn't work.

Despite an inexplicable but handy ability to forecast events and read the intentions of others, he wasn't much given to the metaphysical. His years of hardship and professional climbing had armed him with the notion that if it couldn't be seen, felt, tasted, heard, smelled, or measured, it was mainly irrelevant. He enjoyed ghost stories as much as anyone and had a live-and-let-live tolerance for the world's religionists, but his daily life was essentially consumed by the need to manage the existence he'd been given, with little thought for whatever might lie beyond. Death? Merely another abstruse law of a mysterious universe, to be dealt with and conformed to when it came into play.

But Anson Lunt had had a somewhat spookier, transcendental view of life and death. His decades as a physician and research scientist had convinced him that the human being was an extraordinary, animate computer, designed by a superior intelligence and programmed to perceive and act within certain parameters of a greater reality. He'd told Morton several times that he looked forward to dying, believing as he did that it would introduce him to a whole new level of experience.

So what was to feel bad about?

The local TV news lady, all mascara, tilelike teeth, and lacquered hairdo, wasn't so sanguine, her face and voice remaining determinedly tragic and funereal. Even so, it took no mind reader to detect her private delight over the dreadful occurrence that had made her day.

Behind her, Zieglersville Airport was a cheerless prairie, darkened by low, fast-moving clouds and a drizzle that wanted to be rain. Except for the yellow slickers worn by the gaggle of Federal air safety people—stooping, plucking, and bagging like peasants in a bean field—it was a study in gray-on-gray, a monochromatic figment of Hell.

"Dr. Anson Lunt, renowned Zieglersville cancer specialist, and pilot Bill Rooney died here this morning," the woman singsonged, "when their twin-engine turboprop plane crashed while landing after a flight from New York. Federal authorities are on the scene, searching for clues as to just what caused the accident. So far as is known, there was only one witness to the plane's final moments. He is Albert Margolis, an employee of the Rooney Air Taxi Service."

Margolis, a small, dour man with restless eyes and the air of wariness that comes with a life of folly and desperation, came on-screen.

"Tell me, sir," the woman burbled, "just what you saw here this morning."

"Ain't awful lot to tell," Margolis said, self-conscious. "I was out on the apron, catching a smoke, and Rooney's turboprop came out of the east, its lights blinking. It made a kind of downward turn and came in toward the runway from the south. Then, while it was still pretty high up, settling toward the touchdown zone, props idling, lights on bright, the nose was all of a sudden pointing straight down, and the motors started screaming. There was a kind of screwy wobbling, and the plane went in and blew all to hell out there on the south boundary. Damnedest noise I ever heard, I'll tell you. By then I got myself together and ran for the phone and dialed nine-one-one."

"So then what—"

Morton blew a little raspberry, tapped the button, and cut her off in midquestion. Aloud he said, "Way to go, Anson. You did a great job with your life, and it was a pleasure knowing you. Have a wonderful trip."

He hated himself when he got sentimental like this. He beamed down to the real world by glancing at his watch.

The call should be coming by now.

Literally from birth Morton had this ability to read people and their intentions—an intuition thing. Its first piece of work was to warn him to tighten his buns, because, sure as hell, the midwife was about to slap them good. Probably then, too, he had learned that foreknowledge is okay, but evasion is better. While insight could put him on alert, it wouldn't ease the sting when life held him by the heels and actually registered a hit. The trick was to see the hit coming and not be there when it arrived.

When he transferred to Kenwood Junior High School, for instance, he knew from the minute they first traded glances that Billy Mahler, the honor student, athlete, and pet of all teachers, would try to make his days miserable. It was nothing specific— just an inner awareness that Billy saw him to be some kind of threat.

But what to do about the hassles he knew would follow?

Morton's solution was juvenile CIA stuff. First, he paid Billy's kid sister, Nancy, one candy bar a day to report on whatever she knew of her brother's comings and goings. Next, he got a Polaroid of Freddo Toomey diddling little Janey Fenwick in the cloakroom, a coup which turned Freddo, one of Billy's schoolyard henchmen, into a pretty good overall stoolie. With information flowing in from these sources, Morton was able to second-guess Billy and deflect or neutralize his sneaky little plots, most of the time making Billy, the would-be screw-er, the screw-ee. It worked so well it became Morton's lifelong policy to backstop his sharp eyes and sensitive hunch mechanism with bribery and espionage.

He was smiling at the memories when the phone rang.

"Hello."

"It's Margolis, Mr. Morton."

To the Social Security and IRS people, Margolis was a retired railroader who augmented his pension by working as the night watchman at Rooney Air Taxi Service. To Morton, he was an oily, repulsive son of a bitch whose true income was in the six-figure range, thanks to the blackmail he laid on reputable citizens he had secretly photographed doing disreputable things in certain Mertz Highway motels. Morton knew about his little game, and Margolis and his motel-owner collaborators knew he knew. So to buy his silence they got vocal, and together made up the most zealous squad in Morton's platoon of informants.

"What's up?"

"You see the news? About the crash out at the airport?"

"Who hasn't?"

"Well, I got some computer disks left in the airport office by that nutty doctor, Lunt, before he left for New York last night."

"What do you mean—left in the office?"

"He was waiting in the office while Bill preflighted the plane. He had this locked tote bag with PROPERTY OF LUNT BIO-CHEMICAL LABORATORY stenciled on the side. He put it in Bill's wall locker. That's where passengers park things they don't want to take on a flight. I happened to be looking through the window, and I saw him put it there."

"And when you were alone you took a peek, right?"

"I like to work out with the picks. You never know when you might have to diversify, I always say."

"So what's on the disks?"

"Beats the hell out of me. Lot of scientific stuff. Numbers, signs. Like that. I understood them like I understand my ex-wife. Seeing as how your company is a competitor of Lunt Biotech, I thought you might want to see for yourself what's on them, so I made the copies."

"You're trying to sell them to me?"

"Well, yeah. Man's gotta live."

"Something else you've got to do. You've got to understand that it's not Bradford Chemicals Corporation's policy to buy stuff left lying around by careless competitors."

Margolis did some whining. "You're not even interested?"

"It's unlikely that Lunt could have put anything on those disks I'd want to see or should legally be allowed to see. So turn them in to their rightful owners. You might get a reward."

"Can we talk—?"

"This conversation is finished. Call me when you have something I can use."

2.

Greg Allenby's lean, sandy good looks had long ago eroded into a caricature of a patrician gone to seed. His shoulder sag spoke of decades of grieving over missed opportunities. His eyes tended toward the watery, and his suits were tweedy, vested, and rumpled. His car was an aging Bentley, and his home suggested a Tudor country house, low-slung, with tall casement windows, steep slants of slate roof, chunky chimneys, and subtle tints in its masonry. It sprawled along a ridge under a stand of mature maples in Sylvan Hills, on Zieglersville's northwest hem. He hated the place. Jennifer had chosen it, paid for it, and decorated it, and he never came back to it at day's end without feeling the melancholy distance between what was and what might have been.

He eased the car into the garage, punched the key that closed the door behind him, then sat for a time in the silence, rejecting once again the insistent memory of Joe Reiner, gone one night three years ago in a garage filled with a cloud of burnt high octane.

He shook free of the spell and went into the house. Jennifer was downtown, getting her hair done. The boys were at late soccer practice. Byte, their hypochondriacal Boston terrier, was at the vet's again. Their absence was welcome, promising respite. He hung his topcoat in the foyer closet, then stood for a full minute, listening to the inexplicable creakings in the upper regions of the house, to the faint, whirring duet of the refrigerator and the heating system, to the wind in the trees outside, and dealing with the sorry fact that he had everything a man could want except those things he'd dreamed of having.

In the study he lingered by the large window, watching the twilight descend on the distant hills and struggling against a renewed perception of his decayed marriage and desperately souring career. Mixed with it all was this sense of exile, a kind of apartness from an indefinable something indefinably wonderful.

He was determined not to begin drinking until the proper martini at the proper time before a proper dinner. The TV was of no help: heavy-breathing soaps; more bad news on the weather channel; idiotic game shows. He flipped the off button, then sat behind the desk. He moved the date book from here to there, the list finder from there to here.

The loneliness was intense.

In the quiet, the ding-dong of the doorbell was like a shell burst, startling enough to bring him out of the chair. The reaction was irrational; this was his house, he was alone and minding his own business. He had every right to be here, doing nothing, alone and unhappy. So why should he feel this rush of—What? Panic?

The man at the door was vaguely familiar—flat face, sly eyes, a knowing smile. A leather physician's bag hung from his left hand.

"Evening, Dr. Allenby."

"Hello there. What's up?"

"I'm Al Margolis. You know: the guy who works at Bill Rooney's air taxi service?"

"Oh. Yes. Of course." He added, inane, stalling, "You were on the noon news—"

"Can I come in?"

Allenby hesitated. "Well, I'm expecting my wife anytime now—We're—"

"Should only take a minute or two."

"All right."

Allenby led him to the kitchen, where the tiles and vinyls and chrome would be impervious to the man's dirty smell. Still, some unnameable sense told Allenby to go carefully, to be civil. "I just got home, and was about to make coffee—"

"No need on my account."

They sat on the benches in the breakfast nook and traded wary smiles.

"So what can I do for you, Mr. Margolis?"

"It's what I can do for you." Margolis placed the bag on the plank table between them. "You're with the Lunt lab, aren't you?"

"I'm director of research and development there, yes."

"And you worked with that guy who got killed with Bill Rooney in the crash last night?"

"Dr. Anson Lunt. He owned the laboratory and clinic. He was my employer."

Margolis patted the bag. "He left this in Bill's locker before they took off for New York. He told Bill he didn't want to lug it around the city, so he'd pick it up when they got back." He laughed softly. "'Course, they didn't get back, did they. Leastwise in one piece."

Allenby realized he detested his visitor. "So?"

"I thought maybe you'd like to have the bag. And the stuff that's in it."

"That's very nice of you. Dr. Lunt was more than my boss. He was a friend—"

"In return for a reward, sort of."

Allenby stared. "You're trying to *sell* it to me?"

"Well, finders keepers. I find, you keep. Ha-ha."

Allenby felt a gathering of real anger. "No, I'd say it's property that should be delivered to Dr. Lunt's survivors."

"Ain't none. I checked."

"Or his friends."

"Hell, Dr. Allenby, I'm one of his friends. We was friends ever since he started those New York trips. I'd help him aboard the plane, do little things. He even tipped me now and then. We was friends."

Allenby's face was hot now. "So what's in the bag? Medical instruments? Pills? What?"

"Look for yourself."

Allenby pulled the bag to him, snapped open the clasps, and peered inside. Seeming lost and trivial, like detritus in a forgotten drawer, were a sheaf of unlabeled computer disks and five yellow-topped vials of clear liquid. He stared at these for a time, recognizing the yellow's signal, *Development with Market Potential*, and struggling to hide the consequent rush of excitement, which if seen by this—profiteer—would surely inflate the price.

Avoiding the man's eyes, Allenby said, "It's not much. But it's worth something, I suppose. How does fifty dollars sound?"

"I was thinking more in the five hundred bucks range."

Allenby sniffed, incredulous. "Oh, come now. Surely you can't be serious."

"Bag alone's worth that. Look at the leather—the inside work."

"Fifty dollars, my man. No more."

"Okay." Margolis shrugged, closed the bag, and fastened the clasps. "I'll try it on some other friends. Like Teddy Bradford or his gofer, George Morton, maybe."

"You're a cheap little extortionist."

"Really? How about that."

"Will you take a check?"

"Sorry."

Silent, furious, Allenby took an envelope from a cubbyhole in the desk and counted out five one-hundred-dollar bills.

3.

The Sleepy Hollow Hunt Club was neither in a hollow nor did it have much to do with hunting. It was a scattering of squat, rustic buildings on a hill overlooking a valley called Bigelow's Cut. Its core membership was composed of jaded Establishment graybeards, who, in their days of moving and shaking, had moved Zieglersville from nothing to something by shaking the government money tree. Recent years had seen an influx of jaded Baby Boomers, admitted on the strength of their kindred lust for moving up and shaking down. Precious few among the lot had ever had anything to do with hunting wild game. In truth, most of them—the few NRA types and the even fewer 'Nam and Gulf War vets excepted—didn't know one end of a gun from the other and were appalled by the very idea of searching out and shooting down furries and cuddlies. So the hunt club had become nothing more than a bucolic frat house, where the seniors could doze over highballs on the veranda and the underclassmen could do coke in the game room while trading lies about their sexual conquests.

The club's nod toward convention (beyond the antique rifles and stuffed deer heads hung on its walls) was its skeet field, available by appointment to the tiny claque who actually liked to shoot now and then. The launchers were operated by Toots

Pettigrew, the aging "groundskeeper" who hired the grass mowers and shrubbery trimmers and saw that empty bottles and beer cans were picked up and placed in the trash. And it was Toots who now told Morton and Allenby that they could take position because he was about to activate the skeet towers.

Allenby loaded his twelve-gauge and made excuses in advance, saying that he hadn't shot skeet for almost a year and hoped he wouldn't embarrass Morton, the club champ.

Morton was chivalrous, reminding Allenby that it was only a game, adding some sauce about how, if he got in some practice, he and Teddy Bradford—paired up for the annual New Year's Twosome Shoot—might make a team good enough to take the trophy and the thousand dollars that went with it.

They stepped up to the Number One station and Morton motioned for Allenby to lead off. The pull was called, and the high-house clay bird arced sharply in the stiff breeze. Allenby's autoloader barked, but the target continued on serenely. The low-house bird was a repeat performance.

Morton called his pull, swung his Remington through an easy lead, fired, and powdered the high-house bird before it arrived at centerfield. Likewise the low-house bird.

"See?" Allenby sighed. "I'll embarrass you."

"A game or two and you'll be back in the swing. Besides, we've got a bit of crosswind going today."

Allenby made a face. "You're patronizing me."

"Of course I am. I'm trying to piss you off. To rattle you. I've got to win somehow."

They traded the obligatory smiles.

At the next station, Allenby managed to knock down one out of two.

"Now cut that out," Morton said in his Jack Benny impersonation.

"Up yours, Upjohn."

They laughed and began the counterclockwise stroll around the shooting arc. Allenby's performance did indeed improve. When the doubles had been shot and the game was over, they checked their guns for unload and safe, then moved off to the side and sat on a bench.

"What was the score, Greg?"

"Twenty-five for you, nineteen for me."

"Not bad for a guy who hasn't shot for a year."

"Maybe. But you shot a perfect score."

"I'm having a bad day."

The steward came out of the clubhouse, bringing coffee and beef sandwiches. They ate slowly, watching the progress of a thunderstorm that flickered over the distant valley. Morton gathered his trash, dropped it into a waste can, and asked Allenby—cool, casual—what was on his mind.

The gun club was the most public private place in the county—public, in that there was no cause for suspicion in a twosome idly squirting ammo, even when the two were arch business rivals, and private, in that a conversation on the side of a windy hill wasn't likely to be overheard.

"I've got a great deal for Teddy. A huge plum."

Morton let him see some peevish surprise. "Come on. You're not going back to that old crap, are you?"

Allenby parried the question. "Well, George, you know how phones and letters make me uneasy, and I couldn't justify a business trip to New York on my expense account. So I thought it would be best for you and me to meet here at the club, where we can sit in this lovely sunshine and talk about something that your boss will most surely have a very heavy interest in."

Morton ran a thumb over a smudge on the stock of his shotgun. "How often do I have to tell you, Greg? The market isn't what it used to be. Besides, your prices are high, and the bottom line for us hasn't been all that wonderful."

Allenby gave him a supercilious smile. "Ho-ho. You think the others were high? Wait'll you hear the price on this. Teddy will be running around like a panicky chicken, trying to find the money. I kid you not."

"You're a pain in the ass when you talk like that. For someone who's trying to sell something, you have a lot to learn about salesmanship."

Allenby drew himself up, prissy. "No need to be vulgar."

"Hey, man. Vulgar's my thing. I hold the patent on it."

"Be serious, George. This one stands to make us all as rich as Croesus. It's a breakthrough. A biotech triumph. I discovered it. It's mine. But under my employment agreement with the Lunt organization, it belongs to Lunt, and all I'll get is a pat on the back and maybe a year-end bonus. I want more—lots more—so I'm offering to sell it to Teddy on the q.t."

Morton was incredulous. "You mean you've invented a product on Lunt time and with Lunt resources and the Lunt people don't know what you've been doing? How can they possibly not know? You've got a Ph.D. in magic, or something?"

"Anson Lunt was out of the management loop for a long time. As chief of R&D, I run my own show. I report to no one but myself. And that insufferable administrative chief of his, Melanie Flynn, I might add, is quite easy to outflank."

Morton gave him a wry look. "You're a mighty fancy crook, Greg—one of the fanciest crooks I know—but I'm always surprised when you make it so obvious."

Allenby laughed and compounded clichés. "Takes one to know one. Besides, one man's crook is another man's go-getter."

Morton was truly ticked now. Allenby was effete, egocentric, smug, and representative of all the things in people he loathed. Worse, Allenby's self-absorption carried over into his science, giving him a myopia that enabled him to see the world only through the bottom of a petri dish, to miss the larger fact that the high-risk venture money was drying up. He seemed totally unaware of the massive shifting caused by the fault lines traversing the health care terrain.

"You just don't get it, do you."

"Get what?"

"The downsizing, the race for primacy by way of new drugs, robotics, genetics, information networks and databases and computer-assisted therapies. How, with a home computer, e-mail, and teleconferencing, the patient will soon be able to get the best damned clinical help in the world without leaving his own living room. How Bradford Chemicals—along with all the manufacturers—is gearing up for a medical industry that will deliver its services like pizzas. How today's medicine and hospitals are on the way out. How today's tradition is already tomorrow's Dark Ages. How, how, how. Wake up, for hell's sake."

Allenby made a face. "Pu-lease: give me a break. I get enough of that hot air from Melanie Flynn. You want the formula or not?"

"Bradford Chemicals Corporation is no longer your big teat, Greg. The good old days are gone for good. We've buttoned up our blouse."

Allenby smirked. "And I know how to unbutton it again, you arrogant twit. I've found how to tame the trophoblast."

Morton stared at him, full on.

"Touché, eh?" Allenby laughed again.

Morton said nothing.

"I absolutely kid you not," Allenby burbled. "On my own, after hours, nights, and weekends for damn near ten years, I've worked up the chemistry and attendant dietary therapy that will harness the trophoblast and put it to work as an oncological antitoxin. Tie it together with the traditional treatments—surgery, radiology, and chemo—and we've got ourselves one huge mother of a drug, a gigantic step forward in the control, even the prevention of a whole range of cancers. It's not the magic bullet—not yet—but it's very close to it."

Morton watched the approaching storm for a time. When he spoke, he tried to keep his voice calm, noncommittal. "Well, laddie, the reputables won't buy. They know you belong to Lunt. They'll assume that you're selling property that rightfully belongs to your company. They don't deal in hot goods."

Allenby gave Morton the needle. Smiling primly, he said, "You think that Bradford is the only company that is friendly to hot goods? That you and Teddy are my only clients?"

It was Morton's turn to shrug.

"Georgie, Georgie." Allenby shook his head and sighed the sigh of a long-suffering schoolmarm. "What do you think I've done with the money you've paid me over the years? I've built a mechanism that makes customers think they're buying legitimately from a Toonerville lab. They don't see me, they don't see hot stuff anywhere in the mix. But in this case I'm surfacing to offer Teddy the right of first refusal. I'm doing him the auld lang syne thing."

"Like how?"

"If I stick to my employment contract and turn over the formula to the Lunt people to make and sell, the best I can expect is a little more money and boring anonymity for the rest of my life. That just won't cut it, Georgie. No way. I deserve better than that. I deserve the loot and the fame that go with a major discovery. And now that the late, great Anson Lunt is gone, it can happen. His lab and plant—his business and its assets—are a gorgeous plum, just waiting to be picked by some enlightened, ambitious, and well-heeled organization. An organization like Bradford Chemicals, say. And when Bradford buys Lunt, I'll see that my formula goes with the deal—with the understanding that I get instant retirement, a substantial advance against royalties based on a muscular percentage of the annual gross income earned by whatever Bradford product might be derived from my formula."

"You're making some large assumptions here, Gregory. You're assuming that the Lunt enterprise is for sale. You're assuming that, if Lunt is for sale, Teddy Bradford would be willing to buy it. You're assuming that, if he did buy it, he'd be willing to give you any kind of percent of the gross."

Allenby rolled his eyes. "Willing? Come, now. With this in his hands, Teddy Bradford would soon be running one of the greatest money machines in history."

Morton tried for nonchalance. " 'Soon,' my ass. You may have a formula, a program, but it'll take a decade of patient-testing and case histories and FDA submissions and patenting processes—and forty-nine tons of money—just to move the thing into marketing position."

Allenby shrugged that infuriating shrug again. "You do that much for a freaking cold remedy, chum. Ten years and a ton of money aren't anything special in your business. But here's

where I lay my clincher on you. I've cured a man with metastatic cancer in nine days. From terminal carcinoma in both
lungs and a huge secondary in the left arm to a big appetite and
a readiness to go to work. In nine days, Georgie. *Nine days*.
And you know very well that, with that kind of performance,
the FMAA is going to give it blitz clearance under its special
reg for new drugs that make a difference in life-threatening
illnesses."

Morton humphed. "Nine days? Come on, get real."

"We had a terminal in our clinic, forty-two-year-old man
name of Hicks. I injected a massive dose, because he had nothing to lose and I had to see if the earlier tests on primary cancers
were true indicators of the stuff's efficacy in calamitous conditions. So I gave him an arterial injection of one of the batches
I've produced to date. The patient's pain subsided within six
hours and he was asking for dinner after twenty-four. Up and
walking around a day later. X rays clear by week's end."

"You have records on that?"

"Bet your sweet ass, I do. Live witnesses, too."

"You can duplicate the achievement?"

"Find me the body, and you've got your demo."

Morton gave all this a minute to digest. Then: "So what's
your proposal?"

Allenby shook his head. "No, that's not your line, it's my
line. Teddy has two weeks to come up with an offer. If I don't
like what you put in the collection plate, dear boy, be prepared
to enter Corporate Hell, because I'm most surely going to sell
this gold mine to somebody. Here or abroad. And for mega-
bucks."

Morton stood up, then slipped his shotgun into its padded
carry-case. Without looking at Allenby, he said, "I'll take this
to Teddy, and we'll be back to you in a day or so."

"Well, don't dally, Georgie. How often does your boss get
a chance at rock-bottom, ground-floor control of a major control
of cancer, eh?"

Morton thought: *God, how I hate that laugh of his.*

*   *   *

The road back to town led Morton past Elmwood Manor, and as he cleared the hill and saw the great house spread across the Amish plain below, the inner dam built to contain his perpetual loneliness was ruptured by a flash flood of nostalgia. There Anson had introduced him to Ace at one of those "comedy relief parties" Charles Hamilton used to throw "to break the melancholy of this godforsaken Nowhere that has entrapped us good guys." There she had later led him into deep and tender and rewarding conversations, into zany poolside antics, into moments of silent sharing and understanding. The memories were actually painful, as in the penetration of a spear.

What makes for love? What—or who—decides that this person will love this person? Tens of jillions on this earth, and some cosmic smart-ass generates a special bond, a special and everlasting devotion of one specific jillionth for another specific jillionth. They all have faces, figures, minds, attitudes, auras. They're pretty and ugly and tall and short and fat and skinny; they have smooth skin, wrinkles, straight teeth, no teeth, blue eyes, brown eyes, black eyes, green eyes, big noses, small noses. Some are smart, some are dumb. On and on. So what makes who lock onto whom? Why, for good God's sake, was I locked onto a woman who in no way fit my youthful image of female perfection—and then, after somehow lighting my fuse anyhow, moved on, forever out of reach? What a royal, pluperfect pain in the ass.

He shouted at the windshield, "Knock it the hell off, Morton! Self-pity ain't your style!"

He slapped the car into road-rage gear and launched into a squealing pass at High Top Curve, only to be forced into a semipanic, nose-to-nose halt with a nondescript brown car that had voomed through Elmwood's outermost wrought-iron portcullis.

The other car backed up, then turned in front of him, southbound in the other lane. As it passed, the driver, a pretty blonde, glowered at him through a pair of granny glasses. He took a deep breath, struggling against the self-reproach that told him he couldn't even drive down a lonely country road without pissing somebody off.

As he entered town, there was another wrenching, and he heard himself again.

"It's got to work. It's plain got to work."

When he got back to his place, Morton knocked down a bourbon, took a shower, pulled on fresh jeans and a tee shirt, and made himself an omelette. He'd cleaned up the kitchen and was into the six o'clock news when the phone rang.

It was Burroughs. "Calling like I promised."

"How did you make out?"

"I was downhill from you, in some bushes," Burroughs said. "There was some wind noise, but the video is good, and the conversation is still pretty damned clear."

"Bring the tape to me here as soon as."

"Give me twenty minutes."

4.

Rain, like that which now hissed against the car windows, helped Zieglersville not at all. After dawn the drizzle had become a downpour, which turned the streets into flumes and laid a seething murk over the crags and valleys of the skyline, where even the huge electric date-and-time sign on the Investors Equity Bank building had been reduced to a watery glow. Traffic routinely slowed with the first sprinkle, but this, a Grade A deluge, had transformed the center-city streets into what suggested the world's largest and noisiest car wash. But Morton refused to let the delay ruin his mood, which was fairly good for a change, and after a time he was able to clear the Ninth Street causeway and get onto the Ligonier Pike, where things eased up a bit and gave him a straight shot at Elmwood Manor.

Alicia Cosgrove Emerson was the only issue of the marriage of Frederick T. Emerson, a wealthy Rhode Island socialite, and Margaret L. Cosgrove, the daughter and sole surviving relative of the legendary John M. Cosgrove, founder of International Petroleum Corporation. Emerson had died in a fall from his polo pony, and Margaret, inconsolable, followed soon after, leaving little Alicia to be brought up by "Big John" Cosgrove, her grandfather. Entirely out of his depth, Big John decided that Alicia needed a proper home, so he had commissioned a renowned Munich architect to design one that would not only provide shelter for the kid but also serve to memorialize his apotheosis from ragtag wildcatter to oil baron. The architect had come up with "Elmwood Manor," whose towers and slate roofs and mossy walls foisted an artificial mesa on the gentle plain. A gigantic looming meant to exalt, to inspire, it instead came off as a medieval fortress town with the esthetics of a cruel, dead society. Alicia's husband, Charles Hamilton, in a wheelchair since a traffic accident years earlier, hated the place and refused to live there. Big John's will required Alicia, on pain of disinheritance, to retain Elmwood Manor, Big John's monument to himself, as her official legal residence. Laws notwithstanding, devotion to her grandfather and a personal sense of duty compelled her to live there, keeping her marriage together by flying her own plane twice a month to Florida, where Hamilton filled his days by wheeling and dealing internationally from his "studio"—a twenty-room contemporary on its own half mile of palm-shaded beach.

In the morning storm, Elmwood was a forbidding blear among regiments of rain-misted elms, and Morton understood the unhappiness of those who'd been forced to call it home.

He announced himself to the black box, and the massive wrought-iron gate swung open. He drove to the main entrance, parked behind a muddy Corolla, and was met at the door by Hugo, the requisite butler, whose mortician's welcome suited the time and place. "Mrs. Hamilton is in the solarium, sir."

"Lead on."

They passed through the opulence—low, beamed ceilings; polished mahogany paneling; ranks of lead-paned casements; deep-hued tapestries and gold-framed oils. At the end of the gallery, the solarium, a room built of tinted glass, presented a panorama of meadows and hills under the storm-blotted sky.

As always at first glimpse, he wondered what it was about Alicia that made her so attractive. He'd never had much time for women. In general he respected them, and in earlier times there had been two who not only had lit his fuse but also had shown superior intelligence and exceptional courage. But the games most of the others played, while often fun, were incredibly time-consuming and usually ended up not so much fun. Alicia was a oner, conforming to few of the popular criteria for female beauty. She was handsome, to be sure, with patrician features, auburn hair seeming always to be just this side of tousled, and understated clothes that played precisely to her slimness. For all that, though, there was a childlike unaffectedness that inexplicably translated into sensuality, a fact that never failed to bewilder him. Like now, with her Celtic fairness even more wan, her large hazel eyes bleared by tears, slumped in one of the wicker chairs beside the fountain, she suggested a little girl who had done and seen everything there ever was. A maddening contradiction she was, and even now, in this unnatural situation, his maleness was drawn by her femaleness. Seated across the coffee table from her was a large, bespectacled blonde wearing nurse's white stretch knits, whom he recognized as the woman who had glared at him after the near miss at the Elmwood gate the other day.

The two women gave Morton surprised stares. As always when encountering Alicia in public, he felt the uneasiness of a schoolboy who finds himself sharing an elevator with the headmaster's voluptuous wife.

"Hi, Alicia," he managed. "I had to see how you are. I couldn't stay away. Not now."

Alicia, rarely at a loss for words, appeared to be at a loss for words. She blushed faintly, dabbed her eyes with a handkerchief, then went into the social explanations mode. "Amy, this is George Morton. He is senior vice president of Bradford Chemicals. He and Teddy Bradford were once Anson Lunt's collaborators, but there was a falling-out." She paused, her lower lip trembling. "And, frankly, I don't know exactly how to handle this scene."

The blonde looked him over, noncommittal. Unaccountably, he felt compelled to explain, to the lighten the mood. "Anson and Mrs. Hamilton and I were once pals. But things changed, and they began to see me as an enemy. Which is too bad. I'm really a pretty neat guy when you get to know me."

The nurse remained silent, neutral.

This irked him somehow. "And you are——?"

Alicia's good manners took over. "Amy Cummings. She's a nurse at Zieglersville General and a therapist who helps with my back problem."

They exchanged nods, then the nurse gathered up her gloves and bag, putting on a sudden recollection of a need to be elsewhere. "Takeoff time."

Morton was about to apologize for interrupting her visit, but she made it unnecessary. "It's okay. I was gonna leave anyhow." She patted Alicia's hand. "I'll phone you."

When she'd gone, they confronted their awkward aloneness—the first in months.

"Are you all right? Really?"

"Just this nagging back thing. It comes, goes."

"Come on, now—you know what I mean."

She looked away, her gaze on the rain-washed countryside beyond the tall windows. "I'm having trouble with the reality of it. With the—emptiness. I dearly loved Anson. He was very precious to me."

Morton could only nod.

"Why did you come here, George?"

"Irrational impulse."

She smiled faintly. "One of your chronic ailments."

"Only when it comes to you and your best interests." He paused, then added awkwardly, "I'm sorry, dear lady. I know how terribly hard this is on you."

"Nothing new, really. I've been mourning Anson for years. Ever since you, the others, turned on him. In a way, he died when that happened. I should be immune to grief by now. But it goes on and on."

"Someday you'll understand that I never turned on him. Never. You may not know that, accept that. But he did, I'm glad to say."

"Do you believe there's an afterlife, George?"

She had a way of surprising him with digression. But he was not unarmed, having as he did a knack for seeing a flow and going with it. "Sure. Why not? Anson did. I remember how he put it: 'In this room, all around us, there's music, pictures, chatter. They're real as hell. But we can't hear or see them unless we have TV or radio sets. We can't see or hear what's after death, either. We don't have the right equipment.' "

"That sounds so—Sears, Roebucky."

He reached out and took her hand. "Hey—Why make it so tough on yourself? Let him go, dear. He was a great guy, and wherever he is now he has to be having a better time than he was having here. Don't fret. Be glad."

She was considering this when Hugo came into the solarium, trailed by a youngish man wearing a worn but classy topcoat over his worn but classy business suit. He could have been an English lit teaching assistant, or maybe a midrange bureaucrat. But, Morton's instinct told him instantly that behind this man's polite, campusy facade was a mean-street cop.

Hugo explained. "Mum, this is Detective Sergeant Jacoby of the city police."

Alicia gave Morton a quick, quizzical glance. Then she nodded Hugo's dismissal and turned to regard the policeman with regal gravity. "So, then, Sergeant, what can I do for you?"

"Sorry to intrude, Mrs. Hamilton, but I've been looking into certain angles in the recent plane crash out at the airport. I understand you were a friend of Dr. Lunt and a contributor to his clinic, and I was hoping you could fill me in on some of the things he was doing before he died."

Alicia's uneasiness was apparent. "Well, why would what he was doing at the clinic have to do with the crash?"

"Probably nothing, ma'am. But in my work I got to do a lot of poking around—most of it a waste of time."

"So you are here to waste my time?"

"No way, ma'am. That's not what I meant—"

Morton turned to leave. "I've come at a bad time, I'm afraid—"

The familiar Alicia Hamilton returned. She held up an imperious hand, halting him in his tracks. "I want you to stay for this. I prefer not to talk behind your back."

Morton felt heat in his face. "You plan to talk to the police about me?"

"I can't talk about Anson without you and Teddy coming into it."

"Well, why the hell not?"

Jacoby intervened, calm, pacifying. "Easy, easy. No sense in anybody being upset by my being here." He held out his right hand. "I recognize you from your pictures in the paper. You're George Morton, right?"

Morton shook the hand. "You sure you wouldn't rather talk to Mrs. Hamilton privately?"

"No big deal. Glad to have you sit in." He gave Alicia a peacemaker's smile. "So, then, Mrs. Hamilton, let's talk."

She nodded toward the wicker. "Sit down, please."

They sat, and Jacoby, who sent Morton's mind to the old *Dragnet* TV series, glanced around the leafy room. "Nice place you have here, ma'am." It was like complimenting the queen on Buckingham Palace.

"Thank you." Alicia gave him a tentative glance. "So what would you like to know? Are you familiar with Dr. Lunt and his work?"

"Only what I read in the newspapers. Local medic. His off-beat treatment of cancer patients got him and his clinic a lot of notoriety. That sort of thing."

"Not notoriety. Fame. He was world-famous."

"Well, as I say, I'm not all that up on it." Jacoby took a pad and ballpoint from his jacket pocket. Morton saw that he was framing his next question delicately. Alicia and her husband were a seven on the sociopolitical Richter scale as well as heavy donors to the Police Charity Fund, and so the city's lawmen were not about to handle her casually. "I understand you drove him to the airport that day."

"We'd had a special meeting of the Lunt Foundation's board that afternoon. As the meeting broke up he told me he had an evening engagement in New York and had to hurry if he was to cab to the airport on time. I offered to take him."

"He didn't have a car?"

"His eyesight was poor. He worried that he might cause an accident and hurt people. So he gave up driving some years ago. He was a very considerate man." There was a catch in her voice.

"So did he say anything special?"

Alicia's soft hazel gaze went out to the rainy meadows again. "We talked about the foundation meeting. But then he got very quiet, and when I asked him why, he said, 'I'm finished, Alicia. I'm in the tunnel, and the locomotive is closing fast. They're doing a number on me again, and this time they're going all the way.' Those may not be his exact words, but that's pretty much what he said."

Jacoby made a note. "Any guesses about what he meant?"

Alicia shrugged. "I suppose he was referring to the old quack charges against him. He'd never got over the ridicule—the humiliation of being called a fraud and a snake-oil artist by former friends and colleagues. He couldn't seem to live all that down. But this was different. The way he talked, I got the idea the persecution was still going on."

"Why would that be?"

"He'd never given up his line of study, despite the trouble and loss it had caused him. He believed in what he was doing. And there are those who've never given up waiting to knock him down if he got out of line again."

Jacoby's manner took on an edge. "Names, Mrs. Hamilton? Places? Dates?"

"I am not a gossip, Sergeant."

Jacoby looked out at the sky, which was now laced with lightning. He seemed to be concentrating on maintaining his cool, but it was obvious that he was barely making it. He made a note, and without looking up, asked, "How about you, Mr. Morton? Do you have anything to say about any of this?"

The question was another surprise. Morton had assumed that his presence and his opinions were irrelevant to the sergeant's basic mission, which was to be able to tell his boss that he had dropped in on Mrs. Hamilton and done some official sucking-up. But it was also one of those damned-if-you-do-and-don't questions, so Morton picked his way carefully. He was already kicking himself for coming here in the first place; he didn't need to kick himself for having given the police some stupid answers.

"I'm having a problem understanding just what you're getting at, Sergeant. Why all these questions?"

Jacoby gave him a cool stare. "I'm bothered by the idea that a guy, famous for having an army of enemies, dies in a plane, flown by a very good pilot, that suddenly dives into the ground during a routine landing on a routine arrival on a routine flight from New York. I'd be bothered by any guy dying like that, but my systems start pinging when there's so much angry history, so many hard noses."

"Well, I don't know what we can do to help."

"You can start by telling me how you two, personally, related to Dr. Lunt."

Morton shrugged. "Mrs. Hamilton and I have conflicting views of his biochemical studies. She's always considered Dr. Lunt to be a genius whose work would inevitably bring forth a cure for cancer. I liked him as a man—I especially admired his tenacity—but I thought that, as a scientist, he was chasing rainbows. She's backed up her opinion with contributions of time and money to the Lunt Clinic, and I've backed up my opinion by stating publicly that Dr. Lunt's work was misguided at best, dangerous at worst. Bottom line: Mrs. Hamilton and I are flat-out antagonistic over the work of a man we both happened to like a great deal."

The detective bored in. "Tell me about Lunt's work, Mr. Morton. Just what was he doing that made everybody so mad?"

Morton's problem was to give a straight answer without salting Alicia's wounds. Lunt's death had torn her up, and he didn't want to increase the bleeding.

Damn! Why did I come here?

"It's hard to put in a nutshell," he said. "Basically, Anson Lunt believed that cancer is caused not by an alien attacker kind of thing, like a virus, or whatever, but by a lack of something in the body. He saw cancer as a nutritional deficiency disease, like rickets, or pernicious anemia, or scurvy. His life was dedicated to identifying that deficiency, and when he opened a clinic

to treat cancer sufferers with diets and injections of artificial
vitamins manufactured in his small plant, Teddy Bradford and
I—as did most of the medical and pharmaceutical community—
declared his work to be life-threatening."

"Why, exactly?"

"Well, mainstream medicine believes that there are only
four ways cancer can be treated with any hope of success—
with surgery, with chemotherapy, with radiology, or with a
combination. And the drug manufacturers have, understand-
ably, concentrated on producing medicines that play to these
treatments—make them more efficient and easy to administer.
But Dr. Lunt claimed that these traditional treatments do more
harm than good, and he encouraged his patients to refuse all of
them until his alternative procedure had been tried."

Jacoby glanced at Alicia. "And you believed that Lunt was
right, and the others were wrong?"

"Yes."

"And you, Mr. Morton, thought he was—"

"Plain wrong."

Alicia said bitterly, "You called him a quack."

"Hold on, dammit. Teddy, the Bradford Corporation—even
your own husband—called him a quack. I never used the word,
because I considered him to be a skilled scientist who was stumbling down a really goofy garden path. Being mistaken doesn't
necessarily make someone a quack."

Jacoby revealed a professional's value of facts over a rich
woman's clout. "A little cheeky, isn't it—using your husband's
money to back a guy your husband dissed?"

Her answer was pure Alicia. "Obviously, the Social Register
is another thing you're not all that up on, Sergeant. As the sole
heir of John M. Cosgrove, founder of International Petroleum
Corporation and its many affiliates, I don't have to use my
husband's money for anything."

To his credit, Jacoby didn't roll over and squirm. Deadpan,
he made another note, and persisted. "I still need to know: How
come you were such an Anson Lunt fan—ready to pump up a
guy your own husband, Charles Hamilton, a major force in the

international chemicals business, was trying to take the air out of? I mean, the clippings include a lot of negative things Mr. Hamilton had to say about Lunt and his operations, and here you are—" He left the thought hanging.

Alicia gave Jacoby a lingering stare, as if sorting through possible answers. She went for candor. "I discovered a lump one day, and my Philadelphia physicians wanted to remove the breast. I'd read about the Lunt Clinic for Alternative Oncology and the fuss that surrounded it, and Dr. Lunt seemed to be someone I could relate to. So with nothing to lose, I went to him for an opinion. He explained his treatment—George just described it for you—then gave me some IVs and pills and put me on a carefully regulated diet. The lump eventually disappeared, and I still have the breast. I've since contributed heavily to the clinic. And no one on this earth dares say anything against Dr. Lunt in my presence."

"Does that include your husband?"

The question was presumptuous, intrusive, and entirely wasted. As the ultimate product of a lineage whose conservatism was rooted in Plymouth Colony orthodoxy and subsequently fine-tuned (after Big John's huge oil strike) in the most rigid of denominational schools, Alicia not only surrendered to her inhibitions, she embraced them, made them singularly her own. She'd become an island of conformity and patrician manners in a world awash in revolution and iconoclasm and baloney—a world in which, ironically, Big John Emerson would have been very much at home. She could speak easily on almost any subject external to herself, invariably viewing the matter, large or small, serious or silly, through the prism of her uncompromising sense of responsibility and propriety. But thanks to this same inflexible lens there could be no such thing as a public discussion of things mattering to the inner, deeply private Alicia—her marriage in particular. Popsicles in hell were more likely.

And so her answer to Jacoby: "What my husband and I discuss is none of your business."

Jacoby blinked, and it was apparent that Alicia had finally put a shot through his hull. Obviously, he was under his chief's order to butter up the lady, and he seemed now to realize that, in the heat of the information chase, he'd begun to tick her off, big-time. He snapped his notebook shut and rose from his chair, cool. "Well, I guess we've done all we can do here today. If either of you think of anything that might contribute to an understanding of the airplane crash, please give me a call. Just dial the police number and ask for me."

As Jacoby headed for the door, Morton said, "I'm sorry we couldn't give you whatever you're looking for, Sergeant. But all we've got are opinions, hunches—"

At the door, Jacoby turned and gave them a small smile. "Opinions and hunches are what cops start with. Let me know when you're ready to give me some. Meanwhile, thanks for your time."

He left.

In the silence, Alicia said, "That man could be a problem."

"He already is, dear lady," Morton said dryly.

5.

Burroughs was an expensive information source, but he was worth it. As a technician, he had played a central role in establishing the city government's computer databases and their linkages. As a compulsive gambler with humongous debts, he depended on Morton's cash subsidies to protect himself from the wrath of both the law and the outlaw. In return, he had enabled Morton to access City Hall, the County Building, and the municipal, county, and state police with his personal computer. In robe and slippers in his own den, Morton could monitor virtually every screen in the various bureaucracies, call up law enforcement files, and even perform basic document-editing functions. And that was the routine part. For extra fees, Burroughs would devise and supply clandestine surveillance and wiretaps, and it was this particular service that had proved to be the most useful in the thing Morton had going with Greg and Teddy. But now that Sergeant Jacoby was an unwitting player in the game, Morton decided that he would need to spend more time on the police net, with special attention to the homicide venue.

The screen showed that Jacoby was a tidy, surprisingly literate man. His case files were divided into three basic categories: unsolved homicides dating from 1990; the very active investigation of the gunshot deaths of a convenience store owner and two customers; and now "The Lunt Case," which was little more than a digest of his talks with Lou Mackey, the NATS air-safety prober, with witnesses like Al Margolis and Hank Feeney, a trucker who had been passing the airport at the time, and with Alicia and Morton himself. There was also a series of speculations—dubbed "Backgrounders"—in which he characterized those he had interviewed. Margolis, the airport handyman, was "a shifty spook with dirty fingernails," for instance. Alicia was "a reedy heiress with reddish hair and an absentee husband she doesn't like." He was especially unimpressed with "George Morton, a cocktail party smoothie in two grands' worth of flannel, silk, and cordovan—a glob of Establishment fat, whose major achievement has been a twenty-year rise to the top of the corporate gravy."

This made Morton laugh. *A man is known by the metaphors he keeps, eh?*

He laughed again, turned off the set, and, taking up his briefcase, went to the garage.

Melanie Flynn stood before her desk—cool, correct, a commander beneath a white flag, about to reject the enemy's proposals. She was also a flaxen-haired knockout—composed, groomed to salon perfection, and dignified in her immaculate lab coat—a fact that made it doubly necessary for Morton to focus on his mission. He had admired her from a distance for years, from the evening they'd been introduced at a lavish Elmwood soirée, actually, but until this morning, alone with her, this close, he had never fully appreciated just how truly compelling she was. A lady's man he wasn't, but her nearness now suggested what he might have missed. Or why men leave home.

Steady, fella. The agenda. The agenda. Keep your mind on why the hell you're here. Disassociate yourself. Think cunning. Remain inscrutable. Play the archetypal pain in the kiester. Even if it kills you.

Forcing himself to picture her as merely another benchmark on the terrain of his battleground, he shook her hand, noted that it was a nice morning, and thanked her for giving him some time.

She sat behind her desk and waved him to a chair. "What can I do for you, Mr. Morton?"

He gave her his gravely earnest expression. "I've come personally and, if you will, confidentially, in a final effort to reach an agreement on Bradford Chemicals's purchase of Lunt Biotech."

She gazed back at him, her large eyes, cerulean blue, unblinking. "I've already told your people that the Lunt organization is not for sale to you. And if it were for sale, you wouldn't talk to me, you'd have to talk to the owner, Dr. Lunt. And that's not possible, because he's now in Boise's Shadowlawn Cemetery."

Morton fashioned Prim Smile No. 1. "Dr. Lunt was, of course, a primary player in the scenario. But it's our perception that you, Dr. Flynn, are the one to talk to in the Lunt organization. Dr. Lunt, as he himself admitted publicly, was a moody eccentric. You are noted for your commonsense willingness to meet others halfway."

How it pained him to dish out this kind of blarney. How it pained him to see that she wasn't buying a bit of it.

"Your perception is wrong, Mr. Morton. My responsibilities include talking with many people about many things. But I cannot—will not—talk about the sale of an enterprise solely owned by Dr. Lunt until the lawyers define precisely where things stand now that he's gone."

Morton nodded reasonably. "Our initial overtures were exploratory. Our representatives could only show reasons for deals, not make them."

"And you can?"

She knew, as he did, that it always came down to one-on-one. There was always a flurry, of course: exploratory discussions, proposals, counterproposals, struggles to reach satisfactory common ground, platoons of lawyers haggling, CPAs droning, computers racing, fax machines sending out blizzards, all that sort of thing. But nothing really happened until two individuals with the proper muscle looked each other in the eye, and said, "Okay, it's a deal." Anson had been the sole owner of Lunt Biotech and its affiliate, the Lunt Clinic for Alternative Oncology, and was the top creative force—a physician and a fundamental research scientist with an acknowledged lack of interest in business administration. He left no family, according to his bios in the various *Who's Whos*. It was logical that Dr. Flynn be one of the ones in this particular one-on-one.

Morton waved a haughty hand. "No matter how the estate is settled, it should be obvious to you, as Dr. Lunt's business manager, that now is the time to ally the Lunt organization with new funding and new market direction. You've all along had the authority to speak for Dr. Lunt *in absentia*, and you're the logical one to investigate the various opportunities now open to your organization. I am Bradford's senior vice president, a departmental director, and among those the company has granted check-writing authority. Especially in this case, in which I'm prepared to make a ten-million-dollar cash down payment on Bradford's acquisition of Lunt Biotech, its research laboratory, its clinic, and all of its assets, including those products for which patents are being sought. The remaining principal would be in the form of five hundred thousand shares of Bradford stock valued at eighty-one million, five hundred thousand dollars, payable in whatever increments and over any time span you specify. And, having heard this, you, as the power behind the Lunt throne, can look me in the eye, and say, 'It's a deal.' Is it a deal?"

She said nothing.

"Do you have any questions or comments, Dr. Flynn?"

She continued to stare out the window. "You have a good line on how things are around this shop. How come?"

"I don't understand—"

"How did you know that I've been authorized to speak for Dr. Lunt *in absentia*? How did you know there are products lining up for patents?"

His smile seemed to bother her, so he gave it to her again. "Bradford has a very elaborate program for keeping up on things. Simple logic, to begin with. Then analysis of professional journals, trade magazines, raw material flows, plant activity, fee payments, shipping—any and all of a thousand indicators."

"Industrial espionage, in other words."

"Well—"

"You have a spy in our organization, too?"

He held up a hand of caution and parried the question. "Hold on, Doctor. Let me finish. Any industrial enterprise uses those techniques to keep up with developments. But in your case, Dr. Lunt himself was the source. Bradford has been conducting research in nitrilosides and deduced from papers written sometime ago by Dr. Lunt that he'd long been onto things we were only beginning to understand. The reasoning among our people is that we shouldn't go to the expense and effort to reinvent a wheel you people are ready to patent. Far better to seek an agreement that would make Bradford and Lunt partners, rather than competitors."

"If you can't beat 'em, join 'em. Right?"

"You, as patent holder, would be amply rewarded, and we would save millions."

She surprised him by going directly to the core. "If Bradford did acquire Lunt, what could Lunt employees expect?"

"Very little would be changed, actually. Organizationally, we envision Lunt becoming an operating department, moving en bloc, so to speak, from life under your logo to life under ours. Lunt employees would, therefore, automatically become Bradford employees, with all benefits, including vested retirement funds, being carried over and brought into agreement with the Bradford benefits package—which, as you no doubt know, is considerably more liberal than that which you have here. As for operations, you'd continue with your work as is. The contract would simply stipulate that the marketing and promotion of Lunt products and services would be under the Bradford logo. In addition, a small company would be set up to monitor research and patents in this country and abroad so as to provide an early-warning system against derivatives of Lunt products that might compete."

She was wary. "Even those that originate here?"

"Well, yes. Here, anywhere——"

"Meaning that, if I were to introduce an item the monitor considers to be competitive, you would automatically own the item and any patents as well?"

"Not necessarily. If we deem the item to be beyond the Bradford scope of interest, you'd be free to develop and market it under a logo of your own."

"What if I later get an offer from, say, Magna?"

"Then Bradford would have one month to decide whether to top Magna's offer."

"And if you don't top the offer?"

He laid on her one of his more infuriating smiles. "Unlikely, my dear."

"Well, Mr. Morton," she said slowly, "I don't think this is such a good deal."

"You have a counterproposal, perhaps?"

Her pretty face had turned red. "As a matter of fact, yes. I propose that you stand up, shoot your French cuffs, adjust your Italian tie, take up your English briefcase, go to your German car, and get the hell off our property."

"No need to get angry, Dr. Flynn——"

"This is my cool side. You don't want to see my angry side."

"I think we could come to a satisfactory——"

"Forget it. There's not one person in this company who doesn't resent the Bradford attempts to destroy Anson Lunt. So there is no way the Lunt interests would ever be sold to Bradford. No way. Besides, your proposal offers peanuts for a company and a product line worth——"

He broke in. "We know for a fact that Lunt is on the financial ropes, and if push comes to shove, you'd sell to anybody for the right price."

"You're not hearing me, Mr. Morton. Your price—Bradford's price—could never be right."

A very silent, very tense moment followed. Then he rose from his chair, picked up his briefcase, and marched to the door.

"I'm sorry, Dr. Flynn. It would have been nice to be your friend and collaborator."

"This is our last discussion. The chess game is over."

As he closed the door behind him, he gave her that infuriating smile again. "The game has just begun, my dear."

When he got to his car, Morton threw the briefcase into the backseat, settled himself behind the wheel, and laughed a downtown belly laugh.

"Way to go, Melanie-baby. Way to go."

The rest of the day was given to straightforward Bradford Chemicals business, and Morton lost himself in it, partly as escape from the heavy concentration he'd been giving the Lunt thing, partly to avoid the guilt that always pinched him when he stinted on things he was paid to do. He left the office after six and drove straight home.

Although he had lived and worked in Manhattan for years, he'd kept the Zieglersville house, bought in 1986 for a mere $120,000 during his tour as service superintendent at the plant. The house was worth very much more now. It was a nicely proportioned Williamsburg Colonial on two acres in an area that had since become upscale chic. It was also a bit much for a bachelor, but he liked its feeling of space and solitude. With promotion to the New York offices, he decided that these spiritual returns would be worth the taxes, maintenance, and housekeeping required to keep it as a place to unwind during those times business brought him back to Z'ville.

Driving home, Morton passed Greg Allenby's place on the corner of Myron Boulevard and Greenfield Parkway in Sylvan Hills. In the evening mist the house looked sad and neglected, and Morton thought of Jennifer Allenby and the two boys and how abandoned they were by a husband and father who was so involved in regretting the past and daydreaming about the future he had no time for the good things that filled the present. Greg's solution was to lose himself in the amassing of money and things, honestly when possible, dishonestly when required.

Along the way, when the pursuit of happiness brought nothing but loneliness and guilt, he would drink about it, and glare at the woman and kids who tried hard to love him anyhow.

Well, Morton thought, pulling into his driveway, *don't get all teary about it, George. Allenby is a lousy, thieving son of a bitch who deserves every rotten thing he gets.*

Morton fought his own loneliness with a martini and still another run of the videotape of "Ruff" Cobb's silly damned Fourth of July pool party. On that day three years ago, after all the sparring and games of denial, Ace had put him on infinite hold, had told him, level-eyed and level-voiced in the midst of the drunken clamor, that she wouldn't see him anymore, but even so, there wasn't anybody but him, never had been, never would be, and that the greatest mistake of her life had been to bury that truth in excuses and self-righteousness. It had been a hell of a speech—the last intimate words he'd had from her. The following months were a weird melding of mourning and emancipation. The finality of the breakup had blown him away, and he spent a lot of time stifling an unmanly need to weep. But simultaneously he'd felt liberation—being freed to swim from a sinking wreck that could have pulled him under. So there were attempts at new liaisons. There were women with super looks and superficial brains; there were women with high IQs and even higher opinions of themselves. But only when the Anson Lunt calamity had come full term had he found the chance for a new life. Now, when things got him down, he'd wander back to the video for a one-man pep rally to remind himself of where he'd been and how far he'd come—and of the rationale of his lonely guerrilla war to get her back. And it usually worked. Despite all the footage given to the sophomoric mugging and to the splashing and horseplay by the vacuous, pretty people, he was almost always cheered and set back on course.

Finishing his drink, he put away the tape and went to the computer and reaccessed Jacoby's Lunt Case notebook. The sergeant was working late, obviously, so Morton found himself reading over the cop's shoulder as he punched in his material.

Jacoby was proving to be an interesting type, much beyond the average, as cops go. The fact that he kept careful notes was nothing exceptional—most good homicide detectives do. It was his readiness to speculate, to make guesses, to extrapolate and, above all, to evaluate the character of each of the principals in his investigation that held Morton's attention. A shrink Jacoby was not, but he showed a lot of discernment and a surprising amount of good-natured toleration for the human condition. Morton suspected that, in other times and contexts, Jacoby would have made a great friend.

Why were the municipal police giving so much fidgety attention to Anson Lunt's death? Jacoby's notes offered an answer:

> Chief Stabile agrees with my hunch; there's definitely something peculiar about the crash. He says he'd flown with Rooney a lot and knows for a fact that Rooney held ratings in everything but moon walks, knew every trick of the wind, every bump in the runway, and operated a state-of-the-art flying machine that had state-of-the-art instrumentation. Rooney didn't drink, didn't smoke, didn't gamble, and when he flew he was all business. The chief says he can't believe the crash was caused by pilot error. And he wants me to find out what did cause it—who made it happen, and why. When I mentioned my huge involvement in the convenience store shootings, the chief told me to turn that over to Himmel and spend my time on the Lunt thing.

On Alicia Hamilton:

> Showed the chief the photos of Mrs. Hamilton and Dr. Lunt that turned up in our rummage of Rooney's house—shots of them standing beside a plane and hugging with what seems to be considerable enthusiasm—

and suggested that maybe there was a triangle going
and we ought to look into Mr. Hamilton's attitude on
the relationship between his wife and the Mad Doctor.
The chief isn't all that hot on the idea because he's
been friends with Mrs. Hamilton and her husband for
years and has seen how fond they are of each other.
Besides, she's a devout religionist who takes her marriage vows very seriously. Lunt and Mrs. Hamilton
were longtime associates in medical research, and the
chief says it isn't too outlandish to believe that in the
pictures they could have been simply horsing around,
or maybe saying good-bye or hello. Maybe, but I have
some reservations: Mrs. Hamilton is a mature, damned
good-looking woman, and I can see an older guy like
Lunt getting the hots for her. And if they were all that
innocent, why would Rooney have such pictures
stashed in a bedroom drawer? Can see Mrs. Hamilton,
or Lunt, maybe, having them in their family albums.
But Rooney hiding them? Weird City.

Morton had shut down the computer and was trying to decide
whether to go out for dinner or to go into the microwave mode
when the phone rang. It was Allenby, and he was, as usual, out
of joint, and with his arch, professorial locution replaced by
street raunch, he was most surely drunk.

"Her Highness called me to her office this afternoon, George.
You're fucking up. Things like knowledge of Flynn's *in-absentia*
role, of a patent being readied for a manufactured nitriloside.
Inside shit."

"Well—"

"For hell's sake, be more careful, you asshole."

The phone at the other end slammed down, and Morton listened to the dial tone for a time.

He decided to stay home with the micro.

6.

She struggled to brighten her mood, alternately staring out the window and tapping notes into her personal computer.

The intercom buzzed, and she started. It was 1:20 by the desk clock. *The day half-gone, and all I've done is fret about that slimer, Morton. Get your act together, babe.*

"Yes?"

"Detective Sergeant Jacoby of the city police is here, Dr. Flynn. He would like to see you if you're available."

Staff meeting at one-thirty; one of those dragging conferences with Lawson Beatty of the law firm at two-thirty; meeting with Bill Goudy of Superior Supply at four; ten minutes for signing the day's outgoing paperwork; fifteen minutes for the drive to the Hayloft and cocktails with Tom Radcliff. "Tell him I can give him ten minutes, Helen."

Sergeant—What was it? Jacoby?—was a surprise. He was clean, lean, and rather well set up, looking more like an insurance salesman than anything cop-ish. He strode into the office, smiling at her as if he meant it and apologizing for breaking into her morning. She motioned to the guest chair, then asked the standard question. "What can I do for you, Sergeant?"

"The department is looking into certain aspects of Dr. Lunt's death, and we thought you might be able to help us."

"Like what aspects?"

"Well, I can't really go into the whole of it, ma'am. But answers to a few of our questions could help us understand pieces of it."

This guy's an eel, she thought. "You want me to talk about certain things without telling me why you want to know. Is that it?"

He smiled again, more broadly this time. "I suppose you could put it that way. But you make it sound—sinister. Nothing cute or sneaky here, Doctor. Just a routine part of a routine inquiry. Honest."

He has a nice smile, she decided. *Cops aren't supposed to smile, to look cheerful and reassuring. They're supposed to be all ground down by the grubby realities of their trade, by the sadness and the loss and the cruelty. What the hell kind of cop goes around looking like a happy church usher?*

"Sorry, Sarge. Please give me a little slack. This hasn't been the best of mornings. What are your questions?"

He took a pad from his jacket pocket and made a thing of clicking his ballpoint pen. "You are the director of the Lunt Biotechnical Laboratory, right?"

"Pro tem. I was assistant director at the time of Dr. Lunt's death. Formal succession awaits our lawyers' interpretation of Dr. Lunt's will."

"How long have you been working here?"

"Eleven years."

"Was Dr. Lunt married, have any next of kin our routine inquiries haven't picked up on?"

"He was a bachelor. I'm pretty sure he left no family."

"In your eleven years here, you've obviously seen from inside some of the media flak Dr. Lunt took for his cancer experiments. Right?"

She waved a cautioning hand. "Hold on, Sergeant. There's something you have to understand. Dr. Lunt's research into alternative oncology was conducted entirely apart from his involvements here at the lab. The other employees and I were not privy to his personal studies."

"Like me, you only know what's in the newspapers."

"Well—" She found herself dealing with confusion. "I suppose you can say that—"

"How did he manage to keep the two separate—his work at the lab and his personal cancer research?"

"First, he was directly subsidized by a grant from Alicia Hamilton. He had a whole separate set of books, a whole separate agenda when it came to his cancer research. Second, computers. Everything he did by way of cancer research was kept on computers to which only he had access. Whether or not the material in those computers now belongs to the lab is being determined by our lawyers, who are studying his will and the stipulations of the Alicia Hamilton grant."

Jacoby made a note. "So you don't know anything about his experiments?"

"Experiments isn't the word. In all his thirty years in cancer research, treatment came first. He didn't experiment with patients. Most of his patients consulted him after their personal physicians pronounced them incurable, choosing his alternative treatment over the delaying action of traditional surgery, radiology, and chemotherapy. Some, concerned about their genetic vulnerability to cancer, came on a preventive, precautionary basis. As a physician, Dr. Lunt treated them all, his way, at their specific request; as a researcher, he noted the results."

"Well, it's pretty clear that he took a lot of flak from the medical people for using unorthodox approaches to the treatment of cancer. Denounced as a quack, and all that. How come, when he was keeping things so close to his chest that even his own people didn't have access?"

"In the early days, like any good researcher, he'd report his findings to the various medical journals. His papers were rejected out of hand. He sought FMAA approvals. His applications were denied. And, in the bargain, everybody landed on him like a ton of wet noodles."

"Anybody particular in that everybody?"

This annoyed her. "Just what are you getting at?"

Lips pursed, he put a careful period to another note. "Do

you have any reason to believe that there might have been foul play behind the plane crash that killed Dr. Lunt?"

She thought about that for a moment. Shaking her head, she said, irritably, "Not really. Why? Do you?"

"The media said Lunt had ticked off a bunch of doctors. There was a lot of name-calling. Heat. Could one or more of those doctors have felt that the world would be a better, safer place without him?"

She couldn't hide her astonishment. "You mean, was he murdered by physicians who didn't agree with him?"

"Something like that."

"Popular he wasn't. And a lot of physicians are big-time pains when it comes to turf and status, sure enough. But serious pros—and they're the vast majority—have a strong sense of mission, a nagging itch to make sick people well. A few made life pretty miserable for Dr. Lunt, but it's hard to imagine even those hardcases plotting murder to keep him from doing his thing. I know them, and I know that for all their arrogance and elitism, they're into curing, not killing."

Jacoby shrugged, drawling, "It's my experience that, given sufficient motive, anybody will kill. You got a list of people who've given Dr. Lunt a bad time?"

She shook her head. "Tilt. The conspiracy theory's yours. I'm not about to play casting office."

"Suit yourself. Meanwhile, tell me in your own words what all the shouting was about."

Again she was unable to hide her confusion. "I thought you said you'd read up on it."

"I want to hear it from you. What you saw. Heard. Understood. Whatever Lunt might have told you. Tell me why you think everybody was so durn mad."

"It takes some explaining."

"You mean I'm too dumb to understand?"

She felt heat rising in her cheeks. "Of course not. I didn't mean to sound that way—"

He laughed, suddenly, disarmingly. "Hey, I'm just kidding,

Doctor. As a matter of fact, I probably am too dumb to understand it. Try me anyhow."

She gave him another inspection, slow, wary. "He and I did have some talks about his problems, and I did manage to get an overview. But what I say now is just what I've decided on my own—not what could be considered gospel. Know what I mean?"

"Sure. That's what I want. Your observations, ideas."

She stared at the gloomy day beyond the windows. "As far back as the 1970s, Dr. Lunt's studies of cancer gave him serious doubts about the-tumor-is-the-disease theory. He confirmed the evidence—developed earlier by independent and highly regarded researchers led by Dr. Ernest Krebs—that most humans have cancers many times in their lives. If the body's immunological defense mechanisms are functioning normally, the cancer cells are rapidly destroyed; if the defense mechanism is faulty, a tumor develops. Dr. Lunt said it's obvious that the tumor isn't the cause of the disease, it's merely a symptom."

Jacoby broke in. "Defense mechanisms?"

"The cancer cell is coated with a protein that protects the cell from the body's leukocytes, which are natural enemies of cancer. In the healthy body the enzymes trypsin and chymotrypsin quickly identify and dissolve the protein coating and the leukocytes are able to move in, kill the cancer cell, and nip the tumor in the bud, so to speak. When defenses are impaired or faulty, this either does not occur or occurs ineffectively. You with me?"

"Yep. Except for some spellings."

"There's a second line of defense as well. Some fifteen hundred foods produce substances called nitrilosides. The body's normal cells contain the enzyme rhodenese, which converts nitrilosides into nourishment. But cancer cells—and only cancer cells—contain the enzyme beta-glucosidase. When the nitrilosides come in contact with beta-glucosidase, they break down into two molecules, one of benzaldehyde and one of hydrogen cyanide, both of which are toxic to the cell."

"Cyanide? That'll knock over an elephant—"

She shook her head, and her voice took on the tone of one who had explained a thousand times. "Not in the infinitesimal amounts we're talking about here. And only when cancer cells are present. Nitrilosides, normally benign, turn killer when—and only when—in the presence of cancer cells. So Dr. Lunt, following the route established by Ernest Krebs, reasoned that the root cause of cancer is a breakdown in the body's immunological defense mechanisms and that this failure is usually triggered by poor nutrition. Not only that, but he concluded that the defense systems were often further damaged, even destroyed, by the traditional surgery-chemotherapy-radiation treatment. And he said that with traditional treatment or not, any truly effective control of cancer—whether incipient or advanced—certainly should involve an early introduction of those nutritional ingredients that would help to return the natural defense mechanisms to their proper health and function."

Jacoby turned a leaf in his pad. "And all this is what got him into deep doo-doo with the Establishment?"

"Did it ever. His findings, which led to a substance he called 'Vitam,' instead of arousing interest, were met with stony silence. No professional or trade journal of any standing would publish them. No major foundation or research sponsor would give them credence. And when the mainstream media picked up on the situation and began to run stories on it, the medical and pharmaceutical hotshots they quoted summarily dismissed, often ridiculed, Dr. Lunt and his findings. Worse, those few doctors who eventually read his research papers and decided to design Vitam programs for their cancer patients soon became laughingstocks—even pariahs, like Dr. Lunt. Worse yet, the Feds were persuaded to ban the importation, sale, and use of Vitam, so that Dr. Lunt couldn't arrange its manufacture under license abroad."

She paused, and Jacoby got in another question. "Why would the medical establishment get so upset about something so promising, for cripes sake?"

"Vested interest. Prestige. Huge egos. Dr. Lunt said it right out: The industry's Teddy Bradfords and Charles Hamiltons, with their huge investment in surgery, chemo, and radiation, would rather destroy reputations and muzzle truth than admit that a mere healthy diet and regular doses of specific vitamins might do for pennies what the industry's been trying to do at a cost in the billions."

"That's a pretty heavy-duty accusation—"

"Dr. Lunt was no wimp."

"You aren't either. Right?"

"One does what one can."

"So go on, Doctor."

"Things have turned better recently. Thanks to a court order putting the Feds in their place, Vitam and similar substances are no longer under a total ban in the States. And the National Institutes of Health has opened the Office of Alternative Medicine, which now issues formal reports on the matter. And get this: A study in the *New England Journal of Medicine* found that one in three Americans are seeking some form of alternative medicine to improve their mental and physical health. The *Journal* says—" she raised a hand and drew imaginary lines of type in the air—" 'Alternative medicine is gaining more acceptance in the medical community, too. Once considered the province of so-called health nuts, alternative therapies are now being studied by medical researchers.' Would you believe it?"

"So didn't that make you and Dr. Lunt happy?"

"Not really. Those of us who see real value in the nutritional treatment of cancer are pretty cynical by now. For twenty years it's been impossible to get one word about Dr. Lunt's findings into the medical journals." She lifted her head in an elaborate parody of hauteur and drew more lines in the air. " 'Surgery, chemotherapy, and radiation are the only acceptable methods of treating cancer. We do not publish alternative methods.' A few press releases don't wipe out that kind of prejudice."

There was a pause. Jacoby quickly spoke into it, wanting to keep the information coming. "So now, with Dr. Lunt out of the picture, it's you who will be inheriting the farm. Right?"

She felt her face redden. "Which means?"

"Nothing, really."

"You're saying I did in Dr. Lunt just so I could get all the incoming money?"

"I'm not saying anything of the sort."

"It seems to be quite clear that you are."

"Come on, Doctor. Rhetorical questions, looking for motives, are at the root of any homicide investigation."

"You want motives, pal?" she asked hotly. "Why don't you start browsing around Bradford Chemicals? Motives they got plenty of. Meanwhile, my motive is to get you out of my office this instant. Don't come back without a warrant, or whatever the hell you flatfeet use as a harassing license."

"Hey, don't get sore. There's nothing personal in this."

"Out, Clouseau. Right now."

Jacoby folded his notebook, stood up, and, en route to the door, said, "Anything bugs you, give me a hoot on the hooter. Nice to meet you."

7.

Since the Republic's earliest days, Delaware had demonstrated a benign disinterest in regulating and taxing international wheeling and dealing. Delighted to find a state government that thought the way they did, both the hugely successful and those who aspired to be hugely successful—among them Teddy Bradford's forebears—had trooped to Dover or Wilmington over the years, there to pay the modest fees and file the few papers that would formalize their world-class ambitions.

Annual stockholder meetings in Wilmington had become *de rigueur*. But many boards, presumably because of this same oddball sense of bond with friendly turf, would also hold their nuts-and-bolts quarterly meetings there. Bradford Chemicals was one of them, but for a different reason.

Although the company's main offices were in New York and its plants and business locations were scattered from Muncie to Madras, Theodore Bradford III, chairman and CEO, liked to meet in Wilmington every quarter because it gave him a reason to be in the town Gloria Cadwallader called home.

Extreme wealth, as the propaganda would have lesser mortals believe, has extreme burdens. In Teddy Bradford's case, his burdens were, first, being rendered impotent in the presence of Samantha, his formidable wife, and, second, being both too well known to the public and too well observed by Samantha to sneak in a bit of rejuvenating outside scronch. Greater New York was out, thanks to Samantha's intricate network of chums there. Business trips, in the States and abroad, offered little relief; friends of Samantha either lived in the places he visited or were in his travel party. Happily, though, Samantha boycotted Wilmington, having been snubbed in her private-school years there by Eugenia Fox, snotty granddaughter of Aldo Fox, the city's political boss.

So, come board-meeting time, it was Wilmington-Ho for a liberated Teddy. Gloria, the plain-Jane, socially inept, and hopelessly nymphomaniacal heiress-apparent of the Cadwallader plumbing-fixture millions, would always be available. Her parents, as sorrowing pragmatists, would see to it, because they'd observed that a robust quarterly servicing by a wealthy, sterilized, and safely married Teddy Bradford seemed to be enough to keep Gloria quiescent—and therefore less a target of opportunity for fortune-hunting studs.

Morton knew (by way of a Cadwallader housemaid in his clandestine pay) that the elder Cadwalladers had asked Gloria to supervise the main house of the family estate in nearby Greenville during the week they'd be visiting friends at the Springs—that week containing, by no coincidence, the date of today's quarterly meeting. So, as he sat among those at the boardroom table, Morton was secretly amused by Teddy's thespian efforts to convey an air of brisk all business, knowing as he did that anticipation of the night ahead was turning Teddy's pants into a nuclear oven.

"So, then," Teddy was saying, his chinless face shiny from a fresh shave, his black pompadour aglow with Vitalis, "we come to George Morton and his report on new-acquisition activity. Remember, ladies and gentlemen, this is an open-discussion workshop, with no tapes running or secretaries making notes. So nobody has to worry that he's going on record sounding like he's the village idiot. You got any questions of George, sing out. Okay, George, the meeting is yours."

As vice president and managing director of New Ventures,

Morton headed a staff department peopled by some thirty high-paid advisers in key fields. He would receive the counsel of these specialists, then alone make the department's final decisions, which to all practical purposes made him a one-man executive committee. He'd take that clout to the board of directors, where, as a voting member, it was his duty to recommend for or against proposed acquisitions—be they properties, products, or significant personnel. This made him a big-bore cannon, not only in the company but also in the trade and its various ancillaries, such as the American Chemical League, the National Drug Manufacturers Association, the United States Medical and Surgical Confederation, the Federal Medicine Approval Agency, and many lesser special interest groups. Which made him one of the ruling pharisees of the Church of the Holy Profit, and when he spoke, congregations around the world tended to listen.

Even the Bradford board, which Deke Swanson, legal director, dourly called "Teddy's teddy bears," tended to listen occasionally, but today was clearly not one of those times. They sat unmoving in their plush, high-backed chairs, their glass-button stares fixed on something forty miles beyond Morton's forehead.

"Thank you, Mr. Chairman," Morton said. "As you ladies and gentlemen know from my interim report, mailed to you last month, we have successfully concluded our negotiations with the Hendel-Ajax people and will provide you with copies of the closing papers next January 3. Also, there's been good progress in the discussions with Peterson Surgical Tools, and I hope to have a favorable, concluding report for you by the end of this month." He paused, then slipped into the pitch mode. "The main thing I want to discuss this morning is the situation at Lunt Biotech. Some of you have asked my opinion on what we might do, now that the property is currently in limbo resulting from the tragic death of its founder and chief, Anson Lunt. I'd like to take a few minutes to tell you what I think about that."

The board, smelling a possible dollar, began to drift back from Dreamland. In the interval, Morton's mind produced a fast scrolling of the vulnerabilities to be found among these paragons. Crowell: the sporting arms and ammunition giant, whose fondness for the bottle kept him in and out of pricey, obscure hospitals; Francesca Randall: queen of the cosmetics industry, carrying a hopeless torch for Mandy Simms, the superstar cover girl; Emerson Williams: investment banker with two kids hooked on heroin; Dr. Angelo Mariano: the university president whose defiance of the political correctness agenda laid on him by his faculty would soon cost him his job; Maurice Ledbetter: former congressman and secretary of labor, losing his battle against prostate cancer; Laura Radowski: the voluptuous diet-food mogul, currently involved in a sporadic love affair with Reggie Felton, the profligate but insanely successful movie producer; and Frederick Andrews: the international real estate baron, belabored by desperate cash flow problems.

Every one of them an old pal and courtier of Teddy Bradford. Every one of them a theatrical prop—a stuffed animal used for window dressing.

The real power in this room rested with Teddy, the majority stockholder. What Teddy wanted, Teddy got. The others: on hand simply to impress the stockholders and the Feds, the doters on form and perception, and to give a semblance of parliamentary procedure and democratic fairness to their rubber-stamp approval of what had been preordained in Teddy's despotic mind.

And something else: Unspoken, never admitted or suggested, yet as real as the sunlight in the window, was the challenge that hovered between Teddy Bradford and Morton—an understanding that each saw in the other an implacable predator, and if they had been competitors instead of collaborators, the battle for supremacy would have been to the death. *No doubt about it,* Morton thought now: *It's Teddy's fear of this that has made him keep me on his gravy train.*

So now it was time for Morton to make his move, to shift the inner gears and activate the connivance that would symbolically deliver to Teddy a gargantuan middle finger.

Break a leg, George!

Giving them his most earnest expression, he spoke slowly,

exuding Great Significance. "While on the surface Lunt would seem to be a worthy addition to the Bradford family of companies, I must recommend against its acquisition."

Teddy stared at Morton as if his vice president had suddenly grown a third nostril. "You recommend goddam *what?*"

"That we forget the Lunt thing."

"What the shit are you talking about, George?"

"I can't say it any clearer."

There followed a suspended moment in which Teddy seemed to struggle with apoplexy and the board dealt with its own collective surprise. Then, after a murmuring passed around the table, Laura Radowski, a member who seemed to have a real interest in the affairs of Bradford Chemicals, held up a forefinger and asked the obvious. "You gave us to believe that Lunt was a plum waiting to fall into our basket. What's changed?"

Morton gave her a somber look. "When Dr. Lunt died, most of what was valuable in his company went with him. Without him, we'd be doing little more than buying assets and an inventory. We'd be getting none of the advantage of having Dr. Lunt continuing on with us, guiding the R&D of what would have been the Lunt Division of Bradford Chemicals."

Laura Radowski blinked. "You can't be serious. The record shows that only a few years ago you and Teddy were heaping scorn on Anson Lunt. Now you would have liked to buy his company to *acquire* him?"

Laura, a newcomer to the board, was known to be a favorite of Samantha Bradford and therefore to be treated by all—especially Teddy—with gingerly respect. "It was the only way we could hope to get him into our camp, Laura. He was not available otherwise." He hesitated. "But that was a very pertinent question. Very." Morton glanced at Teddy. "Wouldn't you say so, Mr. Chairman?"

Teddy, still struggling to see what Morton was up to while trying to clear his mind of extravagant visions of the orgy to come, wouldn't have known a pertinent question if it had bitten him in the butt. But he wasn't so confused he failed to see a chance to suck up to Samantha's pal. "Yeah. Laura is most astute."

There was an awkward silence, eventually broken by Laura.

"I see incredible hypocrisy here," she said. "The only person in this room ever to say anything halfway nice about Anson Lunt was George Morton. And even you were insipid, George. Plain insipid."

Teddy, at last realizing that he was now dealing with an unpredictable—and therefore dangerous—George Morton, took back the meeting with some quickly fabricated misrepresentations. "Let me put in a word here. George and I have talked over this matter at length, and it always came back to the central point: Anson Lunt *was* Lunt Biotech. And for us, as it is for everybody these days, creative talent is very hard to come by and is very expensive. Creativity of the magnitude displayed by Anson Lunt is virtually nonexistent on the hiring market, not only because of its rarity but because it's almost never looking for work. I did some groveling twenty years ago and asked Anson to join Bradford. Fabulous salary and perks. Huge resources at his disposal. Virtual autonomy. But he refused. He didn't want, as he put it, 'to be a chained oarsman on Bradford's battle galley.' If he hadn't wanted so damned much to be independent, he'd have been working for us long ago."

The forefinger came up again.

"Yes, Laura?"

"If he was so all-fired great, why did Bradford Chemicals do such a huge number on him back then?"

Teddy did some fancy footwork. "He had developed and written papers on a serum that would, according to his claims, control—even dissipate—some forms of cancer when it was incorporated in a severe dietary regimen. He claimed that cancer was caused by a lack in the body, and that the tumors were symptoms, not the disease, and to concentrate on their removal by surgery and radiology and chemistry was to prolong the patient's suffering and delay his inevitable death. Dr. Allen P. Fulmer, who was head of fundamental research at our Newark lab, ran extensive tests on Lunt's product and theory, both under glass and in animals, and found no validity to the claims. He issued a report which, in essence, said that to abandon many decades of positive research results and successful surgical, radiological, and chemical therapies and replace them with an injection and a restricted diet was nothing short of voodoo—witch-doctoring in its worst form. The media picked up on that, and before long Lunt was catching hell from every quarter. It was not our intention to ruin him, but, sadly, his ruin was the net result. He also went into—"

"Hold on," Radowski broke in. "The way I read the records, Dr. Lunt was not suggesting that the orthodox methods be abandoned. He was suggesting that the orthodoxy be used as a fallback, a last-ditch backup to his serum and the diet therapy. It seems to me there's a big difference."

This woman was sharp. Morton saw that he'd have to go carefully with her.

"And the record shows, too," she was saying, "that at the very time Bradford Chemicals was fanning the fire, making Lunt more disreputable by the minute, both in the media and at the Federal level, Bradford Chemicals was working on a serum very much like Lunt's. It looks to me that we were more interested in beating out his product than we were in saving existing medical technology."

Crowell, silent until now, slapped the table with an angry hand. "Dammit, Laura, that's all ancient history. Let's just drop it and get on with this meeting."

Williams made a noise ostensibly meant as approval.

"I agree," Francesca Randall snapped, obviously feeling a need to put Radowski in her place. "As a relatively new member of this board, Ms. Radowski asks us to spend time on a matter that is long since resolved for the rest of us—something done, beyond retrieval or change."

Radowski wasn't about to play the dumb yardbird recruit. "I suppose you don't want to talk about it, Ms. Randall, because you were among those who heaped the most ridicule on Dr. Lunt." Her glare traveled around the table. "And the rest of you: members of the chorus. Except you, George. And even you pussyfooted around, clucking your tongue like a preacher watching an alley fight."

It was time to get the discussion back on track, so Morton laughed. "And that feeble attempt almost got me fired, Laura. Our chairman was not very happy with me for breaking corporate ranks on that one. Right, Mr. Chairman?"

Teddy was not amused. "I was ready to tie the can to you good and proper for spouting off on TV about your respect for that old phony."

"I had my reason."

"And when I discovered what it was, I decided a man shouldn't be fired for being grateful—even if it's for a silly misconception."

Laura's eyes narrowed with interest. "Grateful, George? You were grateful to Dr. Lunt? Whatever for?"

"My poor old wreck of an uncle. Uncle Denny. My only relative. My only family, actually. He scrimped to help me through college—went broke doing it, I found out later. I was still in college when he went down with inoperable cancer. Uncle Denny had this terrible fear of dying alone and unattended in some charity ward, so I ran around madly, trying to find a place where he could die with dignity. But I didn't have a job or money, and so I struck out and was ready to give up when I heard about Anson Lunt and his work. I went to Anson, and he put Uncle Denny in his clinic and laid huge TLC on him, never even mentioning money during the months it took the old man to reach the end. Later, when everybody was denouncing Lunt as an unfeeling charlatan, I came to his defense. Weakly, I'm ashamed to say, but I did what I could."

Laura gave him a long stare, then pantomimed a kiss. "You just rose a thousand percent in my estimation, pal."

Morton waved a dismissing hand. "No one in this room feels good about what happened in those days, Laura. It was not our finest hour."

Another taut silence followed, and Morton was grateful when Andrews grumped, "I'm hungry. Let's break for lunch."

Teddy coughed gently into his fist, then said, "You're all set up for the executive dining room, but I have to leave. George'll take over the afternoon session, because I've got some deadline business across town."

Morton accompanied Teddy to the ground-floor entrance, where Teddy's rental car awaited. As they stood on the sidewalk in the raw wind, Teddy delivered what Morton called his General Patton stare.

"What the hell are you up to, George?"

Morton pretended worry. "I honest-to-God don't know what to do for you at this point, Teddy. Greg Allenby's proposal is based on your acquisition of the Lunt company. And the Lunt company's not for sale to you."

Hot-eyed impatient, Teddy would have slapped his thigh with a riding crop if he'd had one. "I must acquire that formula. I *will* acquire that formula. And if my company can't buy it openly, I'll buy it myself—under the counter and direct from Greg Allenby."

"Come on, Teddy: Do you have any idea the kind of bucks we're talking here? Three hundred million, at least. And then there's the problem of what the hell you'll do with it once you've got it."

"Those problems are *your* problems, pal. I'm expecting you to find the answers to both."

"But—"

"I'm not exactly a poor man, you know. And Allenby's also got a problem. He's selling hot goods, which automatically cuts his price, real hard. And, since I'm his only likely market, he'll get no more than two hundred million and one percent royalties."

"Still—"

"Godammit, George, stop whining and just set it the hell up! I don't care how you do it—just do it!"

* * *

Late in the afternoon, while waiting for the Metroliner, Morton called Allenby on his private Z'ville line.

"Hello, Greg."

"Hi. Where are you?"

"In Wilmington, waiting for a train. I have to go back to New York tonight."

"So how did it go?"

"The board meeting was over early, and I spent most of the afternoon talking with Teddy. There's a complication."

"What means *complication?*"

"You were right. Melanie Flynn refuses to sell to Bradford. Which confirms that Teddy can't buy the Lunt property to get your formula."

"Well, I must say," Allenby snapped, his tweedy academic accent full of sudden venom. "I'll simply have to work out something else with somebody else, wouldn't you agree?"

"Not so fast. Teddy is ready to buy the formula for himself—direct from you. Under the counter."

"I don't think Teddy has enough. Not for what I want, anyhow."

"How does a hundred million grab you? A hundred million and one percent of any gross eventuating. Providing you can give Teddy a demo, that is."

There was a lengthy silence at the other end, broken when Allenby said bitterly, "The demo's no problem. But the money's not enough."

"So sell it someplace else."

"When will he pay?"

"As soon as you show him that the stuff works."

"So set it up quick, then. A very special Caribbean island is waiting for me."

Morton gave a full minute to some preparation, then dialed New York.

"This is the Bradford residence," the butler intoned.

"Hello, Baker. George Morton here. Is Mrs. Bradford in?"

"Good evening Mr. Morton. Hold for a moment, please. She's in the library, and I'll transfer you there."

There was a click, and she came on, cheery.

"George, dear. What a welcome surprise."

"Hello, Samantha. You're looking beautiful as usual."

She laughed softly. It was their little joke, his pretending he could see her over the phone line.

"Where are you?"

"Still in Wilmington. And I hate to bother you with such a silly request, but you're the only one I could think of who might have the Cadwalladers' unlisted number here. I've got to contact Teddy, but I don't have the number."

A moment of taut silence, then: "Teddy is at the Cadwalladers'?"

"Well, I think so. One of the Cadwallader house staff called me earlier this week to ask me what wine Teddy preferred with lamb. She said Gloria is having him over to discuss her possible purchase of some Bradford common and wanted to surprise him with a little dinner and thought I might know about the wine. He left the board meeting early, and so I suppose that's where he went."

This silence was even longer, tauter.

"Well, I'm sorry, George, but I have no idea what the phone number is. I've been out of touch with the Cadwalladers for sometime now."

"I see. Do you by chance know anybody else who might know? I really have to speak to him."

"I'm sorry. I can't help you."

She hung up.

The sun was rising over Greenville's rolling hills when Teddy awakened. He opened an eye tentatively, studying the winter landscape beyond the windows for a clue as to his whereabouts. Then, remembering, he sat up quickly, both eyes wide with the familiar guilty panic.

Easy, guy. The Cadwalladers are at the Springs, the servants are on leave, the guard has been paid off and is doing coke in the gatehouse. Samantha doesn't expect you until dinner tonight. Not to worry, buddy-boy.

Gloria sprawled naked across the foot of the bed, legs spread, arms thrust outward, deeply unconscious and, in the morning light, suggesting what Rembrandt might have come up with had he decided to paint an exhausted whore.

They'd made it in the foyer, against a wall and still in their topcoats. They left a trail of clothes to the living room, where they'd made it on a sofa. They'd made it on the main stairway, then in the master bath's Jacuzzi, and finally here, in her father's bed, where, in her frenzied climaxes, she kept shouting, "You son of a bitch, you son of a bitch, you son of a bitch."

Taking care not to awaken her, he swung from the bed, sore all over, eyes heavy, mouth dry, and padded off on a search for his clothes. He dressed in one of the downstairs johns, his mind filled with a renewed sense of the uneasy suspicion that had plagued him since the board meeting. He sat on the rim of the tub, consulted his address book, and took down the wall phone, dialing quickly.

"Watson Investigations," the cheery woman announced.

"This is Teddy Bradford. Is he in?"

"Yes, Mr. Bradford," the woman fawned cheerily. "One moment, please."

"Hello, Mr. Bradford." Watson's voice was oily. "What brings me this pleasure?"

"I want you to do a job for me."

"Sure. What kind of job?"

"You know George Morton, don't you?"

"Your vice president? Who doesn't know him?"

"I want you to put him under surveillance. Immediately, and continuing around the clock until I tell you to stop."

"Can you tell me what I'm looking for?"

"No. It's just that I know he's up to something. I think he's trying to beat me out of a deal I'm trying to cut with Greg Allenby, of Lunt Biotech. I don't trust either of those bastards, and I want you to tell me what they're up to."

"Well, that's a bit—diffuse. I'll need a better focus if I'm to deliver useful material—"

"You need nothing. You just get your ass into gear and start watching that son of a bitch Morton. You tell me what he's up to, then I'll tell you what to do about it."

"This is going to be expensive—"

"Don't give me that nickel-and-dime shit, dammit. Just get going. Allenby's got something I want bad. I got the feeling that Morton is trying to keep me from buying it, probably because he wants to get control of it himself. I don't have any time for long-term games because this is a right-now thing. So I don't care what you do or how you do it, but I want you to do whatever it takes to throw Morton out of the game and make me stop worrying about him. Understand?"

"That's a very broad canvas—"

"I didn't call you for a debate, goddammit. Do it."

"I'm on it right now, Mr. Bradford."

8.

The week of wind and rain had ended at dawn. A red sun appeared in the mist over the eastern ridges, and suddenly winter pretended it was spring. The sky brightened, the horizon took on a greenish purple clarity, and out here on Three-Mile Road, upwind from Zieglersville's trademark chemical stinks, the breeze suggested thawing meadows and dripping woodlands. Everything sparkled—the trees, the honeysuckle hedges, the fallow fields, the barn roofs—and Morton thought he could hear, even over the Cadillac's purring, the busy noises of birds flocking. He'd pretty much forgotten how beautiful rural America could be; his professional life was his only life, given to days and nights in the air-conditioned hives where money is made and power is won. So he found himself being grateful for what amounted to an outing, thanks to Peter Van Dyke's wish to meet at his Lancaster County farm instead of at the firm's headquarters in Philly.

Van Dyke had retired from Stevens and Kolb, crème de la crème of the elite Philadelphia law firms, about ten years ago, ostensibly to make room at the top for a nephew. But he'd really made the move to free himself for full-time work as the gatekeeper and manager of dirty tricks for Barnaby Falloon, a multibillionaire usually described by the media as "the shadowy and immensely powerful manipulator." Just what Falloon manipulated, and toward what end, was never made clear, presumably because the media were among those forces he manipulated. But the cognoscenti knew that to be admitted to Falloon's thinking was first to pass muster with Van Dyke; to be admitted to Falloon's presence was, in the words of the late, ill-fated TV commentator Randolph Ridenour, "to persuade Saint Peter Van Dyke that you had a God-size proposition."

Morton's initial entree to Van Dyke had been traditional: He had gone to a university and a graduate school on the approved list, and, while he was a member of the Sphinx— the exclusive New York club that served as the entry-level unit—he was not yet fully credentialed in the hierarchy of private clubs whose memberships decided the economic and political direction the nation would take at any given time. But for Morton, entry-level was good enough, because even the anointed must look to the problem of succession and replacement, and recent years had shown that when there was a lack of suitable bodies from the cadre of Old-Timers and Big Names, promising candidates for the hierarchy's higher strata could occasionally be found among the Sphinx's properly schooled commoners.

Morton understood all this, as he understood that in the one association he'd had with Van Dyke, he had been used more than he had used. But high stakes usually called for high sacrifice, and he had been a willing pawn.

This time would be different.

The driver brought the limousine to a halt at the main entrance of the big stone house at precisely 9:55. A large man in a black suit came out of the shadows and, opening the door, helped Morton from the backseat, taking the opportunity to run expert hands through a fast, subtle frisk.

"Good morning, sir," the man crooned. "Mr. Van Dyke is waiting for you in the library."

"Thank you. Do you want to look at my briefcase?"

"That would be very helpful, sir."

Morton clicked the latches and opened the case wide. "That's a small tape recorder. And the box beside it is a tape that I'll be playing for Mr. Van Dyke."

The man examined the case and its contents. Nodding politely, he swept a hand toward the door. "This way, sir."

In the foyer, the man eased Morton from his topcoat, using the opportunity for another sneaky frisk. Then he led the way to the library, where he took a sentinel's post at the doorway, his dark eyes alert, and announced out of the corner of his mouth, "Mr. Morton is here, Mr. Van Dyke."

Peter Van Dyke, a small man with a bald head and large ears, came around the Shaker desk, his right hand held out in greeting. "Well, George. It's good to see you again. It's been a while, eh?"

Morton shook the hand. "I'm grateful for your willingness to see me on such short notice."

"There is always time on my schedule for you. Come—sit down. Coffee? Cigar?"

"Nothing, thank you."

Van Dyke waited until Morton was settled on the sofa, then returned to his desk chair. His little gray eyes sent a signal to the man in the doorway, who nodded deferentially, stepped into the hall, and closed the heavy door behind him.

"So, George: You're looking fit, as always."

"Life has been good."

"You are still vice president of Bradford Chemicals?"

"Yes. I'm in charge of New Ventures."

Van Dyke laughed, a kind of hissing sound. " 'New Ventures.' What a nice term for muscling in."

"It does have a certain ring, doesn't it."

"I've always said you should be the CEO at Bradford. Teddy is a fossilized nincompoop."

Morton gave him a modest smile. "I'm working on it."

"Need some help, let me know," Van Dyke said amiably.

Morton shifted in his seat and became very sincere. "In a way, that's why I'm here. I need a bit of help in a project—"

"Like we gave you on that Acme Hydrogenation thing several years ago?"

Van Dyke's mention of this prior deal was to be expected. It was a reminder that while Falloon was satisfied with the return on Acme, Morton should go slow in any attempt to add liabilities during his still-existing probation. Falloon was known to have said openly that, in the past, too many of the blow-dried Commerce and Finance types had tried—unsuccessfully, of course—to get cute on deals and expected Sphinx membership to protect them against reprisal.

"Not exactly," Morton said, smiling politely. "The labor union trick isn't feasible in this situation. Here we have to be a little more—circumspect."

"Ah."

"And the stakes are considerably higher."

"Ah."

"Because of the delicacy of the matter, and because of the higher stakes, I feel again much in need of your advice. Your assistance." *God*, the thought flickered, *I sound like something out of* The Godfather.

Van Dyke raised an eyebrow. "Does the Bradford board know of my past work in your behalf?"

Morton shook his head. "Teddy, the board, other layers of management, credit me solely with the successes you have made possible. They have always given me high marks as a negotiator. As a recruiter of top-level executives. As a finder of new product lines. As the scout for promising but weakly financed companies that can, if bought and turned around, be exploited. I've proved many times over how good I am at these kinds of things. They have no reason to believe I received help from you."

"You do have a certain knack."

Morton pushed backed against this needling. "I can read, Peter. I can read the greed that says enough is not enough, the fear that demands more than enough, and the laziness that says there's already enough. I am very quick at picking up on which of those, or which combination of those, prevails at any given time. Only when the lack of time requires fast, direct action do I reach for help. You and I know that I couldn't have achieved such fast results with the Acme thing without your advice and operational assistance. But no one else knows. Nor will anyone else ever know."

Van Dyke cleared his throat and became earnest, businesslike. "So, then, what is this help you need now?"

Morton reached for the briefcase beside his chair. "The research and development director of Lunt Biotech has personally developed a product that stands to bring in an absolute, perishing mountain of money. But Anson Lunt, the owner, has just died, leaving the company in a very wobbly financial condition. The existence of the product has been known only to the inventor, the R&D man, who is preparing to expropriate the formula— which under his employment agreement really belongs to the company—and sell it privately to the highest bidder. Teddy Bradford is interested, and because he prefers to remain invisible in under-the-counter dealings, he has appointed me his liaison with the seller."

Van Dyke was patrician, even when he sneered. "Teddy always was a gutless wonder. His lack of character and spine is precisely why he was never invited into the Sphinx. He is not a classy man."

Morton did not disagree.

"He certainly trusts you, though, eh?"

Morton made a club-type joke. "It's my most terrible weakness, Peter. I've struggled all my life to overcome an absolutely excruciating case of trustworthiness. It's the main reason I'm not rich."

Van Dyke smiled and played to the joke. "How very sad. So how can I help you change all this?"

"Before I answer, may I play a tape for you?"

"Tape?"

"It's a conversation with Greg Allenby, the Lunt R&D man. It sets the stage for what I'm about to propose."

Van Dyke waved a hand of invitation. "Please."

When the skeet-field tape had run its course and Morton had turned off the player, Van Dyke sank back in his chair, making a steeple with his fingers. "So we hear one man admitting to the sidetracking of a new drug and offering to sell it to another man who isn't all that enthusiastic about the idea. So what does this mean?"

"I was deliberately unenthusiastic. As camouflage. To hide my very hot excitement. Truth is, Allenby is offering a major tool in the treatment and control of developing cancers. Also an antitoxin that prevents a wide variety of cancers from developing at all. Whoever owns it will make a freaking fortune. Allenby has to sell it because he has no way to manufacture it on his own. Teddy wants sole personal ownership. But he has the same manufacturing problem. He can probably find the money to buy Allenby's formula, but he needs time to prepare the ground for sliding the stolen goods into his company's product line as a legitimate, in-house development."

Van Dyke asked the logical question. "Teddy Bradford is the major stockholder in his company. Why doesn't he just persuade his board to cut to the chase and buy the whole damn Lunt kaboodle? Buy the cow to get the milk?"

"The heir apparent, a woman scientist who was Lunt's managing director, refuses to sell—especially to Teddy, a very big enemy of her dead boss. Teddy can't buy directly. He has to buy sneakily."

"Up to now this is only academically interesting. Just what are you getting at, George?"

Morton went for broke. "Peabody Chemicals of Chicago is one of your interests, is it not?"

"Yes. It manufactures industrial chemicals and insecticides. That kind of thing."

"I suggest that you quickly form a Peabody subsidiary, announcing that it will begin the manufacture and sale of medicinal drugs. Simultaneously you can name me president and CEO of the subsidiary. I, in turn, will see that the Allenby formula becomes the property of the subsidiary, and as a bond I will put up ten million dollars of my own money—a kind of good-faith, nonreturnable insurance on my own performance."

"You will, in other words, snatch the Allenby formula from under Teddy Bradford's nose and deliver its ownership to us?"

Morton nodded. "After Peabody chemists have refined the

formula, making it uniquely and patentably yours, you and Mr. Falloon—and I, of course—will reap a huge pile of money on what amounts to a peanuts investment."

"How do you propose to acquire the formula from Allenby? Do you have personal backers?"

"No. That's why I'm here. I'm hoping that you and Mr. Falloon will see the huge promise in this drug and finance its acquisition with, say, a clandestine cash payment to Greg Allenby of three hundred million dollars."

Van Dyke smiled, wry. "Nothing shy about you, is there, George."

"I see no reason to screw around."

"We form a subsidiary, put you in charge, then have you sneak three hundred million to Allenby for his invention before Teddy Bradford can move on it. Right?"

"And my ante of ten million keeps me on the straight and narrow from start to finish. It's your control over me, so to speak."

"Pig in a poke, George?"

"No way. You don't put up a dime until I've arranged a demonstration of the drug's effectiveness. A demonstration for you, personally."

Van Dyke stated the obvious. "Still, all this would also make Peabody a dealer in stolen goods."

"That's why you need me. I am Peabody's protection. I position Peabody one huge step removed from a stolen-goods rap. If things were to go wrong—which, God forbid, they won't— Peabody could convincingly declare that it had no way of knowing that the formula had been stolen by Allenby and sold to me. Both Peabody and I could make a real case for having been misled, duped, used, and made unwitting victims of Allenby's crime. We could even, with the help of Stevens and Kolb, join the prosecution and file suit against Allenby. But that's not likely to happen." Morton paused for dramatic effect, then added, "And we'll all go down in history, like Salk with polio; like Fleming, Florey, and Chaim with penicillin."

Van Dyke, unmoved by the drama, stuck with pragmatism. "Who's in the Lunt management?"

"For the time being, the administrative chief, Dr. Melanie Flynn, is serving as managing director until the lawyers sort everything out. She makes all the business decisions."

Van Dyke made some notes on a pad. Then: "As Bradford's chief of New Ventures, have you made any overtures to her? Suggested acquisition?"

"I've made explorations, letting it be known that Bradford chemicals is interested in acquiring the firm and its patents and assets. But, I'm happy to say, Flynn refuses even to discuss the idea."

"She knows nothing of Allenby's invention?"

"Nothing."

Van Dyke shrugged. "So why don't we just hire Allenby and have him develop his product for us?"

"His employment contract again. As research chief, he is forbidden to join a competitor for two years after termination or resignation from Lunt. And he can claim no personal ownership of inventions until after five years' separation, the assumption being that anything he developed in less than five years would involve some carryover of savvy learned on Lunt's time and with Lunt's resources. We'd be adding those years to the time it ordinarily takes to bring a new drug to market. Allenby's optimism in this regard is pure overreach, I'd say."

Van Dyke showed curiosity. "Why does it take so long, for God's sake?"

"Once a new drug is developed, it has to be tested on animals for three, four years. Then the Federal Medicine Approval Agency has to authorize it for testing on humans. The FMAA is a kind of subsidiary FDA—a creation of Washington power brokers who felt the FDA was getting too big for its britches— and it's proved to be nothing but a home for diselected pols, relatives of lobbyists, and a huge wart that drives the straight-shooters and Honest Abes at the FDA into squirting fits of indignant rage every hour on the hour. As a compromise between the FDA and FMAA, at least a year goes into testing the drug on healthy volunteers, then two years are given to testing up to three hundred volunteers who have the ailment targeted by the drug, and then another three years are needed to verify the drug's effectiveness and possible side effects on a thousand or so patients. Then it has to be given Federal approval—a process that's supposed to take six months but, thanks to the FMAA's screwing around, more often takes two, three years. And even if the drug's approved—only one out of four thousand drugs that undergo preclinical testing makes it to market— the manufacturer has to keep feeding the FDA data on adverse reactions, quality control, and long-term effects. And although the inventor of this particular drug has gone through all the crap leading to a patent and FDA approval, we're still talking a major effort here."

Van Dyke rolled his eyes and delivered another club cliché. "That's what comes when the government gets involved."

"As you can see, I'm not in the easiest of businesses. And ten million may not be much to you, but it is to me. So my nerves stand to be tested in all this."

Van Dyke nodded sympathetically. He made another note, then gave Morton a lingering stare. "You're positive that this product has good market potential?"

"Too good, in a way. If Allenby's claims for it bear out, it could have a very destructive effect on a large part of the pharmaceutical business—the high-tech manufacture of medicines, drugs, that are currently used in the treatment of cancer. Aside from the vast curing powers it offers, it's cheap to make. We in the industry have billions invested in drugs designed for use in the treatment of cancer. The Allenby product not only could kill us on price but, worse, promises to make much of our investment and its derivative product lines totally obsolete. The industry could quickly find itself out of business in what has been one of its most lucrative sectors."

An interval passed, during which Van Dyke made a series of notes on his yellow pad, then he looked up, amusement showing briefly in his eyes. "Tell me, George: Why are you being so good to me and Mr. Falloon?"

Morton had been waiting for this one. "This is my chance to get out of the trenches and into some real money and power. I want to move up from the Sphinx. To gain admission to the best clubs. To become a major player."

Van Dyke sank back in his chair and clasped his bejeweled hands on his vest. "You were nominated for membership in the Nordic two years ago. You were rejected. Did you know that?"

Morton pretended surprise. "No," he lied. "No I did not. Such nominations are secret—"

"I'm telling you now because you're proposing a relationship with Mr. Falloon. I think you should know that he was the one who blackballed you. He said that your tongue-in-cheek attitude, the laid-back cynicism that often show through your studied correctness, suggest that you're too clever by far. Worst of all, he said, you've done nothing noteworthy."

"Well—"

"Really, George, this is your chance to withdraw your offer. I'm not at all sure Mr. Falloon has changed his opinion of you."

Morton examined his manicure. "Well, Peter, my laid-back cynicism tells me that this is also my chance to say up your giggy with a hot cross bun. But I'm too clever by far to miss this once-in-a-lifetime opportunity, and I suspect that Falloon will see it my way and not let all the personal frat-house crap get in the way." Laughing softly, he added, "Even he will have to admit that a cancer cure is pretty goddam noteworthy."

Van Dyke turned in his chair, his gaze on the pseudospring beyond the tall windows. Morton could guess what was going on in the little bald head: How should this be presented to the Boss—or should it be presented at all? Van Dyke was Falloon's second-in-command; his primary job was to keep Falloon informed and to plot the courses of action requiring Falloon's decision. If it failed to qualify for presentation at the top, Van Dyke himself would give Morton the bad news. If it qualified, and if Falloon gave the go-ahead, the proposal would be given the maximum in effort and resources.

Morton waited, feeling his heart beat.

Van Dyke raised his pudgy chin and adjusted his necktie. His voice was a purring. "You understand, George, that I'll have to take this question upstairs."

"Of course, Peter. I certainly do understand."

"Where will you be this evening, say, at six o'clock?"

"At my home in Z'ville. I'm putting in the rest of the workday at the plant there."

"I'll call you at six o'clock with the decision. Will that be convenient?"

"Yes. And let me say again, Peter, how much I appreciate your giving personal time and attention to this."

Van Dyke smiled his cat's smile. "And I am pleased that you felt free to come to me."

They rose from their chairs and shook hands at the door.

"Until this evening, then," Van Dyke said. "Let's hope for a positive reaction, eh?"

Morton finished the day in meetings with the Z'ville plant manager and his staff, who were agitating for huge renovations to the storage tank area. Later he drove through a varsity-type thunderstorm to the house, where he changed into a pullover and jeans. Viewing the storm from the library window, sipping Scotch and water and waiting for the usual sense of escape to settle in, he felt instead an indefinable edginess.

He'd never been one to give much time to self-doubts or anxiety. As an orphan living with Uncle Denny in the redbrick, row-house squalor of South Philly, he'd seen that life was a race most often lost by those who expected to lose. That he was someone superior and special, that he would always somehow be on top, was a willful teenager's decision that eventually evolved into an adult conviction as tangible and unbending as a cobblestone.

He'd barely begun to shave when the preparation began. How could he translate the decision into practical achievement? What would it take to climb out? What made the Clean People different? Important answers came from the screen of Uncle Denny's tiny TV set: The cleanest ones, the rich dudes, always walked straight and spoke big words smoothly and wore clothes that looked great but weren't flashy.

Losers always looked like losers—in dress, speech, attitude, and body language.

Like Uncle Denny. Uncle Denny had been a kind, easygoing, funny, and loving father to him, a sweet man who would daily walk twenty blocks to and from his lousy little job at the piano factory so the accrued carfare could go toward "a nice Christmas for Li'l Georgie." Uncle Denny had been the best thing that had ever happened to him, and even today it was hard to think of him without choking up. But Uncle Denny had been a loser—mainly because he thought of himself that way.

Morton had taken one step at a time. No way could he get great clothes, but one thing he could do—perhaps the most important thing—was to learn the big words and how they went together. He could learn how to talk, and the way to do that was to read a lot, listen hard in Miss Gerber's English classes (listen hard in all the classes, for that matter), listen hard to the Cleanest Ones on the TV, listen hard to himself as he imitated those suckers in speeches at the bleary bathroom mirror. Then he would read some more and practice some more, moving into the next step: watching the successful angle-shooters. How did Freddy Bachmann keep his horse parlor running without paying fines and doing time? How did Dolores Meacham operate a house and run the best-looking girls and make it all look squeaky-clean? How had Lou Francini parlayed his neighborhood numbers racket into a legal, multibillion-dollar-a-year, nationwide insurance business? How do banks work? How do you make money by borrowing money? How can people be bought?

Eventually there was the scholarship to Harvard and his introduction to a world in which it could all happen. And it had happened—precisely the way he'd anticipated.

So why was he now feeling so uneasy? Uncertain?

Was this his introduction to panic, finding himself for the first time over his head? So much was riding on nerve, on judgment, on his reading of currents and their point of future confluence.

Unless all of it worked, nothing would be won; there was no partway, no fractional success. The irony was heavy here: He was acknowledged to be the ace of acquisitional aces, the man who could outwait and outwit them all. But in this, the supreme convergence of his physical wants and spiritual needs, he had to prove to Ace, soon, and without coming across as a wart, that her interpretation of auld lang syne must not only be forgot but also seen as something that had never really been.

To make it happen, he was literally risking his life.

Working to smother those depressing thoughts, he went into the study, booted up the computer with the dedicated phone line. He tapped the keys that hacked into the Lunt Biotech system, just to see what might be going on. What was going on was nothing; all computers were inactive, and the laboratory was sleeping. He was contemplating a bit of Internet surfing when the house phone rang. The sound was harsh, and he jumped, startled.

"Hello?"

"Peter Van Dyke here, George. Would it be convenient for you to meet with Mr. Falloon at his home in Philadelphia next Thursday at 3 P.M.?"

"Certainly."

"Good. Will you be coming from New York?"

"Yes. I'll take the noon train."

"Our limo will be at Thirtieth Street Station."

The dial tone sounded.

Morton hung up. He felt a smile, the doubts evaporating, the old self-confidence rushing in.

He was feeling pretty good by the time he showered and got into his pajamas. Too awake for bed, he scanned the TV late news, then took a few minutes to boot up the hacking computer again and to tune in on Sergeant Jacoby's investigations notebook, partly for the hell of it, partly to see how the detective's day had ended.

The glow faded fast when Morton read the closing entry, made only an hour ago:

Mrs. Hamilton called at 10:23 P.M. She was considerably
upset by what she called "an armed prowler." Said she
was writing letters at a desk by a window in her second-
floor bedroom at Elmwood Manor. When she turned
out the light, she says, there was a flash of lightning
outside, and she caught sight of a person wearing a
hooded parkalike coat aiming a pistol at her from the
crotch of a large tree outside the window. She says that
she was sure she would have been shot if she hadn't by
chance turned out the light at just the right moment. I
asked her where the hell her grounds security people
had been when all this was going on and she said only
one guy, Bob Griswold, was on duty tonight, and he'd
been down at the garage, seeing why the burglar alarm
had gone off there.

I asked her if she wanted me to come out there and
she said hell no, what good would that do. I asked her
why she had called me, then, and she said she wanted
to let me know that she'd obviously been added to the
bad guys' hit list.

She's a real piece of work, that lady.

No wonder her husband lives in Florida.

9.

Alicia Hamilton's solution to the problem was simple, called for a minimum of cash, and required no more than a Halloween trick-or-treat audacity. She couldn't go to Fred Stabile, obviously, and she didn't want to hire a private investigator and then be forever worried as to whether he could be trusted. So she visited the Ever-Sure Locksmith and Security Alarm Company, a clean and efficient-looking storefront operation on Caldwell Avenue.

"Can I help you, ma'am?" the pretty redhead at the counter asked.

"I hope so. I'm Alicia Hamilton. I own a small house on River Road, not too far from the airport. I've been renting it to the gentleman who owned the air taxi service, but, as you've probably seen on the news, he died recently when his plane crashed. Unfortunately, I've misplaced my keys to the place and I'm unable to get in and see what has to be done to get it ready for another rental. It occurred to me that you people might escort me out there, let me in, and stand by while I look over things."

"I don't see where that should be a problem, ma'am. Let me talk to Dick." She turned and called through a connecting door, "Yo, Dick. Can you help this customer?"

A crisp young man appeared in the doorway, dressed in well-pressed work clothes with a breast patch proclaiming that he was Dick Forney and boasting that one was ever sure with Ever-Sure.

"Help you, ma'am?"

She repeated her story.

"May I see your driver's license, please?" His gaze went over her red topcoat, tailored tan suit, and black accessories—a dog-show judge examining an entry.

She held out her wallet and his eyes widened slightly when they took in her address.

"You're the Mrs. Hamilton who has the big place on Hollow Tree Road?"

"Yes," she said, part warm, part cool.

He grinned. "We put the new alarm system in that place couple years back."

"Indeed." She smiled tautly and told a lie. "That's why I came here for help."

"I don't suppose you have a copy of your rental contract with you—"

"Sorry, no. It's in a lockbox in our Florida place."

"No prob. You don't look like somebody ready to knock off a house." He peered at her license and scribbled on a pad. "City regs," he explained, handing back the card.

She managed a soft laugh. "If I were planning to burgle a house, young man, I'd most certainly pick one with a more prepossessing address. And I'd be even more certain not to invite somebody as bright as you to come along for the ride."

He beamed. "Where's your car, Mrs. Hamilton?"

She pointed out the plate-glass window. "That black Mercedes parked across the street."

"You lead the way. I'll be in a white Ford pickup." To the girl he said, "Be back in an hour, Molly."

The young man did something to the lock and held the door for her as she stepped through.

"Aren't you coming in with me?"

"No, ma'am. No need to. Just take your time. I'll be in my truck, catching up on some paperwork. I'll lock up when you're finished."

She thanked him and went into the living room, congratulating herself for having had such a great idea. Here she was, about to search a dead man's house, with her personal sentry waiting politely outside. Her mind went to Gramps, who had made a large thing out of addresses and what he'd called "motorcars." His eyebrows would knit severely as he admonished, "If it takes your absolute last penny, kid, always be sure to have a good address and a big, black, shiny motorcar. You can otherwise be as poor as Job's turkey, but if you have a proper address and a motorcar that looks expensive and well kept, you can open any door, get anything you want, because people— especially Americans—are almost always ready to take things at face value. If you look rich, you are automatically thought to be rich. Good things come only to those who look as if they don't need them."

She stood quietly for a moment, dealing with a gathering headache and those damned recurring spots before her eyes. She sighed then and got on with the business at hand.

Bill Rooney had been a bachelor, dedicated to the proposition that women were wonderful so long as their stockings weren't hanging in his bathroom. At least that's what he would say when in his cups and full of all that daredevil-ace crap. But it had occurred to Alicia more than once that the macho pose was a covering compensation for a personality that was basically wimpy and groveling. And his aviating struck her as being old-maidish; as girl and woman, she had logged eleven hundred hours of multiengine time, thanks to a doting Gramps and, later, an indifferent husband, and she'd learned how to read signs along the way. One ride as copilot with Bill Rooney, and she'd had his number: a guy who would have, if it had been technically possible, done all his flying with one foot nice and safe on the ground. And, in the final analysis, his panicky clutching of bachelorhood simply had to have been a fantastic break for any husband-hunter who might have been tempted while passing through his life. Being married to him, she thought now, would have been like doing life in ankle chains with an oily maître d'.

He'd also been a neat-freak, obviously. Except for a few dishes in the kitchen sink and a sweater tossed on the bed, the place was ready for a top sergeant's inspection.

Glancing guiltily over her shoulder in acknowledgment of her trespass, she went quickly through the bedroom chest of drawers, the closet, the writing desk by the window, and even the linen shelves in the bathroom ell. The living-room bookcases, the computer cabinet, the end-table drawers, the dining-room sideboard, the kitchen cupboards, even the tiny workshop in the utility room—none of them produced.

"The office," she murmured in the silence. "Maybe he kept them in his office."

They sure as hell weren't in this house.

She went out to the street, where the white pickup sat in the pale winter sunshine.

"All set, Mr. Forney," she called through the window.

The pane zizzed down, and Forney asked from the inner dusk, "Everything look okay?"

"Just fine. Mr. Rooney kept an immaculate house. I—"

She broke off, because at that moment a black-and-white police cruiser came around the corner and squeaked to a stop, nose-to-nose with the pickup truck. A large woman in natty police blues swung out importantly and came toward them, adjusting her opaque sunglasses. "What's up, Dick?"

Forney leaned out his window, and said, "This here woman, who said she owns this house and was renting to Bill Rooney, got me to let her in for a look-around. I checked with the city on my cellular and they said the house was owned by Bill Rooney and was in estate settlement, and nobody was renting it to anybody. So I followed the suspicious-conditions thing we locksmiths got with you guys and I called Dispatch."

Alicia, struggling to contain her panic, felt the sunglasses focusing on her.

"Let me see your ID, ma'am," the cop said.

Alicia presented her driver's license and auto insurance card. "I'd like to talk to Chief Stabile, Officer." The cop pursed her lips and examined the credentials. She looked up and asked in that bored, superior tone cops think is cool, "What were you doin' in the house, ma'am?"

"Mr. Rooney had some papers belonging to my husband, who is in a nursing home. I admit I used false pretenses to gain access to the house, but I could think of no other way to do it."

The cop used her black sunglasses and bored face to show how unimpressed she was. "You mind if I look in that there purse of yours?"

Alicia handed her the purse. "Of course not. I have stolen nothing, and I have nothing to hide. And again: I want to speak to Chief Stabile."

"Mrs. Hamilton is a very important lady, Paula," Forney put in, hedging. "And I could see though the windows she wasn't up to anything bad."

Paula went through the purse without comment, then handed it back. By this time she was obviously ready to do a bit of hedging of her own, since somebody with an address on Hollow Tree Road and a wad of hundred-dollar bills stuffed in with the lipstick and Kleenex and Mercedes keys could very well have the ear of Chief Stabile.

"If you know Chief Stabile," Paula asked reasonably, "why didn't you call him and ask him to get you into the house? Or your lawyer, maybe."

"Because, obviously, I don't think as clearly as you do, Officer. Besides, Fred Stabile and you police folks have enough to do without running around, opening doors."

Having at last found somebody in this day who appreciated her for the many grinding responsibilities she carried, Paula softened the rest of the way. She turned her glasses toward Forney. "You got this lady's license number and all that on your call to Dispatch?"

"Sure do. I follow regs."

The glasses came back to Alicia. "You done a dumb thing,

ma'am. But I'm not going to take you in because this whole thing's so dumb I gotta believe it. Besides, it looks like you didn't steal anything."

"That's very kind of you, Officer."

"But I still gotta make a report."

"I understand. Please have Fred call me if you need any further information." Glancing at Forney, she asked, "What do I owe you?"

"No charge, Mrs. Hamilton. Didn't want to cause you all this trouble. But I got a business I got to protect."

"Of course you do. And I insist on paying your fee."

"I'll send you the bill."

"I want to pay cash. Now. No bills to my home."

"Sure. That'll be thirty-five dollars. The standard fee for a service call."

Driving away, heading for Main Street and the connector to Ligonier, Alicia screamed a scream of angry relief. It wasn't until the Mercedes crested Hammock Hill that she could think calmly again. Even then she couldn't decide whether to laugh or cry. But as always, the view from this eminence, the great spread of sky it presented—the towering cumulus, the colors without names—returned her to her childhood, when she had peered at the clouds, straining to see the God, who, the Reverend MacIntosh had assured her, lived up there.

Inevitably, her mind segued into her youth, her marriage, and the subsequent affair that pronounced its doom.

There'd been this brilliant, lonely, adorable man who had owned her since the first glance. And the hell of it was that, while every day he was easily within sight and sound, he'd become as reachable as a rock on the far side of Neptune. Worse, there had been absolutely no doubt in her mind: Unless she kept control and held strictly to the course, she would most surely be zapped into the contemporary equivalent of Lot's wife's pillar of salt.

This was no superstition, it was recognition of an immutable, everlasting law under which everything has its flip side. Every pleasure has its price. Every privilege has its obligation. Every gain requires pain.

The only thing that kept her going was the hope that she was now on the bad side of the flip—that she was paying the price, meeting the obligation, feeling the pain, that would eventually bring her through to the good side.

But, dear God almighty, it was sure tough going.

10.

By late afternoon the rain had stopped and, as if that were an omen, Jacoby got to see Chief Stabile without delay.

"Could I ask you a question, Chief?"

Stabile's face showed mild surprise. "Since when do you have to get permission to ask me a question?"

"It's about Mrs. Hamilton."

"You're still stroking her?"

"Not stroking. Following where she and Flynn lead us. Looking into what they say. Something smells. My vibes say Hamilton may have pointed us toward the main stink and that Flynn knows a hell of a lot more than she's saying."

"So what's your question?"

"Well, I get the idea that Mrs. Hamilton is a personal friend of yours, and the question has to do with her, ah, private life. I don't want to—"

Stabile's eyes narrowed. "Cut the State Department crap. What is it?"

"You know she was on yesterday's blotter? For hiring a locksmith to get into Rooney's house?"

"Of course I know she was on the blotter. There's nothing on any blotter I don't read. And she called me about it. She thought Lunt had left some papers with Rooney, and she didn't know how else to look for them. She admits it was a stupid move. So what?"

"Did Mrs. Hamilton and Dr. Lunt have a thing?"

"Thing? You're still poking at that idea?"

"Well, yes, sir."

"I said before: friends, sure. Lovers? Doubtful. So?"

"I'm still bugged by that picture we found in Rooney's house—the one of Lunt and Mrs. Hamilton by the plane. Why would Rooney hide away a picture like that?"

Stabile gave that a moment of thought. Then: "You're suggesting blackmail?"

"Well—"

"Not compromising enough. Alicia and Lunt were good friends. Good friends hug each other once in a while. Especially if one's about to leave in a plane. Hell, she even kisses me on the cheek every time I see her." A smile came and went, shadowlike, across Stabile's lean face. "Now, if they were lying on a wing, say, tearing off a piece, that might be something else."

"Well, how about Mr. Hamilton? Would he mind his wife and Lunt being pals?"

Stabile shrugged. "Could be. Anything's possible. The word I get is he's been too busy being sick to care about much of anything at all." He paused, thinking, then added, "But I agree that Rooney stashing such pictures is a four-star discord. And the picture might have been what Alicia was looking for. So I suggest you crank the photos higher up in your scenario."

"Okay, sir. And thanks for the input."

Returning to his desk, Jacoby called up the Lunt file from Case Records and placed it on the monitor of his terminal. Squinting at the scrolling amber display, he tried to ignore the gloom that had unaccountably gathered at the back of his mind.

The file was basic stuff: Traffic's accident report form; victim IDs; aircraft ID, including engine numbers and FAA registration; site description, photo and sketch file references; medical examiner's preliminary report; statement from the only witness to the crash, Albert T. Margolis; notation that the FAA and NTSB had been notified. All formal, cool, written with the peculiar self-consciousness of cops who know that their words will be studied by legions of fussbudgets.

He picked up the phone and rang the Medical Examiner's Office. Doc Logan answered for a change.

"Jacoby, Doc. I have a question."

"Try Public Relations."

"I've just been going over the accident report on the plane crash. In it, there's a mention that your postmortem on Dr. Lunt turned up—and I quote—'evidence of amyotrophic lateral sclerosis.' "

"So?"

"So what the hell is that?"

"The so-called Lou Gehrig's disease. A very bad number, distinguished by escalating muscle weakness—atrophy—or paralysis, caused by the progressive degeneration of motor nerve cells in the brain and spinal cord."

"Bad number? How bad?"

"There are a lot of lousy ways to die, but this one is among the worst. Lunt's body was a jigsaw puzzle and badly burned, but enough was sufficiently intact to show me that if the crash hadn't killed Lunt the sclerosis would have—sooner rather than later."

"Is it likely that Lunt knew he had the disease?"

"Is it likely that Gehrig knew how to play baseball? The disease is insidious, but Lunt would have noticed tremors and difficulty with fine movements, like writing, handling needles, scalpels, and like that. Unsteadiness in walking, knees that wouldn't bend, a dimming of eyesight. And that's just the beginning. The disease always ends painfully and fatally."

There was a pause.

"Anything else?"

"That's it for now. Thanks, Doc."

"*Gesundheit.*"

Jacoby hung up and, yawning noisily, turned off his computer. Pulling on his topcoat, he went downstairs and out to the twilit employee parking lot.

The department had assigned him a black, unmarked Ford for use while on duty. Policy disallowed his taking the car home. So he had gone into considerable hock a year ago to buy himself a souped-up Mustang that had been in the unmarked patrol car inventory, phased out by the State Police when they converted to the Chevy Caprice. The car had no more than two hundred million hard-driven miles on it and smelled of old tobacco and even older hoagies. But it had the guts of an Indy racer and the build of a tank, and he figured that the trade-off between grubbiness and utility balanced out. Besides, the car had a certain panache—an ostensible junker that could break out of the pack like a Canaveral moon shot—and it played to his secret penchant for the funky. So it was now, as always, with oddball pleasure that he climbed in and started up the beast.

He had a fantasy going these days. He would pull up to Lunt Biotech and Melanie Flynn would come running out to hop into the Mustang beside him, and they would be off to Bronson's, an upscale B&B near Reading, for a weekend of horizontal calisthenics. The fantasy never resolved, thanks to the congenital shyness that caused him still to blush at memories of his panic when Mary Alice Frombacher showed him hers and dared him to show her his that day at the Potter Street Elementary School playground. This inborn diffidence had cursed all his subsequent relationships with females. To be a young man was to be horny, but in his case, the lure of easy scores had been outweighed by the terror triggered by the army's VD films, and where the terror left off, the Mary Alice syndrome took over. Those sacks he'd climbed into had been occupied by women who'd taken the time to gentle him and break him in. When these great souls had passed out of reach due to marriage or other limbos, he would reenter the Square One Zone, where the search for replacements seemed always to end in polite handshaking and dreary promises to "do this again sometime." He'd been wandering about in this crappy wilderness when the beautiful and indifferent Dr. Flynn had come out of the fog to put a random shot straight through his libido, leaving him to bleed daydreams.

He was brooding about all this when, while waiting for a light at Eighth and Main, he saw Pinky Watson push his Cadillac through on the yellow at what seemed to be Mach 6. The man was in a real hurry, and Jacoby's experience had taught him that when a sleazebag private eye was in a hurry, big bucks or big trouble or both were usually waiting at the other end. So curiosity and the prospect of a boring night ahead put him into a sharp right on Eighth and a stimulating high-speed tail job. Wherever Pinky was going in such a hurry was bound to be more interesting than a microwave meat loaf and an evening of net surfing.

Pinky was one of Jacoby's many pet peeves. Watson had been a detective on the Philly force some years back and had left under a cloud generated by unproved claims of corruption. But under prevailing American folkways and mores, a crummy reputation and sleazy acts were often tickets to fame and riches. While Pinky Watson had yet to achieve fame, he most certainly wasn't hurting in the riches department, what with his suite of offices in a tony strip mall, ten-room penthouse in the Baronial Acres high-rise complex, three expensive cars, and two even more expensive mistresses. Jacoby had wondered on several occasions what lousy thing he himself could pull off that might bring him a bunch of money and still let him live with his nineteenth-century conscience. But these musings, too, had proved to be wasted time. He was, in every way, a hopeless, nerdy goddam square.

By the time Pinky's white Caddie pulled into the Berger's Burgers parking lot, Jacoby's mood had progressed from curiosity through envy to resentment and irritability. Curiosity came to the fore again when, watching from his car, he saw Watson enter the restaurant and go directly to a table occupied by none other than Theodore Bradford Two, honcho of the company whose chemical plant stank up the city on damp days. To see Bradford sipping coffee in a fast-food joint was like seeing Van Cliburn doing rhythm in a Front Street Dixieland band—possible, but unlikely, and very much worth looking into.

Bradford and Watson were seated in a corner of a T formed by two planter walls topped by plastic philodendron and English ivy. The adjacent corner was unoccupied, and Jacoby eased into the chair that enabled him to hear everything being said on the other side of the wall. What was being said was also possible, but unlikely, and very much worth looking into.

Bradford: "Why the hell did you pick this place to meet? It's barbaric."

Watson: "It's also busy and noisy and filled with people who never look at each other. It provides first-rate cover."

Bradford: "So what's this big thing you've found out?"

Watson: "Your suspicions about your vice president appear to be well-founded. He's up to something, sure enough."

Bradford: "Like what?"

Watson: "I personally tailed him yesterday. To a very interesting address. I tried to call you right away, but your secretary said you were in a meeting and couldn't be disturbed. She put me off today, too."

Bradford: "Will you cut out the goddam suspense crap and get to the frigging point?"

Watson: "He went to see Peter Van Dyke."

Bradford: "Van Dyke? You mean Falloon's gofer?"

Watson: "A limo picked up Morton at his house right after breakfast and took him to Van Dyke's farm near

Lancaster. He was there for an hour and four minutes. The limo took him back to Z'ville."

Bradford: "I knew it. I knew it. The son of a bitch is after money. He's trying to beat me out on the Allenby thing."

Watson: "I don't know what that means, naturally. Or exactly what it is about Morton that's got you upset. But it was pretty clear to me that something big's going down when Van Dyke gets into the act. Nobody gets carted to Van Dyke's place to talk about the weather. So I thought you ought to know as soon as."

Bradford: "You thought right. And we've got to figure out a better way to communicate."

Watson: "We sure as hell do. We can't have your secretary playing God like that."

Bradford: "I'd fire her ass, but she's the daughter of one of my wife's friends."

Watson: "How about I get us a pair of beepers? We call each other direct when we got something important to say."

Bradford: "No cellulars. Too public—risky."

Watson: "Beepers. We beep, then find the nearest phones."

Bradford: "Set it up. And try to find out exactly what business Morton's doing with Van Dyke and Falloon. You hear anything—anything at all involving Greg Allenby, I want to know immediately. Any time of day or night."

Watson: "You got it."

Bradford: "Now let's get out of this goddam greasy spoon.
            I've had all these yammering peasants I can take."

Jacoby waited until they were gone, then went through the line and bought himself a supper of scrambled eggs, corned beef hash, and a side of pancakes.

Greasy spoon, hell. The food was great.

And he was feeling good.

He'd just picked up a solid reason to drop in on Melanie Flynn.

11.

Peter Van Dyke met Morton's train as agreed, and they were driven to Falloon's Main Line estate in the same stretch Cadillac by the same big man in the black suit. The main house was the classic Pennsylvania farmhouse expanded to the nth power—a fieldstone-and-frame creation with huge chimneys, ranks of dormers with cutesy shutters, arcades, gazebos, garden houses, acres of slate roofing, and miles of brick walkways. The whole appeared to be encircled by high stone walls topped by broken glass, with steel gates attended by other men wearing black suits and dark sunglasses.

They gathered in the library, a cavern of bookcases and pine ceiling beams whose window wall overlooked the rear garden's reflecting pool. Falloon, a giant in slacks, a silk shirt buttoned at the collar, a black cardigan, and glistening loafers, sat in a large leather chair beside the fireplace. Nearby, looking uncomfortable on a straight-backed chair, was Andrew Zachary, a piece of heavy FMAA artillery, whose presence surprised Morton. He knew Falloon had a long reach, but he hadn't realized until now that it went so far up the Federal rectum. But he managed to keep a straight face and took a seat on the sofa beside Van Dyke, who said quietly, like a church usher welcoming a newcomer, "George, you've met Dr. Zachary, I'm sure."

Morton gave Zachary a nod. "Hi, Drew. How are things in Washington?"

"Take a tip, George: Stay away from there in droves."

As if to keep the small talk to a minimum, Van Dyke explained. "Drew has been kind enough to break away from his heavy duties at the FMAA to hear just what's involved in this secret formula you are so excited about. He will listen to the particulars and tell us if this Allenby fellow's invention has a chance of getting government approval."

Falloon was more direct. For all his casual togs, he might well have been wearing an ermine cape and a jeweled crown; he exuded regal power, and his voice was an operatic bass. "What the man is saying is that I want Zachary's expert opinion on whether you're trying to peddle a clinker."

"I'm glad Drew's here," Morton said, unruffled. "We're about to talk up a muscular investment, and you deserve all the advice you can get. I must warn you, though, we might get a bit technical as we go along here—"

"Be as technical as you wish, but I might ask for explanations, interpretations." Falloon's glance instructed Van Dyke to get things going.

Van Dyke purred, "Mr. Morton is with us this afternoon to present a plan which, if developed and activated, could result in large amounts of income and provide a conduit through which additional foreign revenues could be brought into our domestic reserves. I have reviewed his proposition and find it to have sufficient merit to warrant your personal attention." He paused, his small eyes alert to signals from the throne.

The big man turned his gaze slowly to regard Morton with low-lidded curiosity. "Peter has told me something of your proposal, but I want nuts and bolts. Precisely what has this man Allenby come up with? I'm told that it promises important advances against cancer, and that the natural fallout would be unprecedented profits, but just what is it? How did it come about? What does it do?"

Falloon, Morton decided, would want thoughtful. Sincere. He cleared his throat, summoning up the proper voice—smart and cool, slightly pedantic, devoid of condescension. "Cancer is divided into two groups: primary and metastatic. Primary is confined to a single area, with, in some cases, a few adjacent lymph nodes involved. Metastatic is a primary that has spread throughout the body, or to other, distant parts of the body. With early diagnosis and early surgery, and/or radiation, and/or chemotherapy, fifteen percent of patients with primary cancer will live for five years. Which means eighty-five percent will die within that same time. The figures are even more dismal with metastatic: With early diagnosis and treatment with the tripod procedures of surgery, radiation, and chemo, only one patient in a thousand will live another five years. Those are terrible odds. Horrific odds. Our job in the pharmaceutical industry is to devise medicines that will help physicians, surgeons, radiologists, and chemotherapists to better those odds. It's absolutely the most important thing we do."

Morton paused, and Falloon made a little motion with his right hand. "Go on."

"About twenty years ago," Morton said, "proposals for alternative cancer treatment began to surface. Individuals claiming to have conducted extensive research claimed they had evidence showing cancer to be a deficiency disease—like scurvy, or pellagra, or rickets, or pernicious anemia—which is intensified by the lack of certain food compounds in the modern diet. They said cancer could be controlled, maybe even cured, by the systematic restoration of such compounds to the daily intake of food. Dr. Lunt was among those making these claims, and he was very adept at getting publicity for his method of cancer treatment, which subordinated orthodox surgery and radiation and chemo as the only sensible treatments to his serum and supplementary nutritional regimens. But the publicity turned out to be a two-edged sword, so to speak, because it got Lunt denounced as a quack by the FDA and the influential associations."

Morton paused again. Falloon said he wanted technical details. But how technical? Both too much and too little could destroy this thing on its launching pad. Too much could bore the man to death and sound supercilious to boot. Too little would fall short and irritate the hell out of him.

Morton opted for too much.

"For thousands of years, humans have countered rheumatic pains and other maladies by eating figs and chewing willow and poplar barks. The glucosides from figs, the natural aspirin in the barks, and the nitrilosides in some 350 edible plants share a commonality: First, in their active aglycones, or non-sugars, derived by hydrolysis of their respective glucosides by emulsion—beta-glucosidase; second, the consequential production of their nonsugar hydrolysates—o-hydroxybenzaldehyde from barks, benzaldehyde from figs, and bezaldehyde with p-hydroxybenzaldehyde from the nitriloside dhurrin; and third, their identical carcinostatic action in humans and animals in proportion to the benzaldehyde in amygdalin, aspirin, and fig glucosides." Morton paused again. Then: "So, you see, Dr. Lunt's uniqueness wasn't so unique."

Falloon, unfazed by these pyrotechnics, went to the core. "So, then, if it's not so special," he rumbled, "why should we be so anxious to get control of this new formula?"

"Because Allenby, who worked for Lunt, has been able to exploit the trophoblastic thesis and, by coupling it with what amounts to a kind of super amygdalin and attendant nutritional therapies, has developed a practical means of halting, even, in some cases, eradicating both primary and metastatic growths. His formula dramatically changes the odds in both types."

"The what thesis?"

Quick. The man was quick. Impressed, Morton struggled against a smile that wanted to form. "In 1902, an Edinburgh embryologist, John Beard, published a paper in *The Lancet*, a British medical journal, in which he said his research found no difference between cancer cells and trophoblasts, preembryonic cells that during the early stages of pregnancy spread rapidly and prepare a place in the uterus wall where the embryo can attach itself. He concluded that cancer cells are, therefore, trophoblasts. Then a Palo Alto scientist said his research indicated that whenever a trophoblast cell shows up in the body outside of pregnancy, the natural forces that control its spread in a pregnancy are absent, and so it begins uncontrolled proliferation, invasion—in short, it's the onset of cancer. This is a grossly abbreviated explanation of a very complicated process, but it should help you understand what Allenby has done. He has, to put it simply, somehow harnessed trophoblasts and, with other nutritional therapies, put them to restorative work—using cancer to halt cancer, so to speak."

Falloon showed his erudition. "Like dead polio virus is put to work against polio?"

"Well, as you say, polio is a virus. Cancer is a body system running amok. The two aren't really comparable."

"I'm talking concept," Falloon said, suddenly testy. "An illness fighting itself. A concept."

Warned by his tone, Morton did some fast, restorative sucking-up. "Concept-wise, you're quite right, Mr. Falloon."

Zachary joined the chorus. "That is indeed an excellent analogy."

Falloon didn't look at him. "So you think this is viable, Zachary?"

Zachary's trendy eyeglasses glinted in the afternoon light. He asked Morton, "Allenby has done the required clinical work, assembled the necessary case histories?"

"All the data the FMAA insists on."

"How about a demonstration?"

"It can be had. You locate a patient, and we'll gather there for Allenby's show-and-tell."

Zachary gave all this some thought.

"Well?" Falloon didn't like to be kept waiting.

"Pending a successful demo, I predict that this should have no real trouble getting approval, Mr. Falloon."

"How about you, Peter?"

"I believe that this is a remarkable opportunity."

Back to Zachary: "Thank you. Thank you for your time and assistance. Have a nice trip."

Zachary, understanding that he was being excluded from further participation, rose from his chair and pretended nonchalance. "I do have to get back. It's been a pleasure."

They watched as he left the room, stiffly, like a dismissed cadet.

Falloon returned straight to work. "So what you're saying, Morton, is that he who controls the Allenby discovery will eventually control the cancer industry."

"That's right."

"So how does one gain such control?"

Here was the trickiest part of the plan. And here Morton went very carefully.

"The first step is to have your Peabody Chemicals set up a subsidiary. With three hundred million supplied by you, I will buy the formula from Allenby, then join your subsidiary as president and CEO. Under my special orchestration, the Peabody subsidiary will absorb, then present, the Allenby research and development histories as its own, and go immediately into the concluding steps leading to FMAA approval and marketing."

"Peter tells me that you have offered to contribute a sum as a guarantee and for a limited participation."

"Yep. Ten million dollars and the outright donation of my management services for two percent of the gross."

Falloon nodded his large head. "Well, Morton, while ten million is hardly an inconsiderable sum, it's not quite enough for the return implicit in two percent of the gross. One percent, maybe."

Morton shrugged. "I'm a man of somewhat better than average means, but the ten million is all I can manage. If that buys me one percent, I most certainly accept. Actually, the ten million is meant primarily to demonstrate the seriousness with which I view this commitment."

"And that's been noted. Frankly, I've never been comfortable in our dealings with you, Morton. There's something of the angle-shooter about you. I grant that you're intelligent, suave, articulate, amiable. But I sense that's mainly facade. Behind it beats the heart of a stalking Hun. What are you hiding so carefully? Whom are you getting ready to shaft? That's what's always bothered me, Morton."

Morton shrugged. "I've never been all that crazy about you, either."

Van Dyke's shocked intake of breath was audible.

Falloon's brows lowered. "Don't get smart-ass with me, mister. I have men like you for breakfast."

Cool, Morton, cool. He's testing you.

"I've always admired you, Falloon. You are one hell of a capable man. But admiration doesn't translate into ass-kissing. You're tough, sure enough. But so am I. And if you don't think so, watch me walk out of here with the formula."

In the silence that followed, Morton was aware of the tense, stricken look on Van Dyke's face. But he also saw the flicker of a smile on Falloon's.

The lowered brows raised. "Perhaps I was coloring you with the same brush I apply to Teddy Bradford, a man I consider to be devious, insincere, and given over entirely to his own ruthless ambitions."

Morton saw that the crisis had passed, and he had regained control, not only of himself but of the meeting as well. In the manner of one who had already dismissed an irrelevance, he said, "Teddy's all those, sure enough. But he's also vulnerable."

"How so?"

"He's greedy and lazy. Real liabilities. But worst of all, he's a coward. He lays it on heavy, the snorting around as the ruthless, aggressive industrial tycoon, but when you get to know him as well as I do you see he's really a self-indulgent, bullying wimp—all mouth and no balls. Which is surprising, in a way; his father was one tough, hard-swinging dude—as was his grandfather, founder of Bradford Chemicals. But for Teddy there was always a net, ready to catch him if he fell. Big money. An overly protective mother. A screen of sycophants to run interference for him, take the chances, deflect the heat. And among these, I'm the chief of sinners."

Falloon sniffed. "Why have you tied yourself to an idiot like that? Somebody you have so much contempt for?"

"In the beginning it was the need of money. Then it became inertia. Then it became an oddball game of chicken, with me seeing how far I could push him without getting fired and him seeing how far he could push me without my quitting and leaving him to carry the ball on his own. It's a rivalry kind of thing. But now it's a real drag, and I'm looking to peel off."

Falloon gave a moment to deep thought. Then: "Whatever your faults, Morton, you've shown me that you are a man who is willing to share risks with his allies. As a demonstration of your personal confidence and nerve, the ten million is impressive. And I think that your day-to-day management of the whole business is a good idea. You have an excellent reputation in the drug industry. It makes you a logical choice to head up the operation and bring it instant credibility."

Falloon turned his gaze to the sun-drenched reflecting pool outside. Morton shot a quick look at Van Dyke and thought he saw relieved applause in the man's eyes.

Falloon went to the nut. "Are you prepared to put up your ten million dollars now, Mr. Morton?"

"Of course." He took a checkbook from his jacket pocket. "How should I make this out?"

"To Peabody Chemicals."

Morton wrote the check and handed it to Van Dyke. "I'll have the funds transferred to my money market account so that the bank will honor this without delay."

"That won't be necessary. We'll hold the check in escrow until things take better shape and we can work out a final settlement."

Morton struggled against, of all things, a need to giggle. "As you wish," he managed. "The funds will be there when you want them."

Falloon changed the subject. "About this demonstration, Morton: Everything we say or do here depends on our seeing this thing work."

"Naturally."

Falloon glanced at Van Dyke. "Our man Guido has a mother who's dying of cancer, I understand. Where is she?"

"In a nursing home on the Northside somewhere, the last I heard."

Falloon said, "All right. Set it up. Have this man Allenby show us how good his stuff is, how well it works. Peter, buy the nursing home tomorrow and replace its people with ours. Be there. And have Zachary attend the test, too. Allenby isn't likely to try any cute stuff if he knows a fussbudget federal expert's watching. Morton, you supervise and take charge of the video."

Van Dyke put in, "I suggest we put Dr. Pitcairn in charge of the nursing home until we liquidate it, all right? As your personal physician he—"

Falloon nodded. "Good idea, Peter. And I want you to get a head start on the incorporation and banking arrangements. Talk to Paul Downey at Sunrise National in Jacksonville. Tell him to expect Morton's prospectus for the Peabody subsidiary. Set up a meeting."

"All right."

"And provide Morton the encryption matrixes for Peabody's e-mail and faxes. We'll use those for communications on this."

"Very well."

Falloon waved a hand of dismissal. "Keep me informed."

Morton returned to New York, and on the way to the apartment he had the cabbie stop at the Far East, where he picked up a bucket of sweet-and-sour chicken. Showered and in his robe, he ate with chopsticks, directly from the carton, staring out the window at the wintry skyline.

It was about time to drop Gordon Brody into the stew, and he considered various approaches.

Suspense and mystery. They were best. Brody doted on any-thing—literally anything, from news tips to women—that had elements of both.

Morton checked his watch. This should be a good time. Brody, chief anchor for the UBC-TV evening news, would be going off the air about now and heading for his office.

Morton dialed United Broadcasting's Manhattan number, then punched Brody's direct-connect extension.

"Mr. Brody's office."

"George Morton, Lucy. Is Gordon there?"

"Hi, Mr. Morton," Lucy said breezily, "he's just coming in the door. Hold on."

After an interval, Brody's mellow baritone came on the line. "Well, George, long time no see. How the hell are you?"

"Fine, fine. And I know you're okay because I see you every evening, getting jowlier and jowlier, show by show."

"Tell me about it. Makeup people aren't nearly what they used to be." Brody laughed.

"I have an alert for you."

"Business story?"

"Well, in a way. But it's bigger than that. It's very big. Truly network material. International in scope and reach, actually."

"An alert, you say. Can't you give it to me now?"

"Not yet, Gordon. It's still incubating. I'll give it to you twelve hours before it goes into general release."

"You're not talking an embargo, are you?"

"No. I mean you'll have a twelve-hour head start over your opposition. You'll have it on the air when everybody else is just leaving the news conference."

Brody was a fawner. "Sounds good, George. You did the same thing with the Amsterdam cartel thing, and I'll always be grateful. It got me promoted and a raise and a bonus."

"Maybe this one'll do even better for you, eh?"

"I'm sure it'll be chewy stuff. You've never bothered me with crap."

"As soon as it tumbles, I'll get right through to you, no matter where you are or what time it is."

"Okay, George. Appreciate the alert. I'll be waiting to hear from you."

They rang off, and Morton finished up the sweet-and-sour.

12.

On his way to lunch, Morton was inching along in the Main Street traffic when he saw Melanie Flynn striding through the noontime sidewalk crowd. When she disappeared through the entrance to Murphy's Cafeteria he made an impulsive decision, leaving the BMW in the adjacent municipal parking lot and returning to the cafeteria, where he joined the line four customers behind her. She was hungry but prudent, loading her tray with small dishes of green beans, carrots, limas, and spinach, with a chaser of stewed apricots and a glass of ice water. He went for an egg salad on white and a cup of black coffee.

The place was crowded, but she managed to claim a two-seater table in a far corner. Morton ignored singleton seats at several nearby locations and sat in the chair across the table from her.

"*Bon appetit*," he said.

She was less than overjoyed.

"Don't you think you ought to sit at another table?"

"Why?"

"Because I was here first, and it makes me uncomfortable to have you sitting there."

"We're both having lunch. I thought it would be an opportunity to be friendly."

Her dark eyes clouded, and the color in her cheeks deepened. "Now hear this, Mr. Morton: I don't like you, I don't like the way you work, I don't like those you work for, and I don't like your intruding on my lunchtime."

He took a sip of his coffee. "I suppose this means you won't be asking me home to meet your parents."

"I had to tell you what I think," she said, unamused.

"I think you're very nice. I've admired you and your work for a very long time and from a regrettably long distance."

"Why is it I don't believe you?"

"For the same reason you dislike me. Because I work for Teddy Bradford, you assume I am like Teddy Bradford. Which is disappointing, considering that you're a scientist and a practical businesswoman who makes decisions based on carefully established fact."

"Birds of a feather, and all that."

"Whoa." Morton sighed and put down his cup. "By that measure, then, you must be like Anson Lunt—crotchety, morose, withdrawn. The prototypical absentminded professor. Or like Greg Allenby—the self-enamored nerd. Which bird are you like, Dr. Flynn?"

Her eyes grew hot. "Don't get on Greg Allenby's case, dammit. He's difficult at times, but by God, he's loyal and dedicated and ethical. So just back off."

"You have trouble reading people, don't you, Doctor."

"I've got your number, pal."

"So let me hear it. How do you read me?"

She didn't hesitate. "Born into a New England lineage, most likely. Catechized by snobs in big houses with small mortgages. Processed in proper schools where proper associations would lead to proper mating. A father with an Old-Boy linkage to Theodore M. Bradford, the First, founder and spiritual leader of Bradford Chemicals. Hired by Bradford and injected into the management arterial system for the steady rise guaranteed to deft and socially acceptable ass-kissers. Eventual arrival in Executive Alley and emplacement as a howitzer in a deep-carpeted bunker from which rivals—inside the company and out—are either cowed into submission or pounded into professional rubble. How am I doing?"

"You've been rehearsing those lines, haven't you."

"Have I ever. Over and over again."

"But you haven't read any of the *Who's Who*s."

"You aren't that important to me."

"I'm important enough for you to memorize nasty speeches. So why am I not important enough to look up in the books?"

"Just bug off, will you?"

"When I've finished my sandwich."

A stilted pause followed, as if they were listening to the clatter of dishes and bleat of piped music and squawking of babies who wanted nothing more than out of their messy goddam diapers. The wailing took him back to the sad row-house days in Philly, and he had to escape it.

Morton stood, picked up his tray. "I truly like you, Dr. Flynn, and I'd like to be your friend. I'm sorry you won't let me be. Forgive my intrusion. It won't happen again."

He was near the door, clearing his tray, when he realized she was standing beside him.

"Are you driving today, Mr. Morton?"

"My car is in the lot next door."

"I need a ride back to the lab. My car's in the shop, and it's next to impossible to get a cab during the lunch hour in this town."

"Come on."

The taut little truce continued during the drive out Northeast Avenue, the most direct route. They rode in silence, pretending interest in the tackiness all around. It had once been a beautiful area, where regal Victorian homes with turrets and broad porches and stained-glass windows loomed in groves of hundred-year-old oaks. Now the homes were bordellos or saloons or rooming houses, the trees had been replaced by billboards and power poles, and the lawns and gardens had been devoured by strip malls and used-car lots. It never failed to depress Morton.

She stirred in her seat, and said, "If you're so anxious to be pals, why are you muscling me?"

He gave her a sidelong glance. "Muscling?"

"I tell you one day to bug off on buying the Lunt property. The next day a detective pops in and lets me know I'm a suspect in what appears to be Anson Lunt's murder."

"You can't be serious. I don't have any clout with the police."

"You do have clout with the banks."

"What in hell are you getting at?"

"Investors Equity has canceled the Lunt credit line."

He gave her a disbelieving glance. "You think I had something to do with that?"

"You're on the Investors Equity board, aren't you?"

"I play hardball, but those tactics aren't my style. And that's a fact, my dear hard-nosed scientist."

"You better tell your people, then. The credit line was due for renewal. The bank has decided against it." She made quote marks in the air with her fingers. " 'The lab's clouded future, now that Dr. Lunt is gone,' the man said."

"What man?"

"The oily one. Wilmer by name."

"That's all he said?"

She made more quote marks. " 'The many questions regarding Dr. Lunt's death and the tentative position in which it places the whole operation makes your overall financial stability less than certain.' "

"Did you try another bank?"

She shrugged. "I plan to. But these things take time I don't really have."

"Will it affect things at the lab in any way?"

"Well, sure. We buy a huge bunch of supplies, from chemicals to john paper, with money borrowed from the bank."

Morton had known for some time that the Lunt lab had been subsidized over the years by private money—grants, bequests, donations—with the break-even point reached by fees for spe-

cialty piecework ordered by other labs, pharmaceutical companies, foundations, and universities. Then, when Anson decided to
peel off from daily association with the lab to concentrate on cancer research, he'd gotten a huge grant from Alicia Hamilton and
hired Flynn to manage the business. She'd done well, never falling
below the break-even, thanks to strong credit, outside investments, new donors, a corps of clinical outpatients on an as-can-
afford basis, and income from the research and analytical services
provided physicians and other research groups. Flynn had fast-
lane personal credentials, too: magna cum laude in biochemistry,
master's in microbiology, doctorate in pharmacology—fellow in
this, fellow in that. But a credit line was vital to the balance of
things, and without it, she'd need either an alternative source or a
huge increase in her endowments if she hoped to stay in business.

Somebody was setting up a harassment. Who could put that
heavy an arm on bankers? And to accomplish what?

Not Teddy. He'd have nothing to gain, since Flynn would
put Lunt out of business before selling it to him, and Teddy
knew it.

"Do you know Barnaby Falloon?"

"The Manipulator? Heavens no. He's in another galaxy."

"Have you received offers to buy from anybody but me?"

"Nope. Why?"

"I wondered if Falloon or any of his interests had made approaches to you."

"Now there's a fella I'd listen to."

"Bad idea. You think I'm a slick bastard? Falloon makes me
look like Pollyanna's daddy. Credit squeezes are one of his nicer
standard tactics."

She had nothing to say to this. But he gave it some thought.
His proposal to Falloon was still pending, making him no threat
to Falloon. And Falloon needed time if he was planning to cut
him out and shake the Lunt tree himself. Which made no sense
at this stage; Falloon needed him for the grunt work—and his
bet all along was that Falloon wouldn't muscle him out before
the kite was flying.

Who, then? Who was giving Melanie Flynn the elbow?

They finished the ride in silence. He delivered her to the lab, she thanked him for the lift, coolly proper, and he drove off, more than a little peeved.

The Cat's Pee-Jays was a dimly lit, pricey watering hole at the top end of McKinley Avenue, where urban grimy began its mutation into suburban kitsch. Because of its location on the southern perimeter of the shake-shingle, sliding-glass housing tracts that fanned out northward, the place served as a last-chance playpen for homebound breadwinners not yet ready for spousal prime time. During the evening rush hour its parking lot was usually teeming with the middle-aged luxury cars of middle-aged climbers who had not yet climbed high enough to afford the current item. The discord in this evening's rush hour was Morton's huge, Teutonic, top-of-the-line Beemer in arrogant red. For this reason he parked in the shadows of the ornamental shrubs at the far rim of the lot, where he'd be hidden and still able to keep an eye on Bud Wilmer's dark blue Continental.

A manipulator must have patience, because ninety percent of his time is spent waiting for something or somebody. And so Morton considered himself especially blessed, having, as he did, an inborn understanding that time is on the side of the man who waits and that fulfillment is his inevitable reward.

Tonight, though, his patience was running on empty. He was tired, he was hungry, he had to go to the bathroom, and he was plagued by an unanswerable question: How could Wilmer, with three children and a doting mate and a three-hundred-thousand-dollar house no more than two miles away, spend so much time in an armpit like the Cat's Pee-Jays? Even more depressing were those who clustered at the patio bar: archons of Z'ville enterprises—the day's polyester proprieties behind them, hearth and kin awaiting in yonder hills—given now to boozy blathering and furtive gropings.

Wilmer appeared in the café's doorway, lingering with Linda Bianco, whose mouth he ate and whose buttocks he kneaded in extravagant leave-taking.

Morton swung out of the car and quick-stepped through the lot and was standing beside the Continental when Wilmer arrived, fumbling with his key ring.

"Hello, Bud."

"George?"

"Let's get in the car. We need to talk."

"I'm due at home——"

"You were due at home an hour ago. Mrs. Wilmer won't mind waiting dinner another ten minutes."

Wilmer unlocked the doors and climbed behind the wheel. Morton took the front passenger's seat.

"No kidding, George," Wilmer said through a cloud of whiskey fumes, "I really have to burn rubber."

"Answer some questions first, eh?"

"This is harassment, you know——"

"What's so harassing about my asking questions?"

"It's the way you're asking them. One little slip, for crissake, and you'll never let up on me, will you."

"One little slip? Hell, Bud, I just saw you, two minutes ago, giving a state-of-the-art massage to your secretary on the porch of a sleazy saloon. And there are six other so-called slips I've got in my book, not counting that night I caught you pranging a whore in your office."

Wilmer's face was distorted by misery. "Sometimes I think it would have been better if you'd had me fired. At least I wouldn't have you hanging over me like I do."

"I'm not hanging over you. Your conscience is hanging over you. And you should answer my questions out of plain gratitude. As a member of the bank's board, I could have had you crucified. But I didn't make an issue of the matter because I like your wife. She deserves better."

"All right. So what do you want to know?"

"Why did you lift Dr. Flynn's credit line?"

"What?"

"You heard me."

Wilmer whined, "I can't answer that question."

"Why?"

"It's cement-overshoes stuff. One word out of me on that drill, and I'm at the bottom of the Susquehanna."

"We're talking the Mob here, right?"

"You said it, I didn't."

"Who approached you? Where and when?"

"Oh, God—"

"Come on: You can whisper to me or you can get fired and wiped out in a divorce court. The whisper is cheaper and safer. Right?"

"I don't know who the guy was."

"How and when did he approach you?"

Wilmer sighed forlornly. "He made an appointment by phone. Said he was Raymond J. Desmond, an investment broker from Cleveland, and he wanted my advice on a thing here in Z'ville. But when he came into my office, he walked right to my desk and laid them out, straight-up. Photos. Color shots of Linda and me on a motel bed. I have no idea how he got them." He shuddered.

"So then?"

"He was not a chatty guy, believe me. He said he knew Dr. Flynn carried credit with us and he wanted me to write a letter canceling her out. I asked him why, but he just smiled. Then he left, saying he'd see me again sometime. He let me keep the prints, said they were samples of some gorgeous and superexplicit transparencies."

"What did he look like?"

"Hell, I was so shook up I don't really remember. Tall, expensive suit, topcoat. I don't know—"

"Would you know him if you saw him again?"

"I don't know."

"The police have a photo album—a Mafia rogue's gallery. I'll have a copy here tomorrow night at the same time. I want you to look at it and tell me if Mr. Desmond shows up there."

Wilmer groaned. "Oh, come on, George, I'm hosting the Chamber dinner at the Union Club tomorrow night."

Morton swung out of the car. "So I'll see you there."

"George—"

"The Union Club, tomorrow night."

13.

The Union Club was not really a club, nor did it engender much union among Zieglersville's social tongs. But thanks to its centrality and late-nineteenth-century grandeur, the building was a favorite among those agencies and special interest groups that were always looking for excuses to hold seminars and do cocktail networking. Morton had never been comfortable with its gilded columns and rococo furnishings; the smells of age and mold, the shadowy, vaulted ceilings, stirred memories of the do-gooding institutions and arrogant bureaucrats who'd given Uncle Denny so many bad raps for not taking care of him properly.

So now he stood in the mezzanine salon of this building he'd never liked, balancing a highball he didn't want and pretending not to see in the surrounding crush those physicians, surgeons, pharmacists, and hospital notables who had transferred their dislike and fear of Teddy Bradford to him. He had planned to skip the event, pleading business in New York, but Bud Wilmer's involvement had changed his mind. So he pretended to do his duty by the Chamber of Commerce, whose annual Yuletide Charity Party this was, by putting on his black tie and coming by for a glass, aware—but caring not a rat's ass—that he'd be the focus of covert glares and snide asides.

Things turned truly awkward, though, when, in an eddy of

the party's traffic currents, he suddenly found himself nose-to-nose with Alicia. She was stunning in a black sheath, and he felt quick pleasure when he saw that the sole accessory was the gold chain and its baroque locket. As usual, she became instantly oblique, as if fearing that, by looking directly at him, their meeting might appear to be a friendly one. That she continued to be tyrannized by what others might think—an absurdity, considering her Olympian status—was bad enough, but he took it a step further, being more than mildly annoyed by the implication that she cared more about the opinions in the grandstand than she did about the admiration of a principal player like him. After all, there wasn't a man in the room who wouldn't classify her as prime-grade on the Attractive Lure Scale, and no one—man or woman—would be surprised to see the likes of him hovering over her at a party. Or anywhere, for that matter. But Alicia was Alicia, tyrannized by propriety, and so he played her game.

"You look great tonight."

"I saw you come in, and I've been trying to stay clear."

"But you did wear the locket."

She blushed. "It goes well with black."

"I'm surprised you still have it. I'm more surprised that you'd wear it in public."

"No one knows it was a Christmas present from you when we were all openly friendly years ago."

"Well, everybody ought to know. How about I make an announcement? 'Attention, folks: Alicia Hamilton is wearing a gold locket, with her maiden-name initials engraved thereon, given to her, in a fit of extravagant admiration, by George Morton, president of her fan club.' What say?"

"It doesn't help to have you tease me this way."

"Tease? Hell, I'm not teasing. I'm serious. If you're always so worried about what these horses' asses might think, why not tell them, flat out? Then they'll know, and you can stop worrying about them finding out."

She smiled, and it pleased him to see that she hadn't lost her appreciation of the absurd.

"You're a real piece of work, George Morton. And there's no two ways about it: I do miss you. God, how I miss you sometimes." She became quickly serious again. "But then, when you're around, I get upset. I see the unhappiness in your face, and I see what all the rotten years have done to us. How they've changed us—all of us."

He considered that, and in the interval she seemed to realize that she'd painted herself into a corner, and to escape she waved a hand—somewhat theatrically, he thought—and the bespectacled Nurse Cummings, tonight wearing a sensible aqua something, eased through the crowd to take station at her side.

"You remember Amy Cummings, don't you, George?"

He nodded amiably. "I doubt any man could forget her."

The blonde remained stolidly professional. "Is there something I can do, Alicia?"

"I'm getting tired, dear. Will you take me home now, please?"

"Sure." Nurse Cummings took Alicia's elbow in hand and, turning for the door, gave Morton a lingering, enigmatic glance. "Good night, Mr. Morton."

"Good night, Miss Cummings. Take good care of that lady. She's very special to me."

"Not to worry."

The buffet was lavish, and he was standing there, viewing it without enthusiasm, when he got another surprise. Melanie Flynn, resplendent in red and black, materialized beside him.

"Hi," she said.

"Hi."

"I read some backgrounders on you this afternoon. I owe you an apology."

He stared at her, speechless.

"I thought you were to the manner born. I didn't realize that you were—" She groped for the words.

He supplied them. "A Dead End Kid?"

"I was going to say 'a self-made man.' From abandoned child

in the Philly slums to a much-honored Ph.D. and captain of industry—"

There was a moment when he felt a flicker of irritation with himself for being so openly delighted. He'd worked for years to achieve immutable nonchalance, and now, with a few polite words, she was turning him into a blushing schoolboy.

"PR people have a fondness for hyperbole," he said. "I had a lot of help. I couldn't have done it without a kind old man who felt sorry for me and claimed to be my uncle and had nothing to his name but precisely the kind of love I needed. Besides, the experience had its upside: I matured fast, and knew even more at age ten than I do now."

"Well, in the cafeteria I said some pretty tough things. I was being judgmental, and my judgment was terribly wrong. I'm sorry. I'm not usually such an uninformed bitch."

He couldn't help but laugh. "That was one classy apology. People who come right out and admit they might have been wrong are a scarce commodity these days."

She returned a tight smile. "Tell me about it."

Morton handed her a plate, and they attacked the buffet, which he suddenly found to be more inviting. Laying some beef and lettuce on a roll, he said, "I had your credit restored and I'm getting a line on how and why it was lifted. One of the bank's officers is being blackmailed, and for some reason the blackmailer ordered him to cut you off. Any idea why?"

Her glance was quick, sardonic. "I regret to say that in my uneventful life I haven't had the chance to do anything that could be of any possible interest to a blackmailer."

"Not you. The banker. The banker's being blackmailed."

"My statement stands."

He laughed, and they continued to rummage through the goodies, unwilling to shout over the surrounding high-pitched gabbling and canned music and oppressed by the hundreds of competing hair sprays and perfumes.

During a lull, she said, "I can't figure you out. In my office you were so—unlikable, threatening. Now here you are, being nice, helping me—How come?"

"Because I like you very much as a person and admire you as a professional. I told you that in your office, but you were too mad to hear it."

"I still worry about you. You're up to something."

"Welcome to the multitude. You have to wait in line to worry about George Morton."

"God, but it gets to me. All this sneaky stuff. Greed. Ambition. The struggle for ascendancy. You. Credit lines. Detectives watching my every move."

Morton peered across the room and picked out Jacoby, standing by the foyer entrance, uneasy in his rented tuxedo.

Morton smiled. "You really do have trouble reading people, don't you, Dr. Flynn. He's watching your every move, not because he's a cop, but because you absolutely total him."

"You can't be serious."

"Take it from a longtime people watcher: You own that young man."

"You're not only a nerve-wracking enigma, Mr. Morton— you're an outrageous matchmaker."

"Not so. Jacoby is only one of the men who adore you."

She gave him a lingering, penetrating stare. "Now you *are* joking."

"Believe me. I know adore-you when I see it. Been there, done that."

She was surprised, puzzled. "Are you hitting on me?"

He felt the sudden heat in his face. Trying to make a joke, he said, "I know better than to compete with a handsome cop." He took her arm. "Come on. I'll walk you over there. You should take command of your conquest."

"I don't know what to say to a cop. Especially a cop who thinks I'm a murderer."

"He wouldn't be a good cop if he didn't consider that possibility. But he knows you're no murderer. Besides, Jacoby's not just a cop. He's a bright, well-adjusted young man—another scarce commodity in today's society."

*   *   *

Morton checked his watch, and, excusing himself from the tentative conversation begun by Melanie and Jacoby, made for the elevator bay. On the way he traded the ritualistic season's greetings with a group composed of Chief Stabile and his wife and several Chamber types. Bud Wilmer was nearby, turning on the charm for Gladys Malloy, the furniture factory owner, and Morton gave him the signal. Then he boarded an elevator and punched the all-the-way-down button.

Burroughs had provided him with a copy of the make-album on the regional Mafia, which he'd placed in the trunk of the BMW, along with his golf bags and skeet accessories, and Wilmer was to come by for as long as it took to scan the pictures for a possible ID on Raymond Desmond.

It wasn't clear to Morton just what he would do if Wilmer did show him the man. Falloon had no known connection with the Mafia, but was reputed to have enlisted the Mob's help on occasion. And to confront Falloon for any reason at this stage would be to forfeit the game, because Falloon would surely avoid a deal with a man who suspected him—even before the handshake—of a double cross. But, he'd worked his way around a lot of double crosses in his lifetime, so there was no reason to believe that he couldn't beat this one—if Falloon was indeed trying to screw him. Intuition told him that Falloon wasn't, that Falloon was depending on him to get the trick in motion, but he was backing his hunch with some work by Burroughs. Just to be sure.

The garage was dim and cold, and in the half-light the ranks of cars seemed like animals standing, numb and silent, in the dankness of some godforsaken barn. His car was parked in Reserved Slot 10, which was only a few feet from the elevator bay. He was moving the album from the trunk to the front seat when an elevator door sighed open and Wilmer stood there, huddling against the chill and blinking into the gloom.

"Over here." Morton waved and slid behind the wheel.

Wilmer turned up the collar of his dinner jacket and, looking like an elegant panhandler, came to the car and climbed into the front passenger seat. As Morton slowly leafed through the album, he kept shaking his head, making soft negative sounds.

"None of them, eh?" Morton said at the end.

"No. I don't recognize any of those faces. Not one. Like I told you: I think the guy was from out of town."

Morton stared at him through the dim light. "Why is it I don't believe you, Bud?"

"Well, that's just too bad." Wilmer put on a good show of indignation. "You asked me to look at the pictures, I looked at the pictures. What do you expect me to do—pick out one of those goons just to satisfy you?"

"Not just this. I don't believe you big-time. About anything. Why is that?"

"I'm going home." Wilmer, his face showing mixed anger and fear, swung out of the car, slammed the door behind him, and made for his Continental, which was parked, nose out, at the top of the down ramp.

Morton threw the album into the backseat, and watched as Wilmer's car blossomed into light and voomed down the ramp, a straight shot of concrete leading to the River Street exit.

His irritability became incredulousness as the big sedan not only failed to slow for the checkout window but actually picked up speed. Smashing its way through the wooden lift gate, the car raced unswervingly across River Street, bounced over the far curbing, slewed sideways, tore through the ornamental riverwalk railing, and rolled twice in the air before it plunged, upside down, into the ice-covered Susquehanna.

14.

Jacoby's office was a cubicle of translucent plastic in a second-floor corner of the police building. Morton sat on a hard chair beside the one window, looking around and pretending not to listen as Jacoby wound up a phone conversation with someone named Doc. There was a tin desk piled high with file folders, a tin cabinet choked with manuals and indexes and reference books, and a tin table that supported a computer terminal whose primitive screen showed a noncommittal amber menu. A coat tree, a wall calendar matted with paste-up memos, and a stock photo of a palm-lined tropical beach, which had been framed in dime-store brass and propped next to the phone, and that was it.

After a time he placed the phone carefully on its cradle and gave Morton a polite smile. "Sorry to keep you waiting. Mornings tend to get pretty busy around here."

"No problem."

"Are you all right?"

"Certainly. Why?"

"You seemed to be sort of, ah, shaken, when I saw you in the parking garage last night."

"I'm not accustomed to having business associates say good

night, then drive straight over a cliff into the river and die. I'm
sorry it showed."

Jacoby nodded sympathetically and offered coffee. Morton
shook his head, so Jacoby flicked on the tape recorder on the
desk and told it who he was, the date and time, and who was
giving the following statement. Morton gave his Social Security
number and where he lived and what he did for a living. And
then he added a question. "How come a homicide detective is
questioning people about a one-car automobile accident?"

"Because we want to be sure it was an accident."

"Well, why wouldn't it be?"

Jacoby ignored the question by changing the subject. "You
were a close friend of Mr. Wilmer, the deceased?"

"No. He was a vice president of Investors Equity Bank. I'm
a board member there. I knew him mainly in that connection."

"So what were you two doing in the parking garage?"

"I told you last night."

"Tell me again, please."

"We were attending the Chamber of Commerce party upstairs. I had something in my car I wanted him to look at, so
we went down to the garage."

"What did you want him to look at?"

"A document."

"What kind of document?"

"A rogues' gallery. We were trying to identify a guy who
called himelf Raymond Desmond. He'd tried to rip off the bank
recently. We were trying to get a line on him as soon as possible, because he was due to show up again the next day."

"Why hadn't you called the police about Desmond?"

"Because we weren't sure of our suspicions. The last thing
we want to do is face a lawsuit for improper arrest, or whatever."

"So what happened?"

"I got to the car first. When I saw Mr. Wilmer coming from
the elevator bay, I called to him, and he came over and sat in
the front seat beside me."

"You didn't go down to the garage together?"

"As I say, I went first. He came a few minutes later."

"Why?"

"He was talking with some people, and so I went on ahead. No reason other than that."

"Did you see anybody else in the garage?"

"No. It was very quiet there."

"So what happened then?"

"We finished our discussion and he left my car, saying he was going home. I decided I'd go home, too, but I waited for Wilmer to leave first. His car was parked at the top of the ramp and I wanted him out of the way before I backed out of my slot."

"Did you notice anything unusual about his car as he left?"

"No. He just started the motor, turned on the lights, and went straight down the ramp."

"Did he make an effort to stop, or to maneuver in any way?"

"Not that I could see. Just straight down the ramp and—woosh—out across the street, over the sidewalk, through the railing, and into the river. I called nine-one-one on my cell phone, and that was it. In a few minutes the place was teeming with cops, including you."

"Do you think it was an accident, Mr. Morton?"

"What else?"

"Suicide, maybe?"

Morton shook his head. "Not to speak disrespectfully of the dead, but I don't think Wilmer was the type. He was too much in love with his body to destroy it deliberately."

"What do you mean by that?"

"He was a hedonist. He lived for physical gratification. And he was weak, morally and spiritually."

"He had a reputation as a wencher. Did you know that?"

"Of course. I know a lot of things about a lot of people, especially people who work for banks I'm in good measure responsible for."

"Do you think one of his girlfriends might have gotten tired of not being the only one in his life?"

"What difference does it make what I think about that?"

"How about Mrs. Wilmer?"

"What about her?"

"Was she known to be bitter about her husband's, ah, indiscretions?"

"Are you suggesting that she might have sabotaged her husband's car, or something?"

"I'm not suggesting anything. I'm asking."

"All I know is that Mrs. Wilmer adores her children. It's my guess that she's always known her husband was a rake but endured that humiliation to keep a home for the kids. She's a lovely woman who goes to any length to make her marriage work."

"Back to the document, Mr. Morton, that copy of the Mafia Personalities ID Index I glimpsed on the backseat of your car."

"What about it?"

"Where did you get that copy, Mr. Morton?"

"No comment."

"That's a police document. It's not for public use."

"Not so, Sergeant. The police work for the public—the taxpayers. So all police documents not considered evidence in ongoing, confidential criminal investigations are public documents. The Mafia index is not evidence—it's a reference, often shown to citizens in the course of a policeman's day. So anybody has the right to see it."

"But not to take it from headquarters."

"Do you want to test that in court?"

Jacoby turned a page in his notebook. "There are two other matters I'd like to ask you about, Mr. Morton."

"Ask away."

"How much do you know about Linda Bianco?"

"Very little, actually. She's employed by Investors Equity, serves as Wilmer's secretary. I don't get into those personnel things."

"Was she one of Wilmer's playmates?"

"I had that impression, yes. Why?"

"She was found dead in her apartment this morning. In her shower. Her skull was fractured."

Jacoby watched Morton closely, presumably for evidence of shock, or the lack of it. He wasn't disappointed. Morton was indeed shocked, and he let it show. "That's—terrible."

"Yes."

"Did she slip and fall?"

"It has all the earmarks of a bathroom accident. She was naked on the tiles, the water still running. But we're keeping our minds open on that."

"You think it ties in with the Wilmer accident?"

"I'm asking you."

As Morton sat there, dealing with this, Jacoby said, "My second question is this: Did you know that Dr. Melanie Flynn was arrested for drunken driving after leaving the Chamber thing?"

Morton showed him some more shock. "Come on. Melanie Flynn? Drunk? She's a teetotaler. Everybody knows that."

"Well, her car was found on the causeway around ten last night by a prowl car crew. She was barely conscious in the driver's seat. She was incoherent. Reeked of booze."

"How could that be?"

"She claims she was driving across the causeway when a small white car sideswiped her. When she got out to check the damage, the white car's occupant—a tall man in a parka—knocked her down, injected her with something that made her groggy, put her back in her car, then poured booze all over her. The cops took her to St. Vincent's, and the ER people confirmed that she wasn't legally drunk and had been sapped and injected."

"So why are you telling me all this, Sergeant?"

"Dr. Flynn says you've been harassing her."

"Jesus. I don't believe this. All I've done is offer to buy her company. That's harassment?"

"It's like when someone complains to the police about a neighbor's barking dog. We go and ask the neighbor for his side of the story so that we can get a line on what's going on and maybe work out an amicable solution."

"Well, just exactly what is Dr. Flynn's complaint? My barking dog?"

"No, sir. She says that since she rejected your offer to buy her company, her bank credit has been impaired, she's been subjected to false and damaging rumors, and she's actually been accosted and physically assaulted by someone who tried to have her jailed on a DUI. She says she believes you have something to do with all that."

"Well, now, Sergeant, I'm truly sorry to hear that Dr. Flynn's been having such a lousy time. She's a fine woman, talented and capable, and although my company is among her competitors in certain areas, I personally admire the hell out of her. So you can believe this: Even if it were a policy of my company to act in such a rotten manner, I'd be the very last to try to damage her in any way. But that is not my company's policy. My company simply wishes to expand its operations—and in no way wants to endanger or harm a lovely woman."

"All right, sir, I appreciate your comments. It seems to me that there's a misunderstanding here. Maybe you and Dr. Flynn can get together sometime soon and work this out to your mutual satisfaction. Meanwhile, I thank you for your time."

"Is that all?"

"Yes, sir. That's it."

Morton was so furious he did not go to the airport, where the company plane was waiting to return him to New York. Instead he drove back to the house and faxed a message to Peter Van Dyke, care of Peabody Chemicals:

You understand that the lady doctor is not to be personally inconvenienced in any manner. This is an absolute condition of our agreement.

An answer came in while he was making fresh coffee.

Your fax was most confusing. We have no intention of inconveniencing the doctor.

15.

Morton decided against going back to New York and holed up at the house for the rest of the day. He seemed uncommonly tired and dispirited, and the idea of food repelled him. So he sat in the library's deep leather chair and alternately dozed and stared unseeingly at the TV's news and weather channel. Somewhere in the afternoon he fell soundly asleep and didn't awake until midevening.

His loneliness was intense, so he gave it the usual treatment.

Personal computers—one in the apartment, the two here in the Z'ville house—were Morton's family.

For a long time, with Uncle Denny gone, he'd had some pretty heavy bouts with the demoralizing realization that there wasn't anybody, anywhere, to share whatever he was and hoped to be. Worse, the only one he'd ever really wanted to share it with remained maddeningly out of reach. Over the years he had developed many acquaintances, of course, but they all were soldiers in the vast campaigns of corporate warfare and therefore beyond any possible intimacy—as in military life, where it never paid to have a close friend because he might be promoted beyond your handshake or killed before your eyes, leaving you in either case with resentment and heartbreak.

Some sort of compensation came with the advent of the in-

formation highway and the on-line communities. With his PC
and the Net, he could go almost anywhere and share with anybody—anonymously and without commitment. The machine
had confirmed his suspicion that the very damned world itself
was an enormous colony of lonely people and that everywhere,
at any moment, legions needed a bit of listening to, a little
bucking up, a touch of reassurance. Yet there was a paradox:
The universal need for attention and tenderness was outweighed
by a universal fear of involvements that could lead to loss and
hurt. So in the cybersociety, real names and addresses were
usually hidden; contrived screen names were enough. What mat-
tered was the chatter itself, the back-and-forth, the sense that
somebody equally lonely was really out there and paying attention to whatever the hell he was saying.

But this night, full of an unspecific anger, he was in no mood
for the social crap. So instead of going on-line, he went Peeping
Tom, activating the surveillance computer in the den to see what
might be new in Sergeant Jacoby's notes.

The sergeant was skeptical of the consensus that said Wilmer's death was an accident. The car had been hoisted from the
river bottom, but the AI team said its front end and general
systems were so severely damaged it was unlikely that tampering
could be proved. Routine inquiries had been placed with the
FBI and other agencies to see if Bud Wilmer and Linda Bianco
had police histories. A backgrounder noted that, during his in-
terrogation, "George Morton appeared to be hiding something."
In interviews, three whores admitted they'd known Wilmer as
a client but knew nothing about him as a person.

Even more angry, he switched channels to see what might be
going on at the Lunt laboratory. Faintly surprised to find everything lit up, he sat for a time in the glow of the screen and
marveled again at the extraordinary energies and agonies un-
leashed by human greed.

From his frantic midnight surfing, it was clear that Allenby
was puzzled and worried.

Morton imagined Allenby at the console of the main lab computer bank, immersed in the soft light and the gentle sounds.

He could feel Allenby's exasperation as the screen kept returning to the root "Patient Records—Read Only" menu. He watched Allenby's impatient flitting to the LUNT-PERSONAL band, which, when entered, opened to the subdirectory Lunt had designated simply—and inscrutably—"Genes Database."

Only no further access was offered.

The screen would display nothing more than a command, ENTER PASSWORD, and Morton was grimly amused at what this would do to Allenby's thin defenses against his own fiery impatience.

To Allenby it must appear that Anson Lunt had been driven by a paranoid determination to keep his research secure. Yet, ironically, it was Lunt, utilizing funds originated by Alicia Hamilton, who had brought his patient study records, as well as all historical-chemical data derived from work undertaken in the biotech lab, into space-age electronic storage. On the face of it, the system he devised was an enormous blessing for those who toiled in his lab: It stored in a central computer a complete inventory and historical digest of all the drugs, major and minor, that had been tested or sophisticated in the lab, as well as an interfacing network with databases maintained by major hospitals, research laboratories, and cooperating drug companies in Europe and South America. It also provided participating personnel with office terminals via which all the information on each of the patient cases and research subjects figuring in a drug's development—physical data, medical history, genetic characteristics, allergies, and idiosyncratic reactions to specific earlier treatments, along with graphics and pertinent X rays— could be called up and read in a matter of seconds.

But as part of all this, Anson Lunt also had established and encrypted an isolated sector for his personal cancer research and its attendant studies. Access to these files had been denied to all but Lunt himself, thanks to a code based on what appeared to be an elaborate series of passwords. Morton watched as Allenby worked his way through the chain of enigmatic directories and, with a bit of luck, found the file that carried the base. He had done instant printouts and now presumably had in his safe at home a refined consolidation of all the data contained on the floppies—the cancer formula's chemical profile, history of its development, and drawings and descriptions of the specialized hardware Lunt had fabricated for its manufacture. He could also read the medical case histories of the several hundred patients who had verified the drug's effectiveness under FDA's 1989 expedited process—since amended and streamlined even more—which sped up and simplified clinical trials for drugs that showed early promise in treating life-threatening illnesses.

Gallingly missing were the taming data. Unless he could get to those, Allenby was held virtually on Square One.

Morton knew what the problem was. It was directly comparable to the "unlocking enzyme" critical to the original Vitam. When Vitam came in contact with this enzyme a toxicity was generated—a poison that was lethal to no cells but cancer cells. What Allenby seemed to be doing was reinventing Vitam and running with it all the way to the point where the unlocking enzyme shot off into new territory, leaving him with no directions on how to follow to the new, improved Vitam.

Morton sighed and shook his head.

There was even a moment of what might have been pity for the wretched Allenby and his star-crossed family, but Morton subdued it with a yawn and the inward reminder that Allenby was a self-winding jerk who deserved everything he got, including the loss of a wife who could no longer stand him and kids he'd never bothered to know.

The next morning he arose at seven as usual, was back in his plant office at nine, and put in a pile of work until noon, when he closed the door and used his personal cellular to dial Charles Hamilton.

Hamilton's business day was based on Continental time, since Le Tellier, Cie., the hub of his European operations, was headquartered in Paris, and so real-time communications with headquarters had to conform (much to the tacit annoyance of his people in the outlands). At noon, Eastern Standard Time, the

Le Tellier offices were closing for the night, which, Hamilton had explained, was the best time to get the top dogs, fond as they were of opening their office bars and hanging about and talking over the day. Which made it the best time to get him, too, because he'd be at his e-mail, chat rooms, and faxes in Palm Strand.

"Hamilton."

"This is George Morton."

"Are you on an office phone?"

"No. My cellular."

"Office phones make me uneasy. Too many opportunities for eavesdropping." He paused. "I see by the paper you were embroiled in a traffic scrape the other night."

"I was standing in a garage, watching a man drive to his death in the river. I was not embroiled in anything."

"Bad publicity. You should avoid such incidents."

"It wasn't my idea, believe me."

"So what's on your mind, George?"

"I called to tell you that my informant in the FMAA has reviewed the Allenby formula and pronounces it valid."

"So it's legitimate, then, eh?"

"Pure gold. And Allenby's about to sell it to Teddy Bradford."

"That leaves the cartel with only two choices: make a preemption, or make propaganda."

"Yes, that's so."

"Which do you recommend?"

"If I were you, I'd be very much against preemption. It would be messy and hugely expensive."

"It would, on the other hand, put a quick and decisive end to the threat the formula represents."

"And leave open the possibility that somebody else will come up with yet another formula, then another, and another. My FMAA informant says the product is readily derived and easily cloned. I think the only logical route is the one we followed when dealing with Lunt the first time: Smother the formula in ridicule and misinformation. That way you not only put an end to it, you automatically negate any derivatives."

"To do that, we first have to let it become public."

"Yes."

"Allowing Teddy to introduce it?"

"Yes. And then rolling out all the white-coat-and-stethoscope types to denounce the stuff; cutting loose the media specialists; launching the hate mail and word-of-mouth; opening a government campaign to ban the formula or any of its derivative imports."

"I assume, then, that you've already taken steps to see that the introduction takes place, right?"

"No. I'm waiting to see what you want."

"All right. I'll call a meeting of my European people. I'll want you to attend, too, to field questions. I'll let you know when the date's set. Meanwhile, I want you to keep in touch with me at least once a day."

"Very well. But make the meeting soon. Time's running fast toward out."

"Anything else?"

"I insist that, whether you decide to preempt or make propaganda, Dr. Flynn be most carefully protected. Either way, she can serve as a useful patsy. We must consider her to be an asset, and we can't afford to have her hurt."

"I don't follow your thinking. To me, she looks like an impediment."

"I just don't want her hurt."

There was a pause, then Hamilton chuckled softly. "Ah. Good old celibate George has a passion for the beautiful doctor, eh? The man of stone at last has a hard-on, eh?"

Morton's anger was huge, but he contained it. "It's nothing personal."

Hamilton was conciliatory. "Hey, I don't care if you have the hots, George. Have fun. Enjoy. Just don't let it get in the way of our thing."

"We need her. Trust me."

"If I didn't trust you, we wouldn't be having this conversation."

"That's a two-way street, Charles."

"All right. But there's also something I must insist on. I want to talk to your FMAA source. I want to hear him tell me the Allenby formula is legitimate."

"I thought you trust me."

"Don't be so damned touchy. My Paris bankers are going to want to know if I can swear to the formula's validity. I must be able to stare them in the eye and say that I have spoken with an unimpeachable government source and have received unconditional technical confirmation. Otherwise, this whole thing is dead in the water."

"Well, you can understand why I'm reluctant to give out the name of my most valuable paid informant. He's very high in the FMAA pecking order and is as skittish as a cat. He could very well dry up on me."

"I'm quite skilled in these kinds of encounters, George. His skittishness will be soothed by a handsome bonus."

"Well, then, here's the drill: We will be having a demonstration of the formula within a week. It will be attended by my informant. I'll e-mail you as soon as it's over. And at that time you can call Dr. Andrew Zachary on extension eighty-three forty-seven at the FMAA, Washington. Identify yourself as Mr. Holmes. Ask him what you want. But I must warn you that Zachary doesn't enjoy complete privacy, so he won't be likely to welcome any long or elaborate discussions."

"Holmes is a code name, I take it."

"Yes. Both to authenticate and to protect you."

"You understand that I really have to do this, don't you, George?"

"I understand it. But I don't like it."

After hanging up, Morton went to the window and stood, thinking for a time. Then he returned to the desk and dialed Zachary at the FMAA.

"I hate it when you call me here." Zachary's whine sounded

as if he were speaking through a cupped hand. "It's risky, and I hate it."

"And I hate it when you pop little surprises on me, like the meeting in Philly. Like not telling me about your tie-in there."

"I don't have to tell you everything. You don't own me."

"Correction: I own everything you are and got. And if you want to test me, I hope the court allows you a minimum security prison. Although with your secret track record it's unlikely."

Zachary said nothing for a moment. When he spoke, retreat was in his voice. "Well, I'm due at a meeting in three minutes. What's on your mind?"

"You will be getting a call from a Mr. Holmes after the Allenby formula demo. Answer his questions, but tell him only the basics. No improvising. No speeches."

"I'm a scientist, not an orator."

Snotty civil servants annoyed the hell out of Morton. He was especially annoyed when the snotty civil servant was a hugely corrupt horse's ass. "I don't care what you call yourself, Zachary. Just do as I say."

After ringing off, Morton sat there, sipping coffee and smiling to himself.

Since he'd recommended so strongly against it, Hamilton would be sure to preempt. Hamilton was such an egotistical son of a bitch he never followed anybody's recommendations, except, when it pleased him, those of Gerda von Reichmann, his talented mistress.

Achilles' Heel Department, eh?

16.

The Hayloft was a wine-and-dinery fashioned from what had once been a dairy barn. It was a multilevel red thing that sat on a knoll overlooking a sweep of country favored by the fox-hunting crowd. Patrons sat in stalls, surrounded by oil lamps, saddles and hanging harnesses. The chef was an artist, the wait-staff was skilled, the combo was trendy, and, to Jacoby, the prices read like license plates. It was the haunt of younger locals who would pay any price to look hip, but Jacoby came by only on special occasions—partly because he was running on a very lean money mixture, but mainly for fear he'd meet some of the people who'd been at him all day and be compelled to suffer more of their whining with his dining.

Elena liked the place, though, so for her he made an exception. Arriving first, he jollied Felix, the maître d', into giving him a booth in a corner removed from the mainstream clatter. He was nursing a dusty martini and admiring the winter sunset through a cutesy window, when she materialized beside him, smiling her curiously attractive lopsided smile.

"Hi, Jake."

He stood and helped her to a seat. "You look gorgeous, as usual."

She slipped the tailored topcoat from her shoulders and patted her lustrous black hair. As she settled in, she looked him over—warm, direct, amiable. "So do you."

"What are you drinking?"

She nodded at his martini, and he signaled the waiter. As the man made for the bar, Jacoby thanked her for coming. She shrugged an elegant shoulder. "I have a date at seven-thirty. Until seven is yours."

Elena's income came from upscale philanderers, who paid her thousand-dollar-a-night freelance fee, first, because she was classy and immaculate, and, second, because she was discreet—never hinting that she was for sale and never recognizing those who had bought. Introductions were always in order, even if the man had left her bed twenty minutes earlier. She could have based her operation in any city in the world, but her choice was Z'ville because her ailing mother and teenage brother (who thought she got her money from modeling) lived there and needed her. She wasn't your run-of-the-mill stoolie, either; she would talk to Jacoby at any time and about any subject for one reason only: He'd pulled in some markers to pave the way for her kid brother's admission to Boone Hill, the snooty Paoli prep school.

"How's Carlo?"

Her face, heart-shaped and golden, became a study in pleasure. "Super. Just super. He's getting top grades, has made the rowing crew, and—get this—has been nominated for class president."

"Cool." Her delight over all this was contagious, and he felt a glow of his own. "Some things work out right, eh?"

She reached across the little table and squeezed his hand. "We owe you a lot, Carlo and I."

"You owe me only one thing: Don't get busted. It would complicate our relationship. Worse, it would screw up a damned smart kid who's on his way."

She gave Jacoby one of her lingering stares. After a time she pantomimed a smooch, then signaled a change of subject by patting his hand. "So why did you call?"

"Things are going on in my life, and I need some answers. You might have a couple."

She waited, her dark eyes solemn.

"I need to get a line on a bank artist who's been around town the last couple days. Likely to be well-heeled and looking for action."

The waiter brought her martini, and she gazed at it for a moment, her eyes strangely sad, as if remembering something she'd rather forget. "Tell me about him."

"Bank people tell me the name he uses is Raymond Desmond. Claims to be an investment broker from Cleveland. Tall, dark hair, expensive clothes. I'm guessing he's the kind who likes flashy hotels and the health club scene."

She thought about that. "I get no reading. Besides, most Johns like to put on more dog than that. I mean, like Vegas, or L.A., or Chi. Cleveland is to yawn."

"Well, do me a favor and keep your radar going."

She took a sip of her drink.

"Something else, El: Have you picked up any jungle drums on Dr. Anson Lunt?"

She gave a moment to thought. "The gossip, the stuff in the papers. And what Bill Rooney told me. Know something? The doctor sort of interested me—the way he seemed to go about his business no matter what the papers and TV were saying about him. A kind of in-your-face guy, you know? The world is filled with wimps these days, but Lunt came off as someone who didn't blink when it hit the fan." She laughed softly. "I told Bill I'd like to meet the doctor someday, but Bill said I'd be wasting my time—Lunt was on the rebound and had some female action in New York to kill the pain, like. Bill said it didn't seem to help the guy much, though, because he just got grumpier each trip."

"You were one of Rooney's pals?"

"Not really. The only time I ever spent with him was in his airplane. High-roller Johns like to import me, so they'd hire Bill to fly me to the action. New York, Florida, Chicago, even L.A.

a couple of times. I spent a lot of time with Bill, to and from. We talked, you know?"

"Where in Florida?"

She hunched a shoulder. "Beats me. All of Florida looks the same to me. I just got on the plane, chatted with Bill, read some magazines, snoozed, then went to the car when the motors stopped. A hugely rich dude was entertaining some cannons from Europe, and one of them wanted to know what American women are really like. So I got the call."

"You must be something else, to be known all around the country like that."

"Horniness knows no boundaries, as the saying goes."

"Rooney waited, then flew you back from these tricks?"

"Mostly. This time they fixed him up with a girl, and we left together when the party was over."

"So what did Rooney tell you about Lunt?"

"He said that on their trips to and from New York, Lunt was like me. I often sat in the right-hand seat in the cockpit because being back in the cabin was too lonely. Lunt felt the same way, I guess, and so he'd sit up there with Bill, and they'd talk—not a lot, because Lunt was a cold fish, aloof, sort of."

"What's this about action in New York?"

"It was Bill's notion that Lunt was carrying the torch for that rich society do-gooder who gave his lab a pile of money. You know—Alicia Hamilton, the one who's got her picture in the paper all the time. Bill says Hamilton would drive Lunt to the airport a lot, and it was clear that he had a be-e-e-g thing for the lady, but she wasn't able to handle it."

"Clear? How come?"

"He overheard them talking in the hangar one time. She was really upset, Bill said—going on real hard about how she was a married woman and no matter how much her husband ignored her and abused her and no matter how crazy she was about someone else she wasn't about to leave him because her religion wouldn't allow it, period. And Lunt kept telling her she was plain nuts to throw away her life, and they went at it pretty hot there for a while. Finally, Lunt stormed around looking for Bill and told him to crank up the plane and take him to New York, where at least one person cared enough to listen to him."

"What kind of guy was Rooney?"

She thought a moment. Then: "I'm no shrink, but my vibes told me Rooney was a phony. Slick and phony."

"So you didn't like him?"

"Oh, I liked him. He was slick, but, what the hey, most guys who patronize women like me are slick—make like they're hot stuff because they seriously doubt they are, if you know what I mean. What was different about Bill was he was a gentleman. He never talked dirty or tried to feel me up, like so many men do. We had good, serious discussions."

"Did Lunt ever talk to Rooney about his problems—being branded a quack, and all that?"

"Well, yeah. Bill said this one night Lunt was really down, and he told Bill that his whole life had been spent in the boonies. In the world's boonies. In his profession's boonies. He said he'd gone through a whole lifetime of busting his butt to do something great, and all it had gotten him was a reputation as a quack, selling snake oil from the back of a wagon. Rooney said the guy seemed so sad and lonely he got depressed himself."

The idea sobered them, and they made a business of sipping their drinks and listening to the combo.

"Is there anything I can do for you, El? Do you or Carlo need anything?"

She smiled, throwing off the mood. "There is one thing."

"What's that?"

"That music. It's me. How about a dance?"

The music was lilting Latin, and the martini was doing warm things in him. To his own surprise, he stood and took her hand. "I'm the world's lousiest dancer. So you lead, and I'll hang on."

She laughed. "Hey, we're not talking Astaire stuff here. We're talking bouncing and wriggling."

"Well, wriggling's my specialty. Let's go."

*   *   *

The lounge was dimly lit and busy, its dance floor moderately crowded, and as they bounced and wriggled he realized he was having fun. Elena, in her element, was a study in uninhibited delight, and it occurred to him that if he was to make a fool of himself, he was lucky to be doing it with a beautiful woman who expected nothing else or anything better from him. And it was at the height of all this that he found himself momentarily staring straight into Melanie Flynn's eyes. She was alone at a lamplit table close by the dance floor, and her expression was built of amused disbelief.

"Well, hi," he managed.

"Hi."

And then he spun about and bounced away in the wake of his joyously wriggling stoolie.

After waving Elena off in her red Camaro, Jacoby hurried back to the lounge and was pleased to see Dr. Flynn ordering dessert. He adjusted his tie and smoothed his hair, then crossed the room and stood beside the waiter.

"The lady will be having dessert at my table," he said.

"Says who?" she said, poker-faced.

"I have a warrant."

She glanced at the waiter, who waited unhappily, pencil poised over pad. "I'll have the mousse. Bring it and my bill to the gentleman's cell over there in the corner."

"How did you know where—"

"I saw you when you arrived."

As the waiter turned to leave, Jacoby said expansively, "And bring us coffee."

When they had settled in, she said, "You are an interesting man. In my office, you're law enforcement's answer to Baron von Richthofen. At the Union Club, you're Jimmy Stewart. In the roadhouse, you're Joe Fosse. Which one am I looking at now?"

He ignored the question and asked one of his own. "How come you're here alone?"

"I wasn't supposed to be. I got stood up."

"Whoever he is, I owe him."

"Well, now. That sounded like Ashley Wilkes."

"The guy who shot Lincoln?"

They traded smiles.

"I was supposed to meet Ruff Cobb for a drink. He wanted to talk over my Chamber committee assignment. He got called out of town at the last minute. I decided to have dinner anyhow."

"Good ole Ruff."

They listened to the music for a time.

"Who was the girl?"

"Elena Hernandez. I've known her for years. I bought her a drink while she waited for her date tonight."

"She's stunning. And she adores you."

"What you saw was gratitude. I've done her some favors, that's all."

"Whatever you say."

The waiter brought the mousse and coffee, but she had apparently decided against the dessert, pushing it aside. They pantomimed a toast with their cups and pretended to listen to the music again. He used the interval to note how her profile was an interesting composition of gentle curves, of smooth lights and darks, and how her lips—full, deep pink, and erotic—were the most compelling feature of a truly remarkable face. He was fascinated most, though, by a question: How did she manage it? In a world directed by media standards, female beauty was solely physical—shining hair, shadowed eyes, glistening teeth, unblemished skin, rake-handle figure, and couture; intellect and spirit were matters best left to academicians and preachers and had no relevancy to deodorants and panty hose. So how could this woman conform to the stereotype so satisfactorily and yet manage to communicate so much character? By anyone's standards, she was gorgeous, sure as hell; but how come, when looking at her and the pleasant interplay of all the nice physical details, he would also see integrity, guts, and wisdom?

"Tell me something," she said. "What does a homicide detective do when he's not working? Alone in his digs."

"This one plays with a computer—an ancient box declared surplus by the police department right after the War Between the States. A quill pen is speedier. But it has a good capacity, and I have fun with it."

"Doing what?"

"Networking. Ambling down the Information Highway. What does a biochemically trained mousse fan do?"

"Watercolors."

"You studied art, too? It's not in your write-ups."

"Not formally." She sipped some coffee, then said over the cup's rim, "When I was in my early teens and too gawky for self-esteem, too insulated by my daddy's money—we spent a summer in a big old house on the Maine coast." She returned the cup to its saucer. " 'Good for our souls,' Daddy said, 'isolation, salt breezes, gulls crying, surf pounding at the foot of the cliff, the sense of wilderness amalgamating with contemporary comforts, the stuff of personal renewal'—precisely the kind of flapdoodle a kid with exploding gonads doesn't want to hear. I was a good little girl, didn't complain much, but, boy, did I get bored."

"No villages around? No barn dances?"

She smiled. "If there were, I surely didn't know about them. I doubt I'd have been permitted to go to them, even if I had known."

"Your parents were all that tough?"

"Heck no. They never wanted anything but the best for me. But they always seemed to regard me as a cutesy, doll-size Ayn Rand. Which meant they didn't think of me in terms of barn dances. They thought of me in terms of pinafores and straight A's in the Fundamentals of Individualism and the American Experience, as taught at Miss Murgatroyd's School for Refined Women."

He nodded. "So in rebellion you started drawing pictures of naked dudes?"

She laughed. "I would have if I'd known how. But one day in the attic of the big old house—we'd taken it furnished—I found a chest full of water-based paints and how-to books, apparently left behind by the owner's kid. I began dabbling to ease my loneliness, and I've been at it ever since."

"Have you ever sold your work?"

She laughed again. "No. It takes a lot of savvy and time and effort to show and sell art. You've got to be a real pro, and I've already got a career going. So art-wise, I remain a dabbler. How about you? Did you get into computers when you were a lonely little boy enduring a dreary summer?"

"Winter, actually. I was ten, whiling away the hours in Uncle Schnitzel's snowbound Tyrolean mansion, allowing my ski accident to heal. I'd finished reboring the cylinders in the Benz limousine and was looking for something to do when I came upon a cobwebbed IBM in the wine cellar—I was precocious, drinking-wise—and after a few hours of familiarization, I invented a software graphics program for the admirers of naked girls. It's still selling madly, mail-order out of Copenhagen."

"Seriously, what's your story? How did you get into detective work?"

"I'd like to be all kinds of dramatic here, but I can't, because I just sort of fell into this business. All I can report is a normal childhood in a well-adjusted middle-class family where I was loved and expected to take out the trash on Fridays and given an allowance. Good marks in high school, an ROTC scholarship, and easy graduation from Penn State with a degree in journalism, then to the army, where, because they thought journalists are investigators, they trained me as a military policeman. After OCS, I got in some real good police work in the field, both Stateside and with the NATO detachment in Brussels. I was promoted to First John, then to captain when I was assigned as the aide to a horse's ass of a provost marshal because he thought I looked cute opening car doors for him and talked classy when introducing him to chicks at embassy cocktail receptions. But I'd developed a real interest in police work, and when I got out of the service I applied for a job with the force here in Zieglersville."

"Why here? Sort of a comedown, wasn't it?"

"I don't really like big cities or small towns. Z'ville was the right size, and Chief Stabile has a hell of a reputation as a cop's cop—his solving of those religious serial murders here a few years back is still studied at police academies. I kid you not: It's an honor to work with a guy like him."

She thought about that. "Quaint term, *honor*. You don't hear it much anymore."

"Ain't much of it around."

"I went to work for Anson Lunt for the same reason. He was a class act the whole way. There's just no way to count all the people he helped in his lifetime."

"Guy in my line of work gets pretty used to irony. But I'll admit that Lunt's dying of one fatal disease at the same time he was helping so many survive another fatal disease is a real nudge."

She gave him a steady, disbelieving stare. "I—" She coughed, then said in a constricted voice, "You're saying that Anson was dying? Before he was killed?"

"Didn't you know?"

"I—No—What—How—"

"Hey, I'm sorry if I'm springing something on you. I just assumed you knew."

She shook her head slowly.

Jacoby said, "The medical examiner said the PM showed that Dr. Lunt had Lou Gehrig's disease. He was a very uncomfortable gentleman who didn't have too long to live and was lucky the crash did him in, according to Doc Logan."

"My God."

"Really, I'm sorry."

"I'd seen a slight trembling of his hand lately. And he seemed especially careful going down stairs. But when I mentioned it he just smiled and made a joke about being a tired old man."

He could see she was on the verge of tears. "I'm really sorry, Doc. It's a huge kick in the teeth, and I'd have done anything to—"

His cellular chirped.

"Jacoby."

"Dispatch, Jake. The M.E.'s got what looks to be a 187. He wants you to give him a call at his lab. Okay?"

"Right away."

He threw a tip on the table, and they skirted the dance floor and went to the cloakroom. Speechless with indignation over his gaffe, he helped her on with her coat.

She paused at the door to the parking lot. "I'm glad you told me. It brings together a lot of loose strings. And I'm feeling sort of rotten—guilty—right now. I could have been a heck of a lot more helpful to that dear man if I'd known."

"But you didn't know. So what's to be guilty about?"

"It's hard to explain. And I don't think I understand it altogether myself. Anyway, I don't feel very good about it, and I want to go home."

"That's the story of Robert L. 'Jake' Jacoby: Just when things are looking up, things are looking down. I was having a great time, and I blew it."

She patted his shoulder. "You're a nice man. And I hope we get to be good friends. But I'm having trouble handling this right now. Just give me some space, and I'll call you. Okay?"

"I'm already your good friend, Doc. You need me, I'm there. Anytime, anywhere."

17.

"Logan."

"Jake, Doc. You called?"

"There's something down here on my table you might want to see."

"The things I usually see on your table, I'd rather not see."

"The AI guys brought this one in. A drunk, run over a goodly several times on Airport Road tonight."

"I'm not into accident investigations. So why would I want to see this one?"

"Albert T. Margolis. Ring a bell?"

Jacoby sat forward in his chair. "Oo. The sole witness to the airplane crash that killed Lunt and Rooney."

"So I read in the papers. I also see in the papers that he was questioned by you hotshots in Homicide."

"Yeah. You say he was drunk?"

"Man can't get much drunker. He must have had a whole damn quart in his gut. On top of a dab of phenobarb. I mean, this gentleman wasn't out for fun, he was looking for o-bliv-ee-on."

"Sounds like he found it."

"Big-time."

"Cause of death?"

"Multiple trauma. Crushed head and crushed chest among the least noticeable. I mean, this is *yecch*."

"Tonight, you say?"

"I picked up the body around eight. Prelim tells me he was dead for less than an hour before that. Bubba Perkins is here. Want to ask him anything?"

"Yeah. Put him on."

"Hi, Jake."

"Can you give me a line on what happened, Bubba?"

"Dispatch got a nine-one-one at 7:03 P.M. from a truck driver who said there was a body in the road and he had run over it. Bert and I went out there, and it was pretty obvious that this drunk guy had passed out in the middle of the road and because of the heavy damn rain nobody could see him, so he got a pretty good drubbing."

"Just where on Airport Road?"

"Right next to the airport itself. The yellow building where Rooney had his thing, you know? Just outside the fence by the yellow building."

"Anybody report seeing the victim before all this?"

"Not that we've found yet. But it's still early. We'll have an AI team out there in the morning, and some witnesses might turn up."

"Let me know if anything hints foul play, okay?"

"Sure. You want Doc back on the line?"

"Yeah."

"*Was ist, Herr* Obergumshoe?"

"The vibes, Doc. Do the old soldier's vibes tell him anything about this one?"

"There's one thing comes to mind right away. The victim was really clobbered, but it looks to me like only two vehicles did the clobbering—the truck and a car."

"Come again?"

"The tire marks on the feller. The truck caught him across the legs, but either five cars with exactly the same kind of tires did the honors on his upper body or one car went over him five times. I'm ready to bet on the latter."

"So *that's* why you called me. You and your bullshit about the newspapers. You saw right away this guy was a homicide."

"I did?"

"The guy's only claim to fame was his presence at the airplane crash. Besides, why would somebody hit a night watchman? Why hit a retired railroader snoozing away the rest of his life in an after-hours factory?"

Logan sniffed. "You asked for my hunch, you got my hunch. Anything else, don't talk to me about it. Go talk to your suspects. You're the hotshot dick."

Jacoby grinned. "You have a lovely corpseside manner, Doctor. It'll take you far—maybe even to the top of your profession."

"There ain't no top in my profession anymore, buddy. With the socialized medicine we got going here in the United Soviet States of What Used to Be Amurrica for Spacious Skies, the once-proud medical profession is all bottom now."

"Poor ba-a-aby. Let me know soonest what the autopsy shows."

"*Jawohl, Herr* Obergumshoe."

Jacoby hung up and sat quietly at his desk for a time, remembering Margolis, the night watchman who, only nine days ago, had been seated at a worn wooden table in a drafty tin building, telling about the death of an airplane and its contents. He brooded a while about the chaotic, unpredictable process in which a man could on one day be folding his hands, shifting uncomfortably on a hard wooden chair and speculating on another man's life, then the next week be himself stone-cold dead on a rainy highway. Then he called in Ed Burroughs and told him about Margolis.

"Run over to his place at 770 Bolton Street, will you? See if there's anything unusual there. Do a little rummage. If Doc Logan's right, it was a hit. Which means Margolis was more than a night watchman. There may be stuff at his place that tells us something. Meantime, I'm whacked, and I'm calling it a fifteen-hour day."

*   *   *

Burroughs was backing his car out of the driveway when Morton returned to the house about ten. He pulled over and was waiting by the kitchen door after Morton hangared the BMW.

"Hi. Glad I caught you. I was about to leave."

"What's the occasion?"

"I need a drink first. You got a drink?"

Morton opened the door with his key, then turned on the kitchen lights. "Bourbon or Scotch?"

"Bourbon's fine."

Burroughs was a large, meaty man, with heavy-lidded eyes, a thick nose, and a mouth that always seemed set against a gas pain. His bald head glistened under the ceiling lights, and when he talked there was the glitter of a dental appliance in his lower jaw. Despite all this beauty he knew his business, and his business of the moment was what Morton was interested in.

Morton poured two drinks. He and Burroughs touched glasses and drank.

"So what's going down, Ed?"

The cop rolled the bourbon around in his mouth before swallowing—a man who truly enjoyed his booze. "Have you had your police scanner on?"

"No. Why?"

"That stoolie of yours—Al Margolis—went down around seven o'clock."

"You mean—"

"Run over on Airport Road, and it looks like a hit. I been temp-assigned to Homicide because they're so snowed under. Jacoby's sent me to Margolis's place to do a little rummage. I swung by here to make sure you knew about the hit. It'll sorta knock a link out of your chain, won't it?"

"I'll get by. Do the police know that Margolis was in the dirty-picture business?"

Burroughs shook his big head and looked worried. "Not from me, they don't. You told me to keep it quiet. And that's the main reason I came by. I'm sure as hell going to find some dirty pictures. What you want I should do with them?"

Morton thought about that.

"You're alone?"

"Yeah. Jacoby's gone home after a beeg day. The others are doing their thing at headquarters. This is not being treated as the hit of the century."

"All right, then. I'm going to follow you over. I want first look at anything you find."

Burroughs was dubious. "I don't think that's such a hot idea. There'll be people there. It's a duplex, with a landlord, that kind of thing."

"Who's to know I'm not a cop?"

"One thing, no cop drives a Seven-Series Beemer."

"I'll use the Ford pickup."

"Another thing, one of our guys might show up, you know? I'm having hell's own time keeping a lid on my thing with you as it is. What the hell would I say if a cop found you with me on a crime investigation?"

"That I'm not with you. That by coincidence we arrived at the same time—you to investigate, I to ask Margolis how much it would cost me to buy back some negs."

"Whoa. That would put Margolis in the blackmail business and you in a touchy situation."

"I was getting ready to dump him anyway. He was getting too independent, and, a tiresome smart-ass."

"But if you admit being blackmailed by him, that makes you a suspect—"

"I have an alibi. I was having dinner at the Hayloft with three company people from Chicago, and those three people, the maître d', and the waiter will say so."

"So let's go."

The house at 770 Bolton Street was one of those dreary, two-story frame duplexes with identical up-and-down front and back porches that had been so popular back in the twenties. Myron

Cootch, the landlord, a fat baldie with no teeth and a bathrobe that looked as if it had come in on the tide, lived on the ground floor, and he wasn't too pleased to have his TV evening interrupted. He rubbed his eyes, stared at Burroughs's badge for a full ten seconds, then, after glancing back and forth at Burroughs and Morton, wanted to know what the hell this was all about, anyhow.

"Mr. Margolis has been killed," Burroughs said carefully, "and we want to advise his next of kin, if there are any."

The fat man was unmoved, but curious. "Killed? How?"

"Highway accident."

"I told the sumbish he was too old to be driving nights. Told me to stick it in my ear."

"Did he have a live-in girlfriend? Boyfriend?"

"Who'd live with that creep? He didn't like anybody, and nobody liked him. There was something about an ex-wife somewhere, but don't ask me if it was true."

"Do you have a key to his apartment, Mr. Cootch?"

"I'm the landlord, ain't I?"

"Mind if we look around?"

"Only if I'm there when you do."

"Wouldn't have it any other way. But then you'll have to come down to headquarters and make some statements about what you saw us do. Red-tape kind of stuff."

This little invention did not please Cootch. "And if I don't watch you?"

"You're free and clear."

"Shee." Cootch handed Burroughs the key, turned on his heel, and, muttering, disappeared into his digs, slamming the door behind him.

Everything was gray with age and inattention: the woodwork, the walls, the worn carpeting, even the few dented appliances. Unwashed pots packed the sink; a plate with bread crumbs and dried egg smears dominated the tiny kitchen table. The desk was littered with what appeared to be junk mail. There was one bedroom, furnished with a chest of drawers, two straight-backed chairs, a lamp, and an unmade bed. A musty smell filled the place—heavy, oppressive.

In the bathroom, which even in its prime would have earned no raves from *Gracious Living* magazine, the tub, shower, and lavinette had been made over into a small photo-processing lab. It was cramped and absolutely basic, but workable, leaving only one question in Morton's mind: Where in hell had Margolis ever taken a bath?

As if he'd heard the thought, Burroughs said, "So that's why there's a showerhead on that pipe on the back porch."

"Gracious living, eh?"

A TV set, a standard radio and cassette player, a good camera, unloaded, a box containing some undeveloped film rolls, and several stacks of girlie magazines were stuffed into a four-shelf bookcase and combined to suggest the parameters of the late Mr. Margolis's personal jollies. The three closets contained nothing but nondescript clothing.

Burroughs suddenly erupted. "Holy shit!"

"What? What?"

"Look at this."

Burroughs had found a false panel at the side of the bedroom closet. In the niche behind it were three fat, neatly taped packets of thousand-dollar bills.

"Porn pays," Morton said.

"There's gotta be a quarter of a mill here."

"Obviously our friend Margolis didn't believe in banks."

"Don't touch it," Burroughs said nervously.

"I have no intention of touching it."

"I gotta call in about this right now."

"Yes. But give me a few more minutes, and I'll be out of here. Okay?"

The chest of drawers proved to be the place. Each drawer held a layer of mail-order shirts, underwear, socks, and handkerchiefs, and beneath these layers in each drawer was a standard dime-store photo album. The photos themselves were anything but standard.

Burroughs, leafing through one of the albums, whistled softly, marveling. "My God. I didn't think Judge Madison had enough energy to climb a flight of stairs. But look at him here. And with Audrey Nichols, of all people. Pete Nichols would have a squirting fit, he ever sees this, wouldn't you say?" He turned a page and laughed. "And this is even better: City Commissioner Sam Orton and that dipshit news guy, Marley Statts. Gives new meaning to the old, 'Politics makes strange bedfellows', eh?" He laughed again.

Morton was going through his own selection. "The one I really want," he murmured, "would have me in action with a someone I sure wouldn't want anybody to see me with."

Burroughs gave him an amused look. "Male or female?" He laughed, not unkindly. "No matter which, if you stumble in front of a camera operated by this creep, you're just about as dumb as they come."

"You don't know how many times I've told myself that."

"Notice something? Couple of these prints got a phone number on the back."

Morton, considering a shot of Bud Wilmer and Linda Bianco in a steamy, rear-entry situation, turned it over. A phone number, complete with the local area code in tidy parentheses, had been lightly penciled there. He memorized it by repeating it twice in his mind.

Back home, he called the number to see what would happen. It rang seven times. As he was about to hang up, Mary Dugan's voice came on. She didn't sound too happy.

"Waldo's Deli pay phone. What the hell you want?"

Morton hung up. Which, he was sure, ticked off Mary even more.

18.

Mrs. Emma Donnelli, mother of Guido Donnelli, No. 2 driver for Peter Van Dyke, was a piece of human wreckage stored in a small room at the House of Devotion, a ragtag nursing home smelling of urine and old cooking that sat on Northside Avenue. Morton could barely look at her because it brought back Uncle Denny and the terrible time he'd had with his dying.

Only Guido seemed to share his discomfort, standing beside the bed, staring into his mother's waxen, skull-like face, holding her skeletal hand, and fighting to control his lower lip, which showed a tendency to quiver. The others gathered around her agonized, moaning half-consciousness and listened to Allenby's little lecture on metastatic cancer and how, in Mrs. Donnelli's case, it had begun in her left breast as a lump near the armpit, had spread to the lymph nodes, and now was raging through her neck and torso. She had, he guessed, no more than a week.

Allenby's talk was for the benefit of Peter Van Dyke and Zachary, naturally, because he knew they represented Falloon, as did the softly whirring video camera over in a corner, elevated on a tripod and focused on the bed. Unknown to him, though, was the fact that this was also for the secret benefit of Morton, who planned to smuggle copies to Teddy and Charles Hamilton.

Allenby opened his physician's bag and withdrew a vial with a yellow cap, holding it to the light to let the others see its clear liquid contents. "The Allenby Formula," he intoned dramatically.

Morton, much relieved, fought a need to grin. The vial was one of those yellow-tops left by Lunt at the airport. Allenby hadn't even bothered to transfer the serum to a new one. A break. Big-time.

Allenby dampened some gauze with alcohol and dabbed a spot on Mrs. Donnelli's upper left arm. Filling a syringe with the liquid and, holding it aloft like a conductor raising his baton, he said, even more dramatically, "I will now inject the formula directly into an artery."

He made the injection, and they all stood there, gaping.

The camera continued to whir. The room continued to stink. Mrs. Donnelli continued to moan.

Consulting his watch, Allenby said, "Give it five minutes."

As the fourth minute began, Mrs. Donnelli fell silent.

They stared at her.

In the sixth minute, her eyelids fluttered briefly.

Allenby, gazing at his watch, his fingers on the woman's wrist, his lean face set in thought, was a portrait of the noble physician, the great good guy in the white coat taking on the forces of ruin and death.

Morton thought nonsensically: *Wouldn't it be great if he were as great as he looks....*

"She's sleeping," Allenby announced at the end of the tenth minute. "Breathing normal; pulse rate, seventy beats per minute."

"My God," Zachary said.

The others, frozen in awe, were speechless.

Morton was the first to recover, and he went directly into the supervisor's role Falloon had assigned him. "All right, as soon as she's moveable, Guido, take your mother home. Dr. Pitcairn's staff will give you a hand, and, if you need money or anything, see Mr. Van Dyke. Peter, I'll have copies of the video for you and Zachary first thing in the morning."

Allenby cleared his throat. "May I have one, too?"

"Of course. And I'll be back to you on the financial details."

"Don't take too long."

As they filed out the door, Guido called after them, "Gentlemen—Sirs—You are all angels."

They turned to stare.

Morton smiled dimly. "Let me give you a heavenly warning, Guido. If you say a word to anybody about what happened here tonight—say anything at all without Mr. Van Dyke's explicit permission—we angels will turn into devils. Meantime, we're very glad you got your mamma back."

19.

The weather had been marginal all the way. In the Daytona area a thunderstorm had sent her into a small detour over the sea, but by the time she steered the Beech onto the tarmac and shut down the engines, Florida was doing its thing, with a cobalt sky, majestic puff clouds aglow in the sunlight, and an offshore breeze, smelling of the Atlantic and stirring the palm trees. As always, Burton brought the limo alongside the plane and took charge of the luggage while she and Barry Wendel, the maintenance chief, went over those things to be done to the Beech during the week it would be hangared.

Alicia was unaccountably tired. Flying usually set her up, got her blood racing, lifted her mood—even after a tough thousand miles on IFR—but today she seemed drained, dull. And after clearing the Daytona detour her eyes had begun to play tricks, spotting, and, for a frightening interval, blurring to an impenetrable dimness. She went immediately on autopilot, resting back in her seat, closing her eyes, and occasionally rubbing them. The condition cleared as quickly as it had come. Oddly, this made her even more uneasy.

She probably needed glasses. She'd never worn them, and the idea that she might have to now was depressing, a piling of melancholy on the melancholy that had tyrannized her ever since a similar blank-out in the Merriman Mall parking lot two weeks ago.

Signing off on the authorization forms, she went to the car, squinting in the glare and aware of a headache that seemed to reach all the way to her left shoulder. After Burton got them under way she opened the backseat bar and used a glass of soda water to wash down an aspirin tablet. She settled into the cushions, sighed, and closed her eyes, partly against the outside brilliance (which seemed unfazed by the Lincoln's dark-tinted glass), partly because she felt the need to psych herself up for the coming reunion with Charles.

The effort brought up the inevitable snapshot memories of how Charles had used to be. She tried to ignore them, because they reminded her of those depressing flashback sequences in foreign art films. But he had been beautiful, in all departments, no doubt about it; large in mind and body and spirit, a doer and a giver, sharp of wit, bawdy in humor, lusty in appetites, generous with forgiveness and forever the optimist. One hell of a guy who had overwhelmed her with his magnetism and persuaded her that life with him would be a life like nobody'd ever had. No talk of serious love—just come-on-out-and-play. And she'd been so bored and lonely and he was such a hoot, she was ready to follow him to Pluto, no questions asked. Which made it so hard to deal with the thoroughly unconscionable *Kartellmeister* he'd become.

It was extravagant, keeping separate homes of such size. But they had more money than they each could possibly spend, and it would have been awkward and wasteful to ignore the residence requirements of her inheritance. So she continued to operate from Elmwood—explaining his absence as caused by an illness requiring a nursing home. Which wasn't far from the truth. The accident, ironically not a hell of a lot more than a fender-bender, had left him in a wheelchair, commandant of a squad of therapists and aides whose major, and apparently hopeless, task was to relieve him of his colossal self-pity and rage. Seen from that angle, he was, in fact, in a home, and he was being nursed.

Today he was at a table on the oceanside patio, holding his face to the sun and seeming to listen to the lazy surf.

"Hello, Charles," she said, easing into a chair beside him.

He kept his eyes closed. "I didn't realize you were coming. You should have told me. I'm expecting people from Paris and Washington. We have a meeting laid on."

She felt resentment rising. So he was having a meeting. So why did that suggest there wasn't space for her in this twenty-room mausoleum? It was her house, too, goddammit.

"Don't worry. I won't get in your way."

"Well, you should have called or something."

"It was an impulse thing. The forecast for the weekend isn't all that great. So I got to thinking: Why not beat the weather and go now?" She laughed softly. "As it turned out, I had to fly around a squall near Daytona anyhow."

"I worry about you, Al. I don't know what I'd do if you pulled an Amelia Earhart on me."

It was a major absurdity, this claim of his that losing her would be a catastrophe for him. They spent perhaps a maximum of two, maybe three weeks a year in each other's presence, and spoke by phone or traded faxes several times a week. Beyond that there was nothing but memories and playacting. She knew as a fact that he was more comfortable when she wasn't around, and that realization was worse than flat-out rejection.

"Earhart was audacious. I'm a coward. I'll be around for the long haul."

"All the time hating me. Wishing you could leave."

"That isn't true."

He opened his eyes and searched her face. "Do you mean that, Al?"

Next largest absurdity: his anxious suspicions. When his legs had disconnected from his mind, there had also been a severance of whatever nerve, or muscle, it was that enabled him to accept that she was the same person who had doted on him when he was unimpaired. There seemed no way to convince him that their past and the present formed a homogenous whole. Nothing worked to overcome his jealous distrust, which had eventually turned her passion for him into fear of him.

"Why do you think I came all this way to see you?"

"I sometimes wonder how you can do it—keep up this pretense that I mean something to you."

"It's easy, because you do mean something to me."

Absurdity Number Three: This ritual, in which he would quickly parry the obvious solution.

"Charles, why *don't* we end the charade? Why don't I close up Elmwood and come down here and stay with you all the time? We could do exactly what we've been doing. I'd continue our contacts with the Washington and New York people, I'd supervise the house here, administer your aides, I'd do everything that needs to be done—and I'd be right here for you. All the time."

His eyes, glittering, turned to study the distant flat line between sea and sky. "No. Living here would make you exactly what I am—a prisoner. I couldn't have that."

The Penultimate Absurdity: the myth of his imprisonment. He had three cars and a side-lift van to drive or ride in, each with its special controls and accommodations. He had a Lockheed Globester, a personal jet, fully equipped to conform to his handicap, whose crew stood ready to fly him to any city in the world. But he chose almost always to have the world come to him, and so the guesthouse was, more often than not, filled with Frenchmen and Swiss and Japanese and Brits and God knew who else, gathered to bring money and to hear his latest manifestos.

"Well, we can't have it both ways, either—"

"There. See? That tone of yours. Testy. Impatient. You're—enduring me."

She shook her head, her lips compressed.

"You're not having an affair, are you?"

"Oh, come on, Charles: Give me a break."

"I can't bear the thought of you with somebody else."

"There is nobody else."

"You're so attractive to men—"

"Charles, get real. I'm a skinny little over-the-hill corporation widow. Florida is crawling with us. Women with husbands who aren't husbands. Women with everything who have nothing." She had to be careful here. The tiny catch in her voice told her that she was about to gather up her own case of self-pity.

He leaned slightly, reached down, flipped open the hasps of the briefcase beside his chair, and withdrew a folder. From this he took a photograph and handed it to her. "So, then, what does this mean, Alicia?"

She glanced at the picture, feeling a heat in her face. "I'd driven Anson to the airport. He was leaving on a trip to New York. He was ill, and I had the sudden urge to comfort him. He was my friend, and he was hurting, in trouble, alone. And so I held him for a time."

"Why would somebody take a picture like this and send it to me in the mail—anonymously?"

"I swear I don't know, Charles. I got a copy in the mail, too. Somebody's trying to—come between us—"

He looked away, bitter.

"I swear."

After a silent interval, his eyes came around to her again, unblinking, inscrutable, waiting.

"I can't prove anything, Charles. All you have is my word. And you have that—picture. Do you want a divorce?"

His smile was faint, ironic. "No, Alicia, I don't want a divorce. As a practical matter, a divorce would eliminate me as sole heir to your family fortune, and I'm too greedy to allow that to happen. But there's a more important reason, which is that I love you."

Unable to handle this hypocrisy, she said nothing.

Herewith the Final Absurdity: She had been with him less than five minutes and in that time she'd been stunned and humiliated, had her personal fortune coveted, been in and out of divorce, and was looking for the excuse that would take her out of here at the earliest possible moment.

Her special hell.

The Days of Whine and Poses.

*   *   *

She went up the curving marble stairway and followed the mezzanine to her private suite, where she threw off her clothes and
spent most of an hour in the whirlpool tub on the balcony.
Alternately dozing and watching squadrons of pelicans making
lazy sweeps along the surf line, she willed away her anger and
sense of degradation and gave herself to the voluptuous effer-
vescence around her. The breeze was soft, filled with the sounds
and scents of the sea, and they were about to put her to sleep
when the dull thunk of a closing car door brought her up
sharply, instantly alert, like a nodding sentry who has heard the
snapping of a twig.

Craning, she was able to make out a curve of driveway and
the dark blue flank of the Lincoln limo. Burton, whose horizon
blue livery made him look like a movie-set *poilu*, removed a
bag from the car trunk, then nodded politely at his passenger,
who was just out of sight. Lewis, the houseboy, came down the
path to take the bag and carry it to the guesthouse, and Burton
gestured, inviting the visitor toward the main portico.

Alicia rose quickly from the tub, threw the terry robe around
her, then hurried barefoot through the bedroom to ease open
the door that opened onto the mezzanine and its view of the
foyer below. As she watched, Anton, the butler, swung open
the main door and gave a Prussian-type bow.

"Mr. Hamilton is on the patio, Mr. Morton," Anton crooned.
"Please follow me."

George Morton.

Handsome, impeccably dressed, wryly affable as always.

She closed the door and stood there, biting her lip, her heart
sinking, her mind racing.

After a full minute of this, she went to her library and, picking up the phone, dialed Melanie Flynn's personal phone at Lunt
Biotech. Listening to the ringing, she muttered, "Come on, come
on. Be there."

"Dr. Flynn."

"This is Alicia Hamilton, Melanie."

"Well, hi. Nice surprise. I thought you were in Florida."

"I am. And there's something I want you to do for me."

"Just ask."

"Send a fax to my office number here at the beach house. Tell me I'm wanted there immediately to confer with you and the lawyers on the disposition of Lunt Biotech."

"That meeting isn't until next week—"

"I know. But tell me it's to be moved up and that you need to see me tomorrow morning."

"Well—"

"Just do it, will you, please?" She struggled to keep the panic from her voice.

"Well—"

"Do it, dammit!"

"The fax will be on the way in five minutes."

She pressed the reset button, got the dial tone, and punched the button for Barry Wendel at the airport.

"Maintenance. Wendel speaking."

"Alicia Hamilton. You haven't started on my plane yet, have you?"

Barry chuckled. "No, ma'am. She's only been in the hangar for a few minutes—"

"Good. Refuel and preflight. I've got to return to Zieglersville. I'll be at the field in half an hour."

She hung up and buzzed Anton on the intercom.

"Yes, ma'am?"

"I've been faxed back to Elmwood. Since Mr. Hamilton has a meeting in progress, I don't want to interrupt. Tell him after his meeting. No. Make that: Tell him only when he asks where I am. Which should be around dinnertime. Got it?"

"Of course, ma'am."

"If he asks what's up, show him the fax on my machine."

"Yes, ma'am. You can count on me."

"I always have, Anton. You're a class act."

She dressed quickly, repacked her bag, and hurried down the back stairs to the hallway leading to the service wing and garage.

As she made the turn at the foot of the stairway, the powder-room door opened and Morton stepped into the hall directly in her path.

"Well, this is a nice surprise. I didn't know you'd be here, Alicia."

"Damn, damn, damn."

"Charles and I are about to have cocktails by the pool before his board people arrive. Will you be joining us?"

"You know better than that. Where's your head, for God's sake?"

"Well, after all, I'm an invited guest in your home—"

"And you know very damned well that I can't stand to be in the same room with you more than a minute. Out of my way, George."

"Where are you going?"

"Back to Z'ville. And if you really want to do me a favor, you won't let Charles know you've seen me. My life's complicated enough right now."

"Alicia" he blurted, "please let me back in your life."

Real pleading was in his voice, and it held her for a hurtful moment. Then, in a fierce whispering: "George, for God's sake, don't make it more difficult than it is."

"I'm so lonely for you. For the old days—"

"The old days, the sweet old Anson Lunt days, are gone forever. These days are the days we've got. Give it up, George."

She pushed past him and made for the garage. She felt his sad gaze following her.

"Yes?"

"Barry Wendel, Mr. Hamilton. Hope I haven't called at a bad time."

"It's all right. What's up?"

"You said to call if there was any aircraft activity."

"So?"

"Mrs. Hamilton has just taken off for Zieglersville. She's filed a flight plan that gives her an ETA of 2015."

"All right. Thank you, Barry."

*   *   *

"Hello?"

"This is Charles Hamilton."

"Oh, hi."

"My wife is on her way up there. Her ETA at Z'ville airport is 2015. I want you to initiate a constant tail on her, starting with her landing this evening."

"What do you mean, constant?"

"I want to know everything she does, everywhere she goes, everybody she talks to. And I want a daily report."

"Okay. Anything else?"

"Yes. I want her line tapped, and if there are any conversations or any consequent meetings that seem out of the ordinary, I want recordings and transcripts."

"She has a boyfriend, or something?"

"She's being set up for some kind of blackmail, and I want to know who the bastard is so that I can give him a circumcision."

"Okay. I'll set it up."

"There's something else. And I don't want Bruno to handle it. He's too ham-handed for something this delicate. I want you to handle it. Personally."

"What's that?"

"Alicia's friend, Cummings. The nurse. They spend a lot of time together, talk a lot. I consider Cummings to be a loose cannon. For all that professional stoicism she hands out, she's a handwringer. I don't want her talking to the police, giving me another problem I don't need."

"I'll have a word with her."

20.

Jacoby had at last established the reason for Anson Lunt's many flights to New York. This did not surprise Morton; with a policeman as methodical and pragmatic as Jacoby was proving to be, it was inevitable. But it had taken him longer than Morton expected, mainly because of the police department's tight travel budget, which made investigative trips to New York, a hundred crow's flight miles away, as difficult to arrange as an orbit of Neptune. Entries in Jacoby's case file reflected the painful alternative: dependence on the NYPD, which took a week to do what he could have done on a morning's round-trip via the Pennsy Turnpike.

```
E-Mail To: Jacoby, Zieglersville PD
From: O'Malley, NYPD
Subject: Cabstand interviews, re
Dr. Anson Lunt

    Have ID on limo service that provided subject in-
dividual with transport from LaGuardia to Manhattan
and back. Driver, Jerry Molok, says subject always
went to the same place: the Park Avenue office of Dr.
Allyn Gauchat, a specialist in nervous disorders.
```

Would stay there for an hour, sometimes two, with limo
waiting, then would go right back to LaGuardia and the
visiting civil aircraft ramp. Driver says he's never
known the pattern to vary.

Jacoby followed up this advisory with a memo to Chief Stabile:

Called Dr. Allyn Gauchat in New York re weekly
visits of Dr. Anson Lunt. Gauchat was reluctant to discuss reasons for Lunt's visits, but when I pushed in
with the homicide angle and asked whether Lunt's visits were professional or social, she said her only contacts with Lunt had to do with his Gehrig's disease and
her advice on its treatment. She claims that although
she knew Lunt by reputation, she had never met him
prior to his coming to her for consultations. She was
reluctant to discuss details of Lunt's illness, but she
did allow as how it was "in its terminal stages and
that, while he was in great pain, he was determined to
stay out of the hospital as long as possible."

So Rooney's speculations and the various gossip bits on Anson's going to New York for sex had been effectively spiked,
and Morton suspected that Stabile and Jacoby were as relieved
and pleased as he was to get that horse manure off the street.

Meanwhile, a pair of encrypted faxes from Peter Van Dyke
advised him that the paperwork on the new Peabody medical
drug subsidiary was well under way and should be ready for
their meeting with the Sunrise Bank people shortly after New
Year's. The subsidiary would be named Pegasus Pharmaceuticals, and Morton's appointment as president and CEO was to
become effective January 2. Announcements were scheduled for
release to the media the day after Christmas.

Morton had gone over this and a briefcase full of items relating to his departure from Bradford Chemicals while on the
plane to Florida. They had missed the incoming weather, and

the connections were precise, so he was in the limo and on the way to Hamilton's place before he could finish. But finish he did, and he was feeling slightly smug as the car pulled into the driveway.

He'd been genuinely surprised by Alicia's presence in the house and not a bit surprised by her panicky leaving. She was really a piece of engineering, that woman, and if he hadn't been so sad, he might actually have laughed at her Lucille Ball-type exit.

They met in the cool of the gazebo, which perched on a sandy, palm-encircled prominence overlooking miles of sugar white beach. The breeze smelled of gardens and the sea, and its whispering gave the conversation a soft and easy sound.

Charles Hamilton had positioned his chair at the end of the long glass-top table so that he was silhouetted against the seascape. It was apparent that he'd arranged this so as to present an image of dominion and mystery. It worked. Morton sensed a defensiveness among those around the table.

To Hamilton's right were the FMAA's Anthony Dvorak, Congressman Morgan Twitchell, and Gerda von Reichmann, CEO of Le Tellier and, less notably, executive director of Gebrüder Schwarz, the innocuously named Swiss investment firm that was in reality the tip of a colossal subsurface berg which—unknown to all legitimate manufacturers—dominated or influenced every current in the world's pharmaceutical seas. To his left were Dr. Derek Biddle, president of the United States Medical Society; Roger Detwiler, United Nations undersecretary for world medical commerce; and Lucy Costello, a prosecutor for the U.S. Justice Department who, as a protégé of Thomas Adams Wilkerson, patriarch of the predominant Wall Street law firm, wielded power and influence far beyond her ambient bureaucracy. Morton sat facing Hamilton from the opposite end of the table. Everybody wore shorts and tee-shirts and sunglasses, and they sipped at tall drinks and exchanged salty witticisms that showed what regular folks they were, despite their notoriety as elite international string pullers.

"Everybody comfortable?" Hamilton asked genially.

The sucking-up was elaborate, with much nodding and murmured assurance that this was indeed a great place to meet.

"All right, then, let's get to business, which is what to do here in the United States about the impending introduction of the Allenby thing we've just watched on film."

Dr. Biddle shifted in his chair and cleared his throat gently. "I must say that I think the film is a fake. There can be no quick, single cure for cancer. It's an enormously variegated disease that defies a blanket treatment."

Von Reichmann removed the sunglasses from her patrician nose, patted her glossy blond hair, and peered wryly at the physician. "You think that, and we think that. But the world at large does not accept that. And we are here to deal with the world at large, my dear Dr. Biddle."

"Deal with? What means 'deal with'?" Biddle snapped.

" 'Wrangle the common herd' may be a more appropriate way to put it," von Reichmann said condescendingly.

Sensing a developing antagonism, Hamilton took command. "Perhaps we'd better consider the matter in its context. Let me summarize the situation."

"Please do," crooned Detweiler, king of suck-ups.

Hamilton said, "Dr. Gregorv Allenby, director of research and development for Lunt Biotechnical Laboratory, reports that he has secretly managed to tame the trophoblast and, as a consequence of successful testing at all levels—a conclusive one we've seen on the film—plans to auction the formula and its accompanying dietary regimen, which together reduce and, in some cases, eradicate metastatic tumors. Allenby also claims that, when used as a preventive among subjects with a genetic predisposition for cancer, the course serves as a virtual vaccine."

Costello, always the lawyer, held up a forefinger. "May I ask how we came upon this information?"

It was characteristic of Hamilton at these meetings to talk about individual attendees as if they were not at the table but at a sabbatical on Mars. "From George Morton, our guest today, who, as you recall, was of grudging but effective help in our successful effort to discredit Anson Lunt and have his Vitam formula banned in the United States. Morton recently came to me with the news that Allenby is in the process of selling his discovery—a kind of super Vitam Two—to Theodore Bradford, CEO of Bradford Chemicals, who hopes to exploit the product privately. I've asked Morton to sit in, since some of you might have questions on particulars."

Dr. Biddle broke in. "You mean to say that Allenby has actually developed this Super Vitam to the point of patentability? That this product is on tap today?"

Hamilton nodded. "You saw the film."

"A preposterous fake."

Dvorak did some bristling. "Just a damned minute, now, Dr. Biddle. My own trusted lieutenant, Dr. Zachary, personally witnessed the transformation that film covers. He attests to the validity of the film, the case history files, the basic chemistry, the trophoblast thesis, the whole nine yards, and I resent the hell out of you implying that my best man has been hoodwinked."

Biddle didn't give an inch. "Say what you will. I think the whole thing is blue smoke."

"I believe," von Reichmann put in dryly, "that you said the very same thing about Lunt's original Vitam, Doctor."

"And you know what happened to the original Vitam," Biddle shot back tartly.

"Vitam provided overwhelming evidence that vitamin therapy is effective in the treatment of cancer. What happened to Vitam in the United States is us, my dear Doctor. We happened to Vitam." Von Reichmann's tone had taken on an edge.

"Oh, come on," Costello grumped. "This isn't getting us anywhere. Let's—"

Von Reichmann had collected momentum. "Vitam, in combination with dietary regimens, was then, and is today, saving lives in Europe and South America by controlling and, in some cases, eradicating primary and metastatic cancers. But in this country the stigma we created rolls on. Thanks to us, instead of being universally accepted as a primary procedure in oncology, much of American medicine continues to consider Vitam a spit-in-the-wind, last-hope voodoo potion swallowed by those who figure they have nothing to lose. But we here at this table know how truly effective it is, don't we. Eh?"

Costello broke in. "Mr. Chairman—"

But von Reichmann, openly annoyed now, persisted. "Just out of curiosity, I'd like to know how many of us are taking Vitam. Come on—admit it. Who among us is now taking, or has in the past taken Vitam as a preventive? How about a show of hands? Who among us has the honesty to make such an admission, eh?" She raised her right hand.

Hamilton, although obviously amused by this little skirmish, decided it was time to get back on track. He tapped a pencil against his julep glass, saying amiably, "All right, people, I agree with Lucy. This is a digression—"

Von Reichmann interrupted. "I say it is altogether pertinent to our mission here. Our mission here is about monopoly. Absolute pharmaceutical monopoly. The efficacy of Vitam or the Allenby product, or any drug in the universe is entirely secondary to our purpose. Our purpose is to own, control, or constrain all chemical compounds that in any way have a role in the maintenance of health among the world's population. And if we don't own, control, or constrain it, our mission is to destroy it before it can become a competitor."

There was a silence, which Hamilton permitted to linger. After a time, seeing that von Reichmann's preeminence could use a bit of shoring up in the face of Biddle's attack, he said, "Gerda, as usual, has gone straight to the bottom line. I am daily thankful for the support I receive through her quick mind, her pragmatism, her unwillingness to give a millimeter to oppositional forces. And here she has, in her inimitable way, brought us back on track."

Von Reichmann smiled faintly and tilted her glass in an answering salute.

"The question before us," Hamilton continued, "is how we

handle this new thing—this so-called cancer cure. Let me emphasize the importance of the videotape George Morton has provided. We've seen—right here, in my library, and with our own eyes—a dramatic demonstration of the curative powers of the Allenby Formula. We've watched as Allenby injected his product into a patient suffering terminal metastatic cancer. We've seen how, within five minutes, the patient, a fifty-five-year-old woman, was relieved of her intense pain; within ten minutes, she was sleeping, her pulse rate normal. In sequel footage taken the day before yesterday, this patient is seen at home, walking with her son in the garden, obviously in high good humor. I know Dr. Biddle disagrees, but it's my view that this tape proves that the Allenby formula poses a very real threat to our worldwide business vis-à-vis oncology and its many related fields."

"Even though it began with that charlatan, Anson Lunt?" Hamilton's praise of von Reichmann had brought a bright pink to Biddle's smooth-shaven cheeks.

"Dammit, Biddle, why don't you back off?" It was Detweiler's turn to be rankled. "You know very well that Anson Lunt was no charlatan. He was a fine physician and biochemist, with extremely impressive credentials in both fields. We are the ones who made him out to be a charlatan. Where in hell is your memory?"

Even as an outsider, Morton could see that, in the angry pause that followed, the board would have to jettison Derek Biddle. As president of the newest yet most influential medical association on the North American continent, Biddle was quite useful as a symbol of professional rectitude and, on a more practical level, as a malleable leader of opinion, since he rarely evidenced having any opinions of his own. He was readily prompted into papers and speeches authored by the Gebrüder Schwarz PR people and designed to influence physicians and surgeons who were too busy to keep adequately in touch with the explosion in technology and therapies—which was to say virtually every dedicated, hardworking medical professional from Key West to Nome and beyond. *Are mashed poison ivy leaves a cure for bun-*

ions? Have a GS spinmeister write a paper declaring it to be so and then hand it to Biddle, whose PR platoons and network of faxes would soon have the American medical brotherhood accepting it as gospel. Even though he was a jerk, Biddle was showing signs of taking himself seriously—of believing his own publicity—and, worse yet, he was showing signs this afternoon of allowing his personal jealousies (he had always resented Lunt's fantastic press) to get in the way of rational discussion. From Hamilton's expression Morton saw that Biddle would soon be replaced by one of von Reichmann's favorites, Arthur Neff. Neff was another cretinous peacock—a highly touted, photogenic society doctor with no discernible ideas or antagonisms—who nonetheless during last years's convention had proved to be an engaging platform speaker and a delightful spinner of medical yarns as a guest on TV talk shows.

Hamilton drawled, "We'll go around the table counterclockwise. Tony, do you have a suggestion as to how we should proceed?"

Dvorak nodded, his mouth set in a self-satisfied line. He removed his sunglasses, hung them, Malibu-style, in the V neck of his sport shirt, and, glancing about the table, said, "I say we should stick with the tried and true. I say we pull another Vitam on this new baby."

Hamilton regarded Morgan Twitchell. "Congressman, you've been rather quiet. How about it? Any suggestions?"

Twitchell, of course, lived in a world built on deals and compromise, so he was not about to be unequivocal. But with Dvorak's strong opening he obviously felt that he could afford to sound a bit aggressive. "I, too, believe that the Vitam experience can lay out a map for us on this one. I am inclined to agree with Tony."

"Gerda?"

"I'm thinking. I pass right now."

"Lucy?"

"I agree that we should uncork the Vitam strategy."

"Roger?"

"I agree."

"Derek?"

Biddle shrugged and sent a testy glance seaward. "Why not?"

"George, you have no vote, but I think the group would like your opinion."

"I agree that this new thing be squashed."

Hamilton summarized. "So then: With the exception of Gerda, who is still contemplating her navel"—he gave the blonde a wink and a smile—"the vote is that we should discredit the Allenby thing. Tony, you'll prepare an FMAA case against the trophoblastic theory. Set up a panel of physicians and biochemists who will testify that they have researched the procedure and have found it to be without merit. Announce that the trophoblastic therapy is dangerous quackery and those United States citizens who practice or experiment with it—or even advocate its use—are subject to arrest and prosecution. Lucy, you'll backstop all this with bulletins from your department and with photo-op, media-coordinated raids on import centers, ostensibly to intercept foreign-initiated promos and samples. Roger, you will see that the UN proclaims trophoblastic procedures to be a serious threat to the general health and calls for a ban of the international distribution of literature and chemicals that pertain. And you, Derek, will pump out all this on your membership fax and PC systems, set up frequent press conferences, and get fright stuff on major radio and TV talk shows. Questions?"

Gerda von Reichmann waved her hand indolently.

Hamilton smiled again, showing his approval of this remarkable woman. He'd once told Morton in a moment of drunken expansiveness that not only was she a splendid, completely amoral executive but also had proved to him in wondrous ways that his disability was in no way a liability in bed. Morton had no doubt that her tactics for this meeting—making Hamilton's decision, long since firmed up, appear to be hers—had been settled on last night's pillow.

"Ah," Hamilton chuckled, "our esteemed executive director has surfaced. What's your question, Gerda?"

"No question. A better idea."

"Oh?"

"The video makes it clear that we should preempt."

She was suddenly the meeting's focal point.

"I say we make it a French discovery. I say Gebrüder Schwartz buys the Allenby Formula from Teddy Bradford, then takes it to Paris. There it is announced that Le Tellier, Cie., has perfected a trophoblastic treatment that not only cures existing cancers but also inhibits the development of new ones. This establishes a European origin, which not only gives Le Tellier credit for the discovery but also worldwide ownership. From this base we all can share in the initial profits, then later settle into worldwide licensing, from which we get a piece of the action no matter where it occurs. We do not destroy the Allenby Formula, ladies and gentlemen; we claim it as our own by way of France. And in the United States those at the table here will hail it as the greatest medical discovery of all time. Eh?" She laughed softly.

For a long interval the only sounds were that of the breeze, the surf, and the calling of gulls.

Suddenly Charles Hamilton began to laugh. Glances were traded by Dvorak and Costello and Twitchell, then they, too, broke into smiles. Even Biddle and the wimpish Detweiler picked up the mood when Hamilton saluted von Reichmann, then raising his hands high, clapped lazily, and chortled, "Hear, hear."

"Could we ever," Hamilton gasped finally, "find a colleague of greater audacity and vision? I ask you: Could we?"

There was another burst of laughter and applause.

"All right," Hamilton said finally, "we show hands. All in favor of Gerda's plan?"

It was unanimous.

"Very well. All of us will perform the duties just discussed and assigned, except that the emphasis will be positive rather than negative. Which brings us to the final question of how much we are willing to spend for this thing. Do I hear any recommendations?"

Another silence fell, which was natural, since nobody at the

table other than Gerda and Hamilton himself had a direct say
in the allocation or expenditure of GS funds. Hamilton, as chairman, and Gerda, as executive director, were in fact autocratic
overseers of GS's operational budget, a vast sum collected an-
nually from the world membership and held in the Biekmann
Sparkasse in Zurich and drawn on as required. Still, appearances
were important, because it was known that Hamilton and von
Reichmann—for all their dictatorial power—were answerable
to *Crepes* (dubbed "France's answer to the Mafia" by the European underworld), and it wouldn't do to appear to be anything
but unanimous. *Crepes*, it was said, placed great stock in loyalty
and competence and had a long reach when it came to waverers
and bunglers.

Gerda said coolly, "Bradford knows what he has. It will take
an impressive sum to get his attention."

"So what do you recommend, Gerda?"

"Five hundred million U.S. dollars, half on delivery, half on
the day production begins. With a royalty structure and board
membership in Le Tellier, Cie."

Hamilton's gaze moved around the table. "Comments?"

There were none.

"So be it." He smiled at Morton. "George, you will convey
our offer to Bradford and will deliver the formula to me personally when the deal has been cut. I suggest you return to
Zieglersville this evening, so as to keep things moving quickly
and on track."

Morton said, "Teddy Bradford is greedy. What if he holds
out for more?"

"Then, George, you will go into your Marlon Brando mode.
You will tell him that it's an offer he can't refuse." Hamilton
paused. "Any other business?"

None was suggested.

"Very well, ladies and gentlemen, our meeting is closed. If
you wish to stay the night, you're welcome to do so. Meanwhile,
the swimming pool and handball and tennis courts are available,
as are cars that will take you to the airport whenever you care

to leave. I, of course, must return to therapy at once, so I'll say my good-byes now."

Much laughing and applause followed.

When Morton got back to New York it was after midnight, and a light snow was sifting down, turning everything a dirty white and putting hazy coronas around the streetlights. He retrieved the BMW from the airport lot and fell in with the city-bound traffic, hoping to get to his apartment before the dusting got serious and turned into drifts.

He made it all right, and the snow turned to rain. But as he slowed for the turn into the underground garage, he was watching the rearview mirror with much interest.

He was right. The blue Saturn had followed him all the way from the LaGuardia lot to his very damned apartment building and was now parking across the street and dousing its lights.

"Something new, George," he told himself aloud. "Ya done got yo'se'f a ta-yull."

After garaging the Beemer, he ducked out the side door and hurried down the alley to the street, and, crossing the intersection, took cover behind a line of cars parked at the curb to the rear of the Saturn.

It was snowing quite heavily again, large white flakes that came down like an opaque shower of feathers—an advantage, because it gave him additional cover, and a disadvantage because it virtually obscured everything more than six feet away.

He made his way slowly along the sidewalk, squinting.

A car motor started, a rasping in the midnight quiet. Whoever was at the wheel apparently decided it was not so smart to get snowbound.

Morton began to trot toward the sound.

But he hadn't moved fast enough.

The blue car pulled away from the curb without lights, and he saw its license number like he saw the other side of the moon.

PART TWO

21.

Jacoby had just finished a peanut butter sandwich and a glass of milk when the doorbell rang. He dabbed his lips with a paper napkin, then went to the vestibule, threw the lock, and opened the door to confront the tall blonde—the nurse, What's-Her-Face—who had been at Alicia Hamilton's house that morning.

"Hi, there," he said, trying to disguise his surprise.

"Sorry to intrude on you, Sergeant. I'm Amy Cummings. I was at Alicia's that morning." She held out her hand—proper and rosy-cheeked Scandinavian. The granny glasses glittered in the hallway light, and the fur hat, boots, and long black coat seemed to make her even larger.

Jacoby forced himself into diplomatic mode. "Of course. I saw you at the charity cocktail do the other night, too. This is a pleasant surprise. What can I do for you, Miss Cummings?"

"I'm worried about Alicia. And I'd like to talk to you about it—unofficially, sort of."

"Come in."

She kept her hat on, probably because she didn't want to muss her tidy hairdo. While he was hanging her coat in the entrance closet he said, "Try the sofa. Next to my recliner it's the best seat in the house. Drink, maybe?"

"No thanks. I'm on vacation right through the holidays. Big consumption time. I'm trying not to overdo."

"Thou shalt not be happy at happy hour, eh?"

"You got it."

Settling in, they traded smiles, strangers searching for common ground.

"I should probably be doing this scene at police headquarters," she said in her husky voice. "But I'd just as soon keep a low profile, and you come across like a guy who'll know best what to do about the situation. Without stirring things into a federal case, like."

"What situation?"

"The news says you cops are looking into the Lunt airplane crash. That it might have criminal stuff in it, right?"

"Well, you know how emotional those news types get over accidents, disasters. So what's up? Do you have some information about the crash?"

"Not directly. But I overheard something out at Alicia's house a couple of weeks ago. It's been bugging me, because it sounded sort of—well, spooky."

He waited, polite, saying nothing.

"Alicia and I got acquainted eons ago by way of her charity work at Z'ville General. I really got to know her after I began to give her treatments. I'm an RN, but I'm a physical therapist, too, so when she developed some back problems, I began giving her massages and workouts at her house twice a week. She's got her downside—rich-lady arrogance now and then, mainly to cover a rotten self-image, and she's stubborn and opinionated like you wouldn't believe—but she's really a great woman under all that. Kind, warm, generous to a fault, sentimental, all puffed up with a goofy Puritanical sense of duty and honor and that stuff, but mainly just a sweet, wonderful person it's fun to be around. We've had a lot of laughs, done some good stuff together, community service-wise."

She paused, looking at him as if awaiting confirmation.

He went with the flow. "She seems very nice."

"Well, one day a couple months ago I was on a therapy visit

to Elmwood. I arrived early—came in through the servants' entrance in the garage wing, as I always did—and went to the gym. While I was getting my gear ready, I heard her talking with George Morton in the solarium."

"By talking, you mean he was there? Not on the phone?"

"They were in the solarium, which is connected to the gym by a little hall. I was in the gym, and I could hear them—" She hesitated.

"All this is between you and me, right? I mean, I'd die if I thought Alicia knew I was talking behind her back like this. About her personal life—"

"I'm no gossip, if that's what you mean. Cops work on tips, and you're giving me a tip, is the way I look at it."

She glanced at her watch. She was obviously nervous.

"So what were she and Morton talking about?"

"Alicia was really upset. All teary and mad. I got the impression they'd been talking about Anson Lunt and his work—you know, the cancer crap. But when I picked up on it, Morton was telling her what a great woman she is and that she was being wasted by lashing herself down to a life of misery with a greedy, self-pitying asshole who couldn't care less about her, when all she had to do was snap her fingers and a man who adored her would give her a life. But she went on ranting about no matter how crazy she was about someone else, she wasn't about to leave her husband. She was real religious since she was a kid, you know. She kept saying that it was against the Commandments for a married person to lust after someone else, and she wasn't about to tempt God that way. She couldn't get rid of the lust in her heart and mind, she said, but she could sure enough keep from letting it loose."

She paused, looking pained and forlorn.

"What did Morton have to say about all this?"

"Well, he didn't seem to be real large on the God thing, because he started barking around about how she was nuts to louse up her life by hanging on to childish fables that kept her from tossing out cruelty and loneliness and grabbing on to love and fulfillment—that kind of stuff."

Jacoby cut to the chase. "You're telling me Morton and Alicia were having an affair? That he wanted her to leave her husband and move in with him? And she wouldn't do it because of religious beliefs?"

Nurse Cummings shuddered. "Well, I can't really say—It sounds so gross when you put it that way."

This time Jacoby was more firm, clenched, when he asked the question. "Come on—Say what you think."

"I always thought that Alicia had the hots for Lunt, the usual crush-on-the-doctor bit. You know: 'God, Doc, you saved my life and so hop in the sack and I'll show you how grateful I am' kind of thing. But when I heard this argument it sounded like Morton was in the act somehow. It's hard to explain, but I got the impression that Morton was trying to muscle in, and she was being all torn up by her loyalties to her husband—and to Lunt, for that matter."

"So if they weren't actually having an affair, it sounded like he was trying to get one going. Right?"

"Well, I suppose so—"

Jacoby hunched a shoulder. "I don't want to come across as cold and insensitive by saying so what. But so what? What's a case of the hots got to do with the crash?"

Nurse Cummings chose her words carefully. "Well, I hate to put it this way, but there's a huge pile of money in the background of all this. Alicia's money."

He gave her a quick look. "You're saying what?"

"George Morton, for all his laid-back cool, is a very hard man. Take it from me: he's an Olympic-class angle-shooter. And the guy that gets Alicia gets himself rich. So put it together."

"How about her husband?"

"Charles doesn't need her money. He's stinking rich in his own right."

"You think Alicia wanted Lunt but kept him at arm's length because of morals and all that, and Morton was trying to get in between and get next to Alicia's fortune?"

"I'm not saying anything. I'm telling you what I heard and what my reactions were to it, that's all. Hell, you're the cop.

It's up to you to think about my tip and see if it has anything to it."

Jacoby gave all this a moment of thought, then went for the question she hadn't fully answered. "Why did you really come here tonight, Miss Cummings?"

"I told you: I want to keep a real low profile in this stuff. And I thought you would know what to do with the information. Alicia needs help, and my vibes tell me you can give it to her."

"So tell me why you really don't want to talk to me officially, Miss Cummings."

Suddenly testy, she glanced at her wristwatch. "I got to go. I have a date, and I don't want to be late."

"Answer the question."

She thought about it, and he waited. A minute of this, and she sighed and shrugged surrender. "Okay. I came to you because I'm afraid to be seen at headquarters."

"Why?"

"I'm being watched. Somebody's watching me. I'm afraid that if I went to the cops—Well, I think it's dangerous."

"And you don't think it's dangerous to be seen visiting me at home. Is that it?"

"Well, yeah. I go to headquarters, he knows I'm snitching. I come to this apartment building where lots of people live, he doesn't know anything for sure. Who I came to see, and like that."

"He? Who's he?"

"A tall guy in a hooded black storm coat. I see him out of the corner of my eye. In the supermarket. In parking lots. On the street. In a blue Saturn, following my car. I can never see his face. But he's there."

"Why would somebody be following you?"

"You tell me. I don't have anything, own anything, or know anything that anybody in this world could want. Look at me, Sergeant. Do I look like somebody who could cause anybody problems? Or have something somebody wants?" Self-pity sounding, she answered her own question. "No way."

"Well, obviously you've overlooked something. How about Charles Hamilton? Could he resent your relationship with Alicia for any reason?"

She looked surprised. "Well, hey. That never occurred to me. Far as I know, Charles Hamilton doesn't even recognize my existence. I'm a hired hand, and he treats all his hired hands like they're one step below insects."

"It seems to me you're more than a hired hand. You and Alicia have a somewhat intimate relationship."

She stirred, and her Nordic complexion reddened. "Hold on, there. Are you talking lesbians, or something?"

"No. Possibilities. You have intimate knowledge of Alicia's body. Your conversations probably get pretty personal. Hamilton must know this. He could be one of those guys who is threatened by homosexuality—sees it in every handshake. If so, he could easily misread your relationship and want to do something about it."

"Alicia and I are pals, but not that way. We're both hugely hetero. Matter of fact, I've been shacking with the same hunk for three years. Met him five years ago when I was a nurse-medic in an Army Special Forces unit and he was honcho of the demolitions squad. Now he's service manager for Donagan Used Cars, and, believe me, he's also my full-time personal service manager, if you get what I mean."

"Which is something Alicia's probably told her husband a long time ago. So I'm off course on that one."

He went to the desk and opened his notebook. "Tall, wears a black storm coat with a hood. Anything else about this guy? A limp, or beard, or whatever?"

She thought about that, then shook her head.

"Blue Saturn, you say. Sedan?"

"Yes. Light blue."

"Pennsylvania tags?"

"Yes. But I couldn't read the numbers."

He made some notes.

"I'm not sure about anything," she said. "All I know is, I'm scared. And so is Alicia."

He paused in his writing and glanced at her. "Alicia's seen this guy, too?"

"Yep. Outside her bedroom window, of all things. Also while shopping on Main Street."

Jacoby thought about that, then decided to try a little test of just how much Cummings really knew. "Why hasn't she told me about it?"

Nurse Cummings sighed and shrugged. "Beats me. If she hasn't, I suppose it's because she thinks you've written her off as a flaky broad with an overactive imagination."

Jacoby closed the notebook. Obviously Alicia hadn't spoken to Cummings since calling him to report the stalker in the tree. Which wasn't surprising, seeing that Cummings was on vacation. He found himself wondering why he should give a rat's ass about this. "I never write off anybody, Miss Cummings."

She glanced at her watch again, stood up, and laughed nervously. "Well, at least I've given you a starting place if they find me in an alley with my throat cut. Meantime, I'm outa here."

He walked her to the door. "I appreciate your listening without laughing," she said.

"There's nothing funny about a couple of scared, worried women. I consider that very serious business."

She gave him a moment of somber inspection. "Alicia said you're an okay guy. It looks like she's right."

She left, and he went back to the kitchen to put away the sandwich things. He felt suddenly and unaccountably out of his depth. He wasn't accustomed to the feeling, and it bothered the hell out of him.

Later he sat in the easy chair and read through his notebook, adding notes to the notes. The going was slow, because he kept thinking about Melanie Flynn and devising excuses for calling her at this time of night. None was worth a damn, so, to get back on track, he wrote a summary of Nurse Cummings's visit, then pulled himself to his feet and went yawning to the computer.

He was supposed to do this kind of thing only from his office machine, but if he printed it out and took the hard copy to the office file, what the hell would be the difference? He went on-line and addressed his old cyberfriend, Gustav, at Interpol headquarters:

> Please send soonest any and all data on George Morton (NMI), resident Zieglersville, PA, USA. References here list him as vice president of Bradford Chemicals Corp., and active in many ancillary US and European enterprises. We would like to know if there are any involvements, especially those of a dubious nature, that might have come to your attention re this man. Thanks and regards,
>
> F. Stabile, Chief
> per R. L. Jacoby, Sgt.

The answer came while he was still on-line:

> Computer search of master files here produce no negative information on subject MORTON, George (NMI). References here list him as a member of various trade organizations and contributor to third world assistance programs. But criminal databases show him to be clean. Please let us know if we can be of further service. Best wishes. Gustav.

22.

Melanie was worried about Greg Allenby—as if she hadn't enough to worry about already.

As director of research and development, Allenby was titular head of a number of projects that were the stuff of life for Lunt Biotech. In the Gene Drug Section, TBM-1 was showing remarkable potential in the production of adenosine deaminase, the enzyme critical to the body's immune defenses, and in the past seven months there had been notable results in the compound's applications to cystic fibrosis, one of the more common disorders arising from a genetic defect. If the promise shown here were to be realized, the technique could very well contribute importantly to the treatment and prevention of diabetes— even heart disease and other health problems influenced by genes. Yet Allenby seemed to be totally and inexplicably preoccupied with Anson Lunt's files, and she noted that R&D administration was showing some raggedness as a result.

He was even changing physically. His eyes were red and tired these days; he was becoming—What was the word? Grungy? Unkempt? And Phil Gordon, the genes section leader, grumped openly that Greg was turning into a testy horse's ass—an attitude totally alien to his usual on-the-job persona. When she'd reminded Greg that he was overdue for the company-required annual physical exam, he proved Gordon's point by snapping that he would get around to having a physical when he goddam well was ready to and not before. Even an offer of an extended vacation—euphemized as a "sabbatical"—seemed to do nothing but provoke him. It was now so tense between them she hesitated to bring up the question of in-house espionage, which at first had appeared to be one of his primary concerns.

All this since Anson's death.

Could Greg be in a peculiar state of mourning?

Oh, God: Why was everything always so *complicated?*

She returned to the letter she was writing to employees, summarizing the points she'd made this morning in her meetings with the section heads. How many ways could it be said? Which version was the most believable, convincing, from the employee's point of view, when all it amounted to—no matter how it was said—was that Lunt was not to be sold to Bradford or anybody else, despite the rumors flying around town? The owlish stares, the unsmiling faces, the smell of anxiety heavy in the air had told her that her refutations and explanations simply weren't cutting it. And now, after the zillionth try, she couldn't even convince herself with her writing.

Damn that bastard, Morton.

She turned in her swivel chair and stared out the office window at the blustery winter night, her mind going once again— make that inevitably and inexorably—to Jake Jacoby. The thought: *You want complicated? Well now, there's real complicated for you.*

The thought had barely formed when the phone rang, and he was on the line.

"Greetings, Your Doctorship. This is your genuine Jacobean artifact calling."

"Why?"

"Why? What means why?"

"Cops never call unless they're ready to bust somebody, or something."

"I was sort of wondering if I could buy you a late-night snack."

"I'm into some heavy-duty work here."

He kept it friendly, trying to hide the disappointment. "Doing what?"

She sighed. "Grinding away at Anson Lunt's research records, the things he did over the years to put us where we are today."

"Lot of paperwork, eh?"

"Computer work. Everything he did went into encrypted files in a special computer bank. Greg Allenby, our R&D director, has been on it for God knows how long, and he's getting near a nervous breakdown with the frustration of it. So I've been looking in on all of it—sort of doing a spot inspection of what Greg's been doing in enormous detail, seeing if I can pick up on something he might be missing."

"Why was Lunt so damned secretive? Especially when it came to his own people?"

"I don't think he was being secretive as a matter of worry or distrust. There were no real secrets in his work—chemistry is chemistry, nutrition is nutrition, and genetics is genetics. It's just that he carried certain material under passwords, chosen for his own convenience and with no thought as to how they could impede those who might want to follow his work, step by step."

"Everything I hear about him says he was a loner."

"Well, it was the kind of thing he did. He was always on his own. He'd mix up a little of this and that, try it on this and that, make notes, encrypt them under code names or passwords, and start again. His subjects would come into his office, he would examine them and interview them and make notes, notes, notes. He would visit them in their homes, or in hospitals downtown, or anywhere they happened to be, and he'd make more notes. Then, if the mood hit him, he'd give us a progress report."

"You have been able to read some of his stuff, right?"

"Sure. We've gotten into quite a few files beyond the progress report stuff. Most of them case histories. Month after month, referrals, patients—hundreds of them—some failing, some dying, but more and more of them recovering, thanks to his developing therapy. But then, while plodding through the workaday chemistry and genetic linkages, you bump into those infernal ENTER PASSWORD commands. Then it's dead-end alley, because only he knew the passwords."

"All this data is on computers only? No paper?"

"Many notebooks, journals. But the essential details—the few key bits we need the most—are presumably entered in the computer files, because there's no trace of them elsewhere. And I've run into something even more annoying. We've lost track of some of his subjects, people whose medical histories authenticate his research determinations."

"You sure?"

"Yep. I have one of them on my screen right now. Abner J. Theobold. Imperial Apartments. Milwaukee. A walk-in with prostate cancer. Taken on three years ago this August. Then there's the case history of consultations and treatment that I won't belabor you with. But when I tried to call Theobold, he'd moved, presumably from Milwaukee, because the phone people there had no number for him, even unlisted."

"Or he might have died. Right?"

"I checked. There are no death certificates, no obits. He's just disappeared."

"There are others?"

"Theobold is one of two dozen I've phone-sampled in the past several days. Out of the twenty-four, six no longer have phones. Another six of the numbers we have on file are now wrong numbers—assigned to different parties. That's fifty percent. A very awkward gap in our records. But then, that's offset by the most exciting news of all. The other twelve—those I was able to contact—report that they have absolutely no trace of the cancers Dr. Lunt had confirmed and treated. Every damn one of them has been to his personal physician within the past six months—as instructed to do by Dr. Lunt—and examinations reveal no tumors. Can you imagine? Even if those I haven't been able to trace have all died of their cancers, that's still a fifty percent cure."

"Pretty good, eh?"

"*Good?* It's phenomenal. Even with the thin bit of evidence

I've been able to gather, it's absolutely dead sure that Dr. Lunt was on the verge of bringing in a revolutionary drug and therapy program."

"Well, from what you say, it could make a lot of difference to a lot of sore-hurt people."

"Millions. One out of four Americans will have cancer in their lifetimes. A third of a million Americans die of cancer every year. If Dr. Lunt could come that close to a course of medicine and nutrition that contains cancer the way we've learned to contain TB, or polio, he'd have licked one of the most rotten things humans have to suffer. It's absolutely hand-wringing tantalizing, and I can see why Greg's having fits."

Jacoby paused, then decided now was as good a time as ever. "Which reminds me of something I've been wanting to ask you. You consider Allenby a reliable employee, and like that?"

"Well—Sure. What makes you ask?"

"I've got information that says he's doing business with your competitors."

This time the pause was deeply silent and prolonged.

She said finally, "You can't be serious."

"I've done it again, haven't I. First, Anson Lunt's fatal disease, now this. Little ray of sunshine, that's me."

"Greg's my right-hand man. My friend—"

"Makes it even worse."

"What's he done?"

"I don't know exactly. But his name came up in a police-audited conversation between Teddy Bradford and a private eye named Watson. They were talking about George Morton doing business with the biggies, Falloon and Van Dyke—business apparently involving Allenby. Ring any bells?"

"Falloon and Van Dyke? They buy things."

"Yeah."

"That means that Greg is—"

"Selling something, right?"

"But what's to sell? I have a complete rundown, complete oversight, complete control—"

"I'd say you don't, Doc."

"There's no piece he could sell without my knowing about it. It's just not possible."

"Well, Bradford and Watson weren't just passing the time of day. They don't talk anything if they don't talk money. And with Falloon in the scenario, the money's got to be very big indeed."

She shook her head angrily. "Falloon rolls so high he'd buy Fort Knox just to use its men's room. I know for a fact that Lunt isn't anything, owns nothing, that Falloon would even look at."

They fell into a mutual silence, thinking about all of this. She was about to speak when there was a clanging of bells and blaring of horns.

"Oh, my God—"

"Melanie—What the hell is that racket?"

"The fire alarm. I've got a fire going here—"

"I'm off the line and on my way. You call nine-one-one. Right now."

23.

Morton folded the clipping carefully and returned it to the briefcase on the floor beside his chair. According to the item—faxed to him by Billy Edwards, who, as PR manager of the Zieglersville plant, had been instructed to forward all news involving Lunt Biotech—the fire had been a minor one, confined to a storeroom in the laboratory basement. There had been no injuries, no serious loss, except for some water and smoke damage. Fire department officials were looking into the possibility of arson. Lunt's chief, Dr. Melanie Flynn, refused to comment.

The article, heavy with the down-home tone held dear by the determinedly provincial editors of the *Zieglersville Gazette*, unaccountably evoked the old chestnut about the client, who, reporting to his insurance company that his john had been damaged in a fire, noted that fortunately the flames hadn't reached the house.

Even with fire and journalistic yokelism as linkage, Morton could see no correlation between the Lunt lab and a privy. Because his normally systematic mind writhed in the presence of mixed metaphors and non sequiturs, the joke only added to his foul mood, which was, of course, rooted in the upcoming lunch with Teddy.

Most of Teddy's people hated to be required to lunch with

him. It would always be at his club, a bleak Manhattan brown-
stone with towering windows, ceilings in the stratosphere, dark
walnut paneling, thick Oriental rugs, dim-lit lamps, and routinely sullen, brass-buttoned stewards who served up routinely
lousy food. This was to keep peace with Samantha, who, all too
aware of Teddy's propensities, suspected any lunch taken anywhere but at the "men's club" or the company's executive dining
room—where the food was even worse—to be the cover for
an assignation. While he resignedly accepted lunch at the club
as a shklurt of oil on his turbulent domestic sea, Teddy tried to
rope in the unwary to share his dreary noon hours.

"You're early." Teddy, his face grim, strode briskly into the
visitors' waiting salon like a pitchman in one of those TV com-
mercials for warehouse sales. Fighting the urge to say, "No,
you're late—you're always late, you tiresome dipshit," Morton
managed instead, "No problem. It gave me time to do some
thinking."

Teddy said, "Come on. I'm famished. I had a god-awful row
with Samantha last night and one of the side effects of a row
with her is I always want to eat like a pig."

"Well, it'll calm down. Your rows never seem to hang on
very long."

"This one's different. I mean big-time. I've never seen her
like this. The minute I got back from the board meeting she
tore into me."

"Tore into you? About what?"

"That's what's so—weird. Nothing specific. Just a lot of crap
about a phone call from a friend that proves what a sneaky,
two-timing bastard I am."

Morton showed how he wasn't taking this too seriously. He
smiled, and said, "Hell, Teddy, that's no crap. You're the sneak-
iest, two-timing bastard in town."

"This ain't funny, pal. She's really on my case."

"Anything I can do to help?"

"She likes you, George, but she doesn't like you enough to
make a difference on this one. I'm in really deep shit. She's

talking divorce now. She's talking taking me for every penny I got. She never did that before."

"Well, easy does it. One day at a time. Meanwhile, I wish the best for both of you."

They went into the cavernous dining room, which was nearly unoccupied. Four pallid old men, billionaire players in banking, media, electronics, and oil, nibbled in silent boredom in the near corner. Beside a window, two notorious corporation lawyers whispered in agitated debate across the limp wreckage of their meals. Teddy led the way to a table in the geometric center of this luxurious wilderness and took a chair facing the doors to the foyer, as if preparing to challenge whoever else might dare to enter.

The wearisome Bradford self-importance, combined with his own urgent need to escape this oppressive place, compelled Morton to get to business before the soup was served.

"I don't like to impose on your lunch hour, Teddy, but it was the only time in this hellish day that I could find a moment for some quiet conversation."

Teddy sniffed. "Lunch was invented for precisely that reason. So what's on your mind?"

"I have news. Peabody Chem is launching a subsidiary. It will compete in the drug-manufacturing field."

Teddy, unfolding his napkin, froze. "You're joking."

"It's true."

"Peabody? My aching ass: They make ammonia and fertilizer and bug spray. What the hell are they thinking of?"

"Diversification. They want to ride the crest of the new wave in pharmaceuticals and the health industry. They say, what the hell, drugs are chemicals, and we're chemists, so why shouldn't we get in on the action?"

Teddy, his gaze fixed on Morton's, absently refolded his napkin. "Where are you getting this stuff? There's been nothing in the *Journal*, the trades. Not a frigging peep, even in the rumor mill."

"They've kept an incredibly tight lid on it."

"So, then, answer my question."

Morton lifted his tumbler and sipped some ice water, his gaze on the gray day beyond the windows. "They've asked me to head up the new operation as president and CEO. I wanted to have lunch so I could tell you that I've accepted their offer, and I'm resigning from Bradford, effective at the end of the month."

There was a sudden, weighty pause. In the interval, a freshening wind rattled at the windows, and a muted clatter came from the pantry as a steward arranged silver. One of the old men coughed, and a phone rang in some distant room. Teddy, Morton saw, was dealing with what any warrior—of any stripe in any kind of warfare in any century and milieu—must deal with at least once: the dismaying fact that he has been surprised and outmaneuvered. Teddy seemed to be having a difficult time of it, what with the indirection in his eyes, the sheen that had appeared on his brow. "I'm not hearing this," he said suddenly, swiftly, fiercely. "I haven't heard a word you said."

Morton shrugged. "Nonetheless, it's true."

"So this is what you've been up to, you son of a bitch. You've been using my time and my salary to put yourself in position to snatch the Allenby Formula before I can get it. You've been committing treason. Well, you aren't going to get away with it. I'll tear your balls off—"

Morton held up a peacemaker's hand. "Easy, Teddy, easy. Hear me out."

Teddy's face presented a spectacular shade of purple. "Hear you *out*? What's to hear? First you advise my board and me to forget buying Lunt—which would be a very goddam logical thing to do. You tease me with a videotape showing how great the stuff is. Then you sneak around to the competition, line yourself up with money and a new job, then move in on Allenby before I can get my money together. You think I don't see through your shitty little plot?"

"It's a great opportunity—"

Teddy had momentum and he wasn't giving it up. "Are you out of your frigging *mind*? Taking over a second-rate subsidiary of a second-rate company to make drugs in a market where all the manufacturers are already downsizing—cutting two hundred thousand jobs worldwide—and moving away from innovative R&D? You know goddam well how heavy the pressure's gotten on Bradford, all the others, thanks to the pressures of the health maintenance organizations and the pharmaceutical benefits managers—those sons of bitches who buy and distribute drugs for a third of the nation's patients. How the hell do you think you'll make a dollar as a wobbly newcomer in a climate that's already killing us and all the other hardcase veterans in the biz? Opportunity? Your opportunity is the opportunity to screw me, which is something you've been waiting to do for years. Don't think I don't know it."

Morton kept his cool. "You just put your finger on the opportunity I see. Innovation. Peabody's prospectus asserts that the only way the industry can avoid a real slump is to boost the hell out of R&D and create new blockbuster compounds—that all the well-established biggies are doing precisely the wrong thing at the wrong time. If the U.S. part of the industry is to reverse the trend and shove its sales over the two-hundred-billion-a-year mark, it's going to have to be done by way of innovation."

Teddy sneered and angrily buttered a roll. "I don't buy that for a minute. R&D's getting to be a luxury. Gone are the days when profits were so huge we could throw money at the *Star Trek* stuff. When so many profits came from the low-cost assembly-line production of occasional improvements on long-existing compounds we could afford to fart around with the new stuff, the dizzy ideas. Not anymore, pal."

Morton nodded agreement. "You're absolutely right, Teddy. And that's where we at Peabody see not only our opportunity but also your part of the industry's return to health and vigor."

Teddy bit into his roll, and he chewed angrily, his hot eyes averted as he considered this remarkable assertion. "How the hell do you figure that?"

"The answer lies in teaming up. Not just the mergers that have been transforming the industry—they've pretty well run their course. I'm talking teams, alliances, loose affiliations, with the large companies like Bradford leaving the innovations to small outfits like Peabody. Small shops will concentrate on invention, innovation, radical departures, audacious pushing out of the frontiers. You biggies will concentrate on clinical development— bringing the mad doctor stuff to market acceptability. Linkages, out-sourcing, alliances, will be struck up, and everybody will make a nice dollar."

The cadaverous, brass-buttoned steward brought the soup, a colorless fluid touted on the menu as Chicken Delight. (Which, a sip revealed, probably derived from the chicken's delight at having escaped any role in its preparation.)

Teddy glared over the rim of his wineglass. "You're serious about this, aren't you."

"Indeed I am."

"After all I've done for you, treated you like a brother, cared about your welfare and progress, you're screwing me right in the ass."

Morton shrugged and took on an amused tone. "Face it, Teddy: You never treated me like a brother. Fact is, you really don't like me. In most of my twenty-some years with Bradford you've used me to get your dirty work done—a high-priced gofer and patsy. You exploited my ideas, my energy. You always considered me to be a socially inferior wart. Not that I minded too much. The money was good, and, after all, I really had no interest in that weird life-form you call Society, so what the hell, eh?"

Teddy sneered. "You're a wart, George. But you were my wart. You won't last a minute without me—without my carrying you the way I have all these years."

Morton chuckled. "I'm not proposing to get along without you. I'm proposing that we continue to make nice music."

Teddy gave him a quick look. "What's that mean?"

"On my watch, Peabody's subsidiary—to be named Pegasus Pharmaceuticals, by the way—will be actively looking for innovative drugs of all kinds. Its whole thrust will be to come up with avant garde stuff that guys like you will be glad to do the clinical development on. So, if Bradford, say, has a little something they'd like to outsource, you could just give me a jingle, and if it shows merit—if it's at home among the projects we can handle at our small-shop level—we can form an alliance. See what I mean?"

In the sudden, heavy silence, Teddy struggled to absorb this idea. Eventually he gave Morton a lingering, low-lidded stare, and said softly, "Let me ask a just-supposin'."

"Shoot."

"Supposing I, personally, come across an innovation whomped up by some attic chemist. I buy it, just to put a lock on it. I can't offer it to my own company, because there's too few R&D funds to take on the in-house stuff, let alone something from over the transom. But I know the stuff has great potential, and if I can get it to market, it'll be Croesus City." He paused, gathering his thoughts.

Morton made it easy. "You mean the Allenby Formula?"

"Which, thanks to your video of the old lady, I'm already making moves to buy," Teddy reminded defiantly.

"For two hundred million, as I recall."

"Not a penny more."

Morton showed some enthusiasm. "Actually, I'd welcome the Allenby thing. I suggest you buy it, then bring it to me. Directly. I'm the only one in the industry you could talk to, after all's said and done. You not only have to shop for a buyer, you've got to find the right, safe buyer. And that would be me—chief of Pegasus. Peabody has given me carte blanche. We'll talk about it. You and I. If the price is right, we'll work something out."

Teddy leered. "The price to you guys at Pegasus will be four hundred million, plus two percent royalties."

Morton grimaced. "Twice what you paid? That's highway robbery—"

"The hell it is. It's a bargain. And you know it."

Morton pretended amused curiosity. "You plan to deal directly with Allenby now that you don't love me anymore? Pay him the two hundred in a personal meeting?"

As Morton had expected it would, this set Teddy back a notch. There followed a long pause given to Teddy's deliberations. And then he answered exactly as Morton had expected.

"No. You know I don't want that kind of exposure. I'll hire a go-between."

"That'll give you a problem. Probably spook Allenby so much you'll lose him. He made it clear that he'd deal only with me. Or you. He wouldn't trust a stranger."

"What'll I do, then?"

"I think the answer is obvious. You send me. As my last act as a Bradford vice president. As the only intermediary Allenby will accept."

"That'll put you in both camps. You'll represent me in my buy, then you'll represent Pegasus in the buy from me."

Morton smiled.

This pause was a long one. Teddy was obviously running a mental check of the perimeter, considering the entire spread and checking the fences against the incursions of oversight or bad thinking. Which eventually brought him to the inevitable conclusion:

"Hell, you're as big a crook as I am, George."

"Nobody's as big a crook as you are, Teddy."

Another silence ensued, and Teddy's face worked itself into a red mobility that finally erupted in laughter. Morton, too, began to laugh, and the lawyers and the rich old coots glared at them, annoyed. Which made them laugh all the more. After years of rivalry—keen, unspoken one-upmanship—the tension had snapped in an orgasmic rush of closure and relief.

Teddy consulted his watch—abrupt, amiably peevish. "Where's that steward with our lunch?"

"Tell you the truth, Teddy, I'm not hungry anymore."

"I'm not either. Let's get out of this rotten hole."

Teddy didn't waste any time. As they returned to the executive office suite, Morton peeled off at the communications room to check on a fax due from the plant in Chicago. The delay was serendipitous: leaving Communix for his office, he glanced down the corridor and saw H. E. Thomason, the company comptroller, entering the tall carved doors leading to Teddy's suite. Which was Morton's cue to get back to his desk and, using the system Burroughs had taught him, hack into Teddy's private computer—the exclusive one that had total access to the Bradford Chemicals mainframe and ancillary systems.

Teddy was an emperor. As CEO and majority stockholder, he could enter and edit any order of business in the system. Morton couldn't edit, but he could read over his shoulder.

Thanks to this capability, Morton spent most of the afternoon watching as Teddy—obviously with Thomason's coaching—shifted two hundred million dollars from the company's employee retirement fund into a new secret escrow account accessed by him alone under the password "Toto."

Teddy had made himself one huge mother of an illegal short-term loan from the pension cookie jar.

And Thomason, no doubt, was now expecting an unprecedentedly high bonus next award period.

Late in the afternoon, Morton closed up his office and went to the apartment, where the answering machine requested him to call Gordon Brody at UBS.

"Hi, Gordon. George, returning your call."

"Hi, pal. I was wondering what's with the alert you gave me. Anything going down?"

"Not yet. But it's close."

"Anything you or I can do to speed things along? I came out of a ratings briefing today, and they tell me my numbers are slipping. I sure could use a great story about now. An exclusive with muscles."

"You need an exclusive, you got it."

"You mean that?"

"Scout's honor. You'll be the only one I call."

Brody laughed. "Why are you being so nice to me?"

"Because you're the best. You're no talking head. You're a newsman. An honest-to-God, old-fashioned news-goddam reporter, one of the very few left in this whole frigging spin-crazy, propaganda-driven world, and I admire the hell out of you for it. You can tell those onanistic ratings jerks I said so."

"Those ratings jerks never listen to anybody. But thanks for the vote of confidence, pal."

"I mean it, Gordon. You're the best. And it's only a matter of days now—a few days—and I'll call."

Morton returned the phone to its cradle and stared at it for a time.

Aloud, contemptuous, he said, "Jerk."

After a few drinks and a microwave dinner, Morton took a long shower, then wrapped up in his robe, pulled on his slippers, and returned to the library. He opened the package Burroughs had dropped off and took out the videocassette his Florida guy had air-expressed overnight. The label, scrawled with a red ballpoint pen, was "Patio Peeks."

He played the tape twice, visualizing the goings-on in the form of one of those gooey film scripts his ad and PR people were always submitting to him for technical-accuracy checks.

EXT.—POOLSIDE PATIO—NIGHT
The nearby sea, the lush foliage, the tranquil pool are awash in the light of a midnight moon. The glass door of CHARLES HAMILTON'S poolside bedroom slides open, and in the interior dusk WE SEE him sitting on the bed.

ANOTHER ANGLE
A nude, statuesque in the dim light, appears in the doorway, her face obscured by her cloud of golden hair.

LONG SHOT
She crosses the patio and slowly descends the steps into the pool. Backstroking lazily, she blows a kiss toward Hamilton, now watching from his chair, barely visible in the doorway.

Morton sighed and shook his head. "Charles Hamilton, ole buddy," he said aloud, "you may be confined to a chair, but you sure ain't confined to your loyal wife. You are, ole buddy, one king-size, phony son of a bitch."

Then: "You, Morton—you've got to stop talking to yourself like this."

He turned off the player and ejected the cassette, which he placed carefully in the wall safe beside his favorite, "The Lunt Clock Tower Video."

24.

By morning, the snow had turned to slush. Morton drove to Zieglersville through the clouds of dirty mist that swirled about the turnpike traffic, dogged the whole way by the blue Saturn. But when he turned into the plant parking lot, the tail continued on down A Street and disappeared in the haze.

It was quickly apparent that Teddy had already passed the word about his leaving, because Doris, who served as his Z'ville secretary, was indirect and overly polite and his in-box was filled with little but in-house junk mail.

No matter.

He phoned Mona, Burroughs's live-in girlfriend, and asked her to call Burroughs at his office and tell him to meet him at noon at Waldo's. They had this arrangement because they didn't want the police switchboard people wondering why there was so much phone traffic between a headquarters grunt and the vice president of the town's leading industry. Mona was a clothes nut, and she was more than willing to serve as their communications cutout because of the muscular department store gift certificates Morton sent her each month.

Waldo's, a deli around the corner from City Hall, served as home away from home for off-duty cops, media types, and local merchants and government satraps. It gave excellent cover for meetings with Burroughs because it was a cave of thunder, a bedlam of clattering dishes and booming voices and canned music where patrons could barely hear their own conversations, let alone those at the next table.

Morton pushed his way along the edge of the crowd, and, elbowed aside by a fat waiter with a tray held high, he found himself brushing against Amy Cummings, the nurse, who was leaning against the wall, the pay phone cradled in her shoulder, her long forefinger poised over the keypad.

"Sorry, Miss Cummings," he said, voice raised against the din. "I'm a lousy broken field runner."

"No prob."

"How's Alicia?"

The nurse stared at him for a beat, as if trying to decide how to handle him. She opted for semifriendly. "I'm checking on her now, matter of fact. I'm on day duty at the hospital this week. I always give her a noon call when I'm on day duty."

"Ah. Well, then. Give her my regards, will you?"

She showed a small smile, nodded, and, as he moved off, she returned to the phone and began punching in a number.

He managed to nail a booth near the loo, and Mary Dugan, a waitress shaped like a bowling pin, eventually brought him the special, which was a platter of franks, sauerkraut, and mashed potatoes, with rolls, butter, and a small draft, dessert extra. He was pushing things around with his fork when Burroughs, large draft in hand, slid onto the bench across from him.

"You rang, Master?"

"I need your help, Igor. I've picked up a tail."

Burroughs took a sip of beer and looked amused. "Are you doing somebody's wife, or like that?"

"Get serious. I want you to find out who it is and why he's following me."

Burroughs stared into the foam in his glass. "Any ideas?"

"Not one."

"Description?"

"Saturn, light blue. Occupant and plates, I couldn't make out.

It caught me at my apartment and came down the turnpike with me this morning. It's outside right now."

"In front of Waldo's?"

"Across the street and down the block. It picked me up as I left the plant and followed me here."

"I'll look it over on my way out. But I can't back-tail it. This temp assignment to Homicide has me on a very short string."

"Hey, man. Don't give me that."

Burroughs gave Morton one of his thoughtful stares. "You know Pinky Watson?"

"The private eye out on Maxwell Boulevard? No."

"My full-size spare."

"So?"

"So I'll get Pinky to handle this."

"I'm not about to pay any private eye fees on top of the retainer I'm already paying you."

"For me to put time on this would louse me up on the force. And if I louse up on the force, I'll be out, and that won't do either of us any good. So I'll pay Pinky. Like I did when I had my appendix out last year."

"You paid him out of your retainer?"

"He watched over your account for me while I was in the hospital. He don't work for nothing."

Morton, impressed, put a pat of butter on his potatoes. "I like you, and I like your work. So now I like your attitude."

Burroughs looked him straight in the eye. "I'd be Susquehanna silt by now, if it wasn't for you. I ain't got a hell of a lot anymore, but what I got is yours."

Morton forked up a piece of wiener. He chewed for a time, then told the detective, "And what you also got now is a ten percent raise. Plus unusual expenses. Which include Pinky."

Burroughs took a concluding swig of his beer, pushed to his feet, and gave a quick navy-type salute. "I'll check out the Saturn now and set you up with Pinky tonight."

The butter hadn't even melted when Morton noticed everybody in the front of the place moving to the plate-glass windows and craning, peering south on Walker Street. Mary Dugan came by, holding a tray of meals over her head and looking hassled.

"What's going on, Mary?"

"I don't know. They say some guy just got shot in front of Powers shoe store."

Morton was out of there and down the street and pushing through the crowd just as the sirens began to sound in the distance.

Burroughs was lying on his back on the sidewalk, his topcoat flung open, his shirt bloodied, and his blue eyes fixed in a stare into eternity.

Morton sent quick, stricken glances around, but there wasn't a Saturn in sight.

25.

The *Z'ville Gazette* went ballistic over the Burroughs slaying, and, while he'd always been impressed with the detective's technical savvy and occasional bursts of ballsy ingenuity, Morton thought that the news and headline writers, who made Burroughs out to be the greatest detective since Sam Spade, could have shown a little more restraint. *Who killed the city's ace sleuth?* the first-day banner demanded, the implication being that if the perpetrator didn't step up and admit his guilt at once, he faced having his subscription canceled. The local TV people followed their usual form and echoed the *Gazette*. So the cumulative result was a Zieglersville media running off in all directions in full pants-wetting frenzy.

But Morton admitted that they had plenty of reason to, considering the three-week body count: Lunt, Rooney, Wilmer, Bianco, Margolis, and now an assassinated Ed Burroughs. Stir in an assaulted Melanie Flynn, a suspected arson at the Lunt laboratory, and the spooky prowling of a mysterious guy in a hooded storm coat—not to forget the driver of the blue Saturn, who almost certainly killed Burroughs—and it was turning into a memorable holiday brew.

Morton vowed to disassociate himself from the homicidal aspects and to concentrate on the main action. But even as he made the resolution he knew he was kidding himself. It was becoming plainly impossible to walk the high wire, juggling Allenby, Bradford, Falloon, and Hamilton when some nut in the crowd below was intent on setting the tent on fire.

He hadn't been in his office for more than twenty minutes when Doris intercommed the news that Sergeant Jacoby was there and wanted to see him. He invited the sergeant in, waved him to a chair, and offered him coffee. Jacoby shook his head, being not the slightest bit sociable.

"This is a coincidence," Morton said. "I was trying to make up my mind whether to call you. I was reaching for the phone when you arrived."

Jacoby was unimpressed. "Mary Dugan, waitress at Waldo's, says you were talking to Burroughs just before he was shot."

"That's what I was going to call you about."

Jacoby's stare was unblinking. "So why didn't you call me right away? From the scene?"

"Two reasons. Three, I guess. First, I didn't have my cellular with me. Second, I arrived beside Burroughs a minute or two before a whole army of police and rescue-wagon people began swarming about, and I thought my calling would be redundant. Third, I had to go to the bathroom—big-time—so I made a dash for here."

Jacoby continued to stare as if Morton were a slide specimen. "You seem to have a great knack for being in the picture some-place when people manage to die messy."

Morton was in no mood for that crap. "So do you, Sergeant."

Jacoby's mood wasn't any better than Morton's. "Don't give me smart-ass. What were you and Burroughs talking about?"

"I could tell you that it's none of your business. But that would not only be impolite, it would be untrue. It is your busi-ness. But Burroughs said you're all too busy to handle such business, and if I expect otherwise, dream on."

"What the hell are you talking about?"

"I'm being followed. I saw Burroughs while I was at lunch and asked him if the cops could find out who it is and make them stop. He said I should hire a private eye, because you people are too busy for that kind of insignificant stuff. He left, and a few minutes later Mary told me there'd been a shooting. I went to the scene and found Burroughs. And that's it."

Jacoby took out a notebook and made an entry.

"Mary says you and Burroughs often had lunch together there at Waldo's. Why?"

" 'Often' is a relative term, Sergeant. But yes, I've had some lunches there with Burroughs. He was very good at computers. I have a personal computer at my house that sometimes gives me fits. He told me what to do about the problems. I'd pay for his lunch. Is that illegal?"

"What's this about your being followed?"

"I returned to New York from Florida night before last. I drove from the airport to my Manhattan apartment. I worked in New York yesterday, then drove to Z'ville this morning. In both drives I was followed by somebody in a blue Saturn. I saw Burroughs and asked him what I should do about it. He said I should talk to Pinky Watson. I suppose you know Watson."

"I know him."

"Well, do you agree that I should see him? Or would you prefer to take over this mind-boggling problem yourself?"

Jacoby ignored the taunt. "Witnesses say that Burroughs was checking the tags of a blue Saturn. That he was standing on the sidewalk, looking into the car, when there was a shot. That Burroughs staggered, then fell on his back. That after the shot, the Saturn fired up, hung a fast U from the curb, and vanished southbound down Third Street. Would that have been your blue Saturn?"

"If it wasn't, it was sure as hell a cosmic-grade coincidence."

Jacoby stood up, put away his notebook, and made for the door. En route he said, "I don't know what you're up to yet. But I'm going to find out. And I'll nail you."

Quick anger stirred, and Morton decided to box the little bastard's ears. "You shouldn't listen too hard to those horror stories Melanie Flynn keeps feeding you. Neither one of you knows a good guy from a bad guy."

Jacoby turned, glaring. "Leave Flynn out of this. You don't know what you're talking about."

"Another of the many things you've got to learn, buster, is that I know everything about everything that goes on in this town. I have communications that make you cops look like jungle drumbeaters. I always know exactly what I'm talking about. And that includes you and Flynn." Here he threw a bluff on pure Morton intuition. "You've got the hots for each other, but neither of you knows what to do about it. She's zeroed in on her career, and that doesn't leave any room for a lasting thing. You keep trying to talk about it, but she manages to change the subject, and it's driving you nuts. See how much I know?"

Jacoby gaped.

"One more thing," Morton snapped. "I don't know what the hell's going on, either, but I guarantee you: I'll find out before you do. So treat me nice. I just might let you in on it."

Jacoby didn't answer. He turned on his heel and left.

Morton knew he'd landed a Billy Mahler-type hit, though. Jacoby's face had turned the color of the BMW.

He wished he could feel better about it. But that wasn't possible. He'd lost his cool and thrown a lot of bullshit.

"Easy, George," he said under his breath. "You're almost across the wire. This is no time to look down."

26.

Back in the seventies, soon after he'd begun working for Bradford, Morton would take ten percent off the top of anything he earned and put it into a special account. It was a time when it was a lot easier to hide money, what with laws and regulations that offered relatively few obstacles to the establishment of offshore shell companies and the transfer of money through them to secret Swiss bank accounts. And with his modest sums he set up Dix & Co., headquartered in Luxembourg, and retained Heinz Schroeder, a young and hungry Swiss lawyer, to serve as its "managing director." It was all just paper, of course, and Dix was really a file cabinet drawer, with Schroeder doing all the grunt work and serving as Morton's conduit to a secret account in Allgemeine Sparkasse, Geneva. As permitted under Swiss law, the bank—acting in his behalf but in its own name—bought and sold securities, real estate, and other investments and kept Morton's name out of it all. Over the next few years, the money began to pile up, and when he wanted to skim some important cash for needs in the States, Schroeder—or later, when Schroeder became a fat cat himself, his assistant—would hop a plane and courier the funds to Morton, enabling him to evade U.S. income and capital gains taxes. It was no longer so simple these days, of course, so he and Schroeder had set up a

labyrinthine set of trusts in offshore tax havens in which Schroeder, a nonresident alien, owned the trusts and made Morton the
beneficiary. Since all Morton's income as the beneficiary was
earned outside the States by a grantor who was not a U.S.
citizen, it wasn't taxable by the IRS. He and Schroeder had
played a lot of variations on this trust theme to the point where
entirely legal, untaxed wealth continued to pour into them both.

The acrimonious episode with Jacoby had rather racked Morton back, impressing on him once again how little time and
elbow room he had left to tie the dangling strings. So that
afternoon, pointedly reminding himself that Jacoby was still fish-
ing and there was no reason to panic, he nevertheless put in a
call to Schroeder, mainly, he suspected, to make himself feel
that he was doing something specific and useful. Miraculously,
Schroeder was at home, having just returned from an evening
at the theater, and he assured Morton that everything had indeed
been taken care of at his end.

"Have you closed on the boat?"

"Yes, sir," Schroeder said in his Americanized, German-
accented English, "she's all yours now, and is being fitted out
at the Marina del Sol on Catalina Island."

"The paper trail?"

"Dealt with, precisely as you've ordered."

"I've been asked to form the management of a new company
here, and I've been telling everybody that I need a vacation
before I take over."

"Well, the boat'll be ready to take you around the world, if
that's what you'd like to do."

"Two weeks, max. Put out the word."

"Will do. All the necessary people will be put on notice. As
for the *Sea Nymph*, she'll be ready for a sail of two weeks or
two years."

"Tell Captain Rawlings to expect an e-mail from me the first
week in January. To check his computer in-box every morning
and night during that week, okay?"

"Consider it done, sir."

"I appreciate your help on this."

"My pleasure as always, Mr. Morton."

"I hope you have a happy holiday season."

"Thank you, sir. You, too."

Morton pulled the BMW into the alley a few minutes before four and parked just south of Waldo's service and delivery door. At three after four, Mary Dugan came out, glared at the rainy sky, and, hunching into her topcoat and hopscotching puddles, made for Main Street. He started the motor and let the car drift alongside.

"Hi, Mary."

She looked at him, startled. "Mr. Morton. What—"

"Get in the car. I'll drive you home."

"It's only a coupla blocks."

"I know. Get in. I want to talk."

"I got some shoppin' to do—"

"After we talk. Get in."

He stopped the car, and she came around and took the seat beside him. After they were moving and headed west on Third Street, she gave him an uneasy sidelong glance.

"You sore because I put the cops on you?"

"Not really. If not you, somebody would have remembered seeing Burroughs talking to me. And it wasn't all bad. It gave me a chance to clear myself right away."

"Well, I sure didn't want to give you no trouble, all the nice things you done for me. But the cops come on pretty hard, and I felt terrible about Mr. Burroughs. He was another guy treated me good, and I just felt awful—mad and mixed up, sorta."

"Me, too."

While they waited for the light at Third and Locust, she gave him another glance. "What you want to talk about?"

"The pay phone at Waldo's. Who uses it?"

"What kinda question is that? Hell, everybody uses it. It's a public damn phone."

"But you do get a pretty good view of the traffic around it, on your way to and from the kitchen. Right?"

She sighed, an impatient sound. "Well, sure I do. But I also get a good view of the cars and buses and trucks that go up and down the street. So what?"

"I know none of this makes sense to you, Mary, but it's important. So just bear with me. I want you to take a few minutes and think hard about the people you see using the phone. Does any one of them stand out—stick in your mind for any reason?"

She thought, and he waited.

"Not really," she said finally. "Mostly it's lawyers from the courthouse and cops and news guys—you know, answering beepers. Regular people, not so many."

"How about Waldo employees?"

She shook her head. "Naw. Waldo lets us use one of the office phones for important personal calls. It's one of our perks. He's a good guy, that way."

He turned the corner at Brewster and stopped at No. 15.

"You'll probably get these same questions from the police in a day or two. I'd appreciate your not telling them I've been asking about it."

"Okay."

"And do me a favor, will you? Keep an eye on that phone, and if you see anything that doesn't fit a pattern, give me a call."

"Sure will. I owe you."

"On the contrary. You'll find your Christmas stocking to be a little fuller this year."

She opened the door and swung out. "You're a nice man, Mr. Morton." She glanced at the duplex behind her. "By the way: How did you know where I live?"

"High-tech. I looked you up in the phone book."

She shook her head again and laughed. "What'll they think of next, eh?"

Morton's date with Pinky Watson was for five-thirty, at his office, which proved to be a storefront thing in one of the strip malls east of town on Maxwell Boulevard. He'd arranged to meet there because he wanted to size Watson up, and it's easier to get a line on a man when you catch him where he puts his feet up. He might swagger into your office, all natty and cool and coming on as a hotshot, but a peek into his own office can show the messy nincompoop that lurks beneath.

Watson, despite his Runyonesque first name, was no dese-and-dem type. He actually stood up to shake Morton's hand and offer a chair. His suit and shirt were Madison Avenue, his tie was Italian silk of conservative pattern, and his shoes were as shiny as quality leather permits. His haircut was neat and standard, as were his office and his secretary, a brunette of indeterminate age, who, after showing Morton in, made a neat and standard exit.

"I'm sorry we had to meet under these circumstances, Mr. Morton. Ed Burroughs will be missed."

"He was very helpful to me. I understand that you have been, too."

Watson waved a dismissing hand. "Ed asked me to stand in a few times. You are a man with interesting problems."

Morton glanced around the room. "How come? Why out here in the 'burbs, instead of downtown?"

"It reassures my clientele. You'd be surprised how uneasy people get in the shadow of the courthouse, or in a second-floor walk-up on Bail Bond Alley. By the time they decide to see me, they're already uneasy enough. They don't need to be depressed by the architecture, or the adjacency of cops and jails. So I try to look like a yuppie insurance broker, or a Realtor, say."

Morton looked around some more, showing his approval.

Watson cleared his throat delicately. "How can I help?"

"I'm not exactly sure at this point. At the time he left us, Mr. Burroughs was about to ask your help in identifying a blue Saturn that's been following me recently. In fact, he was shot while looking over the car. I assume he was getting the tag number before calling you."

"Actually, he did get the number and he did call me on his

cellular. Moments before he was shot. I've already ID'ed the Saturn."

Morton let his surprise show. "Well, now."

"It won't do you much good, I'm afraid. The car is owned by the Ajax Car Rental Company, whose records show it's been rented on the credit card of a Lewis R. Tompkins, a salesman for the Union Nickel Plating Company of Kansas City. I've checked, and Union Nickel is no more than a post office box number in K.C., and the card is backed by a thousand-dollar checking account in the name of Lewis R. Tompkins, same P.O. address, deposited in the First National Bank there."

"Somebody's going to a lot of trouble to tail me."

Watson smiled. "I said you had interesting problems."

"How much do you know about Burroughs?"

"Only that he was the police force electronics expert, and he moonlighted. I'm assuming that he had some kind of personal problem with money and that you were his guardian angel, for which he provided you with certain services."

"How much did Burroughs tell you about me?"

"Burroughs wasn't a talker. But he made it clear that the Z'ville tom-toms have it right. You are heavy artillery in the international chemical business. You are a full ten on the cool scale. You have an itch to eavesdrop and the big bucks that help you scratch it. Ed said that nobody who knows you is neutral: They either love you or hate you—probably because they can't figure out whether you love or hate them."

"I didn't realize he was a psychologist."

"Don't laugh. He came across as a dumbo flatfoot. But he was a lot deeper than that. And he was the president of your fan club. He said you are a closet good guy."

"Well, for God's sake, don't let it get around."

Watson looked pained by the sarcasm. "I'm afraid this isn't going very well, is it."

"On the contrary. You're looking better by the minute. But, Scout's honor, are you as technically proficient as Mr. Burroughs?"

Watson seemed about ready to write Morton off. "I was using

computers and listening devices," he said, just south of testy, "when Burroughs was dating cheerleaders. And I've supplied most of the specialists he used on your tasks."

"Working for me directly can get hairy."

"So I've noticed. The body count goes up every day."

"It also at times gets a little bit, ah, illegal."

"Mercy me."

"So are you ready to become Ed Burroughs Two?"

"I'm not so sure. Give me a little push, and I could end up being one of those who hate you."

Morton laughed. "Well said. I don't need an Ed Burroughs Two. I need a Pinky Watson One. What's your fee?"

"Two hundred and fifty a day and expenses."

Morton shook his head. "No. That's what you charge jealous husbands to peek through motel windows. We're not talking a two-day tail job here. This is the majors. I want you available whenever I call and I want star-quality performance at all times, on all tasks, from electronic penetrations to motel peeking."

"You're talking retainer?"

"Call it what you will."

"I've got other clients—"

"Do what you want with those. But I come first."

"This won't be cheap."

"So how expensive?"

"Two thousand a week, plus expenses."

Morton took his checkbook and pen from his jacket pocket. "I'll give you the first four weeks up front, just to seal the deal. I make this out to—?"

"Watson Investigations, Inc."

Watson pretended not to watch the movements of the pen. "What would you like me to tackle first, Mr. Morton?"

"Tell me who Lewis R. Tompkins really is. Tell me why he's following me. And then persuade him to stop."

"All right."

"There's another part. My look at the police computers shows that the cops are working like hell on the Burroughs do. If my cop computer gives me anything I think will be useful to you,

I'll either call you or e-mail you an alert. What's your address?"

"PinkyW@ USNet.com."

Morton made a note. "Okay. I'll flash-mail you and set up a private chat room, code name 'jasmine.' "

Watson smiled the smile of a man who thinks he's come out on top in a gorgeous deal. "Sounds good," he said.

It sounded good to Morton, too. He'd been paying Burroughs twenty-five hundred a week. Plus expenses.

After Morton left, Watson picked up his phone and dialed the special number.

There were two rings, then: "What is it?"

"Hi, Mr. Bradford. You're not going to believe the news I've got."

"Well?"

"He just hired me."

"Morton? He just *hired* you? To do what?"

"He wants me to take charge of his sneaky stuff."

Watson waited, smiling to himself, for the explosion of laughter at the other end to subside.

"That's absolutely the weirdest goddam thing I ever heard. Great. Great."

"It is pretty funny, isn't it. Now that we have him in our laps, do you have any special instructions?"

"Not yet. Just go with the flow. And tell me daily what the hell he's up to. Okay?"

"My pleasure, Mr. Bradford."

27.

Melanie sat at her desk, staring out at the wintry noon and trying to concentrate on the lousy question of how to deal with Greg Allenby. He had called in at eight-thirty, complaining that his long hours in the lab had finally caught up with him and that he simply couldn't be in until twelve, at which time he would like to see her in her office. She had managed to keep her voice calm and reasonable, and, luckily, her other phone line had blinked, giving her an excuse to break off the conversation, claiming busyness.

The sense of betrayal cut even more deeply when she remembered the sympathy and concern she had expended on the son of a bitch. Worrying over the deteriorating health and increasing truculence brought on by his long hours at the computer bank; stewing about his perplexing, single-minded determination to penetrate Anson Lunt's files at the expense of the lab's business of the day; pitying him for the now-public disaffections that were costing him his beautiful family. What a huge bunch of five-star horseshit.

How would she handle this?

What would she say when he walked in, and she looked into the bastard's hollow eyes?

*Hi, Greg. I hear you've been selling your soul to the Bradford
Company store.*

*Well, now. There he is: the Lunt Biotech's very own high-tech
Benedict-friggin'-Arnold.*

Get out of my sight, you miserable, sidewinder asshole.

None of the above. All were too polite, too elegant.
Besides, they'd produce only momentary satisfaction.

It would be better to say nothing, pretend to know nothing,
and keep alert.

But was she good enough as an actress to pull it off?

Hell no.

The intercom warbled.

"What is it, Helen?"

"Dr. Allenby is here, Dr. Flynn."

"Good," she lied, feeling anything but good about it, but
aware that he could hear her voice at the other end. "Have him
come in, please. I'm all clear."

*Now remember who's in charge here, Flynn. You're the captain,
and you've got a first mate you can't trust anymore. You're the one
who decides what's going to happen here. What would Jacoby say—
His balls are in your court?*

She felt the nudge of laughter, but she assured herself that it
wasn't hysteria.

Allenby had spent the entire morning preparing for this moment
of—What was it? Encounter? Engagement? Confrontation?
Triumph? He'd showered and shaved and dressed with exceptional care, selecting only those specifics that would promote an
image of conservatism and responsibility: the banker's gray suit
with its vest and gold watch chain; the white oxford-cloth shirt
with button-down collar; the silk tie with regimental striping;
the black wing tips, polished to brilliance. And yet, when he
strode into the room (briskly, confidently, as he'd vowed to
do) he was instantly stricken with the feeling of being naked—
physically denuded, exposed, and vulnerable.

Perhaps it derived from Flynn's remarkable eyes and their

unblinking appraisal. Or maybe it was some kind of resonance with the old days, when Jennifer would consider him with silent, knowing accusation those midnights he'd come home, sodden with liquor and someone else's perfume. He knew with absolute certainty that Flynn, like Jennifer, impossibly beautiful and cool and crisp with the aura of command, could see—godlike—through the flannel and cotton and silk, directly into his gut and the rottenness that festered there. He just knew she knew.

But he got on with the game, because there was nothing else to do.

"Sorry I'm late, Mel, but the old bod seems no longer able to cope with wee-hour involvements."

"Have a seat."

There: that peculiar lack of the warmth that had for so long been so much a part of their association, that air of tacit reproach. He felt unendurably depressed and shaken.

"I asked for this meeting because there's something you must know, and to delay it any longer could only cause you more difficulty and inconvenience."

The level stare wavered not a millimeter. "Oh?"

She was doing him a favor, he decided. She was sparing him the playacting, the pretense that his words and manner were mystifying, disturbing.

"I'm here to tender my resignation. I'm leaving Lunt Biotech, effective the first of the year."

"I see. Is there any particular reason?"

There were many parts to the answer, of course, and they appeared in his mind sequentially, a kind of mad scrolling in which four decades' worth of failures and incompletions and unrequitements tumbled one over the other: a father he could never satisfy, a mother who didn't care; schools he hated that prepared him for a career he didn't want; the craving for recognition greater than his ability to attain it; the awareness of his superiority over the superiors under whom he slaved; interpersonal relationships—crowned by a marriage to a woman he didn't covet, who gave him children he didn't like—that inevitably degenerated into anger, bitterness, disappointment, humiliation, resentment, and a chronic bleeding of the soul. *Any particular reason? Well, let's see. How to answer? Try this: a lifetime of being somebody I really wasn't, doing things I didn't want to do, hourly smothering the compulsion to smash down the fences and run off to a paradise in which I would rule,* I *would determine how to achieve the fulfillment that's been denied me. Now that's been changed. After all my years of grunt work, the Great Doctor was about to deny me a share in the cure. I've claimed the cure as my own, and now I'm off to my private paradise. Want any more particular reasons, babe? I have a hundred million of them in my wall safe.*

His initial uneasiness and—What? Guilt?—had dissipated, as if the reminder of his waiting wealth had given him new strength to deal with this melancholy scene.

"No particular professional reason," he said. "You've probably heard that my private life hasn't been going too well, and along with those—troubles—I've been having an itch to hit out for new horizons, to exchange the old familiar for some new familiars, so to speak."

"You've taken a job someplace else?"

He shook his head. "No. I'm just going to take my part of the family savings and go out and look at the world. Head for the warm country. Find a place where the sky's blue and there are palm trees and a hot sun." He nodded toward the windows. "I don't think I can take another minute of that godforsaken weather out there."

"You and Jennifer are divorcing?"

"Alas, yes. For twenty-five years, she'd go her way, and I'd go her way. No more of that."

"How about the kids?"

"No loss. All they ever did was think up cretinous things to say about me behind my back."

Flynn cleared her throat, and there was a pallor in her face he hadn't noticed before. "Well," she said, her voice low and faltering, "I'm sorry that things have turned out this way. I accept your resignation, of course. And I hope you come into what you deserve."

What a peculiar way to put it, he thought.

"Now if you'll excuse me," she said, glancing at her watch, "I'm due at the Anson Lunt memorial service, and I don't want to be late." She stood up, waiting for him to leave.

"Well," he said, rising from his chair, "good-bye, Mel. I wish you the best of luck."

"Thank you."

He went to the door, hesitating there for further word from her. None came, so he went on.

Odd, he thought. No handshake.

And in the entire conversation, she'd never once spoken his name.

Poor loser.

Morton decided that it had been a mistake to limit his penetration of the Lunt organization to Allenby's verbal reports and to the laboratory computer bank. He should also have had Burroughs tie him into Melanie's home PC and word processor, because it might have given him earlier word on her decision to sell Lunt to Amalgamated Chemical.

Allenby, who had been drifting between his efforts to finalize the disks he would turn over to Teddy and his euphoria over impending idle-richhood, finally woke up enough to slip Morton copies of printouts of a letter Melanie had drafted for dispatch to Lunt employees. She'd written the drafts on her home computer and submitted them to her department heads for comment. Besotted as he was by booze and daydreams, Allenby had failed to see the importance of her intentions, and Morton was so ticked over this lapse he was ready to make Allenby a soprano.

Her decision had apparently been triggered by gossip, widely spread at last week's Rotary Club lunch by the Chamber of Commerce's resident bigmouth, Roger "Ruff" Cobb. According to Cobb, Morton's visit to Melanie's office had been construed by employees to be a closure on Bradford's offer to buy—that Melanie, acting with the approval of Lunt's lawyers, had agreed to sell and had, indeed, signed a letter of understanding Morton had brought along. Morton had missed the lunch, of course, and, since the subjects of gossip are always the last to hear it, it wasn't until Wednesday night, when he got home from his talk with Watson, that he was enlightened by the letter drafts Allenby had dropped off in his mailbox.

Melanie had been given a hellacious problem. How do you convincingly deny such a rumor to the employees of a biotech research organization who are already demoralized by their beloved leader's death? How do you halt the spread of uneasy speculation and prudent ass-covering among the scores of suppliers and vendors from whom you buy on time or with whom you deal on a simple handshake? What do you say to steady the confidence of those backers who have given you years of loyalty and tons of money because they think you are a straight rail carrying important, humanitarian things and would never plan a bugout behind their backs?

And, of course, Morton had been given an even more pressing problem. How do you keep an angry and confused young woman from trying to kill the gossip by doing something hugely dramatic and positive—especially when her dramatics would screw up your own plans?

There was no other way. He'd have to talk to her again.

Level with her, and hope for the best.

If she'd let him anywhere near her, that is.

The Church of the Holy Writ was an institution favored by Zieglersville's well-heeled and socially prominent cadre because God and other embarrassing subjects were rarely discussed on the premises. Here on routine Sundays one sang a few nonpartisan hymns, drowsed through a politically correct sermon, dropped a fat check in the plate, and then, piety thus publicly certified, voomed off for an afternoon of golf. Since there seemed to be a kind of sentimental ecumenism in all this, and since she apparently felt Anson deserved some kind of propitiatory send-off by his erstwhile faultfinders, Alicia had chosen the church as the site of a public memorial service to be held three weeks after Anson's private interment in Boise.

Morton watched the proceedings from the church balcony, well away from the several hundred dignitaries packing the sanctuary below. His lofty perch gave him a God's-eye view of the church's pastor, the Rev. Dr. Alois von Zieg (whom in his more sarcastic moments Morton called *Der Writmeister*), as he eulogized Dr. Anson Lunt as "a friend of the church, a layman with deep pockets, who will be surely and sorely missed." The position also provided an excellent view of Melanie, and it was she who dominated the lenses of Morton's opera glasses.

Odd, how she had seemed so, well, *plastic* at first. She had since changed subtly—still gorgeous and immaculate, still cool and poised, but now softer, warmer.

Thanks to Jacoby, obviously.

She had been mortified by the impaired-driving arrest, and the fact that the hospital tests showed that the amount of alcohol in her blood wouldn't have made a gnat drunk had seemed only to make her more angry, according to Benny Steinberg, a reliable informant who had been on ER duty that night. Pell and Skidmore, the cops who nailed her on the causeway, told Benny she'd been zonked and fragrant, but a chargeable offense had been ruled out when her blood-alcohol content proved to be too low and the lump on her head too big. "This here lady is not drunk—she's been sapped and squirted," Benny had pronounced, not without some pleasure at putting down Pell, with whom he'd never gotten along.

Traversing the crowd with his glasses, Morton had to smile at the recollection of Benny's exultant leer as he'd described the incident over coffee the day after.

Thank God there are signs of intelligent life on earth.

Dr. von Zieg closed the notebook on the lectern before him, gazed around the church with a kind of regal Charlton Heston benignity, and invited a closing prayer. A few actually joined in, but (the glasses showed) most spent the interval taking covert inventory of who was there, with whom, and wearing what. And it was depressing to see the evaluating stares Melanie was sending toward a blushing Jacoby, who tried to be all kinds of professional as he pretended to study the audience from the shadow of a nearby column. Her love life was none of Morton's business, but he hated to see her spending all that wonderful charm and energy on a Rube City cop whose idea of dressing up was a five-year-old gray gabardine suit.

After the service, it took some time to get down from the balcony and through the milling-about at the entrance to the sanctuary. Morton waited, his irritability rising, while Melanie took time to chat with Jacoby. But then Chief Stabile and his wife came out of the crowd and, from the looks of things, Jacoby was asked to escort Mrs. Stabile to the car, because the two of them disappeared down the walk toward the boulevard parking area, leaving the chief to shake hands and banter with Mayor Maloney and a gaggle of lesser pols. Morton began to follow Melanie as she worked her way through the crush and made for the walkway leading to the church parking lot, a spread of macadam and tidy painted lines in a glen surrounded by gentle rises and stately trees. Then, consistent with his generally negative day, she was overtaken by Alicia, who took her arm and led her into the cul-de-sac, where the fountain splashed forlornly in its arc of gray, winter-brittle landscaping.

With no move left to him at the moment, he stepped into the adjacent garden and stood, pretending to contemplate the verities, before the carved-marble crucifix there. This turned out to be a break. The tall evergreen hedge gave him good cover from which to watch the two women and hear what they were saying. "You absolutely must not sell the Lunt properties—to Amalgamated or anyone else," Alicia said sternly. "You have no idea what's at stake, and you have no right to sell anything until Anson's wishes are officially established."

Melanie's astonishment showed. "Who—Who told you about Amalgamated?"

"Greg Allenby called me this morning. He was quite upset, and wanted to know if I could say something to you. Well, I'm saying it: Don't sell Lunt to anybody."

"Greg had no right to tell you that. He violated our company security when he talked to you—"

"Don't sell!"

"The lawyers say I have the authority—"

"Lawyers be damned. I don't care what those sons of bitches say. I'm telling you it would be the mistake of your lifetime to abandon the company at this point. Don't, don't, *don't* sell!"

Melanie's face reddened. "Dammit, Alicia, you don't have to look at the faces of those employees, every one of them knowing that Lunt is on the ropes. Every one of them thinking that I've abandoned ship, selling out to Bradford and leaving them to sink without a trace. The only way I can convince them I haven't is to sell to Amalgamated, a thoroughly excellent company whose offer protects Lunt employees and their vested rights in every conceivable way."

Alicia, more agitated than he'd ever seen her, played her only trump. "All right, if you must sell, then sell to me."

Melanie's eyes softened, and she placed a hand on Alicia's shoulder. "You're a dear, precious woman, Alicia, and I love the hell out of you for your loyalty to Anson and his people. But I'm afraid that you couldn't afford it. The price is very high, and the time frame is small."

"Try me," Alicia said, angrily. "You haven't the foggiest notion of what I can or can't afford. I'm not a person—I'm an economic force."

"My God, Alicia. Are you serious?"

"Never more serious in my life."

"The deal with Amalgamated is almost done—"

"Break it the hell off."

"I'll have to talk to the lawyers—"

"Have them talk to my lawyers. And name your price."

Alicia turned and strode off toward the parking lot, leaving Melanie alone beside the melancholy fountain.

Morton's problem was to remain unnoticed. Alicia had said everything he'd hoped to say and much more, so there was no reason for him to hang around. With all the crap that had been flying between them, he didn't need to have Melanie catch him

244 JACK D. HUNTER

eavesdropping. He looked around quickly for a route that would get him out of the cul-de-sac quietly and unseen.

The clouds had lowered, the wind had picked up, and a scattering of snow was in the air. Against the dark laciness of the trees and shrubs on the rise above him there was a movement, a shadow in the shadows. He considered it briefly, curiously, then the Morton prescience kicked in, and he felt a rush of alarm.

It was not a shadow. It was someone in a black, hooded storm coat, now motionless behind a huge oak.

He squinted, his heart suddenly pounding.

There was another movement, slight, and from around the oak came an arm, and a gloved hand, and in the hand, an automatic pistol—drawing a bead on Melanie, who stood pensive and alone.

He wasn't aware of running and shouting and crashing through the evergreen screen. There was only the flying through the air and sweeping Melanie to the ground, then feeling a hot, imprecise pain, and lying on her, covering her struggling body, hearing her odd little whimpers, the shouts and squealing from the parking lot.

For a moment, the snow-dusted rise and its towering trees expanded and contracted, as if a huge, erratic lens were seeking a focus. Then his eyes settled down, and he saw with absolute clarity the hooded figure leveling the pistol directly at him, preparing for a second shot.

There was a second shot, but it came from the walkway behind him. The hooded figure turned and ran, disappearing on the far side of the rise.

Morton rolled his bulk away and, cupping her face in his hands, peered into Melanie's frightened eyes. "You okay?"

"I think so." Aberrantly, he marveled at how her breath could be so sweet.

Jacoby knelt beside him. "You okay, Morton?"

"My left shoulder hurts like sin." Morton gave him a bleary look. "You got an aspirin?"

Jacoby reholstered his pistol and produced a cellular. "I'm just about to call for one."

28.

She stood under the shower for nearly ten minutes, eyes closed, face raised to the steamy flow, lost in the mix of renascence and gratitude that follows a brush with death. Eventually the thankfulness dissipated, making way for an unfocused anger. So Greg Allenby was a lousy shit, and he was gone, and good riddance. So that creep Morton had knocked her down and wrecked her favorite topcoat and shredded her panty hose and knocked the wind and pee out of her—was there nothing the son of a bitch wouldn't do to ingratiate himself? And Jacoby: rushing her to a hospital for a checkup she didn't need, then bringing her home, where the breakfast dishes were still in the goddam sink and her laundry was piled on the sofa, and then hanging around outside her bathroom like a lovesick schoolboy, pretending to be worried about her state of mind now that she had survived a melodrama that had probably been written, directed, and starred in by a greedy, sidewinding—

Hey, knock it off already. Hysteria ain't your style.

She turned off the shower, dried herself with a huge white towel, then pulled on her terry robe and went barefoot into the living room, where Jacoby, standing by the sofa, was hanging up the phone.

He gave her that grin. "I was about to come in and drag you

out before you shriveled like a prune. You must have used a hundred dollars' worth of hot water."

She said nothing, but stood, staring at him.

He blinked and grinned again. "This phone's been alive. The media guys want to ask you some questions. Being the efficient, high-tech sort of fella I am, I've turned off the ringer."

She strode directly to where he stood and, seizing the lapels of his jacket, pulled him to her and gave him a four-thousand-horsepower kiss on the lips. His reaction to this wasn't really clear, as busy as they were, collapsing on the sofa and rolling to the floor in a cascade of laundry.

Somewhere in the night, she said, "Are you awake?"

"No."

"Tell me something."

"Okay: You're under arrest and have the need to remain silent."

"Tell me: Who the hell are you to think you might have a place in my life?"

"I am your Jacobean genie. Pinch my butt, and I'm at your command."

"I don't need a man in my life."

"The hell you don't. I've got the bruises to prove it."

"I'm not talking sex. I'm talking the life and weal of Melanie Andrews Flynn. All my life I've been up to my eyes in men. His Royal Highness, King Daddy the First and Last. Hot-pants jocks in high school, leering gropers in college, condescending poobahs in industry—God, I've been smothered in men. But you know what? To me they're just a bunch of bit players, shooters of lines in the ongoing, not-so-damned-dramatic drama of my résumé. I take them or leave them, and I mostly leave them, thanks to their self-love and apparent resolve to bore me to death."

He lay in the darkness, thinking about that. "You like girls better, maybe?"

"I've done my share of research. Between Tillie McShane,

who kept lifting my skirts in the cloakroom of Miss Doris Randall's Country Day School, and Gerhardt Repp, a Luftwaffe pilot I got to know on a college vacation in Germany and who was the all-time world champion leave-you-cross-eyed pile driver, I tested my capacity and orientation. I turned out to be reasonably lustful and definitely hetero, and with that settled, I've gone about my mostly abstinent life. Until now. And I'm still wondering whether you're such a hot idea."

He turned and faced her on the pillow. He brushed back her hair and kissed the end of her nose. "I was going to say that you are the coolest, most super, and most all-gone wonderful person there is, and just to know you is the best thing that could ever happen to me."

"You were going to say all that?"

"Give or take a few adjectives."

She was puzzled. "I've known you for less than a month, and in that time you've metamorphosed. First a Boring Boris, then a Princely Presence. I'm not sure why that is."

"Familiarity breeds content, they say."

She persisted. "You've been an imp on my shoulder. One minute you tell me you're bringing all hell my way. The next minute you tell me to stop fearing you and start doing you."

"I like that last part."

They lay silent for a time, holding each other close, listening to the muted sounds of the night outside. Then:

"I don't know what to do about Morton."

"Do about him? What means that?"

"I don't like him. I don't trust him."

"Hey, the man saved your life."

"That's what I mean. How can I be all kinds of grateful to a man I worry about all the time?"

"No big deal. Just tell him thanks."

"Do you think he set all that up? That shooting?"

Jacoby pushed away and gave her an incredulous stare. "Set it up? You mean arranged it—"

"Hired a sharpshooter, maybe, just to scare me and nick him

so that he'd look like a hero and make me fall all over him with gratitude."

"Why the hell would he do that?"

"I think he's got a thing for me. Every time I talk to him, I get the feeling he's hitting on me. That I'm really important to him. Personally."

"Can't blame him for that. You're a beautiful and damn smart woman. And he wants to buy your lab and clinic."

"It's more than that. It's—personal. I keep thinking he set up that shooting, just to get my attention."

Jacoby sighed, the sound of a man amused but a bit impatient. "I'll allow you a tad of paranoia, having gone through what you did and all. But that aside, do you have any idea how much skill it takes to shoot a pistol with accuracy? Especially at the distance involved in this case? Not only distance, but movement, too. It's hard as hell to hit a moving target on a formal pistol range, let alone a target rolling around on a parking lot at the bottom of a hill on a windy day. Morton would have had to hire one of the world's greatest and luckiest sharpshooters to pull off something like that."

"So maybe he did."

Jacoby chuckled. "Well, if he did, I'll have to give him an A-plus for sheer idiotic guts. Any man who'd be willing to have someone try to crease his shoulder with a bullet fired under those conditions is a man asking to get killed."

She thought about that for a time.

Jacoby said suddenly, "This has got to be the weirdest afterglow there ever was. Aren't we supposed to be smoking cigarettes, or noshing at the fridge or something?"

"I don't smoke. And I haven't done my shopping for the week, so the fridge doesn't have anything noshable in it."

"So what else is there to do?"

She rolled over and smiled into his eyes. "Well, now, that's got to be the weirdest afterglow question there ever was."

"Ouch!"

"Get back to work, genie."

29.

Morton hated hospitals.

He'd spent most of his adult life in an industry that provided for hospitals and the people who made them work, but he had never spent a minute in one, as visitor or patient, without feeling sorrow and dread. He supposed it had to do with Uncle Denny. It was unspeakably sad that such a beautiful person had been compelled to do his dying inch by inch in a nowhere corner of a glass-and-plastic labyrinth that stank of antiseptics, loneliness, and fear.

So now he was propped up in a bed in Z'ville General, a bandage on his left shoulder and a chip on his right shoulder, trying unsuccessfully to convince everybody in sight that he was okay and needed only to go home.

The media were having a real time of it, probably because his refusal to be interviewed forced them into the fantasy-fiction mode. The *Gazette*, whose publisher, Ed Johnson, always treated Morton warily because Morton was a friend of Sandra McKinley, matriarch of the much-feared McKinley Supermarket clan and a very heavy print advertiser, did some mainline sucking-up, suggesting that Morton was somewhere between Russell Crowe and Arnold Schwarzenegger. And WZIG-TV's newspeople displayed the Bradford company's glamorized PR portrait while portraying him as "a hero of Zieglerville's bloody war against crime." He was ambivalent about it all himself, secretly pleased that all those horse's asses who considered him to be a horse's ass were forced to see him in a new light, and simultaneously mortified over his consignment to the pantheon of tabloid celebrities.

The doctor's orders, issued by Buck Bascomb, the Bradford staff physician and for years Morton's personal medic, were to rest up and await the results of the four thousand tests he and the hospital honchos had run since yesterday afternoon. Morton argued that allergy tests and proctoscopies and EKGs and urinalyses and Wassermans and CAT scans and, for all he knew, pap smears, really didn't have a lot to do with a bullet crease on the back of his left shoulder. Buck said that the tests were to cover his own ass, not Morton's, and if "the patient doesn't lie still and shut up, there'll be a catheterization with a fire hose." Once the kidding was over, Buck said that the wound was nothing serious, no more than a nasty, two-inch gouge, actually, but Morton was one lucky bastard, because the bullet had been on its way to the nape and must have been deflected just enough by the collar of his chesterfield.

Morton tried to look at his imprisonment as a time for reflection, but that idea went out the window with all the people who came in the door. Visitors he had, from the florists who surrounded him with forests of red roses and white carnations from "Your Friends at Bradford" through *Der Writmeister* von Zieg, who assured in his creamy baritone that God was most pleased by Morton's willingness to give his life for the lovely Melanie, and to Jacoby and Melanie, who now stood beside the bed, uneasy and red-faced.

She took Morton's hand and looked him straight in the eye. "Thank you," she said, very serious.

"You're welcome."

"I would have been dead if you hadn't jumped in and shielded me."

"I didn't shield you. I pushed you down, lost my balance, and fell on you."

"Do you always nearly smother people you fall on?"

"Only when they're young and beautiful. So how about you? Are you okay, Dr. Flynn?"

"I didn't sleep much last night, and I jump when someone slams a door, but I'm pretty much okay."

"Good."

Morton could see that she was trying very hard to resolve the conflict between her dislike of him and her natural need to be courteous and grateful for this bizarre and wholly uncharacteristic thing he'd done. Like, what do you say to the cat burglar who drags you from your bed and carries you from your burning house?

What she said was, "I'm due back at the lab, so I have to run now. Anything I can do for you?"

"Not really. But thanks for asking."

She nodded politely and turned for the door, and Jacoby called after her, "Wait for me in the car."

When she'd gone, Morton said, "Don't tell me you have more questions. Please don't tell me that."

"I won't tell you that. I will tell you, just between us, that I'm grateful as hell for what you did. For getting between Melanie and the shooter. That took balls."

Morton waggled a hand in disagreement. "Not true. I didn't do it for Melanie. I did it for me. I knew that if she got shot when I was anywhere within two miles of her, you'd be all over me, reading me my rights and advising me to call my lawyer. I couldn't afford to have her shot."

Jacoby gave him a steady stare, suppressing a smile. "No way do I believe you're that cynical, Mr. Morton."

"Believe it."

"She and I have this huge interest going, you know."

"That's the quaintest term for a case of the hots I've heard since twenty-three-skiddoo."

Jacoby looked out the window. "It's not just a case of the hots. It's more than that."

"So what the hell do you want? A parental blessing?"

Jacoby regarded Morton somberly. "I know you have a hard time with this—"

"With what?" Morton was annoyed, and let it show.

"Well, it's pretty clear that you have a thing for Melanie, and—"

Morton saw instantly what was developing here. Deadpan, he said, "What the hell are you talking about?"

"The way you look at her, the way you pretend that your only interest in her is a business interest. I saw you watching her at the church yesterday. You couldn't take your eyes off her."

"How do you know? I was using opera glasses."

Jacoby spread his arms. "Hey, man, I'm trying to tell you that you're off the hook with both of us. You're no danger to Melanie—you're just plain all gone over her. Your problem is that she's all gone over me."

Morton had to work to keep from laughing. "Well, have it your way. But I suggest you don't try for Ann Landers's job. As an adviser to the lovelorn you don't cut it."

"I thought I ought to make things clear."

Hearing diffidence in Jacoby's words, Morton decided to turn up the heat under it. "Besides, Melanie Flynn is a classy woman, and there's no way you're going to have the field to yourself. You may be cute, but you ain't rich."

"Like you, you mean?"

"You said it, I didn't."

Jacoby was suddenly grave. "Just don't use her, pal. Just don't set her up for one of your rich man's games."

"I play fair. It's a level field."

"Keep it that way, or I'll be all over you."

Amy Cummings bustled in, all nursey white, clipboard in one hand, a digital thermometer in the other. She gave Jacoby the stony Gestapo eye and told him that he'd have to leave, that the patient was needing some attention.

Jacoby went out, then leaned back through the door to say, "Thanks again for what you did."

Morton shooed him out with both hands.

"The world is filled with cashews, Nurse Cummings."

"You should see it from here."

She took his pulse, patted around him with an ice-cold stethoscope, and poked his ear with the thermometer. As she leaned close, he could smell her cleanliness, her female-ness, and he didn't know where it came from, or why, but he had a momentary teenager's vision of her naked, waiting, the mother of all voluptuous women, and then he thought of Burroughs's tape of the incredible nude sauntering across Hamilton's patio and slipping into the moonlit pool, and he laughed.

"What's so funny?"

"I was thinking of the soldier's myth, the one saying that men enjoy battle because it makes them so horny."

"It's no myth," Cummings said matter-of-factly. "I've known guys who actually got off just watching war movies and prizefights."

"You're joking."

"Nope." She peered down her nose through her granny glasses. "Your experience yesterday: It made you horny?"

He laughed again. "Not that I noticed. It's just that just now I had this sudden—thought."

She nodded reasonably. "I do that to men."

"Well—"

"You don't have to be embarrassed. I'm a weak-eyed beanpole, but I have this other thing. Men are always trying to get into my pants. Ever since I was a kid, men have tried to get into my pants. But I can handle it. No big deal."

She adjusted her glasses, made a note on her clipboard, and folded her stethoscope. "I think you'll live, hero-fella."

He considered her gravely for a moment. "Tell me, Nurse Cummings: Why do you dislike me so much?"

"I don't dislike you, actually. But you worry me. You're too cool, like. I can't read you too well. And guys I can't read make me nervous."

"Why should that worry you? Behind my faro-dealer deadpan lies a nice, peachy-keen, lovable sort of cuddle-bug."

"You're kidding. I'm not." Cummings fussed at a vase of

roses on the bedside table. "It's about Alicia, I guess. Alicia's my best friend, and whenever you're anywhere near her she goes into some kind of tizzy. Whatever you are, or whoever you are, you upset her. And I don't like it when Alicia's upset."

"Well, what am I supposed to do about that?"

"Just back off. Stay away from Alicia."

Morton sighed. "Know something? I'm getting awfully tired of people telling me what I'm supposed to be, what I'm supposed to think and say, who I'm supposed to stay away from."

She shrugged and turned to go. "Tough shit, baby."

"News flash," he shot back, "Alicia's my best friend, too. She and I were best friends when you were squealing over the Beatles. And this just in: If you do anything—anything at all—to make her unhappier than she is, I'll kick that gorgeous ass of yours so hard you'll end up on Pluto."

She paused at the door and sent a bright blue stare into his eyes. "Hey," she said, showing a trace of a smile, "you have some fire behind that belly button after all, don't you."

When she was gone, Morton lay back and closed his eyes, listening to the hospital's faint humming and once again struggling against a flood tide of loneliness.

30.

Morton was released from the hospital the next morning, and as he stepped into the winter sunlight, he found the curb graced by Alicia's big black Mercedes. Its window zizzed down, and she waved him toward her.

"Get in."

"I'm not allowed to," he said, dour. "Cummings, that Nazi nurse of yours, has warned me to stay away from you. I'm supposed to be bad for your health."

Alicia smiled. "Amy? Don't listen to her. She's really over-protective of me, poor dear. Come on, get in."

"I have to get my car. It's still at the church."

"So I'll drive you there."

"That cab—it's waiting for me."

"I've already paid him off."

Morton swung into the front seat, wincing when the shoulder protested. "Why are you being so nice to me?"

"I'm nice to all guys who save Melanie's life."

"I didn't save her life. The man was a lousy shot. That's why he hit me instead of Melanie."

She fingered the gear selector, and the Mercedes glided down the driveway and into the merge with Madison Boulevard with all the fuss of a Pullman car leaving the station.

When they were at cruise speed in the right lane, she glanced at him. "I mean it, George. It was a wonderful thing you did for Melanie, and I'll always be grateful that you were there and knew what to do. But, of course, you always did know what to do about everything."

"Give me a break," he said, suddenly testy. "I'm just not up to taking sarcasm this morning."

Her answer was quick. "I didn't mean to sound sarcastic. Honest. I mean you are always so, well, resourceful, and I admire that in you."

He was enjoying his rotten mood. "Come on, level with me. Why did you pick me up? I know what to do about everything, maybe, but I've rarely ever had the slightest clue as to what to do about you. Especially now. So what's on your mind?"

She completed the turn onto Bixby Street and headed west toward Ligonier.

"I don't know how to put it. Adequately, that is."

"Put what?"

Gaze fixed on the street ahead, she said, "When I saw you lying there in the churchyard, bleeding and in pain and possibly dying, I understood, beyond all the lousy words and posturing and alibis, how much you really mean to me. Your wonderful, manly face, all white, your beautiful eyes glazing. You were fading away, sort of, and I wanted to run to you, hold you, to bring you back, to let you know how sorry I am for all the hurt and loneliness my pride and prudishness have caused you."

Morton, stricken mute by disbelief, gratitude, and elation, rummaged in his mind for a proper answer, but in his astonishment he could find none.

She went on, her cultivated voice wavering, taking on a rambling sound. "When I saw the blood, something happened. I saw you differently. Something precious, slipping away from me, beyond reach, forever. I knew then that no matter what you are—or are not—life without you somewhere close by would be the absolute pits. All this time, I've been so utterly prim—so super-damn-cilious. Telling myself my marriage was a good one. Telling myself my affection for Anson was clean and my affection for you didn't exist. How could I *do* that? A great guy I need in my life. Pretending I didn't even like you. *God!*"

Morton, always awkward in emotional moments, reached out and patted her hand. "In the immortal words of Kojak, 'Who loves ya, baby?' "

"I mean it, George. Every word."

They rode in silence for a time, and eventually he managed, "For reasons I've never been able to figure out, I like the hell out of you, too. And damned if I know why, but I'll always be around."

She sighed, suddenly irritable. "Life is one big gas pain."

"Consider me your Rolaid."

She glanced at him and grimaced, shaking her head.

"There's something else bugging you. Right?"

This glance was wry. "You may be a great guy, but you're also weird. Real mind-reader weird."

"So what is it?"

"It's Melanie. I'm very worried about her. She has so many god-awful problems. I want to help her, but I don't know how. She respects you. Want to give me a hand?"

"Respect? *Moi?* Don't be silly. She looks like she smells something bad whenever I'm around—even when I'm in the hospital bed she should be in."

"Well, a lot of that's her own confusion. She sees you as a threat to her lab, but she also is much impressed by the way you made something of yourself. " 'A guy kind of guy' is the way she puts it. 'Clawed your way out of the slums and into the *Who's Who*s.' " She chuckled. "Melanie doth protest too much. I think she's trying to hide a case of the hots for you, George."

He gave her a look. "Now who's weird? Sheesh."

"Kidding aside, Melanie's not handling anything very well these days. She's got trouble with rumors, trouble with her employees, trouble with Greg Allenby—trouble everywhere. She thinks selling the company is the answer."

"Bad idea."

"Why? Can you give me a real, hard, downtown why?"

He pointed to the elaborate radio and sound system in the burled walnut dash. "Is there a tape recorder in all that fancy junk?"

"Sure. Why?"

"Turn it on. I'll give some reasons why she shouldn't sell. Then you get them typed out, hard copy, and tell Melanie that this is stuff you've picked up from, let's say, floppies Anson made and left with you. Okay?"

"Well—"

"Turn on the damned recorder, will you, please?"

She pulled a virgin cassette from the armrest storage, slid it into the slot, and poked a button or two with an expensively gloved finger. "All right, it's running."

"Instead of sending employees a letter announcing a sale, Melanie should send them a letter that admits offers have been received and studied, but also explains why they should bear with her until she works out a way to solve the financial problems and retain ownership. Here are a few reasons: In Anson's gene drug studies, TBM-1 is showing a lot of clout in the production of adenosine deaminase, the enzyme fundamental to the body's immune defenses. In the past year, Anson's had excellent results in applying the compound to cystic fibrosis, one of the more common disorders arising from a genetic defect. He found that the technique can very well contribute importantly to the treatment and prevention of diabetes—even heart disease and other health problems influenced by genes. And in Anson's botanical fungi work, TBO-2, the active compound derived from crabgrass, shows it can do a real number on arthritis. These two drugs alone, if successful in obtaining Federal approval, can bring in hundreds of millions of dollars—and they're only two of the scores of exciting leads being followed by the Lunt R&D squad. A health care revolution is exploding, with hospitals, doctors, insurers, and medical suppliers turning themselves inside out to downsize, simplify, streamline, and computerize. It's agreed across the board, by all sides and all the cognoscenti, that blockbuster drugs Lunt's working on will almost certainly become health care's heavy artillery. Vast riches are at the Lunt operation's door, so to speak. This is why everybody at Lunt should hang on."

Morton turned off the recorder, and he felt her quick examination. "Where are you getting this stuff, George?"

"Don't ask. Just tell her that's what Anson's floppies say. Tell her to put it all in her letter."

"What if she asks for the floppies?"

"I'll give you some."

"You mean you actually have floppies made by Anson?"

"No. I've got floppies made by me from studies made by Bradford."

"Isn't that illegal?"

"Don't ask."

She fussed about that, as he knew she would. "I won't have you doing anything improper or illegal, George."

"Let's put it this way: Teddy Bradford owes Anson a few things. This information will help bring the account into a better balance. Besides, it's so generalized nobody will know the difference. Especially Teddy."

"Well—"

He changed the subject. "What's the problem with Greg?"

"He's told Melanie that he's going to quit Lunt."

"That's good news. Melanie will be well rid of that oily jerk. Tell her to thank her lucky stars."

Alicia swung the Mercedes onto Burbank and headed into the big-tree 'burbs. She said, "Melanie thinks Greg has stolen something important—something he found while rummaging through Anson's files—and has sold it to Bradford. Now he's ready to abscond. And I agree with her."

"What makes you think that?"

"He told Melanie he was going to take his part of the family savings and head for a warm climate."

"So?"

"He says he doesn't have a job. Apparently, he's just going to go. And I know for a fact that he doesn't have any savings to speak of. Jennifer Allenby has been a friend of mine for years, and she tells me she's divorcing him. She and I had a long heart-to-heart yesterday, and only then, after all the time we've known each other, did she let me know what a bastard he truly is, how rotten he's always treated her and the kids. Which just goes to show you how a person can give you one impression and be something else altogether when he's home."

"So what's the bottom line?"

"So Jennifer says that without her—the inheritance she got from her parents, the house and cars and the other assets that she paid for and are in her name—Greg's just about nowhere. Except for a couple of thousand in a joint savings account, he has nothing but the clothes he's wearing. She says just about everything he earned at Lunt went for booze and women and horse parlors. But he's the kind of man who needs plenty— needs, well, money and comfort. If he has no money and no job, he must really have money, if you follow me. I—Oh, it's so damned *mixed up.*"

"You're supposing, then, that because he's quitting when he has no job and no cash he must have stolen something valuable from Lunt and plans to live on it, right?"

"Don't you think that's a logical deduction?"

"Well, if it is true, Melanie should count it as another blessing. Let him steal what he wants, and good riddance. When his theft becomes evident, put his ass in jail."

Nothing more was said the rest of the way. But when she pulled into the church parking lot, and he climbed out of the car, she said, "Thanks, George. You can be real scary sometimes, but I miss you more than you can imagine."

"Well—"

"Remember what I said a while ago."

"How could I forget? You filled my tank, pal."

"I'm very lonely. I really wonder if I can hold on."

"You will. It'll all shake out soon. If it gets too tough, reach for a Rolaid, eh?"

"I don't want to hold on. I've spent my whole life holding on. I want it all to be over now. Right now."

"Easy does it. Go back to Elmwood and take one of your one-hour baths. It'll cheer you up."

"Can't. I'm on my way to the airstrip. Charles called and wants me to come down."

"Why don't you tell him to shove it?"

"Bye."

"Thanks for the ride."

She pantomimed a kiss, and he sighed and gave her a wave as she drove off.

Uncle Denny had it right, Morton decided: "If you want to make home look especially good, spend some time in a hospital."

It was with a sense of rejoicing that he went about the house, opening windows and French doors and letting the winter air replace what he imagined to be the mustiness his absence had created. Actually the absence hadn't been all that long, and the house's heat-cold pump was a fine one, doing a great job of controlling things during his times away. Besides, Mrs. Mayer, the woman who came once a week to clean the very little mess he made, had done her thing the day before yesterday, and he could still smell the furniture polish. But to hell with all that. Today he wanted to feel and smell and touch his home and savor the fact that it was his, and that he was alive in it.

The mood was intensified by the lingering euphoria brought on by Alicia's confession in the car. It had been such a long time, such an arid time, and at last the wall had been breached. And it just made him feel so damned *good*.

He eventually got over the seizure, closed everything, then went into the library and listened to a string of dreary recorded phone calls advising, hustling, and beseeching him, all of which he erased. Then he went to the fax and retrieved a clutch of messages, each sent by Peter Van Dyke and each dealing with routine matters concerning the new Peabody subsidiary, which, one of them confirmed, would be named Pegasus Pharmaceuticals, Inc.

His shoulder had begun to throb, so he took a couple of aspirin and stretched out on the sofa. He dozed, catlike, but after a time he was up and about, driven by a need to do something useful.

So what was going on at the police department?

He booted up his surveillance computer and scrolled past the interoffice junk and tuned into Jacoby's file on the Lunt Case. The entry on the shooting incident at the Church of the Holy Writ was a marvel of brevity, cast in such careful and sterile terms it virtually shrieked Jacoby's combined relief and alarm over the try on his beloved's life. In one of his backgrounders he said something nice about Morton, too: *Morton is an odd SOB but he's one SOB I'm glad was around when Melanie got in a jam. He thought and acted fast, which you don't find too many guys able to do these days.*

On that high note, he decided to make a pot of coffee.

As he headed for the kitchen there was a soft clatter at the front door when the mail slot opened and a flurry of envelopes cascaded onto the foyer tiles. He gathered them and confirmed his suspicion that they were junk or bills.

All but one—a letter from Mona Lindsay, the live-in girlfriend of the late Ed Burroughs, who was all kinds of grateful for the many things he'd done for her and Ed over the past couple of years. But the final paragraph of her ornate script pulled him up short:

And the neatest thing of all the things you did was to give Eddy that wonderful $50,000 bonus. He told me about it just two days before he died, and he was sort of happy and sad at the same time, saying he was happy to get the money but sad that you decided to call it quits and wouldn't need him anymore for whatever you were doing. He gave the money to me for safekeeping, so I have it now, and it'll be put to good use, believe you me. So thanks again, Mr. Morton, for all your wonderful thoughtyness. Ed liked you a lot, and I think you're the sweetest thing ever.

He read the paragraph twice, but it still came out the same: Somebody had bought Burroughs off his account. Who? Why?

And Burroughs had been very quick to put him onto Pinky Watson. Why? Had Burroughs really wanted to nominate a capable successor? Or was Watson part of the buy-off?

He was pondering all of this when the phone rang.

"Hello?"

"Mr. Morton, I got to make this fast. This is Amy Cummings. Alicia's plane crashed, and she's in intensive care here at Z'ville General. I thought you'd want to know."

She hung up, and he ran down the hall to the garage.

PART THREE

31.

The airstrip at Elmwood was an avenue of hard-packed turf that ran generally westward along the edge of a forest.

The trees served to screen the strip and its single-plane hangar from the main house a quarter of a mile to the north, thus preserving the ambient rurality for the ambient plutocracy. Today they also hid the fire company and rescue gangs swarming over the two acres of splintered timber and blackened metal that marked the final resting place of Alicia Hamilton's twin-engine Beech.

Jacoby and Lou Mackey, the NATS investigator out of D.C., stood at the approximate midpoint of the strip, peering at the ground. Their breathing made little puffs of steam in the cold air.

"Here's where it started," Mackey said, pointing. "See the right tire rut? Deep, and angular, hard right. This is where the swerve began."

Jacoby nodded. "What would make an airplane swerve like that? Turn and go into the woods. Tire blow out, maybe?"

"The rut doesn't show that. The rut shows the skidding turn of a healthy tire."

"Well, what then?"

"Abrupt right engine failure at full takeoff speed, is my guess."

"I thought a plane like that can fly on one engine."

"Fly, sure. But this plane wasn't flying yet. Its full weight was still on the ground. It was going like a son of a bitch, tail high, not quite ready to rotate and lift off. *Poof.* The right engine cuts out. The pilot reaches for and kicks at everything in sight, but there ain't no time to do any correcting, and all that's left is a high-speed slide into a stand of trees."

"Why would an engine cut out like that?"

Mackey peered toward the wreck, squinting. "Ah, yes. Why? That's always the question in a plane crash. Why? And it usually takes weeks—months—to establish the official why. And it may take months to nail down this one. But I think I can tell you unofficially right now."

Jacoby gave him a look. "Yeah?"

Mackey pointed down the strip toward the hangar. "See that little flag I pushed into the ground there? A small piece of metal. Something that looks like a piece of engine cowling. It has no business lying there."

"The whole damned plane is in charcoaled pieces—"

"In the woods. In the woods, pal. So what's a clean piece of cowling doing down there, fifty-some feet from the swerve marks, hundreds of feet from the crash site?"

"So what are you saying, Lou?"

Mackey sighed, the sound of a man completely baffled by the world and the insanity of its human population. "I'll lay you ten to one that there was an explosion. Not a large one, mind you. A small, controlled explosion."

"Controlled?"

"A remote-controlled detonator, probably fastened close to the fuel feed line and its union with the carburetor, which, when it went off, was just enough to sever the line, shatter the carb, and shut down the engine. And start a bad fire, to boot."

"And just enough to blow away the piece of cowling, right?"

"You got it. That wasn't in the plan. The plan was to make this crash look like an accident. To do a small explosion whose cause and effect stood to be lost in the massive destruction of the crash itself." He nodded toward the squad of men prowling through the wreckage. "And I'll bet you anything my guys will find something—tiny as hell, maybe, but something—that'll prove I'm right."

"So that's why you called me."

"Yep. I think you've got yourself a job here. An attempted homicide. Somebody was trying to kill Alicia Hamilton. And if the plane hadn't busted open at the cockpit, if the slewing around a tree hadn't been quite so violent, if her seat hadn't broken away from its moorings, if she hadn't been thrown out of the zone of fire, if she hadn't landed in a cushion of snow-buried underbrush, he'd have succeeded. The would-be killer, my boy, was goosed by the fickle finger of fate."

Jacoby sniffed. "Gee. I sure thank you, Lou. That's what I needed, all right—another case to handle."

"You'll be on hind tit, Jake. We Feds take a dim view of aviation sabotage. The FBI's due here any minute. If you pick up on anything, be nice to them. They need all the help they can get."

"Me, too. So I hope it cuts both ways."

"And I hope you find the bastard soon. I hate people who break up other people's airplanes. Especially when the other people are in them."

Jacoby wasn't anxious to trade platitudes with incoming FBI hotshots, so he wished Mackey well and made a quick retreat to his car, which he'd parked beside the hangar. The crash site was on well-fenced private property, which helped to keep the inevitable gathering of rubbernecks and thrill-seekers parked along County Road 14, a two-lane blacktop a half mile from the crash scene. So he was surprised, while unlocking the car, to realize that a kid was watching him from the hangar's shadow.

"Hi," Jacoby said. "What are you doing here?"

"Are you somebody important, mister?" He was about ten years old and bundled into about ten pounds of snow gear. A pair of ice skates dangled from a thong around his neck.

"Ain't nobody more important than I am, sonny. Trouble is, nobody knows it."

The boy was in no mood for jokes. "I gotta talk to somebody important."

Jacoby showed him his badge. "So here you are, right at the top. What's on your mind?"

"I seen a guy fussing with Mrs. Hamilton's plane."

"Oh? When?"

"Before she tried to take off. And he stood in the trees over there with his TV remote."

"Cool. What's your name, and where do you live?"

"Tommy Ludlow. I live over on County 14."

Jacoby opened the car door. "I'm freezing out here. Climb in, and we'll talk."

"Mom says I should never get in a car with a stranger."

"Good advice." Jacoby held out his hand. "I'm Jake Jacoby, and I'm a sergeant with the Z'ville police. Shake."

The boy slid his mittened hand into Jacoby's grip.

"Now I'm not a stranger. Hop in, fasten the seat belt, and I'll drive you home."

With the boy beside him, Jacoby started the motor, turned the heater up to full, and drove down the lane toward the gate at Hollow Tree Road.

"So tell me about it, Tommy."

The boy turned and twisted in his seat, ogling the car interior. "Is this a cop car?"

"Yep. Watch." Jacoby picked up the transmitter. "Jake here, Dispatch. I'm leaving the Hamilton property and driving Tom Ludlow, a witness, to his home on County 14."

The radio snapped and rasped. "Okay, Jake. Keep us clued."

Tommy was unimpressed. "You didn't use proper radio procedure."

"How do you know that?"

"I watch the TV cop shows."

"Well, we're sort of laid-back in Z'ville. So tell me about it. What did you see?"

Tommy pulled a Baby Ruth bar from his multilayered clothes,

peeled back the wrapper, and held the candy under Jacoby's nose. "Want a bite?"

"No, thanks. It's bad for my tooth."

The boy gave him a sidelong stare. "You only got one tooth?"

"Somewhere in me. In my mouth, I think."

"You are really weird."

"How come you're not in school?"

"Christmas vacation."

Jacoby nodded. "I knew that."

Tommy chomped on the candy, and his face seemed to move in circles as he chewed. "I was skating on Borden pond where it meets the woods. I sat on a log under the trees and had me a candy bar, and was just sort of sitting there when I heard somebody tromping through the woods behind me. I ducked down, because I thought it was Mr. Bleaker, one a the security guys who work for Mrs. Hamilton. Mr. Bleaker's a hardcase, and he always chases me off the property when he sees me. But it wasn't him. It was a tall guy in a black parka thing, with the hood up over his head."

"Did you see his face?"

"Well, yeah. I saw his face."

Jacoby felt a rush of excitement. "Great. What did he look like?"

"It was just a face sort of face. I don't know how to tell you. It was all wrapped up in the parka, and—"

"Would you know the face if you saw it again?"

"Sure."

"Tell you what: I'll get you together with a police artist, and he'll draw the face from what you can tell him. That sound all right to you?"

"Yeah. I seen 'em do that in cop shows. Yeah, I can do that."

Jacoby waited while Tommy swallowed and took another huge bite.

"So then what happened?"

The boy thought about that, chewing.

"The guy went along the tree line, sneaky, like he was making sure nobody could see him. I thought that was sort of weird, so I crawled through the snow behind him to see what he was up to. When he got near the hangar, he made a beeline for the side door, where he fussed with the lock and went in. I—"

"Did he break the lock?"

"I didn't hear nothing break. He used a key, I think."

"Go on."

"So while he was in the hangar, I quick took off my skates and pulled on my galoshes and went around back and peeked in the window. He was in there, doing something with the motor on Mrs. Hamilton's plane."

"The left motor, wasn't it?"

"Well, no. It was on the right wing. The right motor."

"Then what?"

"He closed up the motor, went to the door, and left. I sneaked a look around the back corner and watched him go back into the woods. He stood behind that big yew near the pond and waited. Pretty soon a Jeep shows up, with Mr. Bleaker driving and Mrs. Hamilton with a suitcase on her lap. They parked, and while Mr. Bleaker got the tractor out Mrs. Hamilton slid open the hangar doors, threw her stuff into the plane, and climbed in."

"Didn't she check the motors? Walk around the plane, inspecting things?"

"Nope. Just got in the plane. She seemed like she was in a big hurry, sort of. And after Mr. Bleaker pulled the plane out and unhitched the tractor, she started the motors and let them run a while, warming up. Then she taxied onto the strip and went roaring off. The—"

"What was the guy in the parka doing?"

"I was getting to that," Tommy said, annoyed. "The guy in the parka stayed behind the tree, then held out something that looked like a TV remote. That's when the plane popped a puff of smoke and went *ee-ow kaboom* into the trees. And he went hurrying off through the woods toward County 14. Mr. Bleaker got in the Jeep and just about flew down to where the plane was burning, and I ran like crazy after him. When I got to the wreck, he'd already covered Mrs. Hamilton with his own coat and was on the cellular, yelling like you wouldn't believe. It wasn't too long after that the Borden Fire Department showed up and there were people all over the place. I watched for a long time, and that's when I picked you out."

"Why me?"

Tommy hunched a shoulder. "The other people were running around like Jackie Chan. You looked like a schoolteacher. I could talk to you."

"But you weren't sure I was important, right?"

"Yeah."

Jacoby laughed softly.

"Did I do good?"

"You sure did. But promise me something. Promise me you won't tell any of this to anybody. Even your folks. Don't say a word until I say it's okay. Otherwise, the guy in the parka might come looking for you."

"You trying to scare me?"

"Darn right I am."

"Well, you're doing it. You gonna to put me into one a them witness protection programs?"

"Nothing like that. Just stand by until I get in touch with you. And I'll do that by calling on your folks first. Meantime, you need me for anything, just call the police number and ask for Jake. They'll know who you want. Okay?"

"Okay."

"Is your house far from here?"

"Just up the road. Around that bend."

"I'll let you out here. I don't want anybody seeing you with me until the time's right."

As he stepped into the snow, Tommy held up the tail end of the Baby Ruth bar. "There's one more bite, Jake. It's yours if you want it."

Jacoby winked. "Well, why not. The heck with my tooth."

He took the candy, popped it into his mouth, and drove off, chewing.

32.

Swarming news crews, looking for angles on the Alicia Hamilton crash story, choked the hospital's lobby and elevator bays. Morton, fearing he might be considered an angle, sidled into the gift shop and gave the girl on duty a ten-spot to let him through a back door to a utility stairway. As he entered the second-floor corridor, he nearly collided with Alicia's personal physician, Angelo DeVito, dean of Z'ville surgeons and a frequent skeet partner, who bustled out of the Intensive Care Unit with Nurse Cummings quick-stepping in his wake.

"What's with Mrs. Hamilton, Angie?"

"Are you a relative, George?"

"You know I'm not—"

"Then go downstairs and wait until we have an announcement, like everybody else."

"Hey, Angie, give me a break. There's something I have to tell her—"

DeVito turned to give Morton an unbelieving look. "God, what's with people these days? The lady is unconscious, wired and tubed from here to there, and probably at this moment presenting her passport to the Pearly Gates doorman, and you've got something you want to *tell* her?"

"I want her to know her husband is on his way here. It would mean something to her."

DeVito's exasperation subsided into impatience. "Hell, George, the lady's just hanging on. Her upper left chest has been penetrated by a sliver of fuselage stringer. The piece is now lodged near the heart. There are body and leg contusions, some first-degree burns. She lost a lot of blood and suffered some hypothermia."

"What are her chances, Angie?"

DeVito waggled a hand, signifying a fifty-fifty situation. "We've got some tricky surgery ahead, made trickier by the fact that the sliver tumbled and deformed, and the left lung is partially deflated. Lots of people are living full lives with only one lung, so that in itself isn't too big a deal. But along with deep shock, torn innards, and incipient infection to deal with, she's got another prob. She's got a heart condition—angina pectoris. So she's what I consider to be a very sick citizen."

"Thanks, Angie. I'll tell her husband as soon as he flies in from Florida."

DeVito nudged Cummings. "Come on, Nurse. There are things to do." They turned and hurried off. As they went, Cummings looked back at Morton, nodded meaningfully, and gave him a thumbs-up.

Morton had always prided himself on his ability to keep cool under stress, but Alicia's accident had shaken him down to his soles.

It must be that I'm getting older, not so resilient. Or the load's heavier than I ever thought it would be. Waiting for Anson Lunt to take the final count was no fun, but I'd been prepared for that. Good old Anson had been more than ready in his own mind, tortured as he was by the disease of his body and the loss of his reason for living. But Alicia—everything to live for . . .

There was no compelling reason for him to return to his office at the plant, so he took the elevator to the first floor, where he went into the cafeteria and sat at a table by the big windows, sipping a coffee he didn't really want. He forced his mind off its maudlin rambling by using his cellular to punch up his home answering machine, which announced that Mary Dugan wanted to speak with him and she'd be at Waldo's until five.

"This is Mary. Whatcha want?"

"George Morton, Mary. You called?"

"Oh, hi, Mr. Morton. I been watching the phone, like you asked me to do, and there really ain't a lot to report. Mostly them that use it are lawyers and stuff from the courthouse, and the same one's have been doin' it for years. Nothin' unusual, if you see what I mean."

"You say mostly. What about those that don't fit the mostly?"

"That's really why I called. Two people are a little out of what you'd call the ord'nary, and I thought you might like to know about 'em."

"Sure would."

"One's one a them Santy Clauses that rings bells on Main Street. You know—with the charity kettle, and like that. Well, he comes in a couple times a day and makes calls. Sort of sneaky-like. Talks close to the phone, his back to the room, keeps lookin' over his shoulder at the main entrance."

"What's he look like, Mary?"

"Dumpy little guy. Hard to see all his face, what with that ratty white fake beard he wears. But he's got brown eyes, and they keep dartin' looks around. Know what I mean?"

"Mm."

"Well, today I was clearin' the table next to the phone and I caught a bit of what he was sayin'. Sure as hell, he was placin' bets. On our phone yet. Breakin' the law. And I thought you ought to know. He mean anything to ya?"

"Very helpful information, Mary," Morton lied, trying to keep a serious tone. "How about the other one?"

"A nurse from Z'ville General down the street. She used ta come in pretty often, then I didn't see her for a while. Came in day or so ago—can't remember exactly, because things get so damned busy around here—and sat by the phone."

"Sat? That's all?"

"Why's a nurse come three blocks to wait by a pay phone

when she works in a hospital that has a gazillion phones on
every floor?"

"Privacy, I guess. Calls to and from Z'ville General have to
go through a switchboard that keeps records. Maybe she's
having a love affair and doesn't want to risk leaving a trail."
He paused, and this time let his amusement be audible. "Or
maybe she's taking bets."

Mary didn't get the joke. "That's my point. She almost never
uses the phone—make calls or get 'em. She sits at that table
next the phone, has a cup a coffee, and keeps checkin' her watch.
Those times the phone rings, she always jumps up and grabs it
before anybody else can. That's what was different about this
time. This time she came in, went right to the phone, made a
call, then went hurryin' back out."

"What does she look like?"

"Tall. Blond. Stacked. Granny glasses."

"Ah."

"Mean something?"

"I don't know, Mary."

"So, that's all I got."

"You did very well. Very well indeed."

"You want I should keep watchin'?"

"Absolutely."

"Okay."

"Especially if the nurse comes in again. Try to get a line on
what she's saying, will you? I'd really like that."

"Do my best, Mr. Morton."

He was draining the coffee mug when a shadow fell across the
table.

"Hi. I'm on my break, and I saw you here."

Who said there's no such thing as coincidence? It was Amy
Cummings, monolithic in nurse's whites, regarding him ear-
nestly through her steel-rimmed glasses. Her hair, the color of
corn silk, was sleek and tied in a bun, and the set of her mouth
was somber.

"Speak of the devil."

"What's that mean?"

"I was just thinking about you. I'm due to see you tomorrow to get my bandage changed. Coffee or anything?"

She shook her head and took the chair opposite, her big blue eyes looking into his, a touch of sadness in them. He had a fleeting sense of having seen her at other times, in other contexts, and it annoyed him—he was annoyed at himself, actually—because the image, imprecise, elusive, had again been erotic.

"What were you thinking?"

"How you don't like me, but you like Alicia enough to have called me."

She shrugged. "You said you like Alicia, too."

"You got that right."

She blinked those big eyes, and he thought he saw tears. "This morning's been a bummer. Not only Alicia, but another old friend of mine. Gert Margolis. Hung herself in her garage, the cops say. Dead a couple days. I had to ID her."

"That's tough," Morton said, meaning it. "I'm sorry. I keep saying that. But I am." He paused. "Margolis? Was she—"

Nurse Cummings nodded and completed the thought. "A former nurse here, and the ex-wife of that asshole who got run over on Airport Road the other night."

"I understand the police have been trying to find her."

"Well, they found her, all right. She'd been in the garage since that same night."

"You knew her well, then?"

"Yeah. Gert, Melanie, and Alicia—Mrs. Hamilton—and I have been friends for a long time. We've been through a lot together, in our work, you know. Alicia wasn't in medicine, of course, but she gave a hell of a lot to it in money and time and moral support, like."

She paused, and he let the interval go on, aware that she was building up to something. When it continued too long, he prompted her.

"What was Mrs. Margolis like?"

"Pretty as hell. Sweet and naive little thing with a spine like wet spaghetti. Give you the hair shirt off her back. She was almost always broke, and I don't know what she would have done if it hadn't been for the money and hand-me-down clothes she got from Alicia. I tried to help, but, hey, I have my own financial problems, so the most I could give Gert was moral support, friendship—that kind of crap."

"Why did she divorce Margolis? Any idea?"

"Now there was a real prick. He always treated her like dirt, always was taking what little dough she did make. But what tore it was the pictures."

"Pictures?"

"Margolis was an amateur photographer, and to fatten up his railroad pay he got into some pretty raunchy stuff. You know, like porn. He'd hire whores to pose, and like that. But what tore things was when Gert—poor, love-starved soul—got caught up in an affair with some crumb-bum doctor I won't name. One afternoon Gert and her creep friend were tearing off a piece in her bedroom when she thought Margolis was at work. But he wasn't. He was in the closet, taking pictures of the action. Later she happened on some of the prints, and that did it. She was ready to kill the son of a bitch, but went for a divorce instead, I'm glad to say."

Morton gave her a lingering glance. "Do you think she was capable of killing her husband?"

An expression, fleeting, crossed Nurse Cummings's Nordic face, and he thought of the word *stricken*.

"Mr. Morton, you have no idea how many times I've wondered that. And I can't come up with an answer. If ever anybody needed killing, that bastard Margolis was it. And Gert had been pushed to the wall so many times—But she was such a wimp—Hell, I don't know. I just honestly don't know."

"A lot of people have been offed by people people thought were wimps."

"I suppose."

He sipped some coffee, then decided to ask the question and see where it led. "Tell me something, Miss Cummings: Why do you sit by the pay phone at Waldo's, waiting for calls?"

She gave him a quick look. "How do you know about that?"

"Name's Morton. I know everything."

She was not amused. "That's not any of your business."

"Entirely right."

"So then why do you ask?"

He could see this would go nowhere, because she was getting her back up. There was no sense ticking her off. She might be useful sometime.

"Well, you did me a favor. My turn to do you one."

"Like what?"

"That phone is being used by gamblers to place bets. The police have it under surveillance. I'd hate to have them think you were playing the races. It wouldn't go down very well with the hospital administration if you ended up wearing cuffs in newspaper pictures."

She blinked. "Hey. Wow. Now that's a tip I really appreciate. Thanks a lot." She sighed, pushed away from the table, and stood up. "Well, I've got to get back to work. Thanks again, Mr. Morton."

As she turned and walked away, it came to him, swooping in from nowhere, one of those miracles the human mind seems infinitely capable of. One minute he couldn't remember, the next minute he remembered exactly where he had seen her before.

What do the cops always say? Bingo!

But the revelation was a bummer—one more confirmation of the rottenness and betrayal that lurks in the human soul.

Morton's mood was dark as he drove out of the hospital parking lot. Out of reflex, he checked the rearview mirror for signs of Pinky Watson.

Sure enough, the bastard was there in his white Caddy, drifting along in traffic about five cars behind.

An angry thought: *What if I were to call Pinky's car phone on my car phone, and say, "This is Morton, you dipshit. Did you know your right front tire needs air?"*

33.

Melanie stared apathetically at the pile of unfinished business on her desk, dealing again with the questions that had bedeviled her since the shooting. Somebody had tried to kill her. Actually, no kidding, honest-to-God tried to kill her. Would he try again? And why? What did she represent that caused at least one other human being to see her as a threat so huge that she needed extermination? Or worse, simply so annoying that she was like a bug to be squashed?

The dread was especially heavy this day; she'd awakened with an acute sense of her mortality, an understanding that time is finite and plays out like a roll of film, and she would exist only in a certain sequence of frames whose number and character were beyond her power to establish or control. Like most scientists, she was unsettled by death, antagonistic to the idea that existence and nonexistence were determined by an X-factor she could never see, touch, define, or significantly manipulate. Add murder, which in effect became a capricious editing of the film roll, and the antagonism became outrage. When the murder was potentially her own, outrage melded into fear—a sense of teetering on the rim of eternity.

And now Alicia. One minute vibrant, determined to save a business and the platoons of friends whose lives depended on it.

Then a lapse of attention, or the failure of some tiny part in the gut of an airplane, and all the nuances that made up the entity known as Alicia Cosgrove Emerson Hamilton were about to return to the ooze.

What had the poet written?

Death in itself is nothing. We fear to be we know not what, we know not where.

She was sitting there, her unseeing gaze on the paper hills, waiting for some cosmic second shoe to drop, when the fax machine came to life.

Glad for this call to workaday action, she waited until the machine fell silent, then peeled off the message. Jason Burke, Lunt's lawyer, was reporting that Mrs. Hamilton had authorized her attorneys before the accident to meet the Lunt selling price, whatever it might be. Consequently, as Lunt's counsel, he had formally rejected the Amalgamated offer and accepted Mrs. Hamilton's offer to buy, and settlement procedures were now in process. Copies of the letter of agreement attached hereto, with originals for her signature to be couriered to her office tomorrow morning. Yours truly.

She should have been delighted, of course, but her uneasiness persisted. Why had Alicia been so insistent that Lunt not be sold to anyone but her? Sentiment? Loyalty to a fallen leader? Maybe. But there was something more. An urgency above and beyond these things.

Jake.

She had to hear his voice.

She was reaching for the phone when it rang.

"Doctor Flynn."

"Hi. This is Genie, with the light brown butt."

"Hey. I was just about to call you. You don't know how glad I am to hear your voice."

"I'm about to make you gladder."

"How so?"

"You know Fred Bleaker, don't you?"

"Alicia's grounds and buildings maintenance man. Drives her

when she doesn't feel like fighting the traffic war. Services her cars, and so on. What about him?"

"He and I were going over her Mercedes this morning, and he found a tape in the in-dash recorder—one of those Stuttgart options that cost only a little more than the average house—and he played it, to see if maybe Mrs. Hamilton had left him some instructions. What we heard was something that pretty much involves you."

"You're kidding. You've got it there?"

"Right by the phone. The tape, that is. Not the Mercedes. Chief Stabile forbids us to bring cars into the office."

"So play it."

It was George Morton's voice, and he seemed to be listing reasons why Lunt employees should bear with her while she worked out ways to solve the company's fiscal problems—among them Anson's gene studies of adenosine deaminase and his botanical fungi work targeting arthritis. Blockbuster drugs in the offing. Vast riches at Lunt's door. Everybody should hang on.

Puzzled, she thought aloud: "Morton? What's he doing on Alicia's car tape?

"My guess? He was riding with Mrs. Hamilton, talking about you and her plans to buy you out. She thought she ought to get some of his ideas down."

"How does he know about Anson's work with those things? When even I don't know?"

"George Morton knows everything. He told me so."

"This is creepy. Why would Morton want me to hold on, to persuade our employees to do the same?"

"I'm not all that savvy about the ways of industrial chieftains, but if you ask me to guess again, I'd guess that it's a case of if he can't have you, nobody else can have you." Pause. "The Lunt company, that is."

"And Alicia: She's always complaining about how George Morton makes her so uncomfortable, how she really doesn't feel right when he's around. So what's he doing in her car in the first place?"

"Ah. Now there's where I don't have to guess. Bleaker told me that Mrs. Hamilton told him how grateful she was that Morton had kept a bullet out of your pretty bod. She told Bleaker to roll out the Nazi footlocker so that she could go down to the hospital and drive Morton home."

"Well—"

"Mrs. Hamilton is all gone crazy about you. She is second only to me in that department."

She had wanted him to be her lover, but now that he was, warning bells were sounding. She'd still been in afterglow when the pragmatism that was simultaneously her blessing and curse had begun to move in. She had a career, a life plan, and there was little room in it for domestication and devotion to the long-term needs of someone else. He, too, had an agenda, a calling that required the single-mindedness of a zealot. How could they, once their passion had run its course, hope to find the common purpose, the will to give a hundred percent, the other-mindedness needed to sustain a pact for a lifetime?

Well, to hell with it. One day at a time. Take it while you've got it.

"You're a mushy kind of guy for a cop, aren't you."

"I'll say."

"Will you still be crazy about me when I'm thirty-five?"

"Visit you in the nursing home every day."

"But I'm already thirty-five."

"I'm thirty-six. So it's up to you to visit me."

"How about tonight? Dinner."

"Great. I have a microwave meat loaf dinner in the freezer. We'll split it. Pig out."

"On second thought, let's make it my place. Six-thirty."

"Roger. Over and out."

"You've been watching Ronald Reagan movies, haven't you."

"Want me to bring along a couple?"

She laughed and hung up.

Morton. What in hell is that man up to?

34.

Scanning page one, Morton found that the *Gazette* editors—
having lived so long on a diet of City Commission procedurals,
Highway Department budget analyses, and features on ten-foot
watermelons—continued to delight in the change of pace represented by the city's escalating savagery. Today's installment,
an orgy of screamer heads, boldface outtakes, diagrams of the
site, and photos of the victim being carried from her garage,
was devoted to the hanging death of Gertrude Margolis, ex-wife
of Albert Margolis, himself mysteriously run down on a rainy
highway outside the building where he served as night watchman. The spread was shared by a follow-up on the Alicia Hamilton airplane crash, in which foul play was suspected. Sidebars
were devoted to Mayor Maloney, who decried such violence and
assured the populace that criminal activity of this sort would
simply not be tolerated by this administration. Chief Stabile
had two comments: all of his people were working on all of it
and no, Sergeant Jacoby would not be available for interviews.

He put down the newspaper and sank deeper into his chair,
slippered feet on the hassock, hands folded on his stomach. His
gaze went back to the plain, unmarked packet on the end table
at his elbow.

Three hundred million dollars in negotiables.

A marvel that so much could be represented by so little. Even more marvelous that one man, an arrogant giant named Falloon, could summon up such a sum in so little time. And have it delivered, like a pizza, or a wad of laundry, by a small man named Guido, who stood at the door and became teary all over again as he recited the points of his gratitude, like a bead-saying, for Mr. Morton's huge role in the miraculous recovery of his saintly mother. (Yeah, she's still weak, and is on a god-awful diet, and all, but she gets around on her own now, and even asked to go to the movies last night—and she never even liked movies before, which is really cool, ain't it.)

The phone warbled.

"Morton, here."

"Schroeder, returning your call, Mr. Morton."

"Sorry to bother you in the middle of your evening, Heinz. But I have some things I'd like you to handle."

"No problem, I assure you. It's a quiet, snowy night here in Bern, and I am now home and plan to remain here. What can I do for you?"

"Go on scrambler, will you? This is somewhat delicate."

"One moment, please."

Morton visualized Schroeder going down the marbled hall to his study and taking the scrambler phone from its niche in the towering bookcase there.

"There we are. All set, Mr. Morton."

"I'm sending an injection to our people in the Caymans, over-night express, and I'd like you to blend it into the trust via whatever mechanisms you consider to be the most prudent."

"I take it that the injection is rather heavy, then."

"Three hundred million in negotiables."

"Oh, my. That *is* a decent sum. You've been busy."

"There'll be another hundred million on the way in a day or two, depending on how things break tonight. And then, soon, between now and Christmas, it's possible—if this nagging hunch I have proves to be wrong—I'll have another injection of two hundred and fifty million. This is still very much up for grabs."

Schroeder laughed. "Another two hundred and fifty? The mind boggles."

"Do you think our structure can handle these kinds of jolts? Or do we have to make some alterations?"

"No, we're all right. In the daisy chain I've set up, a half a billion goes in as readily as a half a million. A little more time, maybe; a prudent shuffling of the cards. After all, we've become very widespread and sophisticated, and we've been doing this kind of thing for many years now."

There was a pause as they savored this truth.

"Something else I need, Heinz. I want the trust to deposit in my bank here whatever it takes to enable coverage on a ten-million-dollar check. We'll do it openly, high-profile, and I'll meet whatever tax obligation is involved because I want it to be accepted as absolutely legal by whatever eye might eventually behold it, as the saying goes. In any case, I need a net of ten million in my money market account by tomorrow at 4 P.M., our time."

"Very well. Anything else?"

"Not right now. I'll be in touch with you as things go along."

"Good. So very nice to chat with you, Mr. Morton."

"My regards to Frau Schroeder."

At a quarter to seven, Morton backed the BMW from the garage and drove across town.

Teddy's company sedan, a charcoal green Cadillac with deep-tinted windows, sat oddly forlorn in the dimly lit executive parking lot. Beyond, the Bradford Chemicals Zieglersville plant—a forty-acre conglomeration of pipes, tanks, stacks, towers, tin buildings, twinkling lights, astringent stinks—emitted its incessant snorts, wheezes, and clanks. A behemoth, already stiffening under incipient fossilization, barely erect and panting with the exertions required by size and age and the parasitic hosts that crawled over it daily, expecting always to do less and be fed more. Thumping, chugging, and reeking in its struggle to escape the oncoming leaner and meaner Huns who would downsize it, integrate it, redesign it, and, eventually, kill it, offering up its organs to those who would transplant or recycle.

I'm tired, Morton thought as he steered off the highway and onto the plant approach road. *I'm getting out just in time.*

From habit, he parked in his assigned slot, the rectangle with his name in elegant black letters on a white curbstone. Then he crossed the slush-streaked macadam and climbed into the Cadillac's front passenger seat.

He examined Teddy's face, gaunt in the murk. "You look awful. Are you sick, or something?"

"Am I ever. On top of all this running around, trying to rassle up Greg's money, Samantha's hired that hot shit New York divorce lawyer, Bernard Phipps, who doesn't take a case unless he's sees a seven-figure fee in it."

"Sorry to hear that. It looks as if you'll really need the income from this Allenby thing, eh?"

Teddy raised the steering wheel and, with this additional space, was able to turn in the driver's seat and hold out a hand. "You got the floppies?"

Morton was amiably exasperated. "Come on, Teddy: Are you really that dumb, or are you pulling my leg? You know damned well that Allenby isn't about to part with the floppies until he has your folding green in hand."

Teddy sighed. "Do you have any idea how big a deal it is to sneak together two hundred mill and get it into a satchel? I've been going round and round on this for two days now."

"I've told you a thousand times to tell that dork you call a comptroller to set you up offshore. Everybody else is doing it. Why shouldn't you?"

"Well, Thomason may not be brilliant, but he's safe."

"Crooked, you mean."

"In my league, that's safe, pal."

"I've been in your league for twenty-five goddam years, and if nothing else, it's taught me that even I could be a better comptroller than that idiot."

"You think I'm an idiot, too, don't you, Morton."

"Oh, come on. Let's not get into one of your self-pity fits.

Allenby's waiting for me to close the deal, and I'm about to freeze."

"You're still snug with the Peabody-Pegasus people?"

"I start work in January. And they're waiting for your floppies. So can we get on with it, please?"

Teddy sighed again and lifted a leather satchel from the floor at his feet. "Want to count it?"

Morton laughed. "You may be dumb, Teddy, but you're not dumb enough to try a shortchange act."

"You'll just hand Greg the satchel, and he'll hand you the floppies, right?"

"And then I bring the floppies back to you here. In less than a half hour, you'll hold the cure for cancer, Greg will be a rich man en route to some godforsaken island in the Caribbean, and I'll be on my way to membership in the Nordic Club."

Teddy was mocking. "Oo. The Nordic Club. So that's what you're after. The Sphinx isn't good enough for you."

"I'm sick of being a nobody."

"Hell, I'm not even in the Sphinx, and I'm somebody."

"Correction: Your daddy was a somebody."

"Up yours, Upjohn."

Morton laughed.

"So when do I get the Pegasus payment, George? The three hundred million?"

"It'll be delivered to me the day after tomorrow at 9 A.M. Bring the floppies to the Hunt Club at noon. I'll meet you there, make the buy, and then we'll have lunch and shoot a little skeet. Okay?"

"Don't keep me waiting."

"No way. I've got ten million of my own riding on this thing. I want it sewn up even more than you do. Two hundred mill may not be much to you, but ten million is my life savings, pal."

"You put up ten million?"

"As a guarantee to Pegasus that the deal will sail."

"God, you really do want to be a member of the Nordic, don't you."

"So badly I can taste it."

"Bizarre."

Morton swung out the door, satchel in hand. "So sit tight. I'll be back in half an hour." He turned and peered through the window. "By the way, Teddy, you can do me a favor."

"What's that?"

"You can get that son of bitch Pinky Watson off my case. I'm sick of seeing him in my rearview mirror."

Teddy's eyebrows went up. Then he grinned. "You know about that, eh?"

"Since the beginning."

"I'll pay him off in the morning."

"No. You call his car phone right now. He's parked over there behind that billboard. I see him again, I'll come back and tear your balls off."

Halfway to the Cat's Pee-Jays, Morton pulled the car into the dark and silent gas station at the corner of Fourth and Main. He turned on the map light, opened the satchel, and counted out one hundred million from the stack of bearer bonds. These he put into his briefcase, on the seat beside him. The other hundred million he left in the satchel.

He put the Beemer in gear and eased onto Main Street. It had begun to snow—big wet flakes that looked like moths in the headlight glare.

The lounge's parking lot was, as usual, all slamming doors, racing motors, and high-pitched, drunken palaver.

Greg Allenby's tired Bentley was parked in a far dark corner, as agreed. Morton pulled alongside, putting his window next to the other car's. Allenby was a rumpled and booze-fragrant hulk in the gloom.

"You're one ballsy guy, Greg," Morton said from his open window. "I'm surprised you're still here."

"What's that supposed to mean?"

"Haven't you heard? Melanie Flynn is onto you."

"*What?*"

"She's found out you've been doing business with me. Selling me Lunt-owned goods."

Allenby actually wailed. "Oh, my God, God, *God*."

"That city detective—Jacoby. He's been investigating the Lunt airplane crash, and he overheard a conversation between Teddy and a private eye named Watson. Teddy was bragging about the deals he'd cut with you over the years. The eye told Melanie, and now she's working with the cops to put an all-points out for you. She wants your head on a pike."

Allenby sat, goggling, incapable of speech, for most of a minute. Then: "What am I going to do?"

"If I were you, pal, I'd grab my hundred mill and take to the hills."

"You got the money?"

Morton showed him the satchel. "The floppies?"

"Yeah. Yeah. Here." On the edge of panic, Allenby handed the carry-case out his window, and they made the trade.

"Congratulations, Greg," Morton said. "You are now a very rich man."

"A hundred mill doesn't seem like a hell of a lot for what Teddy's getting."

"Maybe not. But it'll go a very long way for a man who settles on his own little island in the Caribbean. That's still your plan, isn't it? To live on an island?"

Allenby was deeply shaken. "I'm not telling anybody where I'll be. I'm out of here. The man who never was."

"Makes sense. But I'd advise you to get another car. The cops'll be looking for this one."

"Christ, George—What am I going to do? The car and plane won't be available until Saturday."

"Where are they?"

"Car's in Philly. Belongs to a lady friend of mine. The plane'll be waiting at a strip near Chestertown, on the Eastern Shore. The pilot has agreed to fly me to El Paso, where I'll walk across the bridge into Juarez." He reached into the glove compartment, pulled out a pint, and took a long drink.

"Call a cab," Morton said. "Have it pick you up down the

street at Laurel Square and take you to Tri-County Airport. Take the bus from there to Philly."

"I can't just leave my car here," Allenby whined. "All my belongings are in it."

"I'd say you don't have any choice. Besides, you're rich now. Get yourself some new stuff."

Allenby thought about all that. Then he gave Morton a bleary, challenging stare. "What do you get out of all this, George? What do you get for being Teddy's bootlicking gofer?"

"One hell of a bonus, Greg. It's nowhere near your hundred million, but it's enough. And I don't have to live on the lam on some godforsaken sand dune. Good luck—and watch your tail."

He fired up the BMW and drove off.

"God," Teddy said. "I thought you'd never come back."

"Nervous?"

"Who wouldn't be? You drive off with two hundred million of my money, and I don't even have a receipt."

"Here's something better." Morton sat the carry-case on Teddy's lap. "Half a billion's worth of cancer cure. All yours." He laughed. "We're about to go into business, Teddy."

"Day after tomorrow at noon. At the club, right?"

"You got it."

As he crossed town, Morton glanced at the clock tower, barely visible in the strengthening flurry—8:10 P.M. Plenty of time for the next round at the Regency, so he put a call to Laura Radowski in L.A. She answered immediately.

"Hi, Laura. George Morton."

"Hey, man. Ain't cellulars great? I'm waiting in a bar for a call from Barney, and here you are. Why?"

"I'm about to make you president and CEO of Bradford Chemicals Corporation. Replacing Teddy."

She laughed. "I could live with that. How come?"

"You're the smartest one on the board. Next to me, of course. But I'm leaving."

"Sure. But what gives you the power to appoint me to replace Teddy? Teddy's an institution."

"Who has been raiding the employee pension fund. Two hundred millions' worth, as a matter of fact."

"*What?*"

"Look into it, Laura. Look into it, blow the whistle, and you'll end up chairman. I kid you not."

"George—"

He hung up.

35.

Uncle Denny was heavy on Morton's mind. It was the Christmas lights, the seasonal music floating from the sound system in the resort's lobbies and hallways, of course. Uncle Denny had always made a huge thing of Christmas. Morton could never hear a carol or see a lighted tree without remembering him turning on the skimpy string of bulbs on the scrawny triangle of pine branches set up, with great care and affection, in the corner of the tiny living room.

Morton stood at the glass wall in what the brochures called "the gathering room" and gazed out at the snowy undulations of the golf course, made pink and pale yellow and blue by the lights. The Regency Conference Resort consisted of this, the main hostelry and convention center, a hub of stone and glass and clapboard in the contemporary style. From this sprang five spokelike arrangements of "cottages," each cast in the image of the parent structure, with the whole catering to titans of the New York–Washington axis who liked to masquerade their golf outings as tax-deductible business conferences. The place was a brainchild of Charles Hamilton, who had built it in the hard-charging days before his disabling accident and subsequent de-campment to Florida. And it was here, as requested in the fax received at the house, he was to wait this evening until summoned to the Presidential Cottage, where Hamilton and his entourage would be staying during his visit to Alicia, now hovering between life and death at Z'ville General Hospital. Hamilton had chosen to stay here instead of at Elmwood, Morton assumed, because the cottage featured an enormous whirlpool bath that could accommodate Hamilton and the voluptuous therapists in his retinue.

He glanced at his watch. According to his county airport source, Hamilton's jet had landed at 6:11. Hamilton, in his chair, wrapped in blankets against the cold and wearing a hooded black storm coat, had deplaned on the hydraulic lift and, along with two of his nurses, entered a specially equipped van, hastily provided by a Philadelphia firm that served the handicapped. Four other therapists had taken a limousine to the Regency. Hamilton had taken the van to the hospital, where he was wheeled directly to Intensive Care. In the presence of that unit's cadre, he threw back his black hood, took his insensible wife's hand, and murmured unintelligibly for a full minute. He left the hospital at 7:32 and arrived at the Regency at 8:15.

It was now 9:45, and, despite Morton's considerable patience, he was beginning to feel edgy.

At 9:47, a page handed him a phone.

"Morton."

"Mr. Hamilton wonders if you could join him now in the Presidential Cottage." The voice was young, female.

"I'll be right there."

He checked himself in the window reflection. Satisfied, he pulled on his topcoat, picked up the case containing copies of the floppies Teddy now thought to be exclusively his, and went through the revolving door and into the night.

Hamilton, wrapped in a black silk robe, a blanket tucked about his legs, sat beside the fireplace, staring into the lazily flickering flames. Morton was in a leather armchair, the carry-case on the floor beside him, waiting for a sign that would indicate Hamilton's mood. They were alone in the softly lit room, the therapists having been sent off for a late supper.

"My wife," Hamilton said suddenly, "has been very seriously hurt."

"So I understand. And I can't say how sorry I am. Such a terrible thing to happen to such a fine person."

"What do you know about this Dr. DeVito?"

"He's unquestionably the best."

Hamilton said in a matter-of-fact voice, "I spend much of my life manipulating doctors and the tools they work with. Arrogant, pompous jerks who think of themselves as gods, most of them. Then, something like this happens, and you find yourself wondering how godly one of them can be, how able he is to work the miracle needed to save the life of someone you love."

Morton struggled to ignore this outrageous hypocrisy. "Single-minded pros—artists, musicians, writers, teachers, actors, scientists, whatever—often come off as egocentric jerks to those who have no need of their talents."

"Physicians and surgeons are the worst, though."

"Well, with the huge amounts of training and self-discipline required by medicine, they tend to see themselves as a brotherhood, working against hellish odds in a world peopled by idiots and ingrates. Their sense of isolation from the herd makes them lousy communicators. That, in turn, makes them easy to dislike."

Hamilton sniffed. "But they're more than professionals just plying a trade. They deal in human lives. Their failures of omission or commission can ruin, kill. And when one of them fails, they close ranks, fall silent, to protect the ass of the incompetent fraternity brother whose lousy goddam bumbling has blemished them all."

Morton, nodded, feigning deep thought.

"Look at me," Hamilton said. "My life was forever changed by a surgeon who was so sublimely sure of himself he chose to risk my legs rather than submit my case to specialists."

Morton made a sympathetic sound. "Only true jerks can be that cocksure. How come you didn't demand a second opinion?"

"I was unconscious for days, and my poor, distraught wife assumed that the bastard knew what he was doing. And when I was able to protest, I came up against the proverbial stone wall." Hamilton paused, seeming to savor a thought. "And so now I make the decisions that change doctors' lives, destroy doctors' careers, and seal doctors' fates. Doctors twisted my legs, so now I twist their balls."

Morton offered a touch of piety. "Vengeance is hugely attractive. But it also carries risks."

Hamilton smiled faintly. "Do I look like a man who is threatened by risk?"

"Certainly not," Morton said, returning the smile.

Hamilton got down to business. Nodding at the carry-case, he said, "So, then: I assume that the Allenby floppies are in there."

"All ready for your acquisition."

"How are we on time?"

"I understand that the Lunt Biotech people plan to make an announcement on January 3. They're by no means ready to demonstrate, but they're announcing anyhow—just to put a lock on the discovery."

"Which means Gerda and her people have to move faster."

Morton made a little joke. "Fortunately, being European, they don't have to contend with our Federal government."

Hamilton chuckled, appreciating the mot. "We have that advantage, all right." He turned and pressed a button on the telephonics box on the table beside him.

"Yes, Mr. Hamilton?" came the metallic voice.

"Connect me with Gerda von Reichmann in Paris and put us on speakerphone."

The connection was made, and von Reichmann came on, clear, brisk. "Hello, Charles. What's up?"

"George Morton is here with me. He informs me that the Lunt people plan to announce on January 3."

"I see. Can you deliver the floppies soon enough for us to beat that date, Mr. Morton?"

"Allenby has accepted your offer, and I have the floppies with me here."

Hamilton said, "We're about to complete the deal, Gerda. And there are a few things I want you to do."

"Of course. How can I help?"

"First, I want you to tape George's basic explanation of what the Allenby Formula is and what it can do. The bottom-line stuff. Second, I want you to give the tape to Pierre Duval, so that he and his PR people there can pull together an announcement and its accompanying press packet—release date, Christmas Day. We expect Pierre to maximize the drama, the excitement, the incredible implications of this medical discovery, keeping it dignified, of course, but using layman's language—the popular idiom. He might want to call it Le Tellier's Christmas present to the world, for instance. Whatever, we want to saturate the world's media with stories of our brilliance."

Gerda was enthusiastic. "Marvelous. Absolutely marvelous, Charles. And you've definitely decided to make this a Le Tellier product?"

"We could have used Kugel or Holtz, but it's more fitting to have the flagship company in the originator's role, I'd say. And Le Tellier is Europe's prime producer of Vitam, which can be touted as the forerunner of this new thing. Best of all, Le Tellier management is always open to our strategies, while the younger people at Kugel often tend to be awkwardly idealistic."

"You're right, as always."

Hamilton nodded at Morton. "Give us a rundown, George. Understandable to the average yuck, but with enough technical crap to impress the competition. You get the idea."

"Okay."

"Ready with the tape, Gerda?"

"All set, Charles. It's turning, George."

Morton went into his seminar mode. "To put it simply, Le Tellier has broadened, strengthened, the foundation established by Vitam. The new medication goes beyond Vitam. When properly supplemented by a dietary regimen, the new drug not only prevents tumors and arrests the development of existing tumors but also, in some cases, actually makes existing tumors shrivel and disappear.

"Le Tellier has given practical application to the trophoblastic thesis, which has for years intrigued medical scientists but always eluded their efforts to tame it. Trophoblasts arise from the diploid totipotent, which are key to the body's healing processes, but sometimes they can't be turned off after they've done their work, and the result is too much healing—too many scars, so to speak, and they become what we know as cancerous tumors. Le Tellier has devised a way to harness, to hem in, these runaway trophoblasts by altering the steroid hormones that put the totipotency into play. Over the past year, a total of 175 cases, from breast cancers to prostate cancers, were administered the new Tellier compound, and, when coupled with ongoing dosages of B17, zinc, and a rigidly controlled, specially designed diet, ninety-two percent of those cases went into total remission. Not one of the test group has died, although each of the 175 had been pronounced incurable. A typical case is a woman confined to a hospital bed with terminal cancer of the breast who is now—after three weeks on the Le Tellier course of treatment—back with her family and walking to church every weekend. The Le Tellier discovery promises to make cancer as inconsequential as rickets and scurvy." Morton paused, glancing at Hamilton. "Will that do it?"

Hamilton clapped his hands lazily. "Prima! An excellent summary, don't you think so, Gerda?"

"Excellent indeed. Pierre will have a field day."

Morton cleared his throat. "Mind if I ask a question?"

"Of course not."

"Won't the pros at Le Tellier get their backs up? I mean, all of a sudden, in the middle of one of their routine workdays, management announces a wonder product none of them have ever heard of, worked on. Isn't it possible that there might be a whistle-blower, somebody who'll take his suspicions to the media, or to the governmental regulating bodies?"

Hamilton smiled and shook his head. "Not likely. Le Tellier management is very security-conscious, very military-like, and operates on the need-to-know principle. Le Tellier research employees, who work on projects in teams, understand that they may never know what the team in the laboratory next door is working on. The ordinary production worker is quite used to having things sprung on him. No problem there."

"Amazing."

"Not like in the States, eh?"

"Not like in Europe, either, as a matter of fact."

"Well, Le Tellier meets all the laws and regulations in whatever country it operates. But it also enjoys certain exemptions, certain prerogatives, most places."

"You mean it owns a sizable number of politicians and bureaucrats. Right?"

They laughed together, and Gerda said, "On that note, I'll ring off and get to work."

"So then," Hamilton said, holding out a hand, "the floppies."

Morton stood and carried the case to Hamilton, who placed it on his lap and patted it fondly.

"And I," Morton said, "will take Teddy's payment."

Hamilton reached under the blanket and produced a briefcase fabricated in rich brown leather. "Two hundred and fifty million in negotiables."

"Like amount due on the day production begins."

"The briefcase is yours, George. As a kind of bonus."

They laughed again.

"Now if you'll excuse me," Hamilton said, consulting his watch, "I must call the hospital and ask about my wife. I'm quite worried about her."

36.

The next day, as he drove the BMW up the carefully plowed driveway to Falloon's huge house, Morton inexplicably remembered the Phaedrian aphorism, "He who covets what belongs to another deservedly loses his own."

Was he being covetous? He considered his motives, briefly but with resolute honesty, and could find no real evidence of greed—only the good old-fashioned need to fix some bastard's crock. So he must have been thinking of Teddy, now hopelessly trapped in the underbrush of his own ego and greed. Or was it Allenby, the self-destructive, chronic loser? No matter which, he decided testily, as human beings, both were sorry specimens who had been shipwrecked before they'd even set sail.

Falloon was hosting lunch for a gaggle of congressmen and their wives. Big cars were parked in glinting echelons, and big men in bulging overcoats, their breath making steamy halos, patrolled among them. Haughty music, the clinking of glassware, and waves of high-decibel gossip drifted from the solarium, where the bartenders and string ensemble labored in the party's stormy eye.

Morton had been invited because Falloon thought it would be useful to introduce him to the Washington barons as the soon-to-be president and CEO of Pegasus. And Morton had accepted because it offered excellent timing and a perfect rationale for the dropping of his bombshell. But putting on the proper face wasn't easy, given the need to schmooze the pols while simultaneously showing the ever-watchful Van Dyke that bad news had entered the room with him.

Morton shook hands and grinned a lot as he eased through the crowd, but by the time he reached Falloon, who stood in a vortex of guests at the foot of the main staircase, he wore his politely grave expression. "We have to talk. Right now."

Falloon raised an irritable eyebrow, and said from the side of his mouth, "This is a party, Morton. Can't your business wait until tomorrow?"

"This is urgent. It has to do with your announcement here. It could be embarrassing—"

Falloon turned to the large man standing watchfully nearby, and said slowly, "Find Mr. Van Dyke and tell him to join me in the upstairs sitting room." Giving Morton a cool glance, he waved a hand toward the staircase.

They sat in an arc of overstuffed chairs.

Falloon glanced at Van Dyke. "Morton says he has information that bears on today's announcement." He gave Morton a low-lidded stare. "What's up?"

"A very serious development, gentlemen. More than serious. Catastrophic, I'd call it." Morton had never had acting lessons, a fact he regretted at this moment when everything was riding on his ability to portray a man struggling to control a huge case of consternation.

"Well?"

"I got a call from Greg Allenby. On my way out the door to come here. He said that he has closed a deal with Le Tellier. He has decided to sell his formula to the French instead of us."

The silence in the room was palpable. Even the fire seemed to suspend its hissings and snappings, and the muted music from below actually stopped when, in a bizarre coincidence, the ensemble took a break.

Morton cleared his throat. "The price was five hundred million dollars."

Van Dyke was the first to regain his voice. "Five hundred million? That's absurd."

Falloon showed the stuff of leadership. For all his shock and rage, his face was expressionless, his tone philosophical. "The French always were quick to see the true value of things."

Morton played a man left wordless after learning that he has just lost a deposit of ten million dollars.

"We've paid that fellow three hundred million dollars for that formula," Van Dyke said quietly. "We had a deal. He has our money. And now you're telling us that he's killed our deal because he got a better offer from somebody else?"

Morton nodded, sputtering, "Two hundred million more."

Van Dyke shook his head in disbelief. "Why would anybody pay half a billion dollars for a single drug formula?"

"Mr. Falloon's got it right." Morton sighed. "The French realize that even a billion is peanuts in today's competitive market. Hell, drug manufacturers are paying as high as six, seven billion just to acquire little companies that do no more than manage prescription benefit programs for employee health care plans. For the French, paying a half billion for the exclusive ownership of a drug that not only cures cancer but also can be used as a cancer antitoxin is like paying two bucks for all the casinos in Vegas."

"Then how come we offered only three hundred million?"

"Because we knew the property was stolen. The French don't know that."

Falloon's bass was made all the more malevolent by its lack of heat. "Tell me, Morton, did Allenby show any sign of understanding how serious his offense against us is? He's accepted our offer, and we have paid him what he asked, and now he reneges. Does he realize just what he's done?"

Morton made a gesture of exasperation. "The only thing he said was that as soon as he gets his money from Le Tellier he will pay us back."

"I don't accept that," Van Dyke murmured. "He could be planning to abscond with our money."

Morton said miserably, "He's already absconded with mine. I'm forfeiting ten million to you. You have my check. That little bastard has virtually wiped me out."

Another silence gathered while they considered the enormity of Allenby's transgression.

Falloon shifted in his chair, a sign that he was about to pass judgment. Morton was aware of his heart's heavy beating.

"There is no logical reason," Falloon said, "for us to wait for anything. Allenby has three hundred million of our dollars. He has gone back on his agreement with us. He therefore owes us three hundred million dollars immediately—the same three hundred we gave him."

A pause.

Falloon had begun to gather his rage about him, an emperor pronouncing the doom of a miscreant. "Moreover, he must pay a penalty. In addition to the three hundred million, which must be returned to me personally by tomorrow at noon, he will, at such time as he is paid by the French, owe us an additional three hundred million. Unless he pays this debt, he's a dead man."

A longer pause.

Falloon fixed Morton with a stare, his eyes glinting. "I want you to pick up that phone on the table and call Allenby and tell him what I have just said."

"That's not possible. He's on an airplane, en route to Florida and a meeting with the French. I can get him later, after he arrives in Palm Strand, but now, at this moment—"

"Have a call waiting for him when he lands. Tell him that I expect him to bring me our money, personally, by Friday at noon. Here. He brings it here, to my house."

"And if he can't? If it's not logistically possible?"

"Then he's dead. It will be worth three hundred million dollars to me to have him dead. You tell him precisely that. I want him to understand that, to believe that."

There was another pause. Then Falloon said, "Now, let's get back to our guests. Except for you, George. You have a lot of work to do."

"I've got ten million reasons to do a lot of work."

37.

Jacoby picked up Melanie at the Lunt lab at nine, as promised. The Acme Diner was closed for alterations, so they settled for something nearby—a pseudo-Tyrolean steakhouse perched on the bank of Three-Mile Creek. The hostess, a plump little brunette in a phony dirndl, ushered them to a table near the phony tile oven, and, showing them a phony smile, handed them menus shaped like cowbells.

The plump little waiter, wearing *Lederhosen*, knee socks, and a felt hat with a brush plume, announced in phony German inflections, "Tonight idt giffs as our special, pickled pigs' feet mit potato pancakes à la Matterhorn."

Jacoby, using his menu as a screen, feigned nausea, and Melanie, glimpsing this, struggled to keep a straight face.

"I'll have the house salad," she managed. "With wheat toast and unsweetened grape juice."

"Bring me the steak sandwich, medium rare. A side of potato salad and a draft beer. Hold the umlauts."

"Zir?"

"I said I don't want any umlauts on my sandwich."

"As you vish, zir," the man said somberly, gathering the menus, "I'll giff Chef Heinrich by the instructions."

When he marched off for the kitchen, Melanie laughed. "I didn't realize this place had a floor show."

"Sid Caesar did it a lot better."

They laughed some more. As the goofy mood subsided, he looked her over carefully. "You look premium-grade zonked."

She nodded. "I'm tired. I've had to put on another hat now that Greg Allenby has left."

"I've been meaning to ask you: How did Allenby and Lunt get along? You say Lunt was a lone-wolf type, very private, doing his own research-and-invention thing around the shop, and Allenby was responsible for keeping everything organized and tidy around that same shop. Seems to me that kind of a situation could cause a bit of abrasion now and then."

She nodded. "Things got pretty testy sometimes. Greg often complained that Dr. Lunt didn't like him, treated him like a hired hand, that sort of thing."

"Well, hell, he *was* a hired hand."

"It's deeper than that. Greg is a talented, highly trained, highly skilled professional, a fact that certainly never escaped Dr. Lunt but one which he seemed never to be able to acknowledge gracefully. It was sort of—"

"A tacit rivalry, maybe? I see that kind of thing in cops sometimes."

She shrugged. "Could be. But it was clear that Greg thought he wasn't appreciated as much as he should be, and Anson was ticked off by this, describing Greg as 'a pouting egotist who wants to be kissy-kissed all the time.' Personally, I thought they both tended to act like children."

"Why did Lunt keep Allenby around if there was so much tension between them?"

"I once worked up the nerve to ask Anson that very question, and instead of telling me to mind my own damned business, as I expected him to, he was surprisingly frank. He said it was because he was both practical and lazy. He admitted that Allenby is a first-class talent who would be tough to replace. He said that it wouldn't be practical to let little irritations get rid of such a big asset. And it would be damned inconvenient and a lot of hard work to dig up a replacement—who might turn out to be an even bigger pain."

The little man with the hat and bare knees brought their food, and they gave time to getting into it. Jacoby's sandwich turned out to be excellent, and he was halfway through it before he got to more questions. "Did Anson Lunt have any friends at all? I mean, I keep hearing about what a loner he was. How big a loner? Was he a recluse? Was he antisocial?"

"Well, he liked his own company, and he rarely shared his work with anyone beyond the need for administrative support. But I don't think he was antisocial in the normal sense."

"How about girlfriends?"

She gave him an amused look. "Come on. Anson? He never had time for anything but his work—especially after that rotten Vitam episode back in the early days. And romance takes time and effort."

"I wouldn't know."

"And it's like with your parents, you know? How you can't imagine them ever having sex, or fooling around? I saw Anson that way. He was so aloof, so contained, so—arid and self-centered—I have trouble seeing him as somebody's lover."

"How did he get along with Alicia Hamilton?"

She gave him a look.

"I just wondered if they were pals or anything."

"Good friends. She never made any bones about how she admired him and his work, and, as you know, she backed up her admiration with lots of money."

"Speaking of Vitam, was that why Lunt had such a hard nose for George Morton? Morton and the Bradford people roughed him up pretty bad when he was getting into the Vitam-dietary therapy. Was Lunt carrying one of those lifelong grudges?"

Melanie took a sip of juice, giving the question some thought. "I don't know how to answer that one. Anson was outraged by the way Teddy Bradford and his people treated him, no doubt about that. He openly hated Teddy Bradford. But he was sort of restrained when it came to George Morton. I had this strange feeling that Anson and Morton—well, respected each other. I almost said 'liked,' but that's too strong. Anyway, there was something peculiar between those two guys. I never knew George Morton, socially or otherwise. On our first contact, I detested him. The oily way he tried to buy me out. His smug superiority. I later learned that he's got substance, being a self-made man and all. And he was—well—chivalrous when it came to the gunshot in the churchyard. What I'm saying, I guess, is that Morton bothers me more than he ever bothered Dr. Lunt. Don't ask me why."

"Intuition is a hell of a force, all right. I never leave home without it." He took a sip of beer. "It could be that there was a kind of bond between them. Their similar origins, hauling themselves out of poverty, and like that. Maybe each understood what the other guy had had to do to get where he was."

"Could be."

They finished the meal, studiously avoiding further mention of the things that were heavy on their minds. Since she had more work to do, she'd left her car at the lab, so he drove her there over a road that was turning white under a swirling of new snow. When he pulled up to the entrance and she prepared to step out, she paused, giving him a speculative glance. "You're a computer nut. Would you like to come in for a minute—look at our setup?"

Jacoby grinned. "I thought you'd never ask. Where should I park this heap?"

"Just leave it here. There's no traffic at this hour of the night."

They mounted the steps and Melanie used a key to open a section of the plate-glass lobby door. There she signed in at a register overseen by a bored but good-natured security guard who pretended to be all-out, gee-whiz tickled by her announcement that Jacoby was a visiting city detective.

Everything was as Jacoby had expected: polished tile floors; pastel walls; spartan furnishings; glistening glass doors leading to laboratory rooms with acres of glistening chemical equipment;

surgical cleanliness everywhere. At the end of what appeared to be the main corridor, she used an electronic key to unlock a heavy gray metal door labeled, DIRECTOR AND SECTION CHIEFS ONLY. This opened into a softly lighted rectangular room in which two of the walls were lined by computers and printers. The remaining area was given to bookshelves, work desks, and a conference area established by a round-top coffee table circled by easy chairs. She turned on one of the computers, booted up to an opening menu, and scrolled through seemingly endless, esoteric directories: amygdalin and mandelonitriles; enzymes; nitrilosides; beta-glucosidase; antibodies; polymerase chain reaction; differential hybridization; multiparameter flow cytometry; genetics; genomes; marker genes; biotechnology, general; biotechnology, specific; cancer, general; cancers, specific; case histories and patient database.

"Hold it." he said. "What's in that last directory—Case Histories and Patient Database?"

"Mainly the cases Dr. Lunt, in his clinician's role, examined and treated over the years—names, addresses, medical histories, tests, X rays, graphics, that kind of thing."

"Can I take a look at a sample file in that directory?"

"Sorry. That's one of the directories Dr. Lunt blocked with a password demand. But I'll open the graphics file and you can browse through that. Give you a feel for things. Meanwhile, I'm headed for the loo."

The graphics proved to be just that—graphs of all colors and shapes, and all of them incomprehensible. Instantly bored, he quit that file and stared at the menu.

Passwords.

Most computer nuts made it easy on themselves when it came to passwords, choosing a word, a phrase, maybe, that was easy to remember and had a personal connection. Social Security numbers, book titles, movies and actors, birth dates, girlfriends—

Jacoby smiled.

What the hell. Give it a try.

He punched up the Case Histories and Patient Database directory and was instantly met with a snotty ENTER PASSWORD.

He typed in ALICIA.

The password demand disappeared and the screen suddenly showed a list of names and addresses. Each listing included a nutshell description of the patient's diagnosis, treatment, and eventual disposition.

Out of pure curiosity, he tapped the Page Down key and halted at

> Alicia Cosgrove Emerson Hamilton, (Mrs. Charles
> M. H.) Hollow Tree Pike, RD 2, Zieglersville. Walk-
> in 3/17/89. Patient disputed mastectomy prescribed
> by Drs. GHF and KLY, Phila. Diagnosis of primary ma-
> lignancy in left breast confirmed 3/29/89. Formula
> prescribed 4/8/89. Tumor size reduced 96% as of 6/15/
> 89. Total remission as of 9/21/89.

So here, then, in a few electronic lines, were the death sentence and reprieve of an eccentric aristocrat whose millions could buy her anything but impeccable breasts. He thought about her a moment, wondering again what had moved her to pull such a dumb stunt at Bill Rooney's house.

Well, c'est la friggin' guerre . . .

He moved to quit the file but his right pinky hit the Page Up key, and as he moved to redo the quit, his eye fell on:

> Gertrude P. Margolis, 322 Ludlow St., Zieglers-
> ville. Walk-in, 6/4/95. Diagnosis: cervical malig-
> nancy, primary. Formula prescribed 6/10/95. Tumor
> size reduced 90% as of 8/5/94. Total remission as of 4/
> 4/95.

He sat back in the chair, transfixed.

Melanie materialized at his shoulder, smelling of soap. "What's that, Clouseau?"

"You won't believe this. On a whim I answered a password

demand with Alicia's name, and *boing,* I broke through to this list."

"You're kidding."

"No. Look."

He scrolled through the entire list of some two hundred names. With each was the notation that there had been total remission—that the patient had been cured of a variation of cancer after having walked into the Lunt clinic or having been pronounced incurable by physicians and surgeons in cities nationwide.

"My God," Melanie said softly. "I just don't believe this."

"Believe what?"

"Do you see what I see? One hundred percent total cures. A total remission in every one of those two hundred names. That's—incredible—"

"Would Lunt be doing a bit of padding here?"

"Don't be ridiculous. This was his life's work. This was what he was all about. Anson Lunt might have had faults, but self-deception wasn't among them. If he said these people were cured, they were cured."

"Let's find some of them and talk to them." Jacoby reached for the phone and dialed Dispatch.

"Gleason."

"Jacoby, Cal. Is Iris on duty tonight?"

"Sure. Due in ten minutes."

"Good. I'm out at the Lunt laboratory—Dr. Flynn's extension. Tell Iris that she can expect a rather sizable incoming fax from me within the next hour. Tell her that it's for the Margolis homicide investigation and that she should let it feed, so that tomorrow she should check every name on the list—no matter what city—for current address and phone number. I mean, I don't want a mere check of phone books. I want her section to contact the police in those cities and do a real rummage. Have them plug into the Interpol cryptonet and feed us direct from police files, city directories, and especially water departments—people might hide behind unlisted phones, but they can't flush the toilet without paying. Also feed us any mention of the names on switchboard caller-ID files, nine-one-one grids. If listees have since died, get me date, place, and cause of each of the deaths. And I want hard copy of anything sent in, because Dr. Flynn needs to interview as many of those people who are still around."

"Iris ain't gonna like this. This a super project."

"Tell her to complain to Stabile."

"When are you gonna start sending?"

"ASAP. Meanwhile, transfer me to Doc Logan."

There was some snapping and crackling, then: "Logan."

"Hi, Doc. Jake here."

"My hero."

"Tell me: Did your PM of Gertrude Margolis reveal any evidence of cancer, past or present?"

"Let me get her file."

Jacoby listened to the rattling and banging at the other end, his impatience growing. The phone lifted again.

"No such signs, Jake."

"No scars, no anything?"

"Hey, do you want to come down here and redo the post? Or do you want to take my word for it?"

"Sorry, Doc. I'm a bit frazzled tonight."

"Well, if news about Margolis is what you're after, I got some. She was unconscious when she was hung up. Somebody injected her with a jolt of phenobarb, then must've helped her into the rope, because she sure as hell couldn't have done it herself."

"Homicide. Right?"

"Oy boy, are you a case. Of course it's homicide." Logan hung up in disgust.

Jacoby glanced at Melanie. She was still staring at the screen, her eyes wide, her lips parted, her cheeks flushed.

"Are you all right?"

"Do you realize what you've done, Jake?"

"Yeah. I made a lucky guess."

"Anson Lunt had found some kind of cure for some kinds of cancer. A cure, Jake. A one hundred damn percent cure."

"Good, huh?"

"Try the Alicia password on the other directories."

He did, and each time the screen produced data relating to what Lunt had labeled THE CURE.

Each time but one: the directory labeled TROPHICS.

No guess or combination of guesses broke through that directory's demand for a password.

They sat, staring at each other.

The phone rang, and Melanie picked it up, listened, then handed the phone to Jacoby.

"Yo."

"Gleason, Jake. That little kid, Tommy Ludlow, was in with his parents this evening and Ed Blake has finished the sketch that came out of it. Ed says you want to see it as soon as. You want I should fax it to you now?"

"Sure do." He gave Gleason the fax number and turned to Melanie. "*Achtung.* Incoming."

They sat quietly, waiting, their eyes on the machine.

Melanie said abruptly, "That's what Greg has stolen. He's stolen the formula for what brought all those cures."

"Easy. One crisis at a time."

"That's what he stole, dammit."

"Calm down, babe. We'll get to him."

The fax machine whirred into life. When it finished its business and the image was complete, Jacoby tore off the sheet and held it under the desk lamp.

The likeness was remarkable, even when surrounded by the black storm-coat hood.

They traded astonished stares. Then Melanie broke off, took a ballpoint from the pencil caddie on the desk, and drew a pair of circles around the eyes.

"Yes-s-s-s!" Jacoby gloated. "Add some granny glasses, and you've got Amy Cummings."

Melanie, suddenly anxious, lifted the phone and dialed.

"Who you calling?"

"Z'ville General. I want to know where Amy is tonight."

The connection was made, she identified herself, asked the

question, listened, then hung up, pale. "Tonight begins her week for night duty in the Special Cases Wing. Where Alicia is."

Jacoby made for the door. "I'm outa here."

"Not without me, you aren't."

38.

Midnight had settled in, and the hospital itself seemed to doze—lights dim, air vents whispering, phones silent, corridors hushed and devoid of motion. It was especially still in the Special Cases Wing, a section of first-floor luxury suites dedicated to those members of the region's elite who might be bushwhacked by plebeian infirmities.

The suite occupied by Alicia Hamilton (which, Jacoby guessed dourly, had to cost at least a thousand dollars a minute) consisted of a standard hospital room, entered directly from the corridor and furnished with the standard bed and sidebar equipment, which was adjoined by the standard hospital bathroom and closet. Adjacent to this grouping and entered by a connecting door, was a large room containing plush wall-to-wall carpeting, luxurious sofas, easy chairs, coffee tables, softly glowing lamps, TV, and classic art, reproduced and encased in gilt frames. Beyond it were a lavishly appointed guest bedroom, a kitchenette with microwave and wet bar, another bathroom containing a shower, a whirlpool bath, a his-and-her lavinette, a mirror wall, and color-coordinated hopper and bidet. This Eden had its own connection to the outside world via a lockable door opening on a small interior cul-de-sac. The culminating refinement was a one-way mirror in the hospital room, which in the sitting room was a window that enabled aspiring legatees to draw open the drapes, perch on the sofas, and watch with avarice aforethought as dear old intestate Uncle Throckmorton wrestled with his indispositions.

"What are we doing here, Jake?"

"I don't want to flush her. She doesn't know we know. She'll come to us. According to that duty roster you snatched for us, she'll be by to check Alicia sooner or later. I want to see how she handles that. I especially want you to see that."

"Why?"

"With your technical savvy, your familiarity with how doctors, nurses, and hospitals do things, you'll make a great witness. The police sketch links Cummings with Alicia's plane crash. Which means Cummings must want Alicia dead. So how does Cummings act now, with Alicia on the slow mend? A jury will want to know."

Melanie was skeptical. "How could she make a plane crash?"

"She was a Special Forces nurse. Told me that herself. That means she'd have had at least some training in automotive maintenance and basic familiarity with weapons and explosives. And she's been shacking with a used-car dealer who used to be a Special Forces demolition guy. Go figure."

There was motion at the door to Alicia's room. A small brunette in stretch whites came in, checking her wristwatch.

"Who's that?" Jacoby asked tautly.

"Jane Kolb. I know her. A darn good RN." Melanie consulted her clipboard. "She's on the midnight-to-eight shift this week."

"What's she doing?"

"Making the twelve-thirty check. Right now she's reading the patient status sheet, which routinely hangs at the foot of the bed.

"Now she's checking Alicia—her general appearance, the IV insert in the back of her hand, content level of the IV bags, blanketing, pillow placement, bed setting.

"Now she's inserting a digital thermometer in Alicia's ear, checking temperature.

"Now she's taking her pulse.

"Now she notes the two figures on the status sheet.

"Now she's looking over the dressings on Alicia's chest surgery, checking for signs of blood or seepage or whatever.

"Now she's using her stethoscope to tune in on Alicia's lungs and hear how they're working."

"Now she's looking at everything in the room to be sure all's as should be—lights, call button, air vents, window drapes. And a final check of the IV rig, making sure the pump's working properly. Now she's looking into the bathroom to be sure nothing's amiss there, and now she leaves, saying good night to Alicia, even though it's unlikely Alicia could hear a locomotive passing by her bed. Kolb's a good, thorough nurse."

They said nothing further, pretending instead to listen to the hospital's busy silence.

"Heads up. Here she is."

The door to Alicia's hospital room had swung open, and Cummings, after a momentary pause, entered in a brisk, quiet stride, stethoscope at the ready. She crossed the room quickly and tried the door to the guest suite. Finding it locked, she moved close to the mirror and, squinting, attempted to penetrate its opacity.

"God, won't she see us in here?" Melanie whispered.

"No way. I tried it."

Cummings made her next move—a fast turn, curiously graceful, balletic, that took her to the side of Alicia's bed. She bent down, and with both hands, seized Alicia's shoulders and shook them violently.

"Damn it, she's not supposed to do that, Jake—"

When the shaking was repeated, Jacoby said, "Okay, that does it."

He threw the lock and stepped through the door. "Knock it off, Amy. It's show-and-tell time."

The big nurse stood, frozen, speechless, staring at him in shock, the light glinting on her glasses.

"Come on in, Mel, and see to Alicia and get a doctor here." He reached for the handcuffs on his belt. "Turn around, Amy.

Put your hands behind you. You have the right to remain silent—"

Cummings turned around, but it was one of those Chuck Norris turns—a wild, wicked pirouette, one leg high. Her foot caught Jacoby full on the side of the head, and he went careening backward, collapsing against Melanie with a force that took them both to the floor in a welter of toppling IV stands and overturning medicine tables.

Jacoby's head was filled with Klieg lights and fireworks, and in some vast distance he heard his own voice shouting, "Help me up! Help me up, goddammit!"

"I can't, you idiot, you're lying all over me."

"Where'd she go?"

"Get off, dammit. Your elbow is in my face."

He eventually managed to stagger to his feet, a roaring in his head, a blur in his eyes. "Where the hell did she go, Mel?"

Gasping, Melanie wobbled erect and pointed wordlessly down the hall toward the fire exit. She rubbed her head and hurried to the bed and a check of Alicia. Nurse Kolb and two male aides came trotting into the room. "What the hell's going on here—" Kolb was flushed, angry, until she saw Melanie attending to Alicia—"Doctor Flynn?"

"Mrs. Hamilton needs Dr. DeVito right now, Kolb! Have somebody call him!"

"Take care of Alicia," Jacoby said, weaving for the door. "I'll be wanting to ask her a lot of questions."

"She's okay. Now find that goddam Amy, will you?"

Finding Amy was not all that difficult.

Jacoby's intention had been to put out an all-points from his car radio, but as he cleared the fire exit and slipped and slid through the sleeting night, he heard the sizzling of tires on the icy macadam. A brown Corolla was fishtailing up the parking lot's south ramp, and even from where Jake was he could see the white uniform behind the wheel. As he began what was meant to be a dash for the laboring car, his intuition—a weird second sense that seemed to float in on the bitter wind—sent him instead into a wobbling, arm-waving shuffle for his Mustang.

Cummings, the feeling told him, was not just fleeing, she was fleeing *somewhere*.

And he was going to tag along.

The Corolla had made it to the hospital's main driveway by the time he got his car into motion, lights out. Because he had all-weather cop tires and had done a lot of cold-weather driving over the years, it was no trick for him to clear the ramp and fall behind at an unobtrusive distance, thankful that the obviously unpracticed Amy was so busy trying to keep her car on the road she had little time to watch for pursuit.

Henderson Avenue, the main artery from the hospital to the downtown area, had also been sanded, but Cummings's lack of skill and the intermittent traffic flow combined to keep this one of the slowest automobile chases since O.J. She had a close one when she skidded through the Tenth Street red light seconds before a huge semi rig crossed behind her, horn blaring. The light almost caused him to lose her, but he picked up the Corolla's taillights at the Bledsoe traffic circle and followed with relative ease until the brown car careened to a halt in the parking lot at the Cat's Pee-Jays.

The lot was nearly full, because drunks and lechers are rarely put off by rotten weather; but several slots under the boundary trees remained unoccupied, and she took one of them. He drove around the aisles twice—an addled driver looking for a roosting place. Cummings left her car, tall in the black storm coat now, hood thrown back, her nurse's shoes hidden by galoshes. He backed the Mustang into a vacancy two slots away from her car, turned all switches off, and, settling low in the seat, began his surveillance. His head still roared and throbbed.

Cummings made quickly for the bar, and went directly to the pay phone in the lobby. She inserted a coin, punched the numbers, and through the steamy windows he could see her impatience. Finally, she spoke briefly, listened a moment, nodded—visibly agitated—then hung up.

She returned to her car, climbed in, slammed the door, and seemed to begin a watch of her own.

Fifteen minutes passed, during which the parking lot resounded to the hooting and yammering of departing sots, the vooming of engines starting, the slithering of tires on the deepening rime. Jacoby's gaze remained fixed on Cummings, a dim silhouette behind the frosted windows of her car.

A light blue Saturn glided slowly through the lot's entrance, made a single circuit, then, after passing the Corolla, stopped, reversed, and backed into the open slot remaining. A man in a dark topcoat left the Saturn and walked slowly to Cummings's car, stopping beside the driver's door and waiting until the window went down. It was too dark for Jacoby to make out his face, and the parking lot clamor made it impossible to hear what was said.

It wasn't too dark, though, for Jacoby to make out the barrel silencer on the automatic the man drew from his coat.

Jacoby slammed down on the door handle, half fell, half leaped from the car, tore his Glock from its belt holster, and shouted, "Freeze! Police!" at the instant the man's automatic snapped, a nasty sound in the nasty sounds.

The automatic came around, and Jacoby could see its winking and there was a violent tearing of the air next to his head. And then his own pistol was thumping angrily, and the gunman began a sliding run for his car.

Jacoby fired once more, and the man went down, rolling, his pistol slithering across the icy pavement.

Somewhere a woman screeched, and men were shouting.

Shuffling awkwardly, sliding his feet one before the other, Jacoby made his way to the automatic and, scooping it up, slid it into his coat pocket. It was hard to breathe, and his head rang with pain and dizziness, but he got to the crumpled figure and turned the face toward the nightclub's lights.

Pinky Watson.

Jacoby pressed his fingers against Watson's neck, but found no pulse. Then, stumbling his way to the Corolla, he found Cummings slumped in the driver's seat, alternately groaning and gasping. He felt her neck, noted an erratic pulse.

"Hold on, Amy. I'll be right back."

He went to his car, leaned in the door, and snatched up the transmitter. "Car Four—Jacoby. I've got a Code Three at the Cat's Pee-Jays. A 10-57, with one man down and a woman probable. Ambulance, please."

39.

"Jacoby?"

"I'm here."

"Don't move me. Don't touch me. It hurts."

"Let me see the wound."

"It hurts like hell. My right boob."

"Easy. Easy. I'm just unzipping the parka. There. Easy."

"What's that you're doing?"

"Opening my pocketknife. I've got to cut your uniform, your bra straps. I've got to see the wound. Okay?"

"It hurts."

"There we are. There. It doesn't look too bad."

"Bullshit. I'm going to die."

"No you aren't. Help's on the way."

"I want to die."

"That's something else."

"Who are all those people with you?"

"They aren't with me. They're people from the lounge."

"Tell them to stop staring at me."

"There's only one of me, and they'll do what they want."

"That bastard shot me. I was set up."

"I'm turning on my recorder and advising you of your rights. This is Detective Sergeant Robert L. Jacoby, Homicide Division, Zieglersville Police Department. It's 1:16 A.M., December 21. We are in a parked car in the lot of the Cat's Pee-Jays, a bar and lounge. Subject is Amy Cummings, of Ten Peach Street, Zieglersville, charged with attempted homicide, obstructing police in their duties, and resisting arrest by violence. Miss Cummings, anything you say can be used against you in a court of law. You have the right to remain silent—"

"Knock it off. I want to talk."

"You've been wounded. The wound isn't life-threatening, but I suggest you don't talk until we get it fixed up. I'll radio for your lawyer right now, if that's what you want. Meanwhile, you got any doubts at all, say nothing."

"I said I want to talk, goddammit. I was set up, and the bastard isn't going to get away with it. Is the boob ruined?"

"No. A neat hole, up high. Near the shoulder."

"I sure hate to die with one of 'em looking dumb."

"Here's the ambulance. We'll get your statement later."

"I want to die, Jacoby. Somebody as dumb as me ought to die. Let me die."

"In due time, Amy. The state's time."

40.

EXTRACT

Statement of Amy G. Cummings

Interrogator: Det. Sgt. Robert L. Jacoby
Witnesses: Fred M. Stabile, Chief
Carl P. Himmel, Detective
Transcribed by Gladys Keenan, Department Clerk

Q. How did you get involved with Alicia Hamilton?

A. We met at Z'ville Hospital where I went to work after I got out of the army. I was a staff nurse, she was into charity and support work. We hit it off good, and we've been friends since.

Q. When and how did you meet Charles Hamilton?

A. Alicia hired me as a part-time therapist to help Charles after his car accident. Thought what she called my sunny disposition would be good for him.

Q. This was at his home in Florida?

A. Yeah.

Q. Was your therapy successful?

A. Well, yeah, I guess you could say that. Right away he
and I had this big thing for each other, and when Alicia
went back north I helped him get his sex back, and he
helped me see I wasn't the dull shit everybody said I was,
and those were the greatest months of my life, with lots
of sun and a huge house to roam around in and great,
kinky poon whenever I wanted it. But when I suggested
that we make a permanent thing of it, Charles got all upset and told me he was crazy about Alicia and wouldn't
think of breaking off from her. We started arguing a
good bit, and when Alicia came back Charles had her
send me back to Z'ville General.

Q. Did Alicia know about your affair with her husband?

A. Nothing was ever said, but I think she suspected.

Q. Did it affect your friendship?

A. Not so's you'd notice. We still palled around, and had a
lot of laughs, you know? Alicia's a softy, and I think she
knew how lonely I was. And you know something? I
don't think she was ever all that happy in her marriage.
She played it straight, but I don't think her heart was in
it, if you know what I mean. And if I didn't know her so
well, I'd swear she had something else going. Well, not
really going; that's not her style. But there was—something.

Q. So why did you try to kill Mrs. Hamilton?

A. I wanted Charles. Real bad. She was in the way. Everything else I'd tried hadn't worked.

Q. What everything else?

A. I got this idea. When Gert Margolis told me about that
dork of an ex-husband of hers, shooting porn pictures, I
went to him and asked him if he could sort of, well, set
up Alicia.

Q. What do you mean by set up?

A. Get shots of her in a porky situation. My idea was to
send the pix to Charles—you know, anonymously—and
get him mad enough to dump Alicia. Then I'd have an
open track."

Q. Margolis agreed?

A. He had me talk to his boss, Bill Rooney. The two of
them had a blackmail thing going with some of the hot-
bed motels here in town, and Margolis said he couldn't
take on any contracts without Rooney giving the okay.

Q. So what did Rooney say?

A. A thousand bucks, he said, and Alicia would be history,
marriage-wise. So I said okay, and he and Margolis did a
real artsy number. Composites. A porn pic with Alicia's
head on the body of some broad getting jazzed by some
dude. It made her look like the mother of all whores, and
I sent a print off to Charles. But nothing happened.
Nothing. And then Rooney got killed, and things sort of
unraveled. So after waiting a couple of weeks, I took
some vacation and went down to see Charles, and he was
really glad to see me, you know? Said he'd missed me
like crazy, and we had ten days of great grooving. But

the picture obviously hadn't even made a dent on him as far as his feeling for Alicia was concerned.

Q. Did you mention the picture?

A. Hell no. I wasn't supposed to know about it, remember.

Q. Then what happened?

A. I got plenty pissed off, that's what happened. I told Charles that I would never give up on him. That he was the only guy I ever wanted, and I wasn't going to give him up just because he had some kind of sick crush on a woman who wouldn't even let him prang her with the lights on. He said sick crush, hell, it was his interest in inheriting her huge fortune, and if it wasn't for that, I'd be Numero Uno. I went superballistic. I said he already had more money than anybody'd ever want, and he was out of his friggin' mind to turn down me, Amy Cummings—the best piece of ass between here and Jupiter—just to get a couple more jillion when he already had a skillion. See what I mean?

Q. So that's when you decided to kill Alicia?

A. Not right then. That came after Rooney started using the picture to blackmail Alicia, telling her that if she didn't cough up a thousand a week he'd send her husband and society friends some *really* good pictures.

Q. How did you know about that?

A. She told me. I was her friend, remember. She confided in me and Gert, asking us what she ought to do. And then Rooney was killed, and Alicia was off the hook.

Q. But you weren't. Right?

A. That's right. Margolis started blackmailing me. A thousand a month and a lay every week, and he wouldn't tell Alicia that I'd set her up. That's when I flipped. When my first payment was due, I met him at the airport. He was just so, God, disgusting. I knocked him silly with some karate, then dragged him out on the road and ran the car over him a couple times. But I didn't know that Gert— she was as gooey over that asshole as I was over Charles— had ridden to work with him that night just to keep him company, and she'd seen me do him. When she started hollering and screaming, I stuffed her in my car, took her home, and, because by then she was talking about turning me in to the cops, I gave her a shot and took her into her garage and strung her up to make it look like suicide. By then I had the heat and decided that I was in for two killings so I might as well go for three. That's when I decided to do Alicia and make it look like an accident. With her dead, I'd end the blackmail shit and open the road to Charles. So next day I got my housemate—a Special Forces guy I met in the service—to fix me a small remote charge I could hang on the carb of her Beech. I had my guy call her, say he was a Florida cop, and Charles had had an accident. I was ready at the airstrip when she tried to take off.

Q. Who did Bud Wilmer, Bianco, and Burroughs?

A. Pinky Watson.

Q. Why?

A. Charles was trying to scare that Flynn dame into selling her company to one of his outfits—Amalgamated Something. Screw up her credit, get her arrested on a DUI, fire shots at her—that kinda shit. The Lunt lab has a formula he wanted, but he didn't want Flynn to know he was the buyer. Wilmer and Bianco knew too much about this, and other things, so he had Pinky off them. Burroughs was doing some work for George Morton, and Hamilton wanted to get Burroughs out of the way so Morton would hire Pinky.

Q. What kind of work was Pinky doing for Morton?

A. No idea. All I know is, Hamilton wanted to keep a watch on Morton.

Q. How do you know all these things?

A. That's the way Charles is. Every time you help him get his rocks off, he tells you the story of his life. Instead of smoking a cigarette, he makes speeches.

Q. So why did you call Watson when you were running from the arresting officer?

A. Charles told me, you ever get in a jam, just call Pinky Watson, and he'll take care of things. Gave me Watson's private number, said call anytime, day or night. Shee-it. You see what that got me.

Q. No. Tell me.

A. I didn't realize Charles was counting on me to go after Alicia. He knew if he got me mad enough, I'd do Alicia, the others. He was playing me like a fish. He figured sooner or later I'd get in trouble and have to call Watson for help. And when Watson offed me, Charles would not only be rid of both of the women who bugged him, he'd be sitting on top of Alicia's fortune. Did you ever see anybody dumber than me?

41.

They sat at a small glass-topped table in the solarium and were served minestrone and chicken salad sandwiches by an impassive old woman who wore a black dress and a starched white apron. After she had disappeared into the shadows of the inner house, Falloon dipped a glistening spoon into his soup, took a sip, then stared off at the day outside.

"I see they've solved those Zieglersville murders."

Morton understood that Falloon was attempting small talk. A bad sign. It meant the big man was so angry he had to work at maintaining the leader's inscrutable composure.

Morton sought to help out. "A crazy business, all right," he said. "I've met and talked with that nurse. She didn't seem the type to go around slaughtering people. But, as Shakespeare once said, 'Mix hot sex and big money, and murder ain't far behind.' "

Falloon looked up from his soup. "Shakespeare said that?"

"Sam Shakespeare, the bartender at the Cat's Pee-Jays."

The little joke didn't help at all. Instead, it seemed to flip open the lid over Falloon's pent-up rage. He banged the table with a hand and erupted. "Allenby has not returned my three hundred million dollars as demanded!"

"Damn." Morton feigned angry surprise. "I called him at Hamilton's place in Palm Strand and made your expectations quite clear. He was to bring the money to you at once. He promised he would. I believed him. He was very worried."

"We are searching for him."

"Searching?"

"My people have been watching the Allenby place, but there's been no sign of him. Do you have any ideas where he might be?"

Morton had no wish to bring bodily harm to Allenby, but more important, he couldn't chance Allenby's being traced to Mexico and made to talk about the three hundred million he never got. So he shrugged angrily. "I haven't the foggiest. He could be anywh—" He paused, holding up his right hand in a gesture of inspiration. "Hold on. I do have an idea."

"Well?"

"Allenby loves to shoot skeet. It was his main hobby. He would enter competitions everywhere—mainly here on the East Coast and in Canada, but often in Europe. England, Germany, Italy. Every time he would stay in the guest quarters at the host club. Get your people looking at the Canadian and European skeet circuits and they just might find him."

Falloon nodded. "Good idea." He waved at the food. "You're not eating, Morton."

"Well, I have to admit that your news took away my appetite. I don't mind saying that I was looking forward to having Allenby punished. I lost my job and ten million hard-earned dollars on account of that bastard."

Falloon took a small bite of his sandwich. He chewed slowly. "A deal is a deal, and under the deal your money is unreturnable."

"I'm in no way complaining to you. It's Allenby I want to kill—figuratively speaking, of course. My deal with you was made in good faith, and I stand by it. I'd like to continue being your friend."

Falloon said, "Which brings me to why I invited you to lunch." He took another bite of his sandwich, which he helped along with a swig of coffee.

Morton waited.

"I've been impressed with the way you handle yourself, Morton. Despite your veiled propensity for the smart-ass, you show a degree of intelligence, an understanding of how my associates and I operate, a coolness when taking chances, and a no-bitching, I'll-fight-another-day attitude over losses. You are also well-mannered and highly presentable in social situations."

Morton waited some more.

"Enrico Scallini is retiring as CEO of Peabody Chemicals Corporation after thirty years with the company. I want you as his replacement. You would begin your duties on February 1 at a starting salary of 2.2 million dollars a year. Bonuses and other perks to be worked out."

Morton's mind played a trick. As he struggled to conceal the rush of exultation, he remembered a scene from an old movie. There was this bleak, middle-aged clerk in sleeve garters and eyeshade—the symbolic exploited wimp—who, while slaving in the bowels of a huge corporation, learned one day that he had inherited a million dollars. The camera had followed as the little guy closed down his desk, rose twenty floors on an elevator, walked through regiments of secretaries, and entered a grandly gilded door labled PRESIDENT. He went directly to a man behind a huge, ornate desk in the middle of an enormous, paneled room, and asked, "Are you Mr. Smith, the president of this company?" The man nodded. "I am. Who are you, and what do you want?" The clerk drew himself up, stuck out his tongue, and, after delivering a thunderous, blattering raspberry, turned on his heel, went down the elevator to the lobby, strode into the street, and disappeared, never to return again.

Today, raspberries weren't Morton's style.

"Would those perks include membership in the Nordic Club?"

Falloon gave him a wry glance. "You still have a hard nose about my having blackballed you that time?"

"Damn straight, I do. I swore I'd shove that up your kazoo someday. This is someday."

Falloon was said to be incapable of laughter. But, as he had the day they'd met, Morton saw what suggested the beginning of a smile. The impression was fleeting.

"I think we could arrange the Nordic."

They ate in silence again. Then:

"Well, Morton?"

"It's one hell of an offer, and all the Nordic crap aside, I'm damned flattered and grateful. I've been with the chemical industry for nearly a quarter of a century. Started as a manufacturing intern in Bradford's Charleston, West Virginia, plant. Clawed my way upward—line operator, foreman, shift supervisor, superintendent, assistant plant manager, plant manager, division manager, department manager—to a vice presidency and board membership. I've done it all, and your offer tops it off."

"Do I hear a 'but'?"

"I've done nothing at all to discover what's out there"—he waved toward the windows—"and what's in here"—he touched his chest—"and here"—he put a finger to his temple. "I've never been tested. Me, myself. My life's half-gone, and until now I've been an employee, working for someone else to attain goals established by someone else. So now I want to spend the time I have left answering questions about me. Can I build a house, alone in the woods? Can I sail a boat, alone on the sea? Fly a plane, alone in the sky? Can I, in fact, do anything alone? Is there anybody who can look at me without seeing my money and position and what I might be able to do for them? How about women? Can I find one who will like me not only for what I am but also for what I'm not?" He paused. "I'm grateful for your offer, Falloon, but I've got these questions to answer."

Morton fell silent, moved by the sudden realization that he had just delivered one of the few honest speeches of a lifetime.

Falloon dabbed his lips with his napkin, nodded slowly, and, folding the cloth carefully, said, "I understand. Disappointed, maybe. But I understand."

"I suppose most men feel these things, or variations on the theme. But most men never get around to doing anything about it. I've decided I'm going to try."

"What will you do first?"

"Learn to sail."

"Kid playing in a puddle, eh?"

"I once saw a magazine ad. I don't know what it was selling. But it featured a full-color photo of a man and a woman on a small sailboat. It was anchored in a blue tropical lagoon—clear water, palm trees, white sand, all of it. They were sunning, lying side by side on the deck, almost nude, holding hands, eyes closed, smiling. And I got this tremendous yearning to do that, with a woman like that, in a setting like that. The feeling has never left me."

Falloon said, "You surprise me again, Morton. You are a closet romantic."

Morton smiled. "I plead guilty."

"You have money for this, ah, adventure in self-trial?"

"Enough. Not much, but enough. Some cash, a few stocks and bonds, CDs. A house I can sell. Enough to get me to the South Pacific in a boat and a bikini."

Falloon was skeptical. "It's hard to imagine you in a bikini. You're always so—Madison Avenue."

He was about to build on this but was interrupted by the arrival of a very grim Peter Van Dyke, who pulled up a chair and sat facing them across the table. "Have you heard the news? Have you seen the TV? Have you heard what those damned Frenchies have done?"

Falloon said, "We've been here, having lunch. Talking. What's going on?"

"The TV—C-Span, the nets, all the main noontime news shows—have had bulletins out of Paris, and now they're going to run live coverage of the announcement by some frog who heads up Le Tellier, that drug company."

"What announcement?"

Van Dyke held out his arms in a gesture of bitter frustration. "That formula they snatched out from under us: They're saying that they invented the thing. They're saying that French scientists have found the cure for cancer."

Falloon, eyes hot, threw down his napkin. "Paris. That's

where that welching son of a bitch has gone. Get some of our people over there. Find Allenby and kill him."

Van Dyke rose from his chair, turned, and without another word, hurried out of the room.

In the ensuing quiet, Morton concentrated on keeping cool, on keeping his face expressionless. It was hard to do.

It had worked.

It had actually worked.

And now it was time to wrap things up.

When he got back to the house, Morton put in a call to New York.

"Gordon Brody here."

"Hi, Gordon. This is George Morton in Zieglersville."

"Ah. You have something for me?"

"Finally. I'm having a courier bring you a videocassette. It'll blow you away."

"It's mine? Exclusively?"

"You bet. And if you think you're famous now, see what happens after you've aired it."

"It's good, eh?"

"Merry Christmas, Gordon."

42.

Morton had instructed his New York agent to pay off the lease on his Manhattan apartment, and the front lawn of the Zieglersville house now sported a FOR SALE sign. After paying his bills, he'd closed all of his stateside bank accounts, except for the small local one on which he wrote routine checks. The furniture, including the computers, their contents totally deleted, would be auctioned upon sale of the house. Both vehicles were to be shown at Hiram Webster's agency, where, he'd been assured, they should bring in a nice price, being in such great shape.

He was in his robe and slippers, sipping coffee at the table in the breakfast nook and going over his checklist once again. The sunlight coming through the French doors was warm, a hint that the days were numbered for the winter outside, and he looked up, peering around in a sudden rush of sentiment. It had been easy to put the house on the market—an inescapable, practical requirement of his plan—but now that he'd received a rather astonishing offer from that couple relocating from Buffalo, he already missed the place. The house had been a sanctuary and a kind of monument to the one who, in essence, was the only love of his life. Only twice had she walked these rooms, yet there were times in them he imagined he could hear her laughter, catch her scent.

Ah, well, onward and upward, old boy . . . Other days and other places await.

The oven clock showed him it was time, so he turned on the portable TV, which brightened into the credits and theme music of Gordon Brody's program, *Morning Eye-Openers.* It was an hour-long show on the dominant network, had received many awards and citations, and had for more than five years been enormously popular, thanks to Gordon's canny news sense and formidable stable of tipsters and informants. But, Morton suspected, Gordon was suffering incipient burnout, and, since it was no secret that his ratings had begun to slip, he was the logical one to have been given this bombshell—anxiety and gratitude would guarantee his maximum effort. Moreover, the wire services and print syndicates remained almost slavish in the way they picked up his material, so any piece appearing on *Eye-Openers* was virtually assured worldwide, multimedia distribution.

Brody was looking especially Establishmentarian this morning, what with his elegant tweed jacket, button-down shirt, regimental tie, bristling eyebrows, and brigadier's mustache. His deep-set blue eyes, crinkled at the corners, slightly sad, slightly mocking, intimated that he had seen everything there ever was, and his throaty baritone conveyed good-humored toleration of humankind's manifold lunacies.

"Good morning," Brody said somberly. "Cancer is one of the most mysterious and deadly maladies challenging medicine today. One in every four Americans will confront the disease in their lifetimes. A third of a million of us will die of it this year alone. And despite the tremendous expenditures of money and scientific energy, no matter how much we learn, no matter how many advances are made, cancer has remained tauntingly inscrutable, tragically incurable."

The camera angle changed, and Brody was now seen in profile, a study in craggy, jut-jawed intelligence as he went on, encapsulating the history of medicine's ineffectual assault on cancer. Screened behind him as he spoke, a mélange of faces and places and incidents highlighted his account, and a cello duet played under, softly, solemnly.

Cool, glib, Brody made his transition into the dramatic Christmas Eve announcement.

"The world was electrified when one of Europe's largest and most respected pharmaceutical firms declared yesterday that its scientists had at last discovered the so-called 'magic bullet'—a drug that not only cures cancer but also can prevent it.

"France's Le Tellier company claims that after years of laboratory experiments and collateral clinical studies it has been able to eradicate major forms of this curse. The company asserts that the new drug not only prevents tumors and arrests the development of existing tumors but also, in some cases, actually makes existing tumors disappear.

"Le Tellier says its scientists have solved the mystery of the 'trophoblast,' a key to the regenerative, healing processes in the human body and have been able to direct trophoblastic power against cancer cells. 'Vitam Two,' when coupled with doses of vitamin B17, zinc, and a specially designed diet, has brought as high as ninety-two percent remissions in cases of breast and prostate cancers that had previously been pronounced incurable—this, according to Le Tellier officials.

"The announcement has had, of course, an enormous worldwide impact, stunning the medical fraternity, sending shock waves through the therapeutic, chemical, and radiological industries, and causing general rejoicing among those who have looked to them all as the last hope in their battles against this dreaded disease."

There was a pause, the cellos suspended, and the camera closed in on Brody's handsome face as he intoned, "But there is a problem. An *Eye-Opener* of epic proportions, turned up in an investigation conducted by your host."

The cellos struck a heroic, portentous chord.

"Le Tellier has been caught up in what could very well be medical history's greatest and most dramatic sting.

"Le Tellier stands accused—posthumously—by America's renowned and controversial physician and biochemist, Dr. Anson B. Lunt, of the theft and fraudulent exploitation of a pharmaceutical formula which, in its current form, is virtually worthless."

A portrait of Anson Lunt materialized on the screen over Brody's left shoulder.

"After extensive digging, *Morning Eye-Openers* has tracked down a videocassette, produced by Dr. Lunt four months before his death in a plane crash, that predicts the formula's exploitation by Le Tellier. Specifically accused of the theft is Dr. Gregory Allenby, who is now missing and, along with a colleague, Theodore Bradford, CEO of Bradford Chemicals Corporation, the subject of a massive Federal probe just launched."

The camera fell back to a full shot of Brody, looming in his high-backed leather chair, regal, imperious, all-knowing. "Before we discuss the implications and ramifications of this momentous development with a panel of experts, let's first see the Lunt video in its entirety."

The scene marbled, then opened on an office interior. Lunt—brooding, cadaverous—sent his level gaze across the desk directly into the lens. Behind him and to one side was a window, through which could be seen Zieglersville's Prosperity Bank clock tower and its illuminated sign, which set the time and date at 1:27 P.M. on the twelfth of last August.

He began to read from a TelePrompTer.

"I am Anson B. Lunt, a physician and biochemist. I have all the proper credentials, and they are available to anyone who cares to see them. For years, my reputation in both disciplines was excellent, and many authoritative documents attesting to this fact are likewise available.

"Nearly twenty years ago, I introduced Vitam, a compound derived from natural elements that proved in laboratory and clinical tests to be highly effective in the treatment of certain cancer patients. When I attempted to suggest in various medical journals that Vitam might be a valuable supplement to the orthodox surgery, chemotherapy, and radiology used in cancer treatment, my papers were rejected and I soon found myself being denounced in professional and governmental circles as a quack and charlatan. The attacks were fomented by a few corrupt individuals in the pharmaceutical industry and government who sought to protect their commercial and political interests. Their widely publicized ridicule and slanders destroyed my good reputation and very nearly ended my professional career.

"But I persisted, and subsequently I developed the formula for a highly sophisticated form of Vitam, which—as demonstrated in extensive and exacting clinical tests—cures major forms of primary and metastatic cancers and, in fact, shows promise as a preventive.

"Word of this reached the same people who waged war on the original Vitam, but this time the table has been turned.

"If you are seeing this videotape on commercial television, it means that certain events have occurred and specific conditions exist.

"First, the new formula has been stolen and sold to my antagonists by Dr. Gregory Allenby, my chief of research and development, who, I've discovered with great sorrow, has for some years been peddling my company's secrets.

"Second, the formula almost certainly will have been introduced by Le Tellier, Cie., as a discovery of its own.

"And third, the claims made for the Le Tellier product are baseless, because, as their chemists will find when they attempt to manufacture, the stolen formula is incomplete. I have deliberately, and with malice aforethought, lured my enemies into a trap. There is no way they can duplicate my findings or achieve my level of clinical success with the information they have at hand and within the time frame they themselves have set.

"Permit me a homely analogy. Say I've come up with history's first recipe for spaghetti—a meal prepared from natural ingredients mixed in proportion and cooked into a sauce, then spread over precooked noodles. A trusted subordinate steals the recipe and sells it to a restaurateur, who, anxious to claim the invention before I can, rushes the dish onto his menu and boasts widely that he is its originator. But I've foreseen the theft and the restaurateur's fraud. So prior to the theft, I plant an altered recipe, which omits the secret to making pasta. The restaurateur finds that, although the recipe includes a dough made of flour and other ingredients, there's no clue as to how to make noodles. He unhappily discovers, too late, that all he can produce is a pot of tomato sauce and some strange, unappetizing dumplings.

"Before I close, I remind you that the vast majority of the world's physicians and surgeons are decent, hardworking, high-principled, and enormously skilled professionals whose major mission in life is to heal. And by far most of the world's chemical and medical drug manufacturers play squarely by the rules and turn out products of impressive quality and dependability. The demands placed on them are many and uncompromising, and they meet these demands with incredible, reassuring consistency. If what I have done here unintentionally hurts some of them, some of the innocents, I sincerely apologize to them. But what has been done to me by the world's Bradfords and Allenbys, has caused great pain and loss to most of my innocents, as well—my 'innocents' being those thousands who could have been helped, maybe even saved, if I'd been free to practice my therapies in peace.

"In any event, the correct formula for improved Vitam does exist. I've seen to it that, once the thieves have felt the full weight of their disaster, the correct version will be submitted to the proper protocols and procedures. God willing, the marvelous cures it's been found to work will eventually be available world-wide to those poor souls who fall victim to one of the worst of afflictions.

"It would have been my pleasure to make this disclosure personally the day after Le Tellier's announcement. But I'm compelled to take my vengeance this way because I am fatally ill and will not live long enough for the sting to play out.

"My heartfelt thanks to the brave and loyal friend who has helped me to exact my revenge. According to what my beloved parents called *The Good Book*, vengeance belongs to the Lord. If that is so, I hope that he forgives the two of us for the great enjoyment we derive from having done the job for him in this instance."

As the scene segued to Brody, who was preparing to intro-duce his hastily assembled panel of experts, Morton laughed outright and turned off the set.

43.

Morton was placing his suitcases in the hall at the foot of the stairs when the doorbell rang.

"It's open. Come in."

"Morton?"

"Oh. It's you, Jacoby. I thought it was my cabbie."

Jacoby looked around at the nearly empty rooms. "I was on my way to the office from the hospital and stopped by on an impulse."

"How's Alicia?"

"Awake, but she won't make the prom. Where you headed?"

"Retirement, Sergeant. Retirement. Away from here, away from all the rotten memories 'here' represents." Morton considered Jacoby amiably. "You didn't come by on impulse, Sergeant. You came by to ask some questions. Right?"

Jacoby shrugged. "That's my thing."

"So what do I know you'd like to know?"

"I suppose you saw that video of Lunt on the Gordon Brody program."

"Is there anybody who didn't?"

"What did you think of it?"

Morton smiled. "I wish he'd just talked instead of reading that prepared script. He was a warmer, more friendly man than he came across there. And all that palaver about spaghetti. I mean, really."

"Well, it helped folks understand better what he'd pulled off."

"Perhaps. But it was an inexact analogy. And I've learned that 'folks' aren't nearly as dumb as we hotshots tend to think they are."

Jacoby gave him a level stare. "Curious you should say that. I'm one of the folks."

Morton laughed softly. "You make a great case in point. Everybody should be as dumb as you are."

"He really stuck it to Hamilton and his French pals."

"Yep."

"Bradford, too."

Morton humphed. "How could he do that? Teddy Bradford was beyond Anson Lunt's reach."

"But he wasn't beyond your reach."

Morton delivered an amused, lowered-eyebrow glance. "You're suggesting that I caused Teddy to raid the employee pension fund? He listened to me, but not that hard. Besides, I'm a Bradford retiree, and I most certainly wouldn't put Teddy up to stealing my own pension, now, would I?"

"So why did Teddy, a real got-rocks with everything anybody could ever want, think it was a good idea to raid the company pension fund?"

"You tell me, Sergeant. Teddy Bradford's a very greedy guy. But I didn't think he was that dumb."

"I don't suppose you know where he and Allenby are hiding out, do you? There's about two million cops who'd like to know."

"Two million hoods, too, is my guess. They're very unpopular on both sides of the law."

"How do you know?"

Morton laughed and waggled a forefinger. "Uh-uh. You aren't getting me on that one. But if you ask me to guess, I'd say Allenby is drinking his breakfast in some Juarez whorehouse. And maybe if you find Gloria Cadwallader you'll find

Teddy, too. They're good friends, and she's even dumber than he is."

"Gloria Cadwallader?"

"Of the Wilmington, Delaware, toilet manufacturers."

"Is she the one who set Mrs. Bradford's divorce into motion?"

"According to the tabloids."

Jacoby sauntered to the window and stared into the brightening sky. "It'll be spring soon."

"Indeed it will."

Another long pause.

"In that TV talk, Lunt thanked 'a friend' for helping him to set up his sting. It was you, wasn't it, Morton. You were custodian of the tape."

"Where are you getting your information?"

"Were there any other helpers?"

"You think I know?"

"Sure do."

"You think I'd tell?"

"Nope."

"So, then."

"I've figured out the Anson Lunt plane crash, too."

"Oh?"

"Lunt was Alicia's lover. She became very guilty about it. But too late, because Rooney got a picture of them hugging and began to blackmail her. Lunt, sitting in the cockpit during the landing, did the one thing that a fatally sick man could do to protect the reputation of the woman he loved. He grabbed the controls and took Rooney and himself out."

"Murder and suicide, eh?"

"I know it. But I can't prove it."

"You're a good detective, Jacoby. Intuitive. And you know what? I think your guess about what made the plane crash is right on. But I also think your guess about the lovers angle is dead wrong. Alicia made no bones about loving Lunt—but as a fine doctor who saved her life. She wasn't capable of adultery."

Jacoby bored in. "You knew he was going to kill himself and Rooney, didn't you. And you did nothing to stop it."

Morton sighed. "You can't imagine how hard I tried to stop him. I'm not exactly a Tender-Hearted Harry, but physical violence just isn't my thing."

"I could arrest you for complicity, you know."

"So are you going to?"

"Too late. I haven't read you your rights."

Jacoby turned from the window and made for the door.

"Promise me something, Morton."

"Like what?"

"Stay the hell out of my jurisdiction. You come on my turf again, I'm going to be on your butt, finding out what you *really* have pulled off here."

"I'll go you one better. If I ever happen, for any reason, to be forced to come back to this godforsaken town, I'll advise you in advance by registered mail. Send you a formal itinerary and agenda. Spring you to dinner."

"Another thing. Say so much as boo to Melanie Flynn, you're dog meat."

Morton pulled on his cashmere overcoat and, shooting the sleeves and leveling the lapels, he gave Jacoby a genuine grin. "Are you going to marry her?"

"On her birthday next month."

"Got yourself a hell of a woman there, buddy. I'm the president of her fan club. I wish you both the best."

Morton paused, running a finger along his mustache, his eyes on an idea. "I was going to save it for later, but, hell, why wait? I have a wedding present for her from Anson Lunt."

"Present?"

"The computer password that fills in the missing link in the Lunt formula Hamilton thought he had. Tell her to try 'Morton.' Then nail down the patent and get superrich."

Jacoby smiled faintly. " 'Morton'? You're joking."

"Not me. Anson. He had a far-out sense of humor."

There was the squeaking of brakes outside. "There's my cab, Sergeant. Anything else?"

"Have a good trip."

44.

EXTRACT

Statement of Thomas M. "Toots" Pettigrew

Interrogator: Det. Sgt. Robert L. Jacoby
Witmnesses: Fred M. Stabile, Chief
                      Carl P. Himmel, Detective
Transcribed by Gladys Keenan, Department Clerk

Q. You are the groundskeeper at the Sleepy Hollow Hunt
    Club?

A. Yeah. For thirteen years.

Q. You were at work at the club on the morning of December 28, last?

A. Yeah.

Q. Were you alone there?

A. No. Teddy Bradford and Greg Allenby were there, too.

Q. Can you tell us why that was?

A. Well, I never did much understand rich guys and their ways, especially those two, who were always real sort of weird. Bradford had been there for most of a week, sleeping on a cot in the heated room behind the pantry and using the clubhouse employee's john early, before the cook and stewards showed up, and late, when the buildings shut down for the night.

Q. Why was that? The club has several guest suites.

A. Bradford said he didn't want anybody to know he was there. Anybody. Especially his wife and people from the Bradford company.

Q. Did he say why?

A. Nope. But after a couple of days there were stories on the front page of the newspaper, with pictures of Bradford and that high-and-mighty asshole, Allenby, and it was pretty clear that both of 'em were in deep shit, wanted for knocking off pension money and stealing company secrets and God knows what all.

Q. So why didn't you call the police?

A. Bradford told me right up front that if I said anything to anybody he'd blow my balls off. He kept his fancy shotgun in reach the whole time he was there, and I believed that sumbish—I surely did. I figured that sooner or later he'd get tired of rotting in that stupid room and go downtown and turn himself in.

Q. What did he do during the day?

A. Just stayed in the room, locked in, eating hardly anything and drinking a lot.

Q. Did anybody call him, come looking for him?

A. Couple calls from Mrs. Bradford, couple from a guy named Van Dyke. Couple from guys who didn't say their names. Nobody came looking until this morning.

Q. What happened then?

A. I came from home and parked the Ford and was unlocking doors and turning out lights when this beat-up Taurus came through the fog and stopped by the equipment shed, where I'd hid Bradford's car. It was Allenby, and Christ, was he a mess. Stubble beard, stinking of booze and dirty underwear. And he was always such a Dapper-Dan hot-shot. A real mess today, though.

Q. What did he say?

A. Told me to hide the Taurus. Asked me where Bradford was. I stalled, 'course, 'cause I didn't want to get Bradford's shotgun on my case. But he said to cut out the bullshit, Bradford and he'd been on the phone, and Bradford knew he was coming. It was then Bradford came around the corner of the clubhouse, cradling his gun, and told Allenby to come on in, they had to talk.

Q. What did you do then?

A. After they disappeared into the clubhouse, I put the Taurus in the shed next to Bradford's Caddie, then went into the main lounge to replace a couple bulbs that had burned out. While I was fussing around with the stepladder, I heard them doing a lot of yelling back and forth, but I

couldn't understand what they were saying—only a cuss-
word here and there. After a while, Bradford stuck his
head out the kitchen door and asked me had I seen
George Morton lately. I said no, not lately, and he said,
well try to get him on the phone and make some excuse
why he should come out to the club—but not to tell him
that he and Allenby were there. I said what kind of excuse and he said any kind of excuse you dumb shit, just
get Morton out here as soon as possible.

Q. Did you do that—try to get Morton?

A. Oh, yeah. But when I tried his house number, the phone
company's mechanical lady said it'd been disconnected.
His office told me he didn't work with the company anymore and the last they'd heard was that he'd left the
country. When I knocked on the supply room door and
told them that, they both went up in hot, tight spirals,
and Allenby actually threw a whiskey bottle across the
room. That's when we heard the other cars.

Q. Explain that.

A. There was the sound of tires on the gravel driveway
down the hill. We all looked out the window, but the fog
was pretty heavy, and all we could see was the shapes of
some cars—two or three—coming up from the highway.
They didn't have any lights on.

Q. So what happened then?

A. Bradford yelled, 'Oh, shit,' and Allenby said what are we
going to do, and Bradford said get your goddam shotgun
because these guys aren't dropping in for a drink. Allenby
said his gun was still in his car, and Bradford said, well,
get one from the rack in the game room and bring some
shells. Allenby said what the hell, these people may be
cops, and Bradford said if they were cops, they wouldn't

be coming up the hill without lights, they'd be coming up with sirens and flashers, so we got to assume that these guys are collection hoods.

Q. Did they say who might be sending out the collectors?

A. Not that I heard.

Q. Did they say what the collectors were collecting for?

A. Not that I heard.

Q. Did they say anything at all?

A. Bradford said something about their only chance was to show them they got guns and that might cool them down and send them away.

Q. You say their 'only chance.' Did Bradford and Allenby try to recruit you?

A. No. They were so busy running from window to window and being scared, I think they sort of forgot about me. When they went out on the porch, I backed off and ran and hid in the generator house—that's the little shed behind the evergreens beside the driveway.

Q. That gave you a pretty good view of everything, then, didn't it?

A. Yeah.

Q. So what did you see?

A. Bradford and Allenby on the porch, holding their guns at the port-arms position. Two guys getting out of each of the three cars. And—

Q. That's six men all told, right?

A. Yeah. And they sort of fanned out in an arc, like, and I
    could see that these were no ordinary collection guys.
    Each guy had a gun, making four automatics and two
    sawed-offs against two twelve-gauges, and they came
    walking toward the porch, slow across the driveway cir-
    cle, and it was like the O.K. Corral, you know what I
    mean? Then Bradford yells, "Hey, you guys don't want
    us, you want George Morton," but they didn't answer,
    just kept walking through the mist, dark and silent. Then
    Allenby yells, "It's George Morton you want, you
    assholes—go get George Morton." The guy in the black
    overcoat finally speaks, saying, "We want the money, and
    if you don't give us the money, we want you."

Q. Do you have any idea why they would bring George
    Morton into it?

A. Hell, no. George Morton's one fine guy, and he wouldn't
    have anything to do with people like that. I think Brad-
    ford and Allenby were just grabbing at straws, like.

Q. So what happened then?

A. Bradford and Allenby sort of looked at each other, not
    saying anything for a time, then Bradford said, soft, but
    real clear, and sort of sad-like, "Oh what the hell." Then
    he yelled at the top of his voice, "Pull!" And he and Al-
    lenby turned and started shooting. Two of the collectors—
    the one sawed-offer in the black overcoat and the other
    in the trench coat, went down like they was hit by a
    train, but the other four hit the stance and opened up
    with their automatics, pow-pow-pow-pow, and it sounded
    like D day, you know? Bradford and Allenby didn't have
    a chance in all that, and they went right up in the air, off
    their feet, and up against the clubhouse wall, then

bounced back and through the railing into the bushes. The four guys came up, took a close look, kicked Allenby's body a couple times. Then they went and picked up their dead buddies, threw their bodies into the car trunks, and drove off. That's when I ran to the main building and called you guys.

Q. What did you do while waiting for the police?

A. I threw up a lot.

PART FOUR

45.

It was high summer, his favorite time in the Alps. The chalet, while relatively small, was the exemplar—brown timber and broad slants of wood shingling topside, brilliant whitewashed masonry below, all of it accented by geranium-choked window boxes and sunny balconies. He stood in the mountain breeze coming through an upstairs window, cradling a phone on his shoulder and admiring the acres of wildflowers that matted the meadows beyond.

The phone seemed to clear its throat, and a voice came on: "This is Heinz Schroeder. May I help you?"

"George Morton here."

"Oh, Mr. Morton," the lawyer cooed, "I'm so sorry to have kept you waiting. But as a matter of fact I was just discussing your affairs with the New York people."

"So how did it go?"

Schroeder laughed a genteel Genevan laugh, the kind reserved for shady foreigners who place their bundles in those marvelously inscrutable Swiss banks. "The good news is that I spoke directly with the new chairperson, Mrs. Radowski. She's both delighted and dazed by an anonymous gift of two hundred million dollars to the Bradford employee retirement fund. She kept asking, 'Why would anyone *do* that?' Ha-ha."

"Is that all she said?"

"She mostly, well, sputtered, I suppose one would say. But she did mention the coincidence—the fact that the amount was precisely the amount that had been embezzled and lost beyond trace by the late, ill-fated Teddy Bradford."

"It doesn't take much to see that."

The lawyer did some sucking-up. "I don't mind saying, Mr. Morton, that I think it's rather wonderful of you to return that money to the fund."

"Teddy stole it to make a payment. I don't consider it rightfully mine. I used to be a Bradford Chemicals employee, and it's not my style to keep money that belongs to my hardworking former friends."

"So typically American."

Morton thought about that. "So what's the bad news?"

Schroeder coughed gently. "The bad news is that Mr. Hamilton left his entire estate to Gerda von Reichmann. And since she, too, is now deceased and is intestate, there is really no likelihood that the matter of inheritance will soon, if ever, be satisfactorily worked out."

Morton sniffed. "No way is that bad news. It's like the retirement fund money. I really didn't want it cluttering up my life."

Schroeder did some breathing into the phone. Then: "About the *Sea Nymph*—Do you want Captain Rawlings to continue with the South Seas island-hopping plan?"

"No. It's served its purpose. Tell Rawlings to return to Catalina and put the ship on standby. We may want to use it sometime."

Schroeder was polite, but curious. "If you don't mind my asking, why didn't you really do it? Take advantage of all that expensive sailing you were paying for."

"The missus likes mountains. In our marriage we have a great arrangement. She goes her way, and I go her way."

Schroeder pretended amusement, then said carefully, "I still urge you to put your main assets to work. Even with the retirement fund bequest, your overall balance remains at more than a billion, and a sum that size should be out, working, doing things, not simply sitting in the Sparkasse."

"No hurry. Making money's no longer my main thing."

"Yes. Well. I—"

"You're a good collaborator, Heinz. I also appreciate your protecting my privacy. And when I'm ready to put the money in motion, you'll be the first to know."

"I'm most grateful."

Morton hung up and went down the short flight of steps to the main sitting room, where he crossed the gleaming planks and stepped onto the sun-washed balcony. Alicia, trim and tan in her white bikini, was at the outside worktable, peering at the computer screen through her huge sunglasses. He touched her shoulder, and it was like feeling warm satin.

"So, Ace: What you up to?"

She turned her face to him, smiling. "I'm being dazzled by the fact that I can sit here in the Tyrolean Alps and punch a few buttons and read this morning's Zieglersville newspaper, error by error."

"There are plenty of those, all right."

She laughed. "Listen to this picture caption: 'Robert L. Jacoby is congratulated on his promotion to detective lieutenant by Chiep Fred Stabile, while Jacoby's wife, Melanie, president of Lunt Biotech and chair of the Anson Lunt–Alicia Hamilton Anticancer Foundation, looks on approvingly.' "

"Cheap Fred Stabile?"

"Well, it's spelled c-h-i-e-p. Melanie looks terrific here, doesn't she."

"Marriage obviously agrees with her."

"Can you say that about me?"

Morton removed her sunglasses, and taking her chin between his thumb and forefinger, raised her face to the sun. Examining her, he said, "Eighteen-seventy was a good year for women."

She punched him lightly in the belly. "Rat."

"I was just talking to Schroeder."

Her cheeriness diminished. "Oh? So what's the verdict?"

"Charles left his estate to von Reichmann."

She looked off down the valley, a touch of pallor in her golden cheeks, and he waited for her to adjust to this, the ultimate humiliation.

She said at last, "Speaking of rats, eh?"

Morton said nothing. What was there to say? Years of lip-biting devotion to a husband who leaves his fortune to a dead mistress.

"I'm such a jerk, George. How could you possibly have waited so long for a jerk like me?"

"If you could be loyal to a prick like that, you could be loyal to anybody. In my circles, that made you one of the seven wonders of the world."

"All those times Anson bawled me out for not divorcing Charles and marrying you. All my self-righteousness. God, I don't know how you stood me."

Again he said nothing, and she answered her own question. "Well, you couldn't tear down my rationalizations by tearing down his character, I guess." She gave him a wry, sidelong glance. "You've got your own problems with Victorian propriety, don't you, George."

He shrugged.

"Refusing to marry me unless I agreed to live on your pension. Making me put everything but Elmwood Manor in a foundation. Brother. You're a piece of work, you are."

"You got that right." He sat on the bench beside her.

She said, "No kidding. Are we all right in the money department? I don't want ever to do something extravagant and have you not say anything."

"We're okay. My Bradford pension is pretty good, actually. More than enough for two senile citizens."

"With this goofy heart of mine, we might run into some heavy-duty medical expenses down the road."

"My insurance should cover most of it."

She laughed. "Look at me. The Great Alicia, married to a

pensioner whose medical insurance might pay my doctor bills. Whee-hoo."

"Well, at least we know we didn't marry each other for money."

She stretched her bare arms and breathed deeply of the mountain air. "Let's get our clothes on and drive over to that little place in St. Johann and have a couple of those huge fruit salads."

"Great idea."

She made a joke. "Can we afford it?"

"My pension check's due the day after tomorrow."

He finished dressing while she was in the shower, then stood by the window, admiring the incredible alpine view. On impulse, he opened his wallet and took out the clipping from the International News page of *Anglo*, Paris's English-language newspaper:

> PALM STRAND, FL., MAY 22 — (USP) —
>
> Charles Hamilton, head of the investment firm, Gebrüder Schwarz, and Gerda von Reichmann, chief of Le Tellier, Cie., the chemical corporation headquartered in Paris, were found shot to death in their bed here today. Hamilton was free on bond on a charge that he had conspired to murder his wife, heiress Alicia Cosgrove Emerson Hamilton. Both he and Reichmann had been suspended from their jobs pending their companies' probes of a reported loss of millions in last year's attempted theft of Vitam Two, the history-making "silver bullet" cancer cure developed by the U.S. biochemist, Dr. Anson Lunt. Neither firm would comment on tabloid reports that Hamilton and von Reichmann had been assassinated by agents of Crepes, an illicit international drug ring, as

punishment for the losses. Florida police have classified the deaths as homicides.

Morton tore the clipping into tiny pieces, which he held out the window and slowly let loose in the breeze.